"No captain can do very wrong if he places his ship alongside that of the enemy."
- *Horatio Nelson.*

HELL FLEET

Book 5 in the Sliding Void series.

First published in 2018 by Green Nebula Press

Copyright © 2018 by Stephen Hunt

Typeset and designed by Green Nebula Press

To follow Stephen on Twitter:
http://twitter.com/s_hunt_author

To follow Stephen on FaceBook:
http://www.facebook.com/SciFi.Fantasy

To help report any typos, errors and similar in this work, use the form at
http://www.stephenhunt.net/typo/typoform.php

To receive an automatic notification by e-mail when Stephen's new books are available for download, use the free sign-up form at http://www.StephenHunt.net/alerts.php

For further information on Stephen Hunt's novels, see his web site at http://www.StephenHunt.net

PRAISE FOR STEPHEN HUNT'S FICTION

'Hunt's imagination is probably visible from space. He
scatters concepts that other writers would mine for a trilogy
like chocolate-bar wrappers.'
- TOM HOLT

'All manner of bizarre and fantastical extravagance.'
- DAILY MAIL

'Compulsive reading for all ages.'
- GUARDIAN

'Studded with invention.'
-THE INDEPENDENT

'To say this book is action packed is almost an
understatement… a wonderful escapist yarn!'
- INTERZONE

'Hunt has packed the story full of intriguing gimmicks…
affecting and original.'
- PUBLISHERS WEEKLY

'A rip-roaring Indiana Jones-style adventure.'
—RT BOOK REVIEWS

'A curious part-future blend.'
- KIRKUS REVIEWS

'An inventive, ambitious work, full of wonders and
marvels.'
- THE TIMES

'Hunt knows what his audience like and gives it to them
with a sardonic wit and carefully developed tension.'
- TIME OUT

'A ripping yarn … the story pounds along… constant
inventiveness keeps the reader hooked… the finale is a
cracking succession of cliffhangers and surprise comebacks.
Great fun.'
- SFX MAGAZINE

'Put on your seatbelts for a frenetic cat and mouse
encounter... an exciting tale.'
- SF REVU

Also by Stephen Hunt

~ THE FAR-CALLED SERIES ~
In Dark Service (#1)
Foul Tide's Turning (#2)
The Stealers' War (#3)

~ THE JACKELIAN SERIES ~
The Court of the Air (#1)
The Kingdom Beyond the Waves (#2)
Rise of the Iron Moon (#3)
Secrets of the Fire Sea (#4)
Jack Cloudie (#5)
From the Deep of the Dark (#6)

Mission to Mightadore (#7)

~ THE SLIDING VOID SERIES ~
Sliding Void (#1)
Transference Station (#2)
Red Sun Bleeding (#3)
Anomalous Thrust (#4)
Hell Fleet (#5)

Omnibus Collection (#1 & #2 & #3)
Void all the Way Down

**~ THE AGATHA WITCHLEY MYSTERIES
AS STEPHEN A. HUNT ~**
In the Company of Ghosts (#1)
The Plato Club (#2)
The Moon Man's Tale (#3)

Omnibus Collection (#1 & #2 & #3)
Secrets of the Moon

~ THE TRIPLE REALM SERIES ~
For the Crown and the Dragon (#1)
The Fortress in the Frost (#2)

~ OTHER WORKS ~
Six Against the Stars
The Alien who Ate Christmas (children's illustrated)
Empty Between the Stars

http://stephenhunt.net/novels/

Thanks to...

Thanks to my gallant crew of test readers who acted as the final set of eyes on the manuscript.

This includes (in the order of comments and typos returned):

Stuart Robertson.
Jesse Farr.
Julian White.
Todd Rathier.
Ron Olexsak.
Patrick Forhan.
Gary Sopher.
Wolf McTavish.
Eva Sanchez.

-1-

Scrap the Crap

'Got a problem on the brew, sir!'

Commander Adella Vega glanced up from behind her desk, fixing Lieutenant Anders Vistisen with a weary look. *Isn't there always?* 'The kind that sinks ships, or sinks careers in this part of the galaxy…?'

That saying was a standing joke in Adella's corner of Hell-Fleet.

'Any part of the galaxy you know of worse than this one, Commander Vega?' asked Vistisen.

'A system where active ordnance is flying?' suggested Adela. 'This *problem*, Lieutenant, is it on DV-station or dirt-side?' She didn't really need to ask, but she did so anyway.

'It's down on Bardfeld's World, sir. Your presence is requested by the Legion. There's a shuttle prepped and on the launch rail.'

Mighty considerate of you, Vistisen, loading one in the pipe for my slow, continual career death. 'Brief me on the way,' sighed Adella.

Vistisen had operated as her point officer in the station long enough to separate the daily chaff of command from the real issues that arose. Adella was halfway out of her office when Uddin Cesti appeared, rapidly waddling his way towards her doorway before Vistisen could intercept him. *Ah, the assorted problems of my command.* Instances of narcotics-related disorderly conduct quadrupled among her crew every time the corpulent wily merchant slid his ship, the *Shamash*, up to DV-Station to dock. Adella didn't require tasking her station A.I. to work out who was supplying all that contraband.

Nope, I don't need to be Sherlock Holmes to work it out. 'Let me guess, Mr. Cesti, the Provost Marshal has impounded one of your cargoes again and you want me to fix your problem?'

Uddin Cesti raised both his chubby hands in what the man regarded as a placating gesture. 'You impugn my reputation, dear commander. I am here to help you with *your* problem.'

'My problem?' Adella flashed Lieutenant Vistisen an icy glare. 'How the hell are you up on my problems before I am?'

'One hand doesn't clap alone, Commander Vega. I heard because your difficulties are on the surface of Bardfeld's World where my customers are.'

'Yes, your *customers*,' said Adella.

Bardfeld's World below was mostly burning hot desert. The planet's oceans dried up a geological age earlier, long before mankind and its allied species from the Triple Alliance had shown up in orbit. *It's seen better days, but who here can't say that?* Uddin Cesti's clients, the Sand Angels, had been baseline human before the colonists genetically modified their bodies to match the local environment. Sand Angels, after their angel-sized wings which acted as combined solar energy and moisture collectors. Sand Angels didn't need much to live a comfortable nomadic existence, grazing across the endless orange dunes. *Maybe to be left alone?* The one luxury the Fleet seemed determined to deny them. Sometimes, Adella envied how little the tribes dirt-side needed.

'As it is my customers with whom your difficulties arise, dear Commander, I thought you would appreciate my offer to mediate below. With the tribes' salt bricks recently supplied, they will feel more warmly towards me than they do towards the Fleet.'

Ain't that the truth. 'Okay, Mr. Cesti,' said Adella, making for the exit, 'you're with me. Lieutenant, I am afraid Uddin Cesti has stolen your seat on the shuttle. Make a start on that destroyer while I'm dirt-side.'

Lieutenant Vistisen didn't try hiding his delight at not visiting the inhospitable world below. 'Aye aye, skipper! Starting on the *Quickmatch*, sir?'

'That's the one. I have bumped her up on the schedule. Chief found out she has a better shock-proof chilled water plant climate system than ours. It's a keeper.'

Lieutenant Vistisen smiled. 'Sounds like a good time to ask him to fix *my* deck's air conditioning, skipper. Feels as cold as void on the dog watch.'

'You wanted comfort, Lieutenant, you should have signed up with Mr. Cesti, here.'

'We are also a working vessel,' said the merchant captain, sounding offended.

Yeah, working extra hard when our anti-smuggling patrols are running. Adella and the trader made for the station's hangars. DV-station wasn't much of an orbital habitat as far as luxuries go. No parks or biomes or wide-outside spaces to replicate a planetary existence. Originally a battleship, the *Dark Viking* had been modified over the centuries for her new role as an orbital station. A little bit added here. A little bit added there. Components from other ships cannibalised and welded on: generator modules, solar power arrays, habitat drums, carrier hangars, tanker storage. It made getting anywhere fun, navigating a jury-rigged maze built by Fleet engineers. *Sometimes, I think they made it extra hard to get around just for kicks.* Bored Fleet engineers were a dangerous breed.

They reached the central hangar, boarded the shuttle and left its launch rail with a magnetic twang, rotating for planetary insertion. Adella caught a good long look at her station's purpose while on the float. The mother of all ships' graveyards blocked her view of the stars. An orbital debris field of ancient Fleet vessels stripped of every useful component fit for reuse; what was left, scrapped. Everyone here called it the *Ghost Fleet.* Every type of military vessel in various states of decomposition: carriers, planetary assault ships, stealthships, fabships, cruisers, destroyers, frigates, countermeasures ships, tankers, and resupply boats. Bardfeld System was this corner of the galaxy's dedicated ship-breaking facility. Vessel cracking wasn't what Adella had signed up for, but it was the command she had ended up with. The Triple Alliance's navy didn't want retired war vessels falling into the wrong hands. *Plenty of those.* The universe never seemed to lack for pirates, mercenaries, secessionist-minded worlds, enemy states, psychopaths, and criminals. So, this is where ships with teeth went to die when they were decommissioned. And this is where navy careers were scrapped, too. Not an official punishment posting, mind. That was the Fleet brig on Bardfeld's World, below. But when you fell just short of an official court-martial, you ended up on the *scrap-the-crap* detail in Bardfeld system all the same.

Adella strapped herself in. There wasn't a human pilot on the flight, today. This being a routine jaunt, unopposed on the ground, their Naval Aviator was an auto-pilot the size of a shoe-box. She paged the station's main artificial intelligence, Slugger, to formally inform it the Chief now held command of their little orbiting fortress of joy.

'Okay, Mr. Cesti, why don't you tell me what my Problem du Jour is?'

Cesti rubbed his thick beard thoughtfully as he settled into his landing couch. 'Sand Angels are protesting the Fleet's encroachment on one of their holy sites.'

'And why the hell would we be doing that?'

'The last storm uncovered an azzaz's bones outside Fleet headquarters.'

'*Ah,*' said Adella. The azzaz had once been leviathan-sized monsters drifting inside the planet's oceans, sucking up plankton like organic cleaning machines. Now, they were part of the fossil record. Sand Angels believed their world's soul was contained in such holy bones.

'Your beloved leader is not minded to respect the new find. A prisoner detail was already building across the affected area. Your Rear Admiral believes that the Sand Angels' faith is, and I quote, a "comedy made-up religion".'

Adella sighed. Rear Admiral Harper Pullinger, was, as the "Rear" clearly indicated, a prize arse. *This whole system's a joke command for a joke officer. If anyone ever deserved their posting here, it's that fool.*

Their shuttle started to shake and rattle as she crossed the exosphere's atmospheric envelope. Her quivering subsided as their anti-gravity field kicked in, braking their descent. The shuttle had been an assault drop barge, once. Adella had spied the AFD-7 Peregrine-class on an incoming manifest during the decommissioning of a centuries-old troop ship. She'd ensured Chief Kessi got his claw on it before it could be stripped for parts. Assigned for her personal use. Not that Adella looked forward to visiting the surface, what with Rear Admiral Harper Pullinger making his pedantic base of operations there. But any landing you could walk away from was a good one, and they had built assault drop barges so simple and safe that even Fleet Marines used them without killing themselves.

I should be thankful for small mercies. If the Dark Viking's corridors weren't so narrow and our quarters antiquated, I'd be sharing air with our idiot of a leader.

They set down at Dra Dras ten minutes later, a rocky plateau with shuttle landing fields overlooking the local Fleet headquarters below. Acres of connected concrete buildings and physical shields designed to hold back the orange sand sheets beyond. A citadel without end. Dra Dras Base was notionally being constructed as sector command for the Eastern Frontier. Except it wasn't, really. Only a tiny fraction of its constructions were operational, the rest empty and facades for the complex's real purpose. Providing construction work for the prisoners in the Fleet Stockade on the plateau's far side. Hard work on a hard world specifically chosen for occupying a punishment detail's time. Endless sun for solar energy collectors. Endless sand for fabbing concrete and glass. Infinite labour for any Fleet personnel insolent enough or guilty enough to be sentenced to this brig planet. Adella sighed as she disembarked from the shuttle. Like stepping into a blistering oven, after the shuttle's environment control. She started sweating immediately. *The only good thing you can say about Dra Dras Base is that it makes my scrap-the-crap command on the station topside resemble a promotion.*

'So big,' said Uddin Cesti, gazing down on the base. 'So useless. Do you think the Rear Admiral might rent out a few empty buildings as warehouse space? These are my tax tokens at work, after all.'

Adella ducked under the popping metal of her shuttle as it cooled, heading for the landing field's bunker-like ground station. There were two caterpillar-tracked vehicles parked outside and damned if she would walk to the protest site in this heat. 'Mr. Cesti, I'm sure the Alliance tax authorities have seen less of you than a blind crow's seen worms.'

'Ah, dear commander, but the worm is the only animal that never falls down.'

Aren't you the lucky one. Adella boarded the nearest vehicle along with her tame trader and set its drive function to manual. She didn't want to worsen matters by having its auto-pilot classify protesters as a threat. Perhaps run a few down. Military vehicle drive systems were notoriously trigger-happy, even when they didn't have sand in the circuits. Uddin Cesti punched in the coordinates for his customers.

A bumpy, uncomfortable ride to get to the location. Thousands of nomads laying siege to a construction site in the desert. Fab forges on caterpillar tracks for converting sand into concrete blocks, sheets of glass stacked up. Girders that resembled steel but were a composite spun from the dune's minerals. Welding gear, cranes, bulldozers. Dozens of half-completed buildings. In front of it all, a depression in the sand dunes where the bones of the long extinct creature jutted out like a slain giant's ribcage. The Legion had deployed a cordon of soldiers to protect the work crew. Not much work going on, however.

Adella parked her vehicle under one of the half-finished buildings' shade, then dismounted with Uddin Cesti. She approached the cordon. There were as many legionnaires present as tribal protesters. Dozens of species represented among their force. The legionnaires wore light ballistic armour, camo-pattern set bright white to reflect the burning sun. All except the small seven-flame sun insignia — gold against a red and green crest — on their chest-plates. Adella had heard rumours the External Legion deactivated their suits' cooling systems on Bardfeld's World, just for kicks and giggles.

The line of soldiers was mobbed by angry tribespeople. Sand Angels fluttered their solar wings, spears jabbing high in the air, an impassioned song of throat clicking and moans, half prayer and half threat. Their skin looked like tortoise hide, their faces contorted and hostile. A few thrown stones rattled off the soldiers' armour. Wasn't anything bigger to find and toss on the dunes. Today, the External Legion was showing restraint.

Adella marched up to the female officer in charge. 'There're an awful lot of legionnaires here for a guard detail. Do I know you?'

'Very funny, Commander Vega,' said Colonel Scolar Pes. 'You well understand that I am the only Arthian on this planet.'

'Yeah, Sco, but that joke never gets old.'

It was the bear-ish Colonel's fault, really. Like the universe's most intelligent talking Pandas; if Scolar's largely female species had been more fertile, they wouldn't have needed to resort to cloning on an industrial scale. Telling Arth apart was the least of Adella's problems right now. 'I presume it was *you* who called Lieutenant Vistisen about this?'

'Indeed. The Legion has been ordered here in force to protect the stockade crew from the tribes. Your detail is to continue construction work without delay.'

'Well, Colonel, if the Legion wasn't so cheap it needed to share administration costs with Fleet on Bardfeld's World, you could have had a crap dangerous planet all of your own for a training camp and barracks. Barely terraformable worlds aren't expensive in these here parts.'

'I prefer jungle over sand flats, Commander, but there are hundreds of species serving in the External Legion and none of us get to vote on our deployment.'

Adella examined the warbling crowds thrusting their spears in the air. 'So, this is my mess, now? Don't recall getting a vote on that one, either.'

'*Please,*' said Scolar Pes, 'at least let there be one reasonable Fleet officer on Bardfeld's World. Do you know how difficult our lives will become if the tribes turn against us? Our legionnaires come here to train for hostile insurgencies on *other* worlds. Not *this* planet.'

'Make that training of yours a lot more realistic,' said Adella. 'But then, I'd be getting calls like this on a daily basis. Shoot my station's schedule to hell, that.' *On the plus side, perhaps one of those storming Sand Angels could stick a spear up the Rear Admiral's…*'

'So, you will help?'

'What we've got here, Colonel, is a problem of interpretation. The stockade crew has been ordered to continue work without delay. Yet here are all these locals, throwing stones and putting a scare into our work details. That's a delay. So, we need to obey the Rear Admiral's orders by *removing* the delaying obstacle.'

'I don't wish to open fire on the crowds,' growled the Colonel.

'Not my style, either.' *Ain't that the truth.* Adella turned to the merchant. 'Mr. Cesti, how do your customers feel about exhuming sacred bones and moving said relics a hundred clicks north? Say, somewhere a lot less like a building site?'

'Yes, yes, that could work. It is the bones that are held sacred, not their burial ground. A priest would need to be paid to bless the skeleton, first,' said the merchant captain. 'I am certain I can secure the best of deals for you.'

'Oh, please *do.*' Adella looked at the Fleet's construction detail, all happily skiving off duty under the threat of imminent violence. *Yeah, because this world needs more empty concrete bunkers that'll crumble back to sand long before they're ever occupied.* 'And let's move with a purpose.'

Adella was impressed with how quickly priests were procured and the bones blessed. *Suspiciously fast.* She wondered if the local Holy Joes had been hanging around, waiting for their palms to be greased before rescuing the relics? Under their priests' sing-song urgings, the locals descended on the bones and rapidly removed them from the sand. A gang of tribespeople struggled under each rib, bearing the creature's remains away as the rest of the mob screeched in delight.

Did Uddin Cesti arrange this to collect his cut and notch up a favour owed in orbit? Commander Vega didn't like being played for a sucker. *About the only thing I share with…*

An Arikaree-class dropship skimmed the cloudless sky above the site. It hadn't launched hot from space, though – heat sinks sealed closed. Aerial vehicles didn't cope well with the sands on Bardfeld's World. An AFD-21 Arikaree, one of the few birds Fleet operated hardy enough to handle the local environment without spending more time in the maintenance shop than the air. It circled slowly, landing on the safe side of the Legion cordon. The locals had guessed who was on board just as Adella had. Tribespeople started throat-singing about *Zom Staf*, a clueless chieftain from legend who served as the traditional butt of tribal humour. This song concerned the leader allowing warriors to queue outside his tent for his wife, blissfully unaware of what was going on under shade.

Rear Admiral Harper Pullinger strode out of a lowered ramp at the flyer's tail. As always, he wore a full dress uniform heavy with ribbons and braid, in case his staff forgot who was in charge. *Must be sweating, in all that.* Adella noted Pullinger had finally given up on the campaign being fought across his scalp. No more comb-over for those faint wisps of hair. The fully shaved head appeared a marginal improvement; it gleamed like a lighthouse in the burn of the sun. *His reflected glory.*

'Commander Vega! I haven't summoned you down to the base.'

'Sir. I was finalising details with Colonel Pes for the Legion's rotation through the station,' said Adella. *Well, I would have got around to discussing the matter, sooner or later.*

'I am sure you are aware, Rear Admiral,' said Colonel Pes, 'that our resupply vessel has posted late.'

'Of course, I am aware,' hissed Rear Admiral Pullinger, as though the mere suggestion otherwise was a slight against his command. 'If Commander Vega was adequately maintaining our system's comms network, logistics would never have become such an issue. But I suppose I can hope for nothing better from the staff I am sent to work with.'

'Sir. Our comms repair ship is due back within the hour,' said Adella.

'I expect an immediate update, Commander. To have our link with Fleet inoperable for two months is a disgrace!' Pullinger peered short-sightedly at the empty sand in front of the site. 'Where are those infernal fossils from that beast?'

'Disposed of, sir,' said Adella. *A commercial disposal, that's no lie.*

'What, disposed of?' Rear Admiral Pullinger swayed forward, examining the warbling mob, as though their existence had only just impinged upon his consciousness. Adella was fairly sure Pullinger had never bothered mastering the local language. Far beneath his dignity. *Does the Rear Admiral suspect they are singing about him?* 'Colonel, disperse this damnable rabble before they realise their precious relics are in a crusher. This detail is working far too slowly.'

Adella didn't bother correcting the Rear Admiral. *Possibly you could regard these endless dunes as a crusher? They've eroded this world's mountains over the eons.* Also, Pullinger didn't seem to realise that slacking was the stockade prisoners' thing, otherwise these men and women would have more meaningful duties than turning sand to concrete under his command. *Another point I better not correct.*

'An immediate update, Commander!' barked the Rear Admiral as he strode to his waiting dropship.

'I believe I shall interpret his orders as escorting the tribes to the bones' new burial site,' said Colonel Pes, watching the officer's dropship take off.

'Well, legionnaires can never get too much marching,' agreed Adella.

She was about to go back to the ground vehicle when a Sand Angel came scuttling up in front of her. Old, as only old could be without decent life extension technology. Male, swathed in white robes, his translucent solar wings fluttering gently, blue like ancient faded cathedral glass. The fabric of his turban-wrapped head bore a silver badge, a sun nailed with sixteen sharp rays. The Unconquered Sun. One of the priests she'd been conned into paying by Uddin Cesti.

'The Vega, the Vega,' hissed the priest, his gene-edited throat making it hard to form normal words. Well, he hardly needed to eat food anymore. Only take on water.

Commander Vega bowed towards the old man. 'I pray the bones of your azzaz prosper far from this place.'

'The bones go,' croaked the priest. 'The tribes go, too, soon.'

Adella had the strange feeling he was talking of deeper matters than the near-riot that had broken out here. 'Go where, old fellow?'

'Deep desert, far and far,' croaked the priest. He seized her arm. 'You must go, too.'

'Into the deep desert?'

'No. You will not survive where we endure.' He jabbed a finger at the blue cloudless sky. 'Your deeps. Yours! May they protect you.'

The stars? I think this one has been partaking of a little too much pipe in the comfort of his tent. 'Protect me from what?' asked Adella.

'The Old Eaters! May the darkness hide you!' The priest's odd prophecy finished and he rambled away following after his people. *Old Eaters?* Adella used her implant to query FleetNet for any local legends mentioning that term. She drew a blank. Nothing. Just superstitions from a holyman high on more than his cult. *Well, hell, what does someone who survives on solar energy know about eating, anyway?*

***

Adella's take-off pattern swung the assault barge over the External Legion's camp five miles north of the plateau. Low enough to see lines of legionnaires quick-stepping through the desert, a few miscreants buried in the sand, only their heads visible. Boot in the Fleet was tough, but the Legion's ideas on the subject brought a whole new meaning to the concept of "pain".

Adella hummed a line from *None Left*, the Legion's semi-official anthem. 'Let us forget, along with our dropships, Death, which forgets us so little. For we are the Legion.'

'Commander?' said Uddin Cesti.

'Nothing, Mr. Cesti.'

'A successful operation today, then, dear commander.'

'Yes, you might almost say *suspiciously* successful,' said Adella. She was about to confront the wily trader about her misgivings, but the lights on her station's board turned red and Lieutenant Vistisen's voice sounded over the encrypted line into DV-station.

'Got a problem on the brew, sir!'

Of course, you do!

And this time, it really was a *real* humdinger. The kind that sank ships.

-2-

Bad Buoy

It didn't take much to make Master Helmsman Beklum Sakwa seem over-excitable. A crab-like Kaggen, the Fleet officer had been attached to Adella's command for trying to convince his fellow Kaggens he was a saint and deserved worshiping. Said worship to be conducted in the time-honoured fashion of financial donations on the church plate as well as getting other crew to do his work for him. Scams that led to religious unrest in the Fleet weren't kindly looked on. Apart from dubious moral fibre, Master Helmsman Sakwa was an otherwise competent officer. Which made believing what he had to report to Adella all the harder to swallow.

'You've been out checking our comms relays on board the *Graf von Arco* for two months and *this* is the insane story you've got to tell me?'

'Skipper, I swear on my life I am not trying to swindle you.'

'You know your comms repair ship has a transponder on her hull, Master Helmsman. I can pull the *Graf von Arco*'s flight details to find out if you've been off enjoying unauthorised R&R for the last few months.'

Beklum raised both his sets of manipulator arms and fighting claws towards the ceiling of Adella's office, as though beseeching God to intercede on his behalf. 'Skipper, myself and my hardy crew of engineers examined every blessed communication buoy from here to the system's edge. Hundreds of them. We stripped each relay, we tested them. They are all working perfectly. Which is why when we reached system edge, we translated into hyperspace to check the first buoy in the subspace chain.'

'Even though the hyperspace chain is the Fleet Corps of Engineers' responsibility.'

'Thoroughness is next to Holiness, skipper. Also, I believed the Rear

Admiral wouldn't wish to confront the contradiction of not being able to send messages over a functionally operative comms relay.'

Yeah, kind of having problems with that one, myself. 'And inside hyperspace, you found …'

'The first communications buoy in the subspace chain is also in perfect working order. What isn't in working order, however, are the quantum mechanics of hyperspace which allows our buoys to transmit entangled data across the relay chain.'

Adella sighed. 'So, to summarise, you expect me to go back to the Rear Admiral and tell him that every piece of Fleet equipment is functioning perfectly, but the laws of physics in the hyperspace realm have changed, rendering FTL communications impossible?'

'Exactly!'

'You know, Master Helmsman, I might actually find it more comforting to discover you *had* been off on a two-month bender, and that your report results from drug-related religious mania.' Adella was sure that was precisely the conclusion the Rear Admiral would reach for, first. Pullinger already regarded his personnel as a gang of washouts, burnouts, barrack room lawyers, troublemakers and skivers. The bullying popinjay just never possessed sufficient self-awareness to ask why *he* had been put in command of them.

'All our technical observations are uploading from the *Graf von Arco*'s databanks, skipper. I am no theoretical physicist, but as a navigator, I understand enough about hyperspace realm physics to be deeply unsettled with what I recorded.'

Adella didn't doubt it. Kaggens shared some weird beliefs about hyperspace being the mind of God and the gardens of Heaven. If this really played out as advertised, did it mean God had changed her mind about allowing the lowly sentients squabbling across her universe access to her backyard? It wasn't only the Kaggen species who'd have trouble with that. Humanity would go ape-shit, too.

'If this is a physical effect, something we haven't encountered in hyperspace before, do you have any idea about how long it'll disrupt QT signals with the rest of the Fleet? Will it be temporary or permanent? Is it local to Bardfeld's System or affecting all of hyperspace?'

'That I cannot answer, Commander, but we have far larger problems than our signals with Fleet.'

'I don't understand?'

'Commander, it is not just communications which are being disrupted by this phenomenon. G-fold manifestation inside hyperspace has become so faint as to be almost unreadable at a distance. Navigating through hyperspace is impaired to the same degree.'

Adella's heart sank at the implications. Hyperspace and real-space were deeply non-congruent spaces. Navigators relied on gravity mapping, faint impressions – G-folds – between the realms, to navigate a path between two points in the real universe. If G-folds were also being hit by this strange storm …?

'How much hurt are we looking at, Master Helmsman?'

'If the change is universal?' The Kaggen carefully pondered the question before answering. 'A journey through hyperspace which took me a week might take a year, now. I would have to translate into hyperspace, take a local bearing, travel on the course for as long as possible until it fades, then drop back into real-space. Reorient, translate, repeat. Not so much hyperspace jumps anymore, but hyperspace hops.'

Adella's mind spun with the horrific implications. Fuel loads. Wear and tear on jump vanes and Minkowski field generators. 'This fresh horror you bring me, Beklum, at least it explains why the Legion's resupply ship is late.' And why her station had received no new vessels brought in by skeleton crews for junking. *How will Fleet react to this? Ground everything until our scientists came up with an explanation? Essential traffic only? Mass disruption to the Alliance economy, that's for sure.*

Master Helmsman Sakwa clicked his claws; the Kaggen version of a shrug. 'Sorry, skipper. All things considered, I wish I had gone absent without leave, instead of discovering this mess.'

And this disaster wasn't just Adella's. It was *everyone's*.

-3-

Fighting Fleet

Three months had elapsed. About the only thing that made these Emergency SitReps bearable for Adella was the Rear Admiral's strategy for dealing with the crisis which could be best described as 'ignoring it.' Pullinger was dirt-side down in sector command. Oblivious to the fact that if the Eastern Frontier didn't have much of a sector to defend before what was now referred to as the Hyperspace Storm, SecComm truly didn't now. As long as the stockade's "guests" kept tight to their construction rota, building the Rear Admiral's empty base, it would take more than fundamental changes to the physical laws of hyperspace to upset the officer's routine.

DV-station's Operations Room currently hosted Engineering Chief Aralat raz Kessi, Senior Medical Officer Liam Pannel and Master of the Helm, Beklum Sakwa. Colonel Scolar Pes was present for the Legion, a courtesy on account of their shared bases in-system. The trader captain Uddin Cesti was in attendance under sufferance by Adella – spokesperson for a swelling fleet of merchant and civilian vessels seeking sanctuary around Bardfeld's World.

'Chief Kessi,' said Adella, 'your update on logistics…'

The Chief was a Skirl, a humanoid lizard with the formal manners of his race. Humans, Skirls and Kaggens composed the three dominant species of the Triple Alliance. They had faced much together over the centuries and survived it. Adella trusted people would say the same about the Hyperspace Storm, one day.

'Yes, skipper. Good news. The gas giant's steaders are expanding their orbital farms faster than we hoped. We can feed everyone in the system without introducing rationing, now. We're using hulks from the Ghost Fleet to supply basic materials for new farm habitats and our steader neighbours are used to colonising gas giants with far less. With the station's technical assistance, they are growing capacity at a rate of parsecs.'

'That's excellent news,' said Adella. *I can do with some. To think of all the trouble Pullinger went to in trying to evict those steaders when they first turned up in-system.* Without crazy extreme colonisers hugging Novensides – the system's largest gas giant – Adella's command would be begging the Sand Angels for their DNA hack. *Looking to grow me a nice pair of solar collector wings and embrace a new life of nomadic sunbathing.* 'We supply the steaders with junk, they supply us with food. I can think of worse trades. However, the broader intelligence picture is more problematic,' noted Adella. 'All our reports are from crews already in flight when the Hyperspace Storm began. The Legion's resupply vessel, the *Grinder*, only brought fresh mouths to feed when she arrived. The colonist vessel *Marswood*'s captain seems to believe the Hyperspace Storm is stronger around the Eastern Frontier. Their console reads indicate the G-fold fade lessens the closer you travel towards Core. We haven't been able to confirm that data using a second vessel, but the *Marswood*'s sensors have been checked and cleared.'

'So, Commander, there may be large swathes of Alliance space where it is business as usual?' asked Uddin Cesti.

'That's our current working supposition, Mr. Cesti. Which means the Hyperspace Storm might *really* be space weather. The hyperspace equivalent of a localised solar storm or graviton damage from a singularity.' *Of course, in reality, we're all taking a leak in the dark. Why couldn't we have an experimental science station in-system, rather than Pullinger's super sandpit?* 'S.M.O. Pannel, how are our people holding up?'

Their Senior Medical Officer pushed a series of charts onto the hologram space in the centre of their round table. Liam Pannel was handsome enough he could have played a doctor in a sim-series. Tall, dark and swarthy, with the right touch of gravitas. If he wanted extra points for verisimilitude, Pannel could have played a doctor in *Hell-Fleet*, the long-running series detailing the wars, affairs and tribulations of life inside the Alliance navy. Mostly high order bullshit, of course.

Not for the first time, Adella wondered how the man had screwed up to be posted here? An Admiral must have had died on an operating table under Liam's supervision? 'Here's my latest psych reads off the crew's implants. We're holding strong on the station. Better than can be expected, in many ways. The real problem is down inside the stockade. There are crew coming to the end of their sentence expecting rotation out. The Rear Admiral is keeping them on hard construction duty. "No shirkers, here, Doctor," is his diagnosis.'

Why does that not surprise me? 'See if we can reassign post-short personnel to duties up here. Crew manifests are below the Rear Admiral's sensor envelope. And those sailors won't be shirking on board the station, I presume, Chief Kessi?'

'I should say not, Commander. Re-purposing the Ghost Fleet to a purposeful end takes a lot more labour and imagination than simply stripping vessels and de-fanging warships.'

'What about your legionnaires, Colonel?'

'The External Legion go where they are ordered. They are happy when I order them to be happy.'

A very Legion answer. That drew smiles around the table. 'Maybe we should make you morale officer for the entire system, Colonel? Mr. Cesti, how fares the civilian fleet?'

'Its numbers swell to rival your own, Commander,' said Uddin Cesti. 'Besides the *Marswood* we have seen seven new arrivals turn up in the last week alone. Two more free-trader captains, three merchant ships from the large combines, a chartered resupply ship bound for the Berstuk Cluster, and finally, a rare ore bulk carrier returning to Core from the mines on Lady Midday.'

Adella nodded. *I hope they're not disappointed with what they find around Bardfeld's World. A couple of hundred acres of unfurnished concrete doesn't a Sector Command Facility make. And DV-station isn't exactly an orbital fort.* 'And their morale?'

'Better if Chief Kessi hadn't requisitioned the rare ores for use on board your recently recommissioned factory ship.'

'I meant the entire civilian complement's morale, Mr. Cesti.'

'Unlike the good doctor I don't have biometric reads for the civilian crews, but my best evaluation would be a blend of mild terror – sailors' superstitions about hyperspace demons and so forth. Along with a nagging suspicion that where employers' payroll is involved, crews are now firmly off the clock. There has been talk of forming a single large convoy and heading back to the Core worlds.'

'How many ships would make it back to Core without jump vane burnout?'

'My best estimate? Two-thirds will survive. A convoy system will allow us to pull crew out of dead vessels, while still reaching home on the remaining operational ships.'

'That sounds crazy desperate to me, Mr. Cesti.'

'These crews' fears are not purely of hyperspace's shades and shadows, Commander. There were rumours circulating many months before the Hyperspace Storm started. Of colony worlds going dark on the Frontier without explanation. Of normally reliable vessels posted late or missing.'

'This phenomenon explains that, surely?'

Uddin Cesti shrugged. 'Maybe, dear commander. But perhaps...'

'I've heard nothing of those ghost stories before today,' said Adella.

'With respect, Commander Vega, the Fleet Intelligence Service's reporting lines are directed–' the trader pointed down to the metal deck.

Rear Admiral Pullinger! Adella sighed. *Of course.* If Pullinger received a Fleet packet from F.I.S. saying that one Commander Adella Vega had won a trillion on the Tri-Homeworlds Lottery, she'd only find out about her winnings from her family a few years down the line. 'Somewhat restricted.' *As tight as the noose that should be strung around that man's neck...*

Cesti's rumours sounded almost as mad as the civilians' convoy plan. But the smuggler and reprobate had his own grapevine to rival Fleet Intelligence. And this far into Frontier space, Adella knew whose network she'd rather rely on for educated guesswork.

That's when alarms went off in the station's Operations Room; a shrieking of sirens and rotating lights fit to wake up crew deep frozen in a cryo-sleep chamber. And *educated guesswork* suddenly got upgraded to *working threat analysis.*

- 4 -

Down the Enchantress

'Triple Alliance Ship Enchantress, this is Dark Viking Station at SecComm East, we are tracking your emergency transponder, please respond.' Lieutenant Vistisen's voice was croaking out, repeating that message like a mantra for the last hour. 'Triple Alliance Ship Enchantress, this is Dark Viking Station at SecComm East, we are–'

'–unable to respond,' said Adella. 'Here's initial imagery from the early QT section.' Adella shifted the images with attached analysis onto the central well. QT buoys' telescopes were designed for as near a realtime combat picture as could be formed across a solar system. More than adequate to reveal the slagged bow of the incoming warship, exactly where her communications array should be.

'Sweet Heavens,' swore Master Helmsman Sakwa, peering in to examine the vessel's horrific damage.

'Well I never, that's a Meteor-27 Class,' said Chief Kessi. 'Last time I heard, that cruiser was still a blueprint on a shipyard database.'

It had been a few years since they had caught the Chief taking backhanders from corporate houses for awarding naval contracts in the shipyards. BuDocks had transferred the Chief to the galaxy's sinkhole at Bardfeld's rather than cashiering him and risking a scandal breaking across the news networks. But, even so. It was the nature of the beast that Bardfeld's World rarely got to greet anything modern. More worrying for Adella that the freshest tech on the Alliance's newest cruiser was incoming hot in a worse state than the last M-10 Class they'd received for decommissioning – and she had been half a millennium old!

'Nothing wrong with the *Enchantress's* engines, though,' said Adella. 'That's a hell of a fast burn.'

'Do you believe they are running from a fight?' asked Scolar Pes, sounding shocked. To the Colonel, the only type of ship that counted came with "troop" in front of it. A ride to the next hot-spot for the Legion to orbital insert.

'I believe she's attached to a battle group,' explained Adella. 'And I think she's acting as their scout.' It's what Adella would do, with disrupted communications and short-hop jumps the new style of transit. Straight back to the tactics of old Earth's cavalry forces.

'If that's what they've sent ahead to scout, I would not wish to see the state of her flotilla,' noted Uddin Cesti.

And you're still here, why? 'Mr. Cesti, we're now at battle stations; clear the Operations Room. I am sure there are a great many civilian captains in orbit who will be seeking reassurance.'

'Dear commander, I only wish I had some to give them.' The trader captain winked slyly at Adella and left.

Sadly, he's not wrong.

Their Skirl Chief of Engineering ran a practiced eye over the military telemetry. 'She's taken particle weapon engine damage, rail-gun strikes *and* missile explosions.'

Yes, the Holy Trinity. It was a tribute to the *Enchantress's* composite armour layers, shielding and point defence systems that she could still slide void. 'She might not have a comms array up front, but her laser turrets can be dialled down for code flash. Lieutenant Vistisen, break out the codebook and prepare for a tried and tested sight-to-sight when the *Enchantress* is within light effective range.'

'Aye-aye, skipper. It's turning out to be an old-school afternoon.'

'Sharp sticks and harsh language, Lieutenant.' And which of the two had the *Enchantress* offered to the enemy that had slagged her so thoroughly, Adella wondered?

***

Sight-to-sight laser flash lacked bandwidth, but even so, Adella's communications with the Enchantress had bordered on the ridiculously terse. Mainly a priority request to receive injured at DV-station's medical facility. That Adella could do; along with brooding over her lack of intelligence on what the Enchantress had tangled with. There were plenty of pirates along the Eastern Frontier, but few capable of ambushing an Alliance cruiser. Not unless the border privateers had seriously upped their game. So, Adella kicked her heels on the central docking ring with Senior Medical Officer Liam Pannel and his staff. Worrying came free.

'I see you've drawn your medical drones out of storage, doc,' Adella noted.

A company of drone medics skittered about the deck in front of the line of massive Fleet-sized airlocks, multiple units assigned to each member of the station's medical corps. The standard Fleet med-drone resembled a metal spider below the waist and a metal octopus above the waist. Painted white, naturally, with a Red Crystal emblem on the spinal battery back. Each spherical head contained a face that projected whichever customised features wounded personnel would find most reassuring. In Adella's case, she'd settle for S.M.O. Pannel's rugged visage. A low hum came from stretchers floating on mag-grav units, their path cleared all the way to the medical theaters and sickbay. Along with Commander Vega's medics, the station's damage control team and small marine complement were ready for action too. *I'm taking no chances today.*

'I've put Bardfeld's hospital on notice,' said the doctor. 'More for their surgical staff than the base's beds. Our sickbay is battleship-sized, even if our team are a little rusty. Last serious injury we received was when one of the Chief's engineers cut her arm off with a laser welder for a bet, and she was so drunk we barely needed to use anaesthetic reattaching her limb.'

Adella thought of the damage on those images of the *Enchantress*. 'Damned if this one is self-inflicted, Doctor Pannel.'

'No news on the *who*, I suppose…?'

'Not from our cruiser. Perhaps the Rear Admiral will be able to tell us?' suggested Adella. Although, given Pullinger was currently scrambling for a shuttle up to the station – and Adella bet his current priority was selecting whichever uniform had the most ornamental braided cord – her suggestion was mainly made in mischief.

'That would be nice, sir,' said the doctor, managing to keep a straight face. 'You're ready for action, too, I see.'

Adella tapped her armoured hard-suit. Like the station's marines and emergency team, it was standard Tactical Assault Light Operator Naval exo-armour: the ubiquitous Fleet-issue TALON suit. 'Always prepared, doc. Maybe there're a few classified reports rattling around the Rear Admiral's office to put flesh on Uddin Cesti's frontier ghosts?'

'I was under the impression this system held the only Ghost Fleet in our sector.'

'You know, so was I.' Proximity docking alarms sounded. Adella heard the thump of mechanical locks unfurling to mate with the *Enchantress*. Clack-clack-clack of magnetic locking. Then the hiss of atmospheres matching.

'Acute Assessment Teams to the front!' barked Pannel. 'Clear passage to sickbay. Prepare for crash receipt!'

Massive armoured circular doors rolled back. Prepared calm collided with utter chaos. Black smoke poured out of the *Enchantress*. DV-station's emergency venting system kicked into action with all the subtlety of a hovering strike jet, sucking up smoke and discharging it directly into vacuum. Fleet crew flowed out of the broken vessel, limping, bearing wounded on improvised stretchers, many carrying others free by hand. Screams for help and calls for medics, station doctors running forward surrounded by platoons of clacking drones to attend the injured. Damage control teams sealed their powered exo-suits and charged into the mist, the Marines likewise, searching for sailors to rescue and fires to put out.

Adella spotted a woman in a Third Engineer's uniform dragging a cadet out of the chaos. She appeared uninjured, but the cadet looked like a rail projectile strike had shredded his left leg. The name-tag sewed onto her shipsuit read ANSGAR. The cadet fair fell onto the mag-grav stretcher pushed by three drones, a stream of screeching medical alerts immediately filling the stretcher's diagnostics panel. 'I'm dying,' whispered the young man.

'Stow it,' growled the woman. 'You're going to make it. I promised you.'

Adella grabbed the Third Engineer's attention. 'Ansgar, where's your Chief Engineer, where's your bridge crew?'

'All gone. Bridge went down on the way in,' coughed the woman. 'No power. Trapped, I think.'

<Cellular degradation by autophagy,> announced the nearest med-drone, scanning the Third Engineer with one of its eight limbs. <Radiation toxicity. Immediate decontamination protocol!>

'Warhead flash,' moaned the woman. 'I knew it.'

Adella left the unfortunate Third Engineer to the drones descending on her; paging the station's damage control team to make for the *Enchantress's* bridge. Then the Commander sealed her suit and sprinted inside the cruiser. Adella had a job to do, too, and apart from saving as many crew as possible, the bridge was her best bet for answers. Black smoke everywhere inside, burning circuits exposed on torn walls, emergency bulkheads blocking various passages. Adella requested a current schematic of the cruiser's layout, but the ship's Main A.I. was as dead as the *Enchantress's* environmental controls. She made do with a basic cruiser map sent by Slugger; the station A.I. adding its elevated concern about the ship in dock's fate. *Yeah, me too, Slugs. With knobs on.* Adella's helmet filtered the worst of the sooty fog from her visuals, overlaying breadcrumbs from the damage control crews preceding her.

Adella ran down a corridor where the alert systems were still operational. <Fire, venting. Fire, venting>. It wasn't. And apart from the Commander, there were only dead bodies scattered about the deck to hear the warning. She never got used to the shocking sight of corpses in Fleet uniforms. Action in the void was frequently distant and impersonal. Drones, missiles and particle beams exchanged at distances so vast you had to wait for light to catch up before viewing the results of the interplay. And the Triple Alliance was the biggest, baddest brute on the block. They were accustomed to winning; of victory without even trying. *So, what's changed?*

She had to clamber up the lift shaft towards the bridge, keeping her power armour's sensitivity dialled down so she didn't rip out ladder rungs in her haste to climb. Adella discovered her Captain of Marines outside the bridge's lock with the damage control team. Yong Xue was part of the 1st Marine Logistics Group. Bardfeld's World wasn't used as a punishment posting by the Marines, more of a pre-retirement rotation. Captain of Marines Xue had been born on Kap7, a triple-gravity bone crusher on Kapteyn's Star. The squat veteran was so strong he hardly needed the Marine-issue hard-suit to break necks. Old age hadn't slowed him down much, either.

Xue saluted when he saw his Commander and stepped aside, revealing the DCT hard at work trying to run a patch override on the bridge's heavy armoured hatch. She noted he'd also brought his unit's own combat medics along with him. There weren't many of *Cap's Kaps* in the system, but they had served their time and knew their onions.

'She's combat sealed fast, skipper!'

Which means breaching charges and laser torches will take far too long. 'We can patch a runaround, Cap?'

'That we can, sir. First day I've ever been glad DV-Station is an engineer's paradise. There're more black-hat hardware hackers serving time on the decommissioning crews than I have hard-suits to fit them.' He gave a friendly tap on the shoulders of the pair crouching by an exposed bulkhead, running circuit-boards into the *Enchantress's* deck systems. 'Why, take these two scamps, here. Developed a taste for the hard stuff in the base commander's mess at Fort Ross 556. Fleet locks and surveillance system not much of an obstacle at all.'

They barely halted to acknowledge the Marine officer's ironic praise; exchanging arcane mutters between each other, STAIC source code exploits and the like. Xue wasn't the only one glad for the scrap-the-crap crew's checkered personnel files when the large locking mechanism retracted.

Adella immediately saw why her comms with the *Enchantress* hadn't tended towards the verbose. Bridge had taken a heavy targeted rail-gun strike. Hundreds of physical projectiles cutting through her like a laser scalpel poking tunnels in butter. Self-healing hull layers had foamed-up exposure to vacuum, resealing integrity, but that hadn't been enough to save most her bridge crew from the ball-bearing sized blast. They were still coffin-sealed by their seats, chairs armoured-up and field-protected for active combat. The majority of seats had been turned into real coffins by projectile impacts. *Lucky strike, or did someone know where to target inside our cruiser?* Adella's intuition swung towards the latter. Adella, the Marines and the DCT team moved at speed between each bridge position, running cables into chairs' life support to discover whether survivors lay within.

'Live one inside Target Acquisition!' called one of the rescue team.

'Skipper's seat contains vitals, too!' confirmed Adella.

Captain of Marines Xue set his combat medics onto both crew. 'Pop the seats and connect mag-grav ... we'll slide them direct to surgery!'

Adella dug into the medical subsystems for the *Enchantress's* captain. This chair was designed as combined armour, fighting position interface, surgical stabiliser and emergency lifeboat with cryo-sleep if necessary. Not one officer had ejected from the cruiser, though. The survivors would have fried-and-died if the ship hadn't docked in time with DV-Station. Bio-readings flowed into Adella's suit. She swayed in shock, having to grip the capsule's side to stop herself tumbling over.

'Commander!' barked Xue. 'Are you–?'

Adella raised her hand. 'I'm fine, Cap!'

And so was Adella's younger sister, Captain Arlinne Vega, who it appeared had been promoted to command of the *Enchantress* during Adella's exile to Ghost Fleet.

- 5 -

Sister Fact

'What's the verdict, doc?' asked Adella.

Doctor Parnell wiped his hands on his surgical greens. 'She's responding to standard lysergic acid diethylamide micro-dosing. From her neural activity, I'd say Captain Vega's vessel was in continuous active combat for a couple of days.'

The blood on the Doc's uniform didn't belong to Adella's sister – albeit there was plenty of it to go around among the cruiser's casualties. Captain Arlinne Vega's bridge position had suffered no strikes during the attack. However, Adella's sister *was* suffering from extended CIF – Combat Interface Fatigue; pumped full of drugs and augment-induced time compression. Basically, Arlinne's brain and nervous system had been seriously overclocked, placed into sync with the ship's AI during combat manoeuvering. From a relative consciousness point-of-view, an exchange of fire which took seconds could feel like an hour to the bridge crew. Adella had suffered CIF herself. Running as a human supercomputer seemed like fun when you were flinging missiles and predicting where the enemy would turn when you dropped particle beams in front of her. Your sticker shock came later, and boy did it ever arrive.

'Two days? Hell of an enemy contact.' With the cruiser's database corrupted by an EMP blast, Adella hadn't needed to prioritise her sister's place in the triage queue. The Captain's recovery was intel-critical.

'You can see her now. Normally, I would give your sister more rest, but…'

'Thanks, doc.'

Adella left Parnell to his other charges, heading to the small bay holding Arlinne Vega. Even with its size, DV's sickbay was full. Bed after bed filled. Multi-limbed medical systems slid around ceiling girders, dropping down on wounded, stitching, drugging, operating in a near blur of activity. Blood synthesisers were running low with the sudden influx, so manual donors from the station crew provided refills – a line formed for each of the three species composing the bulk of the *Enchantress*'s complement.

Adella's sister lay propped up against pillows. Her skin was mottled black all over from bruising. Captain Vega looked like cleaners had mopped her out of a boxing ring. In reality, that was accelerated blood flow bruising her from the inside.

'You look mighty fine today, Captain Vega.'

'CIF kiss will do that, Commander. I wondered whether you might still be at Bardfeld's when we set course for SecComm East.'

Adella smiled. 'Congrats on *your* promotion. Oddly, Fleet hasn't given me back my captaincy. Maybe the Admiralty thought it would confuse having two Captain Vegas from the same clan on the Fleet's officer list?'

'That must be it. I know you have a thousand questions for debriefing, but before we get into it, you need to dispatch your fastest ship to system edge and drop a signal buoy in hyperspace. I'll give you the codes to load into it.'

Adella paged Lieutenant Vistisen to load a signal buoy and prep the corvette *Scorcher* for that run. They might list *Scorcher* as a training vessel, but in reality, the corvette was what Engineering's gear-heads kept in hangar for engine mods and stretch-performance cranking. 'Done! What's your transmit?'

'That SecComm East is still here and hasn't been overrun, yet. The *Enchantress* is operating as a scout for the Second and Third Fleet.'

Adella stared in disbelief at her sister. *I must have misheard her. That would be thousands of ships,* 'You mean the Third Battlegroup *of* the Second Fleet?'

'No, I mean both full fleets. As in, fully deployed and combined.'

'That's insane! Who are we fighting, the whole rest of the universe?'

'No! You haven't heard…?'

'Arlinne, we've been comms dark here for months. All we've been collecting are refugee ships – merchants and colonists caught short when the Hyperspace Storm overtook the Frontier. In a good year, all we see are a single Legion re-supply ship and a couple of flotillas of Fleet's antique scrap incoming on autopilot and skeleton crews. You're the first real Navy to pass through Bardfeld's System for twenty-six months.'

'Dear God, no wonder you don't have a picket line on system edge. Adella, there's a full war raging in this corner of the galaxy!'

'Against whom, exactly?'

'A species from beyond the Frontier stars called the Quazalrats. We have little intelligence on the size or shape of their empire, but given how much trouble they're giving us, the Quazzie Imperium's territory must be truly massive.'

'But, a *war*? What kind of messed-up first contact situation led to that? Didn't we send in negotiators?'

'Of course, we did. Diplomatic Service sent a major delegation along with the Vice-President herself and a group of senators from TA council. The Quazzies were kind enough to ensure *one* of our delegation arrived back in Alliance space. A diplomatic protection service agent allowed to tape the feast where our representatives were cooked alive and served in a variety of styles. After the agent finished filming, they lasered off his arms and legs for their spread. Figured he didn't require limbs anymore. Quazzies are amphibious: think of a frog from your worst nightmare crossbred with a sentient velociraptor. They prefer eating insects the size of dogs, but apparently, they consider it a fine honour for filthy foreigners to intermingle with Quazalrat bodies via an act of sanctified consumption.'

Adella stared in disbelief at her sister.

'I know,' said Captain Vega. 'The Quazzies did much the same on at least twelve colonies along the Frontier we're aware of. Force Reconnaissance did a stealth insert on Kussel, the first colony to go offline. What they found was a scene from Hell. Population reduced down to a couple of percent of its original. Survivors farmed for food, a few more highly skilled colonists enslaved with neural staples and suicide collars. Every world terraformed to a tropical model which we presume is the Quazalrat homeworld's base climate. Mass pollution. Mass local species die-off.'

Adella felt sick. 'They need to be stopped.'

'Ain't that the truth. We've been trying, sis. Your Hyperspace Storm, it isn't a storm at all! It's a Quazalrat super-weapon. They can jam QT transmissions in hyperspace and down inside system space, too. Whatever tech they're using redacts G-Fold navigation by a ninety percent degrade. As far as we can tell, the Quazzies can counteract the jamming field for their own localised ship navigation, but can't circumvent it for comms.'

'So, their ships might not be able to swap message transmits, but they can still run rings around us when it comes to making hyperspace jumps.'

Adella's mind spun with the implications for ship combat. Two equally armed opponents with broken radios, but one force's weapons were on board sailing ships while the enemy navy had mounted theirs on rocket-driven hydrofoils. *Rings. Run around us.*

Captain Vega lifted herself forward of her pillows, groaning with the effort. 'It's worse than that even, I'm afraid. Quazzies can use their jamming field as a sensor mesh, too. Our ships are getting intercepted in hyperspace. We're fighting actions *inside* hyperspace for the first time, ever!'

Adella groaned. *Okay, so the rocket-driven hydrofoils have sonar and radar, too, while all Fleet has is stiff canvas and prayers for a decent breeze.* 'So, make my day, tell me this race of psychopathic frog-like serial-killers also shoot stealth missiles able to slip past our point defenses as if they don't exist?'

'Well, we certainly *had* the best weapons.'

And that was when the *Enchantress*'s Captain told Adella what had happened to the Third and Second Fleet. And Adella learned what bad news *actually* sounded like.

- 6 -

Command Glory

Adella arrived at sickbay to check on her sister's progress and give her the news. The first ship from the rag-tag retreating flotilla – all that was left of the Second and Third Fleet – had just dropped at system edge and was burning for DV-Station. The battlecruiser Little Warden. More vessels would join her, soon. Not the day's only good news. Captain Arlinne Vega had been judged well enough for discharge back to active service. All she needed now was a vessel; the Enchantress wasn't even fit for the yard to de-fang and clip for spare parts. A magnetic grapple and a tug burn towards the sun would do. As sad an end as any, but Enchantress would melt inside the system's star having discharged her duty. Who can ask for more?

'Captain without a command, then,' said Arlinne Vega.

You get used to it. Then, something occurred to Adella. 'It's time to dust off the plans for Operation Xerxes.'

'Just what is *that*?' asked her sister.

'A little distraction for keeping my crew on their toes and mentally occupied during the station's slow periods,' said Adella.

Although in truth, her notional war-game exercises had only ever envisaged an assault on Pullinger's sandpit by a pirate flotilla of ten ships at most. The vessels criminals, outlaws and insurgents might lay their hands on. Hijacked in-system patrol craft, re-purposed freighters and maybe a frigate lost to a mutiny at most. That is what Adella had previously regarded as a serious threat to her system. *Oh, for such happier days of innocence.*

'Is this mischief your Rear Admiral will disapprove of?' asked Arlinne.

'Only if he finds out. You up for some trouble?'

'You know,' said Arlinne, 'I think my crew *could* do with honest work to take their minds off the fact we recently got handed our arse on a plate.'

'*Captain* Vega.'

There was one thing you could say about having thousands of decommissioned hunks-of-junk floating as a dense artificial asteroid field. Plenty of room to conceal a few vessels written off by Fleet decades ago. Toys for her engineers to play with and active void-time logged for the crew. *It's only fair.* Rear Admiral Pullinger had the infinite architectural challenge of his sandpit to occupy his time. So, the station also needed its projects to pay honour to that old adage – the Devil makes work for idle hands. Pretty much everyone in Bardfeld's system knew service here meant they had screwed up. *Pullinger aside, perhaps.* Left to itself, that became a festering wound eating away at morale. Fights, drunkenness, brawling, self-medicating with every substance known to the Alliance – and a few more besides when it came to illegal synthesisers and bio-printing.

Adella might be Commander of the end of the universe. But she still held the title of Commander, which meant that crap going sideways out here, was *her* crap going sideways out here. Anything and everything Adella could do to ease such difficulties, she would.

***

'Maybe you'll get a medal for bringing the Enchantress home,' Adella said to her sister.

Unfortunately for her, Rear Admiral Pullinger was close enough to overhear the remark. 'Don't be ridiculous, Commander. Medals are awarded for ensuring the enemy loses ships, not for almost losing your own vessel.'

Adella bit her tongue. Her sister rolled her eyes, knowing he couldn't see her face. *Nor are they presented for filling an unwanted world in an unloved system with unnecessary buildings.*

Pullinger had insisted that they lay on a formal piping-in for the flagship about to slide into dock. *Cap's Kaps* were in their dress blues, and the Rear Admiral had also insisted on dress uniforms for the station staff greeting the newcomers. Captain Vega had mentioned that this was sure to annoy Admiral Bartosz Blackstar, CIC of the Combined Fleet. Or, rather, what was left of Blackstar's fleet. Out of the thousands of vessels that had departed CoreComm, there were now fewer than a hundred fighting ships limping into system. Even so, *Dark Viking* station had needed to work around the clock upgrading their temporary docking frames for full life support, cargo transfer and refuel facilities. Mooring war wagons that required an appraisal for scrap-and-strip turned out to be a lot less demanding than vessels actually expecting to ship out and fight again.

Requests for spare parts and damage repairs already flooded in. Adella suspected the captains were going to be rather disappointed with the antique replacements about to be bolted, welded and screwed into place onto their precious Void Steel.

Oddly, my sister's thoughts on dress uniforms and a formal reception don't seem to have made their way into the Rear Admiral's daily briefing. I wonder how that foul-up happened?

As a dreadnought, the TAS *Heart of Plasma* filled up a full two storeys of transfer locks at the station. Adella hoped Admiral Blackstar came out on the upper floor as planned, or Pullinger would greet the catering crew as Marines piped them on board. As amusing as that might prove, Adella had her own reasons for wanting to demonstrate to the Admiral that her posting wasn't the big-top for Fleet's clowns.

Locks rolled back, and the *Heart of Plasma's* crew came flooding out. In good order this time, albeit bemused by the formal piping and Marine honour guard awaiting them. Lettering on their staff caps had been abbreviated to HOP which inevitably led to the crew being referred to as *hoppies*, and the ship, informally, as the *Hoppy*. Admiral Blackstar led the way, with his bridge officers following. One significant addition to Blackstar's uniform since the last time his path had crossed with Adella's: a medical exo-skeleton surrounded the officer's body. A metal composite cage; a heavy, clomping mess of sickbay interfaces, drug injectors and cables feeding into the Admiral's body.

'That's new,' whispered Adella's sister.

One thing is certain, Adella thought, *if someone forced Bartosz Blackstar into that ugly contraption, he's been seriously dinged during the recent action.*

Blackstar marched down the line of Marines, giving Captain of Marines Xue a proper salute. More heartfelt than the one he returned to Rear Admiral Pullinger, at any rate.

'Your parade then, Rear Admiral?' asked Blackstar.

'Welcome on board *Dark Viking Station*, sir. We have quarters at SecComm East prepared for you and the Fleet's officers,' said Pullinger, pausing as he noticed the Admiral's frown, 'down on Bardfeld's World.'

'You found the space there, did you? Very thoughtful. However, at the moment, the Fleet's officers will be stationed on their ships for repair and turnaround.' Blackstar saluted Adella's sister. 'Captain Vega. Quite a battering for the *Enchantress*. I saw her state on the way in.'

Arlinne saluted sharply back. 'Yes, sir. You were right on the money. Given how many Quazzies came after us, we set off every tripwire they laid inside hyperspace.'

'Mission accomplished, this time. Send my personal thanks to all your officers and crew. In different circumstances, I would ensure you all received the Cluster of Honour. I know cruiser skippers love tooling around, but I can't afford to sacrifice ships laying false trails every time the fleet jumps. Not unless I want the *Heart of Plasma* as the sole survivor to reach home.'

'You *are* home, Admiral,' Pullinger pointed out.

'I fear we'll lose this system in short order, Rear Admiral. It won't take long for the enemy to track us down here.'

'SecComm East will stand, sir.'

'Yes, yes, quite the orbital fort you have here.' Blackstar grunted in what Adella was sure was irony. 'There will be a briefing for SecComm East's senior officers at seventeen hundred hours; concerning the invaders and what we know of them.'

Bartosz Blackstar appeared to notice Adella Vega for the first time, nodded coolly towards her, then left.

Rear Admiral Pullinger departed quickly, too, now there was nobody important enough remaining to occupy his attention. Adella was fairly sure Sector Command East's leader went muttering something about *defeatist nonsense.*

Well, one man's defeatist is another man's realist.

Captain Vega grimaced, watching Pullinger stride away on his pipe-cleaner-long legs. 'How many years have you been out at Bardfeld's World? If anyone deserves the Cluster of Honour, here, I think it should be you, sis.'

Adella shrugged. *Yeah, but you don't get medals for screwing up. However deep they bury you for it.*

***

The operations room on board the Heart of Plasma wasn't as busy as it could have been. Staff from Dark Viking Station in attendance as well as Rear Admiral Pullinger and a few stuffed shirts from sector command. Colonel Pes represented the External Legion. Adella ensured all her people were here, despite the Rear Admiral's best efforts to the contrary. The briefing's purpose, to update the locals on the state-of-play regarding what Fleet knew of the Quazzies' capabilities. Similar to the station's own operations room, a circular table sat in the chamber's centre with a hologram projection system ready to run over the findings.

Admiral Blackstar opened, covering much of the same ground Adella had heard from her sister inside sickbay – how the Quazzies launched a surprise attack across the Frontier after several opening skirmishes. Then came their failed diplomatic mission; hell, you might as well call it the Diplomatic Service's least successful luncheon. The dispatch of the Second and Third fleet in a combined force along with a priceless cache of Heezy weaponry; the kind capable of slagging star systems off navigation charts. Fleet's unexpected ambush in hyperspace by the Quazzies. The near total loss of half of the Triple Alliance's fighting vessels within an hour. Finally, the survivors' final long desperate withdrawal. Tiny hops, retreating, always retreating. Wagons being picked off. Dying on the jump, dying during hyperspace flight, landing in-system to find the enemy already there, Quazzie invaders deployed for another massacre.

Adella focused in when Admiral Blackstar detailed matters new to her. For a start, one of the staff sitting around the table was the Admiral's nephew. A pilot in Fleet Carrier Wing, one Colonel Kal Blackstar. Dark-haired with narrow eyes and an easy white smile that could have jumped from a dental advert, Blackstar-the-Younger looked every inch the hard-charging pilot stereotype. But Kal launched with a hell of a surprise weapons package under his wings. The Colonel had been genetically edited to serve as master gunner for the Heezy super-weapons carried by Fleet! Not that you could tell, but Kal Blackstar's DNA helix was now partially Heezy. Quite an achievement given that the ancient elder race had been missing from the universe for millions of years.

The Colonel followed up on his Uncle's introduction with a general summary of the Heezy weapons lost in the Quazzie ambush; notable more for what was left out, Adella suspected, than what was left in. She marked a Fleet Doctor hovering near the officer. *Just how high maintenance is it, running as a partial human-Heezy hybrid?* There was more to the Colonel than a set of experimental DNA edits; something that Adella couldn't quite put her finger on. A curious mixture of naivety and the hard-bitten edge of a flight officer she found oddly appealing. *Shut that shizzle down, girl.*

Adella had an unexpected ally in bringing her mind back to business when the Admiral brought up a rotating image of a naked Quazzie into the holo-well. Admiral Blackstar nodded in sympathy as the officers present made various disgusted sounds. *Indeed,* exactly like a sturdy green-skinned frog had mated with a very slippery velociraptor. *Arlinne, you were right on the money.* A three-eyed monstrosity. Two saucer-curious orbs at the front, one small eye on the back of its neck for 360 vision. Stocky build at around five-feet-tall, a pair of legs ending in splayed amphibious-looking feet. Although mostly green-skinned, it bore bright flashes of colour, like an Amazonian toad. It shipped with four arms, two upper limbs that passed for humanoid, each ending in a hand with an opposable thumb and three fingers. Two lower arms dangled like limp, curled tentacles.

The Admiral indicated the holo-model's tentacles. 'A Quazzie's lower limbs can lash out to fifteen feet; loaded with a nerve poison effective against all major Alliance species. This one is a female. The males aren't much different to look at, although *they* can't give birth to three hundred little Quazzies at a time. Our astrobiologists' profile suggests their significant spawning size feeds into their race's territorial and dominance instincts. Bear this in mind when we move onto fleet tactics.

'We haven't identified their home system, yet, but back-fitting from their DNA and biology, we know it's largely wet and tropical. Likely a Hell World-class, with super-predators and highly hostile Flora. Quazzies are amphibians and can stay underwater for between five and seven hours. The Quazzie Imperium's social system is extraordinarily unified. We're talking close to ants in terms of their willingness to sacrifice individual lives for the species. Obviously a byproduct of being one among hundreds in a single birthing-batch. We have seen ceremonial indicators with ritual significance that indicate a belief in gods. These mainly involve eating other sentients, as well as their own dead. We're unsure of the Quazzies' political system, or even if they have one, but a theocracy and a cleansing mission to dominate the universe is our best simulation fit.'

Colonel Pes spoke up. 'These monsters aren't allied with other species, Admiral?'

Blackstar wearily shook his head in response. 'Special Operations Command sent a stealthship poking into deep Quazzie space. Their findings convinced our politicians to send Fleet out in force. Every world Special Reconnaissance encountered in the Imperium is terraformed to Quazalrat standard. Indigenous sentients are farmed for food, with a tiny percentage of usefuls nerve-stapled as slaves. You do find these critters on board Quazzie ships, however...'

Admiral Blackstar recalled a holo of something that looked like a pint-sized Quazalrat. The main difference apart from diminished size was that the creature had four humanoid arms, rather than one pair of limbs as stinger weapons.

'We call these things Quaz Dogs. They operate on Quazzie ships in a subservient role. We think this race came out of the Quazzie homeworld, too. As if the Homo Floresiensi hobbits our palaeontologists found in Indonesia had survived long enough to be tamed and enslaved by humanity.'

Blackstar invited a science team member allocated to the Heezy weapon systems to speak about the new operating environment. Every bit as bad as Adella's sister had detailed. A disruption mesh turning single jump voyages into dozens of tiny hyper-hops, jamming Fleet's QT relay buoys and doubling up as some kind of sensor grid inside hyperspace. As to the science behind the field, while the best physicists the Alliance possessed were attached to the Heezy weapons, for all their insight, they might as well be five-year-olds grappling with infinite-dimensional Hilbert spaces and spin wavefunctions.

The Admiral moved onto ships, tech and vessel tactics, loading up tapes and sims from the Combined Fleet's encounters to date. 'Quazzie ships possess the same basic offensive and defensive systems as our own. But how they are deployed couldn't be more different. Only one class of Quaz vessel possesses jump vanes, their largest. This one, which we call a War-Wheel.'

A massive wheel-shaped vessel formed inside the holo-well. She resembled an old-style rotating space station. Adella couldn't see jump vanes on her, but then the Commander realised the thing was itself one massive jump vane!

'And this is what a Quazzie War-Wheel looks like fully laden...'

The projection morphed to show the wheel acting as a force carrier with hundreds of smaller vessels docked under its circumference.

'All the warships attached to her possess no individual hyperspace capability. No retreat is possible by individual craft. They fight and win, or they are abandoned to die; whether that's in hyperspace or in-system. You remember what Spartan mothers told their sons as they marched to war? Come back with your shield – or on it. This is the Quazzie equivalent.'

'More space to pack in weapons and armour, then,' said Adella.

'Exactly, Commander, although the Quazzies' ships are highly specialised. Every sub-unit carried by that War-Wheel, no matter what her size, falls into one of three basic vessel classes. Shield-ships, which are almost entirely heavy armour and energy screen projectors. Scout ships, which are essentially engines and communications arrays. And finally, what we've classified as Lancer ships, which are dedicated weapon platforms.'

'That's preposterous,' said Rear Admiral Pullinger. 'How would such bizarrely specialist ships fight?'

'In a highly coordinated manner,' explained Blackstar. 'When Quazzies translate into a system they immediately jam any local QT comms network, denying a realtime battle area view to our vessels. We understand the War Wheels carry these quantum jammers. Their scouts spread out, using laser-flash signals to coordinate the engagement. Shield-ship formations then protect attacking lancer ship wings. Here's what we modelled up after the fleet's hyperspace ambush. We were approaching the drop-out point to Skiturn 26F5, the largest colony inside the Frontier worlds when they jumped us.'

Adella watched with a mixture of awe and horror as the battle unfolded. She imagined the shock on the part of individual captains. First, you lose navigation as your gravity folds evaporate around you. Then you lose QT comms. Then something which was previously regarded as statistically unlikely bordering on impossible occurs. You're ambushed inside hyperspace for a mass fleet-level engagement!

War Wheels appearing, thousands of individual ships launching on top of you. War Wheels pulling back as Lancers released hell. Particle beams, missiles, rail-gun broadsides, a barrage from your worst nightmare. Vessel after vessel in the Combined Fleet exploding while crews struggled to reorient vessels for combat, spin up energy shields never needed within the collision-free vaults of hyperspace. Weapons hastily booted out of sleep mode, firing on this bizarre attacking swarm. Too unfocused and too late to penetrate a shield wall composed of nothing *but* energy shields and armour.

Adella could only stare in bewilderment as the engagement replayed in miniature in front of her. The Quazzies fought without quarter, demonstrating suicidal tendencies and no care for individual fleet elements at countless points during the action. The Commander shivered. *My sister survived that slaughter. She lived through the retreat, too. Dear God.*

'I know,' said Admiral Blackstar, as the simulation faded away. 'By comparison, it makes Pearl Harbour look like a pair of children squabbling with catapults. The enemy took the measure of us while overrunning the Frontier. But the Triple Alliance's vessels must seem as alien to the Quazalrats as the reverse. Every major ship with her own jump capability, rail guns, shields, and armour; able to operate independently. We must seek our advantage there, search for ways to exploit the Quazzie's group mentality. Astrobiology speculates their three-ship-class design is a throwback to tactics Quazalrat land forces used against super-predators on their homeworld. If that's the case, it shows an inflexibility of innovation ripe for exploitation by our officers.'

'What's the current operating strategy for the remaining components of the Combined Fleet, sir?' asked Adella.

'I thought it would be obvious,' said an exasperated Rear Admiral Pullinger.

Admiral Blackstar raised an eyebrow towards Pullinger. 'Is that so? Perhaps *you* will be so good as to explain then, Rear Admiral?'

For a moment Adella thought Pullinger might have the grace to blush, but on reflection, he was probably just finding his ridiculously stiff dress uniform a little too uncomfortable for the dreadnought's warm air conditioning. All the other officers present wore working shipsuits. Prepared for combat, not a parade.

'Very well, sir,' said the Rear Admiral without a trace of irony, as though the baton had been intentionally passed to him. 'Given our current set of operating circumstances, Sector Command East will deploy as a re-grouping point. Our vessel-breaking facilities will be tasked as a shipyard to repair the surviving elements of the Second and Third Fleet. These vessels will then recombine for a surprise attack against the enemy.'

There were a few suppressed titters from some of the Admiral's staff, mostly disguised as coughing.

'I believe that would indeed be a surprise, Rear Admiral,' said Blackstar. 'As much to our own officers as to the enemy, in this particular instance. No, my operating strategy at this point is to push back to SecComm Core, give them a complete account of what we ran into. After we develop a new game plan and re-tool our tech in light of the opening engagement, we will return with the full force of the First and Fourth Fleet.'

Pullinger shook his head, sadly, as though he'd been given the wrong answer in class. He obviously had different ideas for prosecuting this unwanted war. It stunned Adella. She'd always pegged Pullinger as someone who kissed ass up while kicking down. But, no. His condescension was dished out on an equal opportunities basis.

'I believe, sir, that would just be playing into the enemy's hands.'

'Rear Admiral, we lost most of our Heezy weaponry when the dreadnought Valhalla went down. She self-destructed when it became obvious that herself and her attached carrier group were about to be boarded by the Quazzies. We believe the Quazzies detected the weapon signatures of our Heezy technology and concentrated fire on the Valhalla first. It was disabling fire; their intention for our Heezy tech to fall into *their* hands. Right now, the most valuable thing we have on board this station is my nephew. We have additional Heezy weaponry protected beneath the great fort at Mars. What we don't have is another operator capable of firing it.'

'I'm sure your nephew is a very fine fellow and a highly gifted pilot,' said Pullinger, 'but surely another volunteer can be found for Heezy hybridisation to launch these weapons?'

'Heezy weapons are, as I understand it, almost living creatures. The Heezy civilization was so advanced it makes us and our current state of technology appear like bacteria by comparison. For a bacterium to hack a human genetic code and pass off as one is a not insignificant achievement. Trust me on this, Rear Admiral Pullinger, if Fleet Weapons Division could have provided every one of my ships with a Heezy weapon operator, every one of my goddamn ships would have *had* a Heezy weapons operator!'

Harper Pullinger made a strangled snorting sound but otherwise held his fire. He bridled at the Admiral's slap-down. Rear Admiral Pullinger's silence was far more dangerous than his peacock strutting and superciliousness. On that sour note, the briefing finished and the exit corridors out of Ops became everyone's favourite place to be.

Admiral Blackstar intercepted Adella before she made it home safe. 'Station Commander. A moment of your time if you please.'

So courteous. Nothing like our last encounter. The Admiral ushered Adella into his private ready room next to Ops.

'I'm surprised you want to see me, sir, given the circumstances of our previous meeting,' said Adella.

Blackstar shrugged. 'How surprised would you be if I told you that the real skirmish was fought *before* your board of inquiry convened? My intervention led to you being posted here, rather than completely cashiered out of the service.'

Adella *was* taken aback, in fact, she was astonished. She always believed Admiral Blackstar had been one of the driving forces behind her years exiled at this scrap-yard posting.

'I seem to remember you saying at my board that the Fleet has limited uses for an officer who can't follow orders.'

'That very much depends on the circumstances. There were thousands of ships-of-the line with my combined force where officers followed orders and protocols and fleet procedures. It's a telling commentary on our systems that most of the ships that came limping back to SecComm East were the ones whose skippers applied a little creative thinking out in the void.'

'With the best will in the world, that battle you replayed was high-grade TARFU. How many impossibles can a skipper be expected to accommodate during a single engagement? QT comms unable to function? Hyperspace jumps reduced to skipping rope and a navigator's best guess? Ambushes inside hyperspace?'

'You are being far too kind, Commander. Warfare has always been the art of the unexpected. It's about innovating tech and changing-up your strategies. We forgot that. Fleet got sloppy and grew too used to a peacetime rulebook.'

'Is that what you wanted to tell me?' asked Adella.

'A limited apology, perhaps,' said Admiral Blackstar. 'From one officer to another, you were ordered to do something very difficult.'

Adella had to stop herself grimacing. Actually, what she wanted to do was sob, but she would never expose herself in front of the brass. *Yes, opening fire on a pirate warship when they were using a passenger liner as a hostage vessel. Practically welded together.* But it would have been a lot easier if the liner's captain *hadn't* been Adella's husband, Eskandar. 'Doing difficult things is a Fleet officer's duty.'

'The politicians scapegoated you. If that pirate madman Blue Barnier hadn't used the liner as a distraction, you would have been hailed as the steel-nerved Fleet bitch whose calm resolve under fire led to the rescue of thousands of passengers.'

Distraction? That was one word for it. Eskandar's liner had been jury-rigged as a kinetic warhead and flung against one continent to make the looting of the rare metal reserves on the opposite hemisphere easy meat. In the end, Adella hadn't saved Eskandar or his voyagers but had added a death toll of 20,000 on the world of Strabane. *All because of my hesitance to fire.*

'You're wrong, sir. I deserve to be here. I should have cut that liner in half and relied on her damage control systems to compartmentalise her. My Marines could have stormed what was left of both liner and Blue Barnier's warship.' *Eskandar would still be alive. Along with many thousands of innocents who didn't deserve my finger on the trigger.*

'Second-guessing decisions doesn't win victories. Blue Barnier knew the liner's skipper was your husband. He knew *you* led the anti-piracy group. That's why Blue Barnier singled out the *Countess of Jupiter* as a hijack target. Cunning is the criminal's strongest shield. Fleet command is an isolated, lonely duty. The distances ships operate at mean that our Captains must always be the ones calling the shots. If we didn't want human mistakes, we'd put goddamn artificial intelligences in control of our vessels make this Fleet a drone operation.'

'I didn't realise you spoke for me at the board of inquiry, Admiral. Thank you for your support.'

'I thought you deserved to hear why you ended up at Bardfeld's World from me sooner rather than later,' said Admiral Blackstar. He tapped his medical exoskeleton frame. 'Later's warping beyond the rainbow bridge for these old bones. I was on the dreadnought *Excalibur* during our ambush. We caught an x-ray warhead flash too close for our shielding to protect us. They wrecked her, much like they wrecked me. My veins are full of more anti-radiation meds than blood right now.'

Adella understood. The damage she could see on the outside was nothing compared to the mutilation of the man's interior. A little like herself. Except she hadn't expired from her hurt, yet. However much it felt as though she wanted to and needed to. Poor Admiral Blackstar; dead man exo-walking. 'How long, sir?'

'It's mostly guesswork given how little we know about the enemy's nuclear yields. My CMO thinks I have anywhere between three days and two weeks left.'

'I would say sorry, Admiral, but I bet you've heard quite a lot of that.'

'Too much. I don't require your sorrow, Commander, I need your head in this fight. Your mind and your heart. Because with our communications and transit technology severely degraded, those two organs are about the only advantages the Triple Alliance has over these bastard Quazzies.'

Adella saluted. 'Yes, sir!'

'Telling you the truth about your board wasn't the only reason I wanted to talk with you, Commander. What is your evaluation of Rear Admiral Pullinger.'

There's a loaded question. 'Why, I believe he's ideally suited to command over SecComm East, sir.'

Blackstar winked back at her, smiling. 'Yes. I understand everyone in the Admiralty feels exactly the same way.'

- 7 -

Meet the Sun

Adella went through the next few days in a blur. A constant battle to stay on top of the repairs needed by the unexpected influx of vessels. Their factory ship now operated 24-7 to turn ships around as fast as was humanly possible; ditto Adella's tired and overstretched engineering crews. The entire operation would have been near impossible if the station's old routine hadn't been cutting antique Void Steel into spare parts for stockpiling. Of course, Fleet, with its normal bureaucratic nimbleness only collected those spare parts every five years or so. Perhaps to rub in the fact that the main purpose of Bardfeld's World was make-work for reprobates who weren't required by the rest of the Alliance. That snub, however, was about to save the tattered remains of two fleets.

The Commander had only just rotated off one of her long shifts when the news she had been dreading arrived in a page. Admiral Blackstar had passed away. And perhaps even more disturbing was the notification that command of the Combined Fleet had passed too. Into Rear Admiral Harper Pullinger's not so capable hands. Pullinger's sandpit exchanged for a toy-box filled with real working ships for him to push about. And where he might push them, Adella didn't want to dwell.

Admiral Blackstar, it transpired, had requested his body be interred on board the *Enchantress* when the wrecked old cruiser tumbled into the sun.

Adella brought forward the date for the *Enchantress*'s final voyage. She also ensured that all sailors killed in action who'd sought a burial in space were taken out of the morgue and made ready to join the broken cruiser. It took a lot of effort to patch the dead vessel; weld on a tug's drive unit, bolt on adequate control systems and reinstall the ship's A.I.

backup – *Meg*, to the sailors who'd served on board *Enchantress*. But there were some jobs you didn't scrape on.

Evening Watch a couple of days later, when the station's staff gathered at parade rest alongside the fleet's survivors. DV's docking levels were packed solid with neat formations of personnel. Nobody needed to be told to wear dress uniforms this time. A pity the Rear Admiral was far too busy with the demands of his new command to shuttle up to the station. *The braids and medals on show here would have made him happy for the rest of the week.*

A magnetic conveyor line ran through the station onto the *Enchantress* and inside her armoury. A torpedo for each coffin, draped with the Fleet's flag. Casket bearers carried each of the fallen to the mag-line, where the torpedoes remained hovering while Fleet chaplains intoned Unified Faith prayers.

After the scripture readings finished, Adella stepped forward to read from the ancient paper poetry book. She'd been given the tome by her mother after graduating from the Academy.

'Sunset and evening star. And one clear call for me! And may there be no moaning of the bar, when I put out to sea.

'But such a tide as moving seems asleep, too full for sound and foam. When that which drew from out the boundless deep, turns again home.

'Twilight and evening bell, and after that the dark! And may there be no sadness of farewell, when I embark.

'For though from out our bourne of Time and Place, the flood may bear me far, I hope to see my Pilot face to face, when I have crossed the bar.'

Marines stood on either side of the mag-line. Captain of Marines Xue's people drew lots against the ships' Marine force to determine who would hold the honour of making the line. Well, lots were what they had reported back to Adella. They'd probably wrestled for it.

Xue flourished his sabre before barking, 'Firing party, present arms!'

Marines raised rail-rifles as one and released a three-volley salute into the air. Crack-crack-crack. A bugler stamped forward. Taps' mournful sound echoed across the locks while the line of coffins slowly loaded on board the *Enchantress*. After the last body passed, Adella switched the podium's command link to audio over the dock's speakers for everyone assembled to hear; the Solar Walk a tradition as old as any inside Hell-Fleet. Adella turned to find her sister standing in the squad of officers behind.

Captain Vega stepped forward and took the podium. The cruiser was Arlinne's command and so too the vessel's Solar Walk. 'Meg, this is Captain Vega. Confirm your orders, please.'

<To meet the sun, Captain.>

'Go gentle into that star, Meg. The *Enchantress* is a good ship and you carry a fine crew.'

<Aye-aye, Captain. Plot confirmed. Boosters, go. Fido, go. Retro, go. Guidance, go.>

'*Enchantress,* you may launch.'

<Burn initiated. Tug aux-drive holding stable. Goodbye, Captain Vega.>

A rattle of docking clamps released, then the ruined cruiser began to push away from the station, glimpses of holed hull and melted equipment. Her bulk disappeared through the wheel locks' armoured glass panels, dwindling to nothing.

***

When Adella spotted the grim look on her sister's face the next morning, she knew what the Captain had to say wouldn't be good. She opened the door to her quarters and beckoned Arlinne inside.

'Okay, tell me.'

'Rear Admiral Pullinger is planning to take the fleet out,' said Captain Vega.

'As Blackstar planned, you mean? Jumping for Core alongside our convoy of civilians?'

'No, he's come up with the genius plan of a surprise attack against the Quazzies. He intends to lead the fleet and draw the Quazzies onto the star around Shiddes 22. Lure them with some fast cruiser hops, make the frogs think we're planning to retake the occupied colony world at Shiddes. Then he aims to deal with the Quazzies in-system.'

Adella groaned. It was exactly the same nonsense spouted by the Rear Admiral inside Blackstar's intelligence briefing. Pullinger wanted to shave the *Rear* off his title, bucking for full Admiral. And it seemed he didn't care how many Alliance ships or crew he needed to spend to win his promotion. 'But that's madness! If Blackstar couldn't beat the enemy with two full fleets, what chance does Pullinger think he has with a hundred beaten-up survivors?'

Captain Vega imitated Pullinger's supercilious tone. 'Defeatism? I won't hear defeatism in the ranks. It is bad for morale and a fleet floats on morale. We have surprise on our side. The same surprise that Hannibal carried with his elephants over the Alps.'

'Yeah, the same surprised look that crossed General Custer's face, too.'

'I'm shipping out with the fleet,' said Adella's sister. 'I've been given First Officer's position on the flagship. Poor old Corinna Reinhilde warped over the rainbow bridge after she took a shrapnel shard through the skull.'

And how Rear Admiral Pullinger must have loved that. Demoting Adella's sister from an operational captain to commander, forcing her to jump every time he coughed. 'You could request a transfer...'

'Who from, your boss? From the pen-pushers at SecComm East? No, the First Officer's seat on the *Heart of Plasma* is actually where I need to be. I may be able to mitigate the worst of whatever tactical TARFU this operation generates.'

'You just be careful out there, sis,' said Adella. *It hardly seems fair.* Captain Vega had already survived more misfortune than most officers saw in a lifetime of service. Simply arriving safe at *Dark Viking Station* should have been victory enough.

'I understand Pullinger's planning to strip your station's Marines out and deploy them with him on the *Heart of Plasma*. You won't have any Jarheads to rely on when your system sees its first frogs.'

'You might almost form the impression the Rear Admiral's trying to undermine my command,' said Adella. 'He's also poached Lieutenant Anders for his flagship. At this rate, I will be promoting mess-hall cooks up to line operations.'

'It's not just your people you need to watch out for. You make sure those suspiciously intact wrecks floating out in Ghost Fleet aren't spotted by the Rear Admiral or any of his toadies. Or all you will have for a System Defence Force will be harsh language plus a few steel girders from that building-site to load into your rail-cannons.'

Adella knew the Captain spoke the truth. If anyone was about to launch a surprise action, Adella had better make sure it was *her*. Or nobody would leave Bardfeld's System alive.

- 8 -

Dead Man's Stick

Adella was confused to find Colonel Kal Blackstar sitting in the station's mess, along with the medical aide who seemed surgically implanted to the Colonel's side; Doctor Delorey.

Adella collected her food from the auto-serves in the wall and sat down on the bench opposite the fly-boy and his medic. 'Colonel, you are not on board the *Heart of Plasma*?'

'The Admiral left me a set of sealed orders to process on the occasion of specific events. One of those was his death. He instructed me to remain safe on station until Fleet can escort me to Core. I suppose that's fair enough. We lost all our Heezy weaponry during the ambush. The addition of an extra carrier pilot to the force won't sway the battle one way or the other.'

'I wager the Rear Admiral wasn't happy about you being grounded!'

'I also had sealed orders to pass across to the Rear Admiral. I dare say they reiterated what my Uncle wrote to me. I'm to stay out of harm's way until I make it back alive to SecComm Core.'

Most zoomies of the Commander's acquaintance were Gung Ho to the point of near suicidal, so it shocked Adella to hear the Colonel sounding so fatalistic about being left off the mission.

'Perhaps the Admiral wanted to protect you. As *you*, I mean. His nephew rather than a trigger for super weapons.'

'No, he wanted to protect his trigger, not his nephew. It's hard to say. My thoughts get very clouded, confused.'

'It is quite natural,' fussed the doctor, reaching inside his medical bag for an injector stick which he loaded into the Colonel's exposed arm. 'This is the first time we've ever blended human DNA with an extinct species, let alone a species as strange and alien as the Heezy. The side-effects need constant management. Without me by the Colonel's side,

I'm afraid the dear boy would pass away within a month.'

'You will be able to fix the Colonel though – stabilise him back to base human after we win?'

'*If* we win,' said the Colonel.

Well, Kal is at least together enough to realise how slim our chances are, at any rate.

'Oh, yes. Fleet medical are ready to mitigate the worst of his symptoms. Right now, I'm afraid the Colonel is of more use to the Alliance war effort as a befuddled half-Heezy, rather than a fully compos mentis human.'

There was something slippery about Doctor Delorey which Adella found it hard to trust. *Why is that, I wonder*? She made a note to herself to seek a second opinion from Doc Parnell the next time she visited sickbay.

Adella leaned over the table. 'They say staying active is the best medicine, Colonel. If you want work to do, I've got an old carrier waiting on the scrap list; the *Smiter.* It wouldn't hurt to have someone on the detail who knows their way around one.'

'I'm not sure if that would be a good idea,' said Doctor Delorey.

Yeah, well, I'm not inviting you. 'It won't be too taxing, work-wise. Hell, most of what we do is directing drones to do the heavy lifting, anyway.'

'I think it will help me,' said Blackstar. 'Having something to do, to focus on.'

'There we go, then. It's settled,' said Adella, enjoying the look of discomfort crossing the Doctor's face. *What have you got against real work, Mr. Delorey?*

***

' I need to receive a titanium-plated report from you, Chief. What ships are running operational?' asked Adella, drumming her fingers on the desk.

Talking to the humanoid lizard was actually a pleasure after long solitary hours replaying combat sims from the ambush. Seeking all the insights she could from the engagement. Every angle analysed. Watching each ship murdered repeatedly. If you could learn more lessons from defeat than victory, losing two whole Alliance fleets left Adella with a university education to compress into what little time she had remaining. Work gave Adella something to do other than worry about her younger sister's fate with the fleet. Fret about how many lives Adella carried in her own hands, here, both Fleet and civilians, everyone waiting for the first Quazzies to arrive. *And how badly I messed up the last time I held an operational command running combat-active.*

'The refinery ship *Spacewise Giant,* and the factory vessel *Takasaki* are fully operative,' reported Aralat raz Kessi. Her office chair had auto-adjusted to accommodate the Skirl's thick stubby tail. Kessi might resemble a humanoid Tyrannosaurus Rex, but like most of his race, he projected the refined manners of a country squire. Adella once read the Skirls' elaborate mores resulted from a low-grade desert ecosystem which prioritised rituals as a social survival mechanism. Ditto, the species' enterprising and buccaneering natures.

Two ships? Very much the official line, Chief. But the Rear Admiral wasn't sitting alongside them inside Adella's office. Adella would actually welcome the senior officer's presence for once, as it'd mean Pullinger *wasn't* off teasing the enemy with the remains of the Alliance's naval capability in this corner of the galaxy.

'The twins have been keeping us in fuel and spare parts for years,' said Commander Vega. 'But I'm talking about some Operation Xerxes-style manoeuvres.'

'Ah, you're referring to those dashed ships that keep on slipping off the decommissioning database?'

It's not a bug in the software, it's a feature. Hackers needed their practice as much as engineers and sailors. 'Exactly those ones.'

'As it stands,' said the Chief, 'we have two cruisers, three destroyers, and a stealth ship on the operational list. They are the *Escapade*, and *Gypsy*; the *Persistent*, *Grappler*, and *Talisman*; and the *Voidwolf*. Captain Vega and her crew were very supportive in helping us brush the cobwebs off the *Voidwolf*, as it happens. There're also a variety of smaller support vessels and five corvettes. And of course, there's still the *Dark Viking* herself. You will find the station's weapons, main drive and jump vanes suspiciously well-serviced and viable, given she's fired nothing except orbital adjustment thrusters for the last century. She won't look elegant flying, but aerodynamics aren't an issue and merely the sight of us should give most sane enemies a few seconds' pause.'

A battleship's weight is never to be sniffed at. But I'm not sure how sane a species of baked-in psychopaths like the Quazzies can be considered, though. 'Thank you for your update, Chief. By an amazing quirk of fate, your operational list almost exactly matches the combined effective experience of the crew manifest inside Bardfeld's System. What about that sweet carrier which keeps on getting deleted from our malfunctioning database?'

'The *Smiter* isn't the problem, Commander. She was more or less functional when Fleet hauled her here. The issue is her missing fighters. Fleet does so love stripping fast-movers for spare parts before we ever get to lay a laser-welder on a single carrier hull plate. I suspect it's because the flight deck's Void Boss recycles old parts while selling new replacements on the black market. Shocking, I know, but…'

'And a carrier without fighters is a void-faring chocolate tea-pot.'

'Precisely. Of course, with additional time I might be able to arrange a shipping error with my contacts back in the naval shipyards. Perhaps a couple of squadrons of Darkstar X-12s accidentally stored inside the next inbound scrap flotilla?'

'Chief, you know of all the thousands of staff here, you're the only officer the Master-at-Arms' office keeps on wanting to send investigators after to ask a few "additional questions"?'

Chief Kessi gave a brief flash of his razor-sharp teeth. 'Once those blighters get a bone in their mouth they don't like letting go, do they?'

'They seem to believe your bone is a few billion hidden away in untraceable funds.'

'That would be such a nice problem to have,' nodded the Skirl officer, as agreeable as he ever was. 'Although, as a point of fact, fungible funds are almost always traceable given enough time. A thoughtful chap or chapess would conceal their loot in commodity-based instruments. Like tracing individual sand grains on my homeworld, those devils.'

Adella sighed. 'If we had that extra time, maybe you could just *buy* me a couple of art-state fighter wings from a manufacturing combine?'

'As it happens,' said the Chief, 'one of the curious side-effects of a good war is how it tickles up commodity values.' He rubbed his scaled hands together. 'Every dark cloud...'

Chief Kessi was likely to die the richest Skirl in the Fleet as well as the most crooked. The real trick for Adella would be ensuring he *didn't* die – along with everyone else when the first Quazzies turned up at Bardfeld's System.

***

'Doctor Parnell, have you had a chance to review that information I sent over to you yet?' asked Adella as she entered the side office off sickbay.

'An interesting case, commander,' said the doctor. 'In more ways than one.'

'Do tell...'

'You have to remember that as far as DNA analysis of extinct species goes, I am parsecs away from being an expert. However, there are a great many things about this data from your Colonel Blackstar's vitals that make very little sense to me.'

Adella stared expectantly at the doctor until he continued.

'There certainly is something written into your young officer's DNA that is utterly inhuman and foreign to us. It may well be Heezy, although the data that would prove that is far beyond the reach of my security clearance.'

'Isn't everything as we'd expect, then?'

'Yes and no. Recent gene edits leave a whole suite of markers in the blood. And your Kal Blackstar possesses none of them as best I can test. It is as though he inherited the Heezy genes which allow him to operate the ancients' equipment with such ease.'

'That makes little sense? If the Alliance had people with the baked-in ability to fire Heezy weapons technology for generations, the one thing

I *can* guarantee you is that Fleet would have got around to live testing their toys before a major shooting war broke out.'

'That is as maybe, Commander, but there's also the matter of the treatment regime sickbay has been supplying to Doctor Delorey. It does not, in my estimation, reflect what would be required to stabilise a human-alien hybrid. There are no immunosuppressants on the list, for instance.'

Adella was puzzled. 'So, what *does* his therapy regime support?'

'Well that, Commander, is where things get really strange. Some of the Colonel's drugs I might use to treat depression, multiple personality disorder, or severe post-traumatic stress disorder. But then again, I could also apply a couple of the items on Delorey's prescription to an enemy combatant during enhanced interrogation if you ordered me to do so. I could tell you a lot more with access to the medical stream from the Colonel's Fleet implant, but…'

'But, that stream is classified to Doctor Delorey.'

'Indeed. So, let us move on to the good Doctor Delorey. Bear in mind that our database shard hasn't been synchronised with SecComm Core for a couple of years, but I can find no records of the doctor with the Fleet Medical Office. He might have transferred in late after decades in private practice, but…'

'But this kind of shtick is usually associated with Black Ops' laundry,' finished Adella. *I knew I didn't trust him.* 'Thank you for your help. And it goes without saying…'

The doctor tapped the side of his nose. 'Consider this conversation covered by doctor-patient confidentiality. Although, in truth, I really don't know what to make of *any* of this.'

That makes two of us, Doctor. Adella left medical and went to her own cabin. The computer access facilities at home were slightly more customised than elsewhere on the station. Adella was sure that the same hacks in place on her system were also installed for the members of Engineering who had given her a "practical demonstration" of why they'd been exiled to Bardfeld's.

'Slugger,' she spoke to *Dark Viking*'s main AI, 'command override *Vega Culture Crash Five Beta Zulu.*'

<Private line established. Data recording terminated. Full access to all files. Full trail deletion after line closure.>

'Access Fleet's military records for Colonel Kal Blackstar.'

<Established, commander.>

'Recall data chain.'

<Colonel Kal Blackstar's military record added to personnel shard at *Dark Viking Station* after synchronisation update with vessels of Combined Fleet.>

'So, no record of a Colonel Kal Blackstar serving with Fleet Air-Space Command before that date?'

<No, commander.>

'Please confirm date of the last full database synchronisation prior to Combined Fleet's arrival.'

<Two years, three months and 14 days.>

Adella grunted to herself. So, a doctor inserted out of nowhere and a carrier Colonel with zero service record who seemed to have been able to sign up, graduate Academy, then be promoted to a flying Colonel at Fleet air-space wing within a couple of years? *Yeah, nothing much suspicious about that.* 'Slugger, access Admiral Blackstar's last positive vetting by FIS. Cross-query family history, existing relatives.'

<Bartosz Blackstar, unmarried. No children. Admiral Blackstar's parents predeceased him by 31 years. Admiral Blackstar has one sister, Janina Blackstar, still alive, aged 176.>

'How many children does Janina Blackstar have?'

<Janina Blackstar has two daughters, Marysia and Danuta Blackstar, both still alive.>

'Has Janina Blackstar ever produced any male heirs?'

<Yes. Kaleb Blackstar, predeceased by 121 years. Died aged seventeen in a mountain climbing accident at Arsia Mons, Mars while attending Chryse Military Academy.>

Adella tutted to herself. As well as Heezy-human hybridisation, whoever Doctor Delorey really was, he also seemed to have perfected the resurrection of long-dead college kids. *What a neat trick. This keeps getting better and better.*

'Slugger, does Doctor Delorey have a private data store set up on your core?'

<Yes, Commander. Fully Encrypted.>

'Load DataAxe and run decryption.'

That data-cracker was totally illegal. But then, Adella was one of the few people that knew three of the malware's four co-authors were currently posted inside Bardfeld's System.

<Unlock in two hours and ten minutes.>

Adella set an alarm to remind her to check back in. When the time expired, she unspooled the cracked results. Most of it was medical data which, when she cross-checked it, seemed to confirm the Doc's concerns about Blackstar the younger's highly unusual treatment regime. There was also a whole lot of data that correlated to mental corrective systems – mostly banned on civilised Alliance worlds. Including a long cipher key to unlock something running on a Fleet-issue brain augment. *What's this for, then?* Was either the Doctor or Blackstar walking around with a secret courier cache inside their mind? *Does this relate to the Heezy weaponry? This is some full-on Black Ops crap, right here.*

By rights, Adella should toss both the doctor and the Colonel into the brig as a risk to the security of her System Defence Force. Of course, if she did that, there was a pretty high chance that the doctor would produce some damnable Fleet priority authorisation handing him effective control of her station. Adella would end up thrown in the brig for hacking inside classified archives and records. *So, what am I meant to do? Pretend I don't know? Allow those two clowns to run around doing God knows what behind my back?* She would have to find a way out of this quandary if she was to stay sane.

So, Kal Blackstar, just who the hell are you?

- 9 -

The Smiter

It felt good to be on the carrier Smiter doing honest work. It was one of the saving graces of scrap-the-crap duty. Nothing like hard physical labour to drive worries and cobwebs away from an overactive mind. As a special bonus, Doctor Delorey had been left off the shuttle rota call; he wasn't here to interfere in Adella's interactions with Colonel Blackstar. Whatever mystery lay behind the Colonel's unusual background, she was fairly sure that Doctor was up to his neck in that mischief.

Adella told herself that understanding the mystery was why she was here. Nothing at all to do with the handsome Colonel or the unlikely feelings he awoke in her. *No, nothing to do with that at all.* It was her duty to the station to get to the bottom of this. A situation that might very well pose a threat to her System. Well, not much more of a threat than an ongoing alien invasion of the Frontier, if truth be told.

Kal Blackstar wandered down the starboard launch hangar of the old bird. A scattering of crew worked across the cavernous space; welding plates, stripping out broken gear, and controlling swarms of engineering drones – ranging from rodent-sized spot welders to lumbering troll-sized construction robots. Like most Alliance carriers, the *Smiter* had four discrete carrier sections constructed on a rotating ring midships of the vessel; one for each of her accompanying fighter wings. Each squadron could land and launch at any angle on the 360° rotation depending on combat operation requirements.

'I thought you said that the *Smiter* was listed for demolition,' noted the Colonel. 'I see none of the key systems stripped out for recycling. If anything, she appears to have been patched up.'

'I might have misspoken,' said Adella. 'I didn't want to bore your Doctor Delorey with unnecessary details.'

'What, details like a spare war group being assembled on the side?'

Adella shrugged. She moved out of the way for a loader drone to stomp past with a case full of pipes. 'I don't understand what you mean.'

'Well, those parts coming across inside our shuttle were obviously stripped out of a dreadnought. What's that old saying about robbing Peter to pay Paul?'

'We try to keep an active home defence force,' explained Adella. 'It's good for morale. And you never know when you might actually need one.'

'A top tip for carrier operations: a carrier with no fighters will not get you very far.'

'I'm so glad I brought you across, 'said Adella, sarcastically. 'It was exactly for those insights that we tagged you for this duty.'

Colonel Blackstar pointed out a line of large reactors stacked at the end of the chamber. 'I thought you might be planning to launch those, instead. If only into the sun to minimise radiation hazard.'

'These old carriers have the largest hangers of anything that's brought here for mothballing or scrapping. We use this empty space to dismantle specialist equipment for parts we want to keep. We could decommission it outside on the float, but—'

'—working in vacuum suits that can be damaged and breached is more dangerous than doing it inside in an artificial gravity field.'

'Exactly,' said Adella. 'So, what you think, really?'

Blackstar pointed to a line of magnetic rails mounted on turntables. Everything a fully crewed carrier needed to put a squadron into space. 'If you had fighters, you'd be able to do the job. The launch systems are as well-maintained as the carrier I flew into the Frontier on. Not as modern, of course. But in good shape.'

'I am glad to hear you say it. We've had continual problems with the primary gun deck on the *Smiter*, though.'

Colonel Blackstar raised a hand to the crew lift off to the side. 'Lead on.'

They rode the lift across and down to the carrier's central gun-house deck. Each massive cannon had an automated projectile hoist and feed, with three chairs for gunners to interface with the A.I. systems, as perfect a human-machine melding as Fleet engineering could provide. Kal went up to a position and booted up its system, an orrery of hologram diagnostic icons rotating into life. He pushed the diagnostics about, getting deep into the system's guts.

'This is an old CVN-301 class carrier,' said Kal, halting the reporting line for Adella to see the section being examined. 'Their rail cannons have an undocumented problem with sabot and armature discards. You need to patch the software here to handle that, or you'll experience jammed roller paths on the magazine load.'

'You train as a Fleet engineer, too?'

'No, but they surely do bitch loudly enough about design issues inside the mess.'

'Don't they just,' said Adella.

'You remind me of someone,' said Kal, 'but I can't quite place who.'

Adella smiled. 'As long as it's not your sister or your mother.'

'Everything becomes so strange when I think of the past. I remember my time at college and in the Academy, but whenever I see my family, all I seem to conjure up is a snowstorm.'

'It's probably a side-effect of your Heezy DNA edits,' said Adella. *Let's be subtle about this Adella. The best interrogations are the ones where the subject does not even realise they are being interrogated.* 'It must feel like walking with two bodies. The real you and an ancient extinct you coexisting in the same form.'

'The thing is,' said the Colonel, 'when I say snowstorm, I don't mean a fuzzy head. I mean a *literal* snowstorm; I see trees bending under the weight of ice; the ferocity of a wind cutting through the forest.'

'Perhaps you're remembering skiing holidays from your youth?' Adella suggested.

'I spent most my time in private schools of the boarding variety from what I remember.'

'Did the Heezy prefer cold worlds out on the system edge?' asked Adella.

Kal shook his head as he closed the rail cannon's interface. 'I don't think they cared. To the Heezy, their physical bodies were just clothes in a wardrobe. They swapped consciousness between whichever body suited the task at hand – sometimes riding more than one body simultaneously.'

Adella leaned in and kissed Kal, almost immediately regretting the impulsiveness of her act.

'That's the second ambush I've been in recently,' said the Colonel, but not unkindly.

'I'm hoping it's not quite as traumatic as having your carrier shot out from under you by the Quazzies.'

Kal pulled her in close and returned her manoeuvre in kind. 'No, not as totally traumatic as that.'

In short order, they were both deploying the gun-house deck in an unexpected mobilisation that would certainly have surprised – and definitely entertained – the Fleet's engineers, if any had been present to observe it.

***

Adella was drifting off into a deep sleep, trying to delete her accumulation of mysteries and worries, when the alarm erupted on her bedside monitor. She awoke in a flash. Old habits die hard. Adella swung her feet off her mattress and paged the system to serve her audio only. *How many years have I been in charge of this* station, and this must be the first time I've had my Dog Watch interrupted by an emergency alert? Very much a sign of the times.

'Vega, here.'

'Commander, it's Lieutenant Stanislava, there's incoming flash traffic.'

Adella trembled. News of her sister and the Combined Fleet under the Rear Admiral's command? 'Dispatches from the *Heart of Plasma?*'

'No, Commander. It's a free-trader vessel. I believe you will want to hear what they have to say all the same.'

What, another ship for Uddin Cesti's convoy—more supporters for his ragbag trade union movement of disgruntled merchants and frustrated colonists. 'On my way.'

Kal Blackstar pushed his head out from her duvet. 'Do you think this'll warrant a general-quarters alarm?'

'Go back to sleep, fly-boy. You've seen enough action for today. With any luck, it'll be some nervy civilian skipper spooked by ghost reads in hyperspace.'

Kal Blackstar hadn't proved quite the antidote Adella had hoped he would. She'd started having the dreams again. Of her life with Eskandar; a reality where Adella had never served with the Anti-piracy Group, where she had children and a home and a comfortable desk job in an orbital dry dock. Dreams which teased Adella with an ordinariness she could never grasp. A life that would never be hers. If only they didn't feel so incredibly real. Each time Adella awoke there was always a point of terrible balance where she wasn't sure if she was a widow dreaming of her husband, or a wife having a nightmare of becoming a widow. A Schrödinger's cat moment with both possibilities equally true and false. Then her heart sank as she realised the truth of her existence. May you live in interesting times was the ancient curse. May you never live in boring ones, was the corollary.

Adella strode into the Operations Room, yawning, and slipped the radio out of the hand of the operator on the communications desk. Then she turned to the officer currently occupying the Ops command chair. 'Lieutenant Stanislava, who is at the other end of this?'

'A Captain Ayo Okereke of the free-trader *Neutron Dance* registered out of the Edge. They translated in-system half an hour ago and went comms active as soon as they were within range. We're allowing them access to our QT network for realtime transmission.'

The Edge? That was about as far away from the Eastern Frontier as it was possible to get. Literally the other end of known space. The Frontier's ugly twin sister, in many ways. Unexplored stars and dirt-poor colonies. One unlucky spacer, then, ending up all the way out here during the Mother of all shooting wars. 'Captain Okereke, this is *Dark Viking* actual at SecComm East. You requested to talk with the Station Commander: speak …'

A male voice came through fuzzy and faint, audio upscaled by the comms-link to compensate for the lossy nature of Fleet's quantum entanglement buoys. His words fed through the chamber's speakers for everyone to hear. 'Commander, this is Captain Okereke of the *Neutron Dance*. We passed through the tail-end of a Fleet engagement in hyperspace during our passage towards Bardfeld's System. Six days back, that would be. We were passing relative-congruent to Shiddes 22 at the time, but it's hard to tell which way's up inside hyperspace, now.'

Adella heard the intake of breath among the Ops watch. Unlucky for the *Neutron Dance* to be in this sector, but damnable lucky to cross through a war-zone without her hull being holed like Swiss cheese.

'Your update is welcome, Captain. Could you estimate which force held the upper hand during your pass-through of the engagement?'

Scoffing laughter sounded over the line. 'Commander, sorry to say, but Hell-Fleet was mostly a debris field bouncing off our collision shields. The *Neutron Dance* is hightailing it deep-core, but we decided we better drop out at Bardfeld's to warn you. In a few weeks, there will be a big-ass alien invasion fleet landing on your doorstep! The Devil Frogs would already be here, but the bloody monsters appear congenitally unable to pass a world by without stopping to commit a little light genocide on its surface!'

Adella made her face a blank mask. *Shut it down. Shut it down tight.*

What was left of the Combined Fleet frittered away on the Rear Admiral's ego-trip. Arlinne's luck pushed beyond its natural limits, along with many thousands of other crew sacrificed alongside Adella's sister.

We're as good as finished!

- 10 -

Votes of Faith

Adella listened to Colonel Pes's report on the surface situation. His words brought back the memory of the strange prophecy the priest whispered to Adella on Bardfeld's World. *The old eaters are coming.* A lucky guess? Or did the people of the dunes understand something the Commander didn't about their enemy?

'I have spoken with the leaders of the tribes as you asked,' said the Colonel. 'None of them are willing to be transported offworld. They are scattering, retreating to the deep deserts.'

Adella considered this. *Well, given Sand Angels only need their wings to collect moisture and convert sunlight into energy, they're probably the universe's most mobile and potent guerrilla army.* They could teach the Marines' Recon Force a few things about desert environment camouflage. If they remained dispersed, there wouldn't become an effective target for orbital forces to bombard from space. 'Have you decided whether to dig-in or come with us?'

'Our transport ship will attach itself to your fleet, Commander. Unlike the Sand Angels, without airspace supremacy, the External Legion will prove too tempting a bull's-eye. The first time we revealed ourselves in force would be our last.'

'I'm very glad to hear that, because your legionnaires are a lot more valuable to me than to the locals down there. What about the Fleet stockade?'

'As you suggested, Commander, I left the main gates "accidentally" unguarded last night. Approximately ten percent of the Fleet's prison population absconded into the surrounding settlements by morning roll call.'

Excellent. Because it's better that they pin their colours to the mast on Bardfeld's World than with us in space the first-moment things get hairy. 'Oh dear, that is certainly unfortunate.' *Still, I need every hand left to help man our little skeleton fleet.* In fact, Adella had already spent long days poring over the stockade prisoner list, working out where to place the surface crew. It helped that anyone court-martialled and sentenced for serious crimes were transferred to civilian prison authorities to serve their time. Fleet stockade was meant for malcontents, rebels, barrack-room lawyers, shirkers and general screw-ups. Hopefully, their "gate test" had just weeded out the worst of the weasels. Those left, she would use; the Fleet would use them. Hell, the three species of the Triple Alliance were not in any position to be fussy right now. The main difference between stockade crew and those in orbit? The sandpit's workforce had been unlucky enough to be caught. Hers were mainly suspected with not enough evidence to prosecute.

'The deserters are fools,' said the Colonel. 'This system will not be a safe place after you depart.'

Hell, I'm not entirely sure how safe we are now. Adella shrugged in agreement anyway. *At least the escapees will have plenty of empty real estate to hide in at sector command.* Maybe Pullinger's sandpit would prove useful in a way its architects had never planned for.

'I received word from the gas giant settlers an hour ago, Colonel. There was a fierce argument about whether they should dive deep and ride things out or ship out with us. It looks like the vote went to the refugee faction because they're also coming with.'

'A move, I suspect, the settlers will live to never regret.'

Pray God, thought Adella, *pray God that be true.*

***

Adella intended to gather the disparate flock of civilian ship owners and captains on board the Dark Viking's flight deck, herding cats pretty much where their shuttles landed. Uddin Cesti's shuttle was first to land, of course. The merchant Captain seemed to revel in his newfound power and popularity as the ragtag refugee vessels' unofficial trade union leader. *Why does that not surprise me?*

'There are a great many worried officers about to join us here, dear commander,' said Cesti as he sidled up to her. His white merchant robes which appeared so appropriate on the surface of Bardfeld's World seemed a comical fancy dress costume amongst the cold steel of the deck and dangerous-looking fighters and assault barges loaded into the *Dark Viking's* hangar. Of course, there were advantages of adding to the battleship over the course of a century. Her hangar unit might be a bolt-on, but Adella would take it. In fact, the Commander would take it and fill it to the brim with as much useful equipment as she could strip, steal and borrow in their short remaining time.

'Do you think they are right to be worried, Mr. Cesti?'

'I think they would be a lot happier if the vessels your Rear Admiral led out were protecting them on their voyage home.'

Adella sighed to herself. *Truth to tell so would I.* Without knowing what had transpired to her sister, without having the fleet's fate confirmed by more than a chance encounter by a trader from the Edge, all Adella could do was bury herself in work and duty. If her own experiences were anything to go by, chance miracles were something that happened to families other than the Vega's. 'The *Dark Viking* never stopped being a battleship.'

The merchant stared theatrically at the nebula glowing behind the hangar's vacuum-sealed gates. 'Do not think I haven't noticed how many surprisingly ship-worthy vessels are maneuvering out of Ghost Fleet.'

'You know this station, Mr. Cesti. Always catching up with our workload. So many ships yet-to-scrap ready to be recommissioned in a tight pinch.'

'Fleet officers are a lot like the merchant variety in my experience, Commander. Luck comes to those who put themselves in positions where it may settle.'

Adella didn't point out that if luck had settled on the Ghost Fleet, then it was certainly a first.

In another half an hour a mob of civilian skippers and their hangers-on filled the hangar. Adella tapped the microphone pinned to her tunic and a rattling sound emitted over the announcement system.

'Captains, thank you for taking the time to attend here in person. I have an official statement to make, which many of you have no doubt been expecting.' An understatement; rumours of the disaster befallen the surviving fleet had swept through the system like a cureless plague. 'We have had no communications from the battle group led by Rear Admiral Pullinger since its departure. Based on intelligence received, we are working on the assumption that the main force protecting Sector Command East has been lost to the enemy.'

An undercurrent of muttering and shocked gasps ran through the crowd. 'It is my analysis that Bardfeld's World – and indeed this system – are indefensible given the vessel strength composing our System Defence Force. That being the case, my command will leave SecComm East with our remaining warships. I intend to honour the original plan of action developed by Admiral Blackstar. We will return to the Triple Alliance core systems with the intelligence and associated assets gathered by Admiral Blackstar during his enemy contacts. You are welcome to form a convoy and accompany Fleet. If you choose to travel with us, know that while we will defend your lives and property in the best traditions of the Fleet, my force's key goal is to survive intact and deliver the Admiral's intelligence. That mission must take first priority.'

One man wearing a skipper's cap shoved his way forward to the front of the crowd, his face already puffy and angry. 'I know who you are!

The Fleet's Jonah! You couldn't protect your own husband in that pirate shootout at Strabane. And you want me to entrust my ship to you? What a joke! The first sign of trouble, you'll clear out and leave us dangling for bait.'

His sentiments cut deeper than they should have done. *Nothing you haven't heard a hundred times before, or worse, from thousands of families at Strabane.* 'Alternatively,' Adella pressed on, 'you might form the view that a civilian convoy will stand more chance if you split off and allow enemy forces operating in this sector to pursue my force, instead. My recommendation, however, is that your best chance of survival lies with accompanying my wagons.'

As soon as she'd finished speaking there was a slow-motion riot among the civilians. Yells, cries and shoving exchanged between those wanting to shelter behind the Alliance Navy, and others eager to take off on their own account and let the Commander's warships act as Quazzie missile magnets. Adella waved her fingers at Colonel Pes, leading a line of legionnaires lined up at the back of the hangar. She nodded and stood easy for the moment. No need to crack heads just yet.

In the end, the civilian skippers remained split fifty-fifty. Half voted to head off in a separate convoy and let Fleet act as missile catchers. Half voted to accompany the System Force and shelter under Fleet's shields and cannons.

Uddin Cesti waddled up to Adella as shuttles began to lift off and clear away to their home ships.

'Mr. Cesti. Are you minded to ship out with the Fleet's Jonah, or are you hoping the Quazzies will use her wagons for a little light target practice, instead?'

'My *Shamash* will fly under your force's protection, dear Commander. Did you ever doubt otherwise?'

Well, a vote of confidence from a slippery survivor like Uddin Cesti was the best she could hope for, today. 'Very good.'

'You know, Commander, you might extend the Fleet's Martial Law provisions to the civilian vessels in orbit here. Conscript them. Compel them to push core-ward under your guns. It worries me more than a little that you doubt your capacity to command; allowing the sheep to decide for themselves how best to avoid the wolf.'

'What I'm worried about, Mr. Cesti, are unwilling Captains fleeing down-range of my rail-cannons as soon as the first bloody Quazzies jump in.'

'We are not passengers on the *Countess of Jupiter* or innocents at Strabane, Commander Vega. History never fully repeats, it only rhymes. I have full faith in your abilities. You might say I am betting the *Shamash* on you.'

'That's sweet.'

'I am too tired to appreciate your irony. I was in my cabin last night fretting for a long time. What occupied me is a retreating force's detectability by the enemy inside hyperspace. A cunning officer would plan an indirect route home; two jumps forward, one back, then another to the side, to avoid finding a Quazzie fleet waiting in ambush for them.'

'A cunning officer would wonder how a merchant possibly knew so damn much when he wasn't in Admiral Blackstar's briefing!' Adella growled.

'Ah, but knowledge is the commodity the wise person values most. My point is, Commander, in the days when hyperspace worked as it should, the majority of vessels travelled by the most direct route. Not always easy, given the non-congruent mapping between hyperspace and our universe.'

Navigation's a bitch. Tell me something I don't know. 'The *majority* of vessels...?'

'Well, there are other vessels who value hyperspace's less direct routes. The back-routes folded and twisted like a knotty crossword clue.'

'You mean the kind of vessels who didn't want to risk triggering a transponder read off Fleet's network of comms buoys, or indeed, another ship. Like, say, *smugglers?*'

'No, no! Let us agree to say ships with enterprising owners and clients who valued discretion and privacy over short voyage times and efficient fuel costs. I am certain I could tease out the knowledge of such knotty routes from my associates and feed them into your plan of retreat. Maximising our chances of survival is in the common interest.'

'Fleet doesn't retreat, Mr. Cesti, it reloads. We rearm in a rear-facing vector from the enemy.'

'Possibly you can do such a thing with the routes I speak of?'

'Survival maximisation is what I'm all about, Mr. Cesti.'

Adella smiled for the first time since she'd heard about the loss of the fleet; watching the sly trader board his shuttle and take off for the *Shamash*. Then it suddenly struck her. If Uddin Cesti was giving up the smugglers' maze of secret hidey-holes in hyperspace, he must believe the Alliance would *never* retake the Frontier.

***

Adella thought she had got rid of all the civilian skippers with Cesti's departure, but then she saw a man and woman in civvies ducking under one of the assault barges lined up inside her hangar. 'Commander Vega.'

Adella recognised the voice from the scratchy QT transmission she'd heard in Ops. 'Captain Ayo Okereke of the *Neutron Dance*.'

He was a tall, handsome man of early middle-age, with skin as dark and lustrous as the nebula beyond the hangar airlock. There didn't seem many pretensions about him. He wore a workaday ship suit with no captain's cap. Although to be fair, a cap wouldn't have fitted over his Afro. The man reached out his hand to shake hers. A steel-strong grip.

'Yes, Commander. The same. I hope you don't intend to shoot the messenger.'

'I would, but I'm stockpiling ordnance for the Quazzies,' said Adella. 'If you've come seeking additional assurances before making your mind up about whose convoy to join, I can only reiterate what I told the group. My System Defence Force will protect you to the best of our abilities, up to and until that interferes with our mission objective.'

'Oh, I get that. As a point of fact, we're here to do *you* a solid.' Captain Okereke indicated the woman by his side. 'This is Professor Alison Sebba. She was my client on this jaunt before everything went sideways.'

'I'm an archaeologist,' explained the Professor. 'My specialty is Heezy-era society and systems. We were out at a dig beyond the Frontier when the Devil Frogs activated their hyperspace disruption field.'

'You have my sympathy, Professor. But right now, my concerns run a little wider than a spoiled archaeological dig.'

'My field has practical applications that will prove useful to you,' insisted the woman. 'It is my belief that the Quazzies' disruption of hyperspace is only made possible by Heezy artifacts fallen into their empire's possession.'

'What leads you to think that?'

'I wrote a paper on this very thing. The Heezy colonised multiple galaxies during their hegemony. Translations of recovered texts lead me to believe the Heezy used planet-sized engines to flash gravity waves between galaxies as a way of communicating. These were very tight beam communications to cross the immense distances involved, travelling at almost unimaginable velocities. But, if you widened such a wave and projected it through hyperspace, you would see effects very similar to an erasure of g-folds and disruption of quantum entangled particles. Wide-beam gravity waves could also be deployed as a sensor mesh – a radar system that actually functions in hyperspace. Heezy vessels probably used a scaled-down form of gravity wave communication to signal between each other, too. If *that* technology had also been discovered by the Quazzies during their conquests, then it could form the basis of a localised field allowing vessels to negate the disruption field around their own ships.'

Adella nodded intently. What the academic had to say on matters made sense. In fact, it tied up many of the loose ends. How the Quazzies possessed advanced tech that messed up hyperspace navigation and comms, yet fielded fleets with standard weaponry and tactics stripped out of a medieval warlord's playbook. None of this was Quazzie super-science. They had discovered it on worlds they had invaded. Just as humanity found its initial cache of elder race goodies buried deep below Neptune's ice. It also explained the Quazzies awareness of and fascination with the ancients' weaponry carried by Fleet; lost with the bulk of the Alliance's naval force. Kal, she was certain, would be interested to hear these insights. She'd just have to make sure Doctor Delorey wasn't in the vicinity when she updated Kal.

'That is valuable intelligence indeed, Professor. Dare I ask if the *Neutron Dance* will accompany us? The Heezy tech specialists on board *Dark Viking* would very much appreciate picking your brains during our voyage home.'

'The answer to that question is trickier than a straight yes or no,' said Captain Okereke.

'I don't see how it can be.'

'Well, let's just say that throwing light on the enemy's technology isn't the only thing we have to bring to the party. Right now, me and my crew are more for throwing in with you, rather than taking off with the others.'

'I sense a "but "coming.'

'Yeah, *but*,' the skipper continued, 'the whole retreat from Stalingrad action you've got planned doesn't really do it for me. Not when there's an alternative. In fact, before we dropped out of hyperspace at Bardfeld's to warn you, said alternative is where we were heading. A shortcut home, rather than this hop-hop-hop death by a thousand cuts gig the Quazzies want to lay on us.'

'Shortcut? Currently, it makes operational sense to go sideways instead of direct.'

'Have you heard of the Comet People, Commander?'

'Yes, although I've never encountered one of their world ships directly.'

Adella rubbed her head. The Comet People were space nomads. Never putting roots down in any system for more than a couple of weeks. Their society born inside Sol, back in the day when interstellar travel meant generation ships and centuries of transit. They had colonised comets looping around the solar system, the ultimate expression of the independent "screw you" culture. Dependent on nobody and nothing except their own resources and wits. Like every nomad tribe from the Romani to the American Indians, they'd ended up the subject of fear, rumours and downright hostility from their more settled neighbours. With jump drives, the Comet People had left that far behind them, skipping from system to system, each as uninhabited or habited as the fancy took them. A quick transit, skimming gas giants for fuel and barren moons for minerals, then gone.

'I *have* met them, Commander. And, one thing to remember is that they never employ Kaggen navigators. Comet People have human Masters of the Helm and their navigators don't need g-folds to orient. They use the Lucky Gene."

Adella snorted. 'That's just some crazy legend. Jumping around the galaxy and *hope* you land in the right place? I mean come on...'

'Nope, I've been down with those cats, and let me tell you the Lucky Gene is as real as the slimy psychopathic toads coming to ace this system.'

'And you know where the nearest Comet People are to ask them for a lend of one of these mystical wunderkinds?'

'Nobody knows where the nearest Comet People are, commander. That's kind of the point of being them. But I do know where the nearest Comet *person* is. A mope called Ossian Joyce. Said fella possessing the Lucky Gene and all. And Ossian owes me a favour. If this isn't the time to collect, then I'm not certain when is.'

'Okay, Captain Okereke, I'll bite. Where were you heading before you dropped out at Bardfeld's World?'

'The Floating Port, baby, the Floating Port!'

Adella's eyes widened in shock.

Two crazy legends in one day. The Floating Port – the only harbour owned and run exclusively for pirates. Hidden for centuries in hyperspace, always moving, constantly shifting position. Adella had heard of it, of course. Hell, she had *hunted* it, even as a hobby project stuck out here at SecComm East. Ever since Fleet Intelligence Service released a classified report suggesting that the current head of the port was one Blue Barnier. The same son-of-a-bitch who had murdered Adella's husband, killed half a world and put down her career.

- 11 -

Rear-facing Vector

Beklum Sakwa sidled up to Commander Vega inside her Ready Room. She needed to keep this meeting brief. They were burning hard for system edge, what everyone had simply started calling the Home Fleet, rather than the official designation generated by the system logs on Bardfeld's, Force SCE-456. As in, please God, see us home safe without getting our ass shot off.

'I can assure you, Commander,' Beklum began, 'rumours that Kaggens with the Fleet have declared me a Saint have no foundation. Any funds recently accrued by me are solely the result of gambling wins, not illegal tithing.'

'Master of the Helm, if you stand good with the higher forces of the Unified Church, then you can put in a word for this battle group. I have more pressing concerns, currently.'

Beklum Sakwa's understanding of the hyperspace realm went beyond mastery of mere physics, navigation, transit, and jump. Adella updated the Kag officer on what the good ship *Neutron Dance*'s skipper and archaeologist client had told her.

'So,' said Adella as she finished, 'what do you think?'

Sakwa rattled his fighting claws as he pondered his answer. 'There are many layers inside hyperspace, the varied Circles of Heaven. I have heard tales of the Comet People and those born to their tribe with the Lucky Gene. It always struck me likely that their manner of navigation simply accesses a higher level of paradise than I can. But I have two concerns...'

Adella waved him to continue.

'Kaggens make excellent navigators because of our hardy neurochemistry. Humans don't, because the mental load of repeated translations between the mortal universe and hyperspace eventually sends members of your species insane. How "lucky" is a jump that lands your ship where you want to be, but could end up with your navigator, this Ossian Joyce, left as a gibbering wreck and your vessel effectively stranded?'

Well, Captain Okereke warned me that his Comet Person is a "little eccentric." 'And your second concern…?'

'What sort of infernal ship are we dealing with that she has ready access to the Floating Port?'

'The way Captain Okereke tells it, a year ago the *Neutron Dance* was tracked by a competitor while shipping high-value cargo. Said unfriendly competitor was in league with a pirate ship, using black hats to jump their rivals and then splitting the booty. Captain Okereke turned the tables on the pirates and their disreputable allies. Okereke came out intact *and* with the pirate's secure key generator for the Floating Port. So now, Okereke can spot out cryptographical-generated output for the Port's nav coordinates at will. Currently, the Floating Port is congruent with the Frontier zone. Barnier's scum sidled into this corner of the galaxy smelling blood in the water with all our vessels posted missing and colony worlds going silent. But the pirates bit off a little more than they could chew after the Quazzies blew up hyperspace.'

Sakwa let out a very human-sounding whistle. 'I know how they feel. In better times, possession of that blessed key generator would mean every officer at Bardfeld could extract their choice of posting, commission, and vessel from the Admiralty.'

'Yeah, medals and forgiveness all around.'

And a shot at killing that son-of-a-bitch, Barnier. Finish the Floating Port off once and for all. But right now, all the key generator meant was a fighting chance at returning home to hand over her intel to Fleet.

'Might I ask what you intend to do with this opportunity, Commander?'

Adella sighed. She had ordered their factory ship and engineers to help disguise the *Neutron Dance* as a pirate, but this still resembled a solo-vessel suicide mission to her. 'Trying to grab up the most valuable human navigator alive from a legendary pirate nest during the worst Alliance-alien conflict for a millennium? What can go wrong?'

'Such opportunities, Commander, are how the Lady of All Things presents her love for us.'

I'd take a friendly carrier group jumping in to back us up. 'I've given my permission for the *Neutron Dance* to attempt the mission, Helm Master. After a couple of jumps alongside Home Fleet, Captain Okereke will be lined up for a straight translation for the Floating Port. Worst-case scenario, the mission fails and we don't grab up a Lucky Gene for our bridge crew. We have to slow-jump back towards Core as currently charted. This mission feels like no-win no-fee to me.'

As if to prove both Adella wrong, the Ready Room switched to combat lighting when the first alarm screeched. Adella hadn't heard a general quarters siren for quite a while. *Enemy contact! Hell, life is what happens while you are busy making other plans.*

***

'Our QT buoy line has gone dark,' called a lieutenant on sensor desk as Adella strode out into Ops. 'Here's final imagery from our zero-perimeter before it went off-line.'

A familiar sight rose up inside the hologram well; recognisable from the Admiral's briefing. It was a massive Quazalrat war-wheel, hundreds of smaller vessels burning out from under her docking clamps. Already heading fast towards the inner system. From here on in, Fleet's realtime intelligence advantage had been lost to the Quazzie jamming systems. It felt every bit as uncomfortable flying blind as Adella imagined.

'Order astrogation to put telescopes on those coordinates,' commanded Adella. They would need to wait for the enemy's light to cross the system to get an exact confirmation on where the Quazzies were heading. Always running half an hour behind the realtime picture, until the Quazalrat vessels were danger-close.

Commander Vega thanked Lady Luck that Home Fleet was only a few minutes away from clearing Bardfeld's gravity well at the system's edge. Where they could generate a stable singularity and breach into hyperspace. 'Master of the Helm, commence jump vane spin-up. I'm sending your console our nav coordinates. When you have a solution loaded, please transmit to the rest of the fleet, including civilian vessels. Monitor confirmation of receipt, we don't want to be leaving anybody behind today.'

'Aye-aye, Commander.' The crablike officer fed her solution through his board. 'This surely is a knotty one, sir.'

'Courtesy of Mr. Cesti, Helm Master. Once we have reached Core, you'll be able to buy your way out of the service and set up shop as a smuggler if the whimsy takes you. '

'Smuggling's a surprisingly low-margin business, sir.'

Well, Adella had things on her mind other than the economics of the black-market. Next, Adella fed a boot-up protocol into her board, activating Operation Xerxes. She double-checked the transponder cloud surrounding the *Dark Viking*, making sure every vessel which should accompany Home Fleet was. Bardfeld's independent convoy had cleared out the day before, not needing to rearm and provision to the same level as a fighting fleet. *Lucky them.* Adella remained worried the civilians wouldn't clear ten hops before they ended up ambushed and overrun inside some system on their way home. *Maybe Uddin Cesti had a point.* Martial law provisions – conscripting and attaching the traders to the Home Fleet – might have been the better choice.

Dark Viking crossed the edge of the gravity interference line.

'Will this be a wide jump or threading the needle, sir?' asked the Master of the Helm.

Commander Vega had already decided. A fleet possessed two choices when making a coordinated mass jump. Every ship could spin up her own vanes, create a separate singularity, and ride it into hyperspace. This method was fast but unreliably messy. Multiple singularities interfered with each other when ship spacing was too close. It guaranteed fleet arrival in hyperspace spread out, possibly too wide to reform in a reasonable amount of time – if at all. The alternative was threading the needle. The first vessel created a singularity using her jump vanes and translated out, while the next vessel in the chain picked up the pre-formed tunnel punched through into hyperspace and made it her own. That required skill and discipline; slower, too, with ships needing to queue. It was a task Adella's crews had repeatedly trained for until the meticulous manoeuvres became second nature.

'You know my preference for that, Helm Master,' said Adella. Of course, threading the needle was a hell of a lot easier when you *didn't* have an enemy attack force burning up towards your stern. 'Have the refinery ship *Spacewise Giant* open a singularity, passing tunnel formation to our factory ship, then each of the civilian vessels in alphabetical order.' Adella made a note to alternate between descending and ascending order at each star system they cleared, to avoid pissing off any free-trader that happened to be called the *Zulu Zebra*. 'Fleet vessels will clear in battle array order. *Smiter* and the *Dark Viking* to go through last. Stand us high and close to the singularity in case any civilian ship master slips. Be ready to pick up slack on their needlework.'

Adella had skeleton-crewed the toothless carrier *Smiter*, hoping to save using her as missile magnet until a real pickle. Adella hadn't hoped to see that level of action quite *this* quickly.

'Yes, Commander.'

Adella could have taken the rank of acting captain as soon as the *Dark Viking* left orbit of Bardfeld's World as a warship. But she had been a captain once, and the title tasted like ashes in her mouth after finishing up on the scrap-the-crap gang. And inside Bardfeld's System, as far as her crew were concerned, the rank of Commander had been superior to Rear Admiral for the last decade. Fleet had made her Commander Vega, and Adella would fight and die under that rank. *Nobody will be calling me AC Vega anytime soon.*

Spacewise Giant created a singularity as sharp and beautiful as any vessel could. In essence, an artificial black-hole large enough to pass the *Giant's* bulk, and therefore every other ship of the line. Adella monitored the increased load on their main drive as *Dark Viking* pulled back from the portal drilled across two universes. It came as an intermittent shaking of Operations' deck. Slugger automatically adjusted power loads as the singularity flexed inside – what was to it – the alien realm of real-space. Next came the factory vessel, the

Takasaki's jump vanes fixing and holding the singularity like reins in the fingers of an expert cavalryman. Adella felt pride in her crew. *Not bad for a bunch of exiled screw-ups.*

She found herself checking sensor data behind their stern. Growing nervous about how close the enemy was getting, now.

'Commander,' said the communications desk officer. 'I'm receiving a stream of telemetry data, but our QT buoys are still non-functional—?'

Aralat raz Kessi sat in the heavily armoured drive chamber, but the Chief kept an augmented presence active on the bridge. He appeared as a blue ghost in their field of vision. 'Commander, exactly as I promised you...'

'Thank-you, Chief. Enjoy it, ladies and gentlemen, because this is strictly a one-shot home-turf advantage,' Adella told her bridge crew.

It had taken the Chief and his engineers days to string a network of automated laser-flash communication drones through the entire system. Longer still to design and built them, in the weeks before. *Might as well be sending smoke signals across the prairies, but a battle area view that's light-delayed is still better than no view at all.* 'Let's see what we can see.'

Slugger filtered the data and set it up in the central well.

The bad news was that the initial war-wheel wasn't the only incoming mothership. She had been joined by two more massive vessels. The original force carrier had dropped in far-and-wide at the opposite end of the system. Exactly where Adella predicted her enemy's first transit. The other two motherships had translated out of hyperspace high and low above the star. Those two points were the quickest exits from the system. It's where a desperate fleet and fleeing individual vessels would make a break for it. Celestial North was where the independent civilian fleet had jumped out a day earlier. *Ah, well. No decent hunting for the Quazzies, today.*

Adella chose a Kuiper Belt-scraper for her exit, named after humanity's home system rim. You needed to be unlucky to run into an enemy jumping out on a KB-scraper, given there was 360° of system disk edge to choose from. Adella wondered if the Quazzies would study her methods and techniques. Try to second-guess her during future encounters? Adjust-up their game? It's what a human adversary would do, but the thing about aliens was that many of them really were *quite* alien. The three central species of the Triple Alliance bonded on similarities of thought, humour, and philosophy, rather than physical appearance. If you could crack wise with an extra-terrestrial you could rub alongside their kind on orbital stations and shared worlds. *Don't see myself swapping war-stories with a Quazalrat in a bar anytime soon.*

Adella examined the three war-wheels. If she was the Quazzies' Fleet Queen or whatever hell-damned chain of command those monsters operated, she would launch her fast-movers from the war-wheels inserted Celestial North and Celestial South against the Home

Fleet, saving her far-edge forces for probing Bardfeld's System.

The Commander ran the enemy positions against Home Fleet's, comparing known vessel acceleration and weapon ranges. It would be damnable tight, but most of Home Fleet should all have jumped out in time to avoid a real firefight. *Not going to be a cake-walk for the last few to shut the door, though.*

'Ships of the line to form a defensive screen behind our escorted convoy,' ordered Adella. 'We'll be taking energy weapons, missiles, and iron before we clear.'

All Adella could do was nervously wait, willing the queued civilian ships to thread the needle a little bit faster. *This is about as organised and planned as it's going to get, too. Next time we might be making a whole-fleet jump on the fly under fire from a force-multiplier enemy.* Adella had counted all the ships in and now she counted them all out again. Gone the *Shamash*. Gone the *Neutron Dance* and their dangerous scheme to short-cut the voyage home. Gone the Legion's assault ship, the *Trojan*. Gone the free-traders and colonists without safe worlds to settle.

The more time passed, the more frequently Beklum Sakwa needed to step in, stabilising the singularity with the *Dark Viking*'s jump vanes. Skippers were growing nervous. They didn't need access to Adella's home-brew drone network to follow the approaching Quazzies, now. Starlight carried across the sobering sight. Hundreds of vessels ranging from fighter-size up to lumbering battleships, burning hell-for-leather towards Adella's force.

'Slugger, update on the three enemy motherships.'

'The war-wheels transiting Celestial North and Low have withdrawn back into hyperspace. The enemy fleet approaching Celestial North is the closest force intercepting with us. We will have first contact with them twenty minutes before their Celestial South force joins the engagement. The war-wheel at opposite system edge is holding on her entry position; her sub-units are on an approach vector towards Bardfeld's World.'

Too far away for us to scuff the big bird's paintwork, eh? That's frankly insulting.

Beklum Sakwa spoke up again. 'I've been monitoring the free-traders to ensure we don't develop any stragglers. But my observations suggest the opposite is the case. Some of the civilian fleet's vessels aren't handling like ships in their class would be expected to, Commander.'

'For example…?'

'The *Shamash* and the *Neutron Dance* stand out.'

Why doesn't that surprise me? 'They've been boosted for smuggling runs…?'

'Possibly that would explain some of their flight-handling characteristics.'

'Given how far we are from Alliance oversight on the Frontier, I'm only surprised half the free-traders in Home Fleet aren't manoeuvering like Jack Rabbits,' sighed Adella.

'Missile launches detected!' called the sensor station officer.

Which means they've already laid down beams and rail-cannon fire. 'Check your shield loads. Deploy early point-defence and activate counter-measures.'

'Permission to return fire?"

'Rail-cannons, only, for the moment,' ordered Adella. 'Lay down some tacks in front of them. Let's test their shields and manoeuvering thrusters.'

A dull thumping sounded from the battleship's depths. The *Dark Viking*'s heaviest cannons were 1000-megajoule brutes, the largest Fleet had ever developed and deployed. Big Aces in the navy vernacular. Modern battleships adopted a more elegant edge with their weaponry fit-out, but there was a damn good reason they had nicknamed the battleship's A.I. Slugger. *Punch a hole in a star and leave it leaking plasma like blood.* You could feel her ship's fury during action. *Hell-Fleet for us. Hell-Fleet for you. Speed kills. Velocitas Eradico!*

'I'm reading elevated infrared signatures from their Lancers.'

'They're testing their own nail-guns against us! Laser-line to hedgehog.'

A secondary image formed in the central well – a storm of incoming metal, the *Dark Viking*'s laser-point defence layering an equally dense cloud of targeting priorities over the cloud. Which projectiles were decoy scrap and which were the real deal. What metal to vaporise first; hot-slap-gas for their energy shields to suck on. A low gurgling as liquid-refrigeration systems speeded circulation, cooling the ship's energy weapons as laser systems deployed.

The barrage of incoming projectiles thinned out across the sensor picture. Adella had to stop herself laughing. *God, I missed this. The raw bloody barbarism of murder and calling it duty.* 'Are they hiding missiles inside their opening salvo?'

'None detected, Commander. Missile-front is incoming behind their iron.'

That's how you do it: let your tacks take the flack. Keep your expensive items a la carte. 'God, they're arrogant shits, today. I really don't think they rate us.' Adella checked her convoy ducks. Only five merchant vessels left to thread the needle.

'Shields are heating. We have beams on high deflect.'

And they know we can't dodge while we're jumping out. They're not totally stupid, these Quazzies. 'Inform me when our suntan starts to smart.'

'Commander,' called Beklum Sakwa, 'we have degrade on our singularity, it's wobbling!'

'Pick up the slack on that thread, Helm Master – perfectly understandable that the last few civilians in our queue are losing their nerve.'

'This wobble's from constructive interference, sir. Someone is dropping out from hyperspace danger-close.'

Damn, perhaps I'm the one underestimating the Quazzies, today. Is this something new they're throwing at us? I thought these Devil Frogs were traditionalists? 'All ships and systems re-task for a broadside. Prepare for ramming by the enemy! Quarter-armour to starboard.'

Quarter-armour was a heavy rotating shield of extra shielding carried by battleships, dreadnoughts and super-carriers – multiple layers of concrete, sand, water, steel, diamond-mesh, hex-cell, and just about every bullet-stopper known to humanity and its allied species. You dropped it where you needed enemy ordnance to bounce.

Beklum Sakwa bobbed inside his chair. 'This is the dirtiest squeeze-through I've witnessed outside of an Academy training simulation, Commander. I don't believe these are incoming Quazalrat war vessels at all.'

If it's civilians seeking sanctuary at SecComm East, they've sure picked the wrong week to flee here. 'Hold our singularity steady, Helm Master. Ready a full broadside on my command.'

A flare of exotic particles exploded from another universe as a large ship exited hyperspace. A brief tear in the space-time fabric almost immediately mended. She came in tumbling at an angle as though her stabilisation thrusters were non-functional. Not the only damaged thing about her. The vessel looked like an Alliance carrier, shot up to hell and leaking atmosphere from thousands of rail projectile impacts. Her main drive was unlit and if her cannon belt feeders still carried tacks, she kept her powder dry in the face of the approaching onslaught.

'Get me a transponder ID read.'

'The *TAS Wager*, sir. One of the carriers the Rear Admiral led out.'

Oh, Sweet Lord. Adella cycled through Slugger's scans and damage estimates. *Wager*'s jump vanes had been shot off. She wasn't fit for any journey apart from the Solar Walk. The incoming Quazzie fleet would save Bardfeld's Star the bother, long before that last voyage came to pass. 'Helm, swap singularity control with our cruisers. They're to stand and hold. Destroyers and support vessels, start threading the needle – free-fire to the rear. *Smiter*, you're with *Dark Viking*. Helm, lay us directly between the Quazzies and the *Wager*. We'll shield both carriers while the *Smiter* lands all fighters, boats and escape pods fit to pogo from the *Wager*.'

Come on, carrier girl. You were alive enough to translate here. 'Do we have comms?'

'Negative, Commander. I think *Wager*'s bridge is holed. Her comms array is blown away, too. I'm running control trace from the drive-room. They're flying from the engine room and primed to capsule out.'

'Let's give them a soft landing field. Raise the *Smiter*.'

Acting Captain Liz Dunmon answered the hail. 'Commander Vega.'

'AC Dunmon, your skeleton crew's mess is about to get a lot more crowded. Are you ready to receive planes and people?'

'Confirm, that. Two empty hangars and a sick-bay filled with more medical drones than *Smiter* currently holds crew.'

'It's going to cut-up rough out there, Liz. You recover their crew fast and it only counts when you jump safe, too. *Dark Viking* to act as your sun-screen and we'll hold the door open for you on the way out.'

'Appreciated.'

Adella killed the connection and monitored the burn as the *Smiter* and *Dark Viking* maneuvered away from the singularity and towards the stricken carrier. Dunmon had been a propulsion specialist before Adella weighted the officer down with a combat promotion. *Some favour.*

'Missiles incoming!'

Yeah, that was something Adella noted during long hours spent poring over engagement logs. Quazzies had the hots for carriers. Priority targeting. She suspected it was because Quazzies believed the fighter-spewing vessels to be an undersized war-wheel. A prime piece for removal from the Quazalrat Chess Board.

'Lay us shielding both carriers. Now, we're worth it!'

Two nests, but the enemy didn't yet know one of the carriers was empty of chicks and the other listing dead-on-the-float.

'Main batteries, load scrammers from our secondary magazine.'

Of course, not every scrammer drone loaded for hyper-acceleration carried scram-jets for planetary insertion. But scrammers were what Fleet called them, anyway. More booming from below-decks as their 1000-megajoule salute sent smart ordinance powering towards the enemy's missile-front. You could pick an individual scrammer and ride it down on top of a Quazzie missile. Duelling artificial intelligences – Quazzie missile warhead versus Alliance hunter-drone. A screech of electronic countermeasure fields, machines trying to mimic each other, launching sub-munitions and decoys, feeding out false echo strengths. Adella watched the terrible flash of nuclear warheads detonated by her drones. The same class of warhead that had cooked Admiral Blackstar during the Combined Fleet's ambush.

Adella checked the time. *Right about now.*

'Commander, something is happening on opposite system edge. It's a … ship-to-ship engagement?'

Yeah, that would be half an hour ago. The exact time, light-adjusted, it took the stealth-ship *Voidwolf* to wait for the war-wheel's launch fleet to pass by and beyond weapons range; then rise out of the gas giant's hydrogen-helium soup and sneak over to the mothership. Even *Voidwolf's* torpedoes ran optical camouflage and carried a smaller heat signature than houseflies. 'It's a good thing the enemy brought three war-wheels with them because the bastards just lost one.'

And by the time the Quazzie Lancers realised their mistake and beat a passage back, *Voidwolf* would be long gone and making for the Home Fleet's initial system hop.

Near-space was getting mind boggle-level busy. Rail-cannons from both sides emptying iron. Missiles traded. Smart drones exchanged.

Point-def flinging down waves of chain-fed missile munchers. Laser-line turning the Quazzie's iron into hot-gas-farts. Particle beams meshed as fire lines swapped. Adella could see Home Fleet's output flaring up against the incoming wall of Shield-ships. *Damn, but those beasts can take a beating.* Perfectly coordinated as they dipped aside and let their Lancers open fire before thrusting back into defensive posture. It looked beautiful, like a flock of birds dancing above a farmer's field. A random walk, hard for Fleet to slip any nasties past. The first patter of metal shards rattled impacting against *Dark Viking*'s hull armour, a sign that the volleys were too large now for the laser-line to melt everything heading their way.

'Armour-up!' ordered Adella. 'Prepare for combat-active MSOP.'

Mind Ship Operations sounded a lot cleaner than what the crew called it. *Coffin Time.*

Slugger's voice cut across every corridor and chamber in the ship, alongside the alarms. 'Prepare for rapid combat drive executions and artificial gravity-field loss. All crew to priority couch positions and safety seating.'

Plates of composite armour snapped around Adella's seat, a whine as crash fields surrounded her position. Felt like wearing candy-floss. Marines could open fire on her coffin point-blank with a machine-gun and only scratch it. Trouble was, Blackstar's recordings indicated even the smallest Quazzie Lancer mounted a 300-megajoule rail-cannon. And at those velocities, her personal seat shielding might as well be candy-floss. When to armour-up during an engagement always had been a fine-line command decision. Too late and you were the meat filling in a corpse-ship sandwich. Too early and you'd be losing officers to anaphylaxis, psychosis, and micro-strokes long before your action ended.

Drug injectors hummed out of the chair's interior and slipped Adella her first combat-cocktail at the same moment as her brain's augment dropped into sync with the *Dark Viking*'s systems. Time slowed to a crawl, and Adella felt the *Dark Viking* as Slugger must feel her. A mailed glove wrapped around her fist.

'Commander, second fleet moving inside combat envelope,' warned the sensor desk officer.

Adella checked the *Smiter* off their starboard. Slugger's transfer update model made it look like a hundred lines of thread hung between both carriers. Every line, a fast-mover, shuttle, escape pod or vac-pack crew cluster desperately making the leap between the *Smiter* and *Wager*.

'Port batteries, lay some iron on the road for the Devil Frogs burning from Celestial South.' I *don't want them to feel left out.*

Dark Viking's big-guns spoke again. A massage to accompany the ship's serving of complimentary cocktails. Another death rattle against the hull as leftovers from the second volley accelerated through their laser-line. Adella felt the hits like paper-cuts, pain as the self-healing layer inside their heavy composite armour closed up each hole. Little spouts of air froze as icicles outside the hull, marking every wound. Damage reports fed through as the battleship reported which systems had absorbed the metal splinters, listing personnel lying dead or bleeding with iron shards embedded across their seat positions.

Wager's crew had jumped the void – but not all of them had abandoned ship. Her drive lit up. A final gasp of fuel reserves as the carrier turned and pushed out towards the incoming Quazzie fleet. Armoured weapon ports slipped open, too, exposing a line of rail-cannons above her launch hangars. Whoever was acting as *Wager*'s skipper had courageously remained inside the engine room, staying on those cloned bridge controls. The crew left onboard were operating their carrier pretty much as Adella intended using *Smiter*, too. *An empty hangar missile magnet! She's buying us the time we need to thread the needle. You poor brave souls.*

'Acting Captain Dunmon, withdraw the *Smiter*! We're closing the line up behind you.'

The huge crippled carrier had sufficient juice for main drive, but not enough for energy shields in tandem. *Wager*'s laser-line and point-defence guns opened fire overwhelmed, hundreds of intense flashes sparking across her hull as she ate up the enemy barrage. But even a civilian trader's drive section came ridiculously shielded – if only to shield the rest of the vessel from malfunctioning reactors. Ditto naval vessels, with knobs on to protect against enemy action. That's where the survivors on board had hunkered down. They took the beating and accelerated towards the Quazzie's Shield-ships. It was as though the *Wager* wanted the Devil Frogs to beat down on her. Adella guessed her crew did. The faster the Quazzies poured fire against Wager, the more gaps the enemy created in their shield wall for Lancer Ships to aim through.

Wager didn't have the same heavy fit-out as the *Dark Viking*, but she carried a deck of Long Sixes, 600-megajoule rail-cannons, launching canister-drones designed to pierce enemy shields, before raining hundreds of kinetic energy penetrators down hard against hull armour. *Wager* had kept her powder dry, but she finally flashed fangs fit to rip the enemy. CDs zapped out, meant for cross-system exchanges, long distance probe-and-play. At this short a range the canister-drones whipped through the gaps in the shield wall and flowered behind the line, only half the drones downed by counter-fire, the survivors scouring enemy hulls. Dozens of Quazzie vessels tumbled out of the neat accelerating formation, Devil Frog crews and systems peppered by hot penetrator shrapnel. *That's how you kill the enemy.*

Wager had little left in her defence but angry defiance. She continued speeding up, facing down two full incoming fleets, more and more hot-sparking from her hull as their foes lit her up. Her death appeared beautiful, a tree wrapped in fairy-lights. The only reasons the Quazzies didn't finish the carrier off with a nuke was that its radiation flash would claim as many lives on their side, by this late stage. Finally, even the armoured bulk of the carrier's drive section couldn't stand the barrage. Reactor explosions ripped the carrier apart starting from the stern, rippling out across the rest of the carrier. When *Wager* passed through the Quazalrat shield wall, she'd be nothing but a tumbling mess of broken steel and void-frozen flesh.

Slugger updated the battle area view inside the well and a pretty picture it was not. The *Wager*'s fate was about to become theirs. Home Fleet was heavily outnumbered and soon to be overwhelmed by incoming fury spat by two fast-approaching Quazzie fleets.

Adella checked the singularity. Her two cruisers, the *Escapade*, and *Gypsy* held the line and kept the door open for them. Everyone else in the queue had jumped out. '*Gypsy*, thread the needle. *Escapade*, prepare to swap singularity control with the *Smiter* and pass likewise. *Dark Viking* is taking rear station assignment. Our turn to close the door, today. Helm, hold us port-broadside out as we close in on the singularity. Gunnery, load sail-drones from secondary magazine.'

Adella's gunnery officer gave an aye-aye in exactly the same shaded tone of voice she'd use acknowledging such a pointless order. Sail-drones could pop a mile of square-sail configuration shielding, perfect for absorbing and dispersing concentrated energy weapon barrages; like a solar-sail racer in reverse. But this close, the fastest, easiest way to slaughter your opponent was a hard pounding trading hot iron, not particle weapons.

'Deploy! Activate at three thousand yards.'

Her holo-well showed sail-drones tearing out, then multiple square miles of meta-materials blossoming around the *Dark Viking*. Like opening an umbrella to try to stop a machine gun at this range. Blackstar's briefing hadn't mentioned whether the Quazzies possessed a laugh-reflex, but if they did, Adella bet that deployment had them rolling about their bridges in tears. She watched cannon-fire start to shred the sails just for kicks.

Both cruisers had threaded the needle. *Smiter*'s turn, next. Adella prayed the enemy didn't target the *Dark Viking*'s jump vanes. Stranded in-system wasn't about to be a healthy option; more so than the Quazzies realised.

'Slugger, transfer temporary trigger control for *Xerxes' Gift* from Base Control Station at SecComm East to my console.'

'Transfer initiated, Commander.'

Smiter threaded the needle, a smear lost to the eye as the physics of two disparate universes interacted. The *Dark Viking*'s crimson bridge lighting flickered as additional power diverted to the battleship's rotating jump vanes.

'Quarter-armour to the rear. Reinforce chaser shields. Line us up for hyperspace translation.'

Both enemy fleets let loose with everything they had. Saving ammo wasn't the Quazzies' priority anymore. Killing the *Dark Viking* was.

'Commander, the Quazalrats are targeting our vanes and drive!'

Adella grunted. She felt the deck tremble as point defence systems went into overdrive, laying down as much counter-metal into the void as her belts could feed through. Laser-line flashing like a paparazzi media drone hovering outside a nightclub.

There wasn't a great deal a skipper could control with certainty during fleet engagements. But the coordinates for your exit jump was one lockup. Which meant you knew where you would be at a certain point in time, and in that point of data, the vectors which made for best enemy intercept.

Adella saw her station flash with receipt of temporary trigger control from SecComm East. She entered her firing solution on the board and rolled it live. It would be unfair to label what the Chief had spent his team's time constructing as *mines,* exactly. Hollowing out asteroids with mining-nano wasn't standard procedure. But that's the depth of rock shielding you needed to cloak a couple of hundred dirty reactors stripped from Ghost Fleet and wired together before they were stuffed inside chunks of harmless-looking space debris.

The Quazzies' flying shield wall had a great many things going for it, but their tactic carried one major disadvantage, too. *Front Toward Enemy.* 'Helm, slip us through the needle at haste. Comms, transmit the following message wide-beam to all Devil Frog vessels. "This is what the galaxy's largest Claymore looks like!"'

'Sent, Commander.'

It was a stupendous explosion, but then, frogs were made to boil, even the Devil Frog variety. A dozen suns blossomed into life behind the pair of enemy fleets – the full Nova Breakfast served up. The level of detonation you were only too glad to witness to your rear as you were swallowed up by a tunnel into another universe. Right about now, the Quazzies were wishing two things. One, that their Shield-ships were formed *behind* their main force instead of in *front* of it. And two, that maybe shield-armour concentration on a single vessel class wasn't such a neat trick after all. Quazzies' void steel spun inside the shock-wave, two perfectly coordinated fleets reduced to a spinning, melting radioactive ballet of madness. A twin debris zone to keep Ghost Fleet company, now that its Alliance personnel were jumping for home.

Adella had only triggered the closest mines, too. Barely seven percent of the reactor-stuffed rocks scattered across the system for SecComm East's base A.I to use for its tripwire defence. *Mr. Frog will be real careful how he slides void inside Bardfeld's System for the foreseeable future*, Adella grinned. Teach the filthy Quazzies the value of caution next time they dropped into an Alliance system with genocide on their mind. *Slow down their advance through our space, too.*

Dark Viking's sail-drone rigging glowed from the ferocity of the expanding blast-front, heat-exchangers on overdrive as they shed rads. Then the sail-drones started popping like bugs slamming into an electrical discharge insect control system.

'Helm, anytime now would be just fine!'

The whine from *Dark Viking*'s overloading energy shields almost overwhelmed Beklum Sakwa's reply. 'Translation in three — two — one —'

Drug injectors inside Adella's coffin slapped her cerebrum out from under her for the duration of the jump, leaving the hardy kaggen navigator and Slugger as the only conscious bridge crew. After running overclocked for so long, that darkness arrived like shore leave for Commander Vega.

- 12 -

Rules of Evidence

A della was still woozy from running overclocked for so long inside her private coffin. Try not to throw up in front of your officers, Adella. That is never a good look. And as far as the great fleet battles of history went, their recent engagement was barely a short sharp blip. Many of the bridge crew headed for the restrooms and a discreet cubicle to sick up inside.

The strange blank canvas of hyperspace lay outside her battleship. In the past, that would have signalled a long uneventful voyage until they reached their destination. Now, it felt like being a fly dancing along a spiderweb. A short hop until they lost their navigation bearings, then dropping back into real-space. It was all Uddin Cesti's spaghetti jumble of smugglers routes from here on in.

The whole Home Fleet had successfully threaded the needle and stayed together within hyperspace. No mean feat. She tried to occupy herself by paging through the damage reports and sickbay list feeding through to her station. After the high of combat, came the low. And it didn't get much lower than this. *Nothing except a fleet engagement lost can be half so melancholy as a fleet engagement won.*

Adella started receiving strange communications from the hangar deck. Some kind of trouble from what she could make out. It looked like the *Smiter* hadn't been the only vessel to take on board crew abandoning the *Wager*. It had been a helluva confused situation during the firefight interrupting the evacuation, but even so, they had lined up an empty carrier's hangars as close as imaginable to carry the swap out as risk-free as possible during a fierce fleet-level pounding.

Commander Vega passed bridge control to the Master of the Helm, put her own trip to the bathroom on hold, and rode the lift from Operations Room to the hangar decks welded onto the battleship's centre-line. Adella heard what sounded like a thundering argument through the locks into the starboard-side chamber.

Adella winced as she realised she recognised the pedantic cadence of the loudest voice. *Oh no, not him!* Of all the people to have survived the *Wager*'s loss, couldn't fate have added one more to the casualty count? She passed through the lock and found the Hangar Boss and his crew being harangued by Rear Admiral Pullinger. Adella wasn't sure what the issue at hand was? Maybe the Hangar Boss wore greasy overalls, rather than dress blues. It didn't matter, as soon as SecComm East's senior officer spotted Commander Vega, he broke away and stormed across to her.

She noted the official Admiralty shuttle once belonging to Admiral Blackstar had crashed on landing; presumably, in the Rear Admiral's haste to abandon his dying, broken carrier. The man's retinue of headquarters officers had been reduced to four or five as well as a small squad of Marines; either by combat erosion or that was all he could fit inside his launch.

'Commander Vega, who precisely gave you the authority to abandon Sector Command East?' Pullinger's face was puffy and red, unusually pugnacious. But most of that was probably down to particle weapon exposure during the *Wager*'s perilous flight back to base.

'I did, *precisely*, acting in my legitimate capacity as Senior System Commander.'

'You have overreached yourself! This is cowardice in the face of the enemy.'

Adella hardly believed what she heard. 'You were on the *Wager*, is that correct, Rear Admiral?'

'Of course, I was on board her as you very well know!'

'Yes, *the* carrier you abandoned in the face of enemy action, allowing your engine room officers to assume command and sacrifice themselves to save your crew.' She threw it in his face not caring that his sycophants were there to witness it. They needed to hear it; they deserved to hear it, as did everybody inside the hangar.

'What are you saying?' Pullinger spluttered, as though the awareness of everyone he had senselessly killed through his stupidity had only just settled on him.

'That if there are charges of cowardice in the face of the enemy, Rear Admiral Pullinger, they deserve to be levelled against yourself. Along with the charges of incompetence of command. Abandoning Admiral Blackstar's strategy of asset preservation, leaving SecComm East as good as undefended, losing the Combined Fleet and endangering your command to no proper purpose.'

Pullinger didn't need a particle beam suntan to turn purple now. 'How dare you speak to me with such impertinence! I am the ranking officer for this entire sector and you will show me the respect I am due. If it wasn't for your rank cowardice in abandoning our sector headquarters, we would still have a secure location to retreat to. To hold the enemy off until reinforcements arrive. I carried the fight to the enemy in the best traditions of the Fleet. I did not flee and abandon headquarters without orders at the initial sighting of the Quazalrats!'

Oh, I am showing you the respect you are owed. For the first time in many a year. 'Where is my sister, Captain Vega? She shipped out with you on board the *Heart of Plasma* as First Officer. Where is your flag vessel and where is my sister?'

'The apple doesn't fall very far from the tree, does it?' Rear Admiral Pullinger jabbed a finger into the chest of Adella's tunic. 'I confined your sister to quarters pending a court-martial on charges of insubordination, refusing to respect the chain of command and wilfully disobeying the lawful orders of a superior commissioned officer. Do you want to know where your sister is? She most likely died inside her cabin when the *Heart of Plasma* went down. A more honourable fate than the dishonourable discharge the bitch had coming to her!'

It didn't even feel like Adella's fist that drove into Pullinger's face, breaking his nose; her body hard on top of his, her hand lashing into him again and again. All she saw was a raw red rage. A loathing so intense she drowned inside it. It took all three Marines with the Rear Admiral's party of sycophants to pull her off him. Harper Pullinger lay on the deck, stunned and glowering up at her, a hatred of such strength that if he had saved it for the Quazzies, he might have limped back with more than a single broken carrier.

'During a time of war, during a time of war!' Pullinger warbled before pulling himself together enough to sound coherent. 'Assaulting a superior officer in the course of executing their office is a court-martial offense. I'll see you dead for this! It won't be a dishonourable discharge for you, it will be a bloody firing squad, Vega.'

Suddenly Adella realised exactly what she had done. In retrospect, running into the Rear Admiral when she was still under the influence of the *Dark Viking*'s combat cocktail was not the smartest move she could have made. But it might very well be her last.

- 13 -

Duty's Absence

The Dark Viking's crew called her brig the Stewbox with good reason. Adella had a typical cell. Containing only a hard bunk able to convert into a crash couch during combat, a dirty head, and a door with a 5-inch-wide viewing slit and a hatch at the bottom which might pass as a catflap if your pet was really, really small. No entertainment as such, unless you counted the many ways she imagined ending the Rear Admiral's life and career. From accidentally opening an airlock with its safety protocols damaged during the stand-off against the Quazzie fleet – to out-and-out fragging the scuzzer. Adella was certain she wasn't the only officer under the Rear Admiral's sway who stayed warm at night with dreams of rolling a grenade through his cabin door. Her daily routine comprised three squares a day. She was fairly sure that Pullinger would have foregone her feeds, too, if Slugger's brig subsystem wasn't counting her calories like every prisoner. For a Commander used to having agency over her destiny, this was as Hell-Fleet as Hell-Fleet got.

Adella wondered if Pullinger had the balls to hold a field court-martial using the pretext of the Quazzie invasion to push ahead with it? The board wouldn't be any better than a Kangaroo court. Adella had already experienced a real board if inquiry and found the experience greatly lacking on the justice front, as far as she was concerned. And she doubted if Home Fleet and the civilian vessels escorted by the group had any lawyers with an understanding of naval protocols, jurisdiction, and case-books. Not that there wouldn't be countless officers from Adella's side willing to stand as her representative.

Adella's dark musings were interrupted by a fluttering of the catflap. She lacked a clock, but her rumbling stomach told her it could be lunchtime. Instead of a steel plate filled with greasy rations, Adella caught sight of a familiar face. *Lieutenant Anders Vistisen*. So, at least one person had survived the *Wager*'s destruction who deserved to.

'Lieutenant, good to see you. Are you on mess duty, now?'

Vistisen spoke *sotto voce*, not wanting to attract attention. 'I had to come and visit you, Commander. You need to know what happened to your sister.'

'That's why I'm here, Lieutenant. I clocked our dear Rear Admiral after I discovered how he abandoned her on board the *Heart of Plasma*.'

'You didn't hear the whole story then,' whispered the Lieutenant through the hatch. 'Pullinger had Captain Vega locked up after she came across the contents of Admiral Blackstar's sealed orders to him. Blackstar made it clear that the Rear Admiral needed to stand and hold at Sector Command inside Bardfeld's System. What was left of the Combined Fleet was to head back to Core under your authority!'

Under my authority? Adella could hardly believe what she was hearing. 'Does that make any sense…?'

'It did to Captain Vega, and for that matter to the rest of us, too. Not to Pullinger, though. When your sister confronted the Rear Admiral about failing to follow orders, he prevaricated. He told her that Blackstar was suffering from severe radiation poisoning and not in his right mind when he wrote those orders. Pullinger said as senior officer it was his duty to take over the Combined Fleet and lead us in a counter-offensive against the enemy. Captain Vega attempted to relieve the dog of his command, but he had her arrested and locked up. When it came to the first engagement at Shiddes 22, the battle was a turkey shoot. Pullinger basically circled the wagons. He didn't deploy the carriers early enough or make use of our cruisers' maneuverability. All we could do was pound their Shield-ships. And up close, broadside-to-broadside, the Quazzies' shield wall has every advantage in that sport. In the end, Pullinger cut and run. After *Heart of Plasma* had her jump vanes sliced off, Pullinger pulled his bridge staff and pogoed to the *Wager*. The Quazzies fielded three fleets in-system, with a further three War-Wheels squatting in hyperspace waiting for us to translate out of Shiddes 22. Pullinger ordered all our surviving vessels to form up and hold the line in hyperspace while the *Wager* sped off.'

'*Wait*, you're saying the Rear Admiral abandoned what was left of the Combined Fleet while the yellow bastard showed the Quazalrats his bloody heels?'

'I doubt Pullinger will paint it like that,' said Lieutenant Vistisen. 'In fact, he's trying to hang the whole debacle on you and your sister. His headquarters toadies are hacking records to make it look as though *Wager* received comms from a courier packet that Home Fleet was bailing out of Bardfeld's System. You'll be Pullinger's excuse for abandoning his vessels. He needed to come running to save the day at Sector Command. He's also rewriting the files so it appears as if your sister's "mutiny" was a lot larger and more successful than it went down. Captain Vega will shoulder liability for Pullinger's decisions that led to the Combined Fleet's loss.'

Adella barely contained her fury. Bad enough Pullinger was planning to frame Adella for his disastrous campaign. But to try to pin the blame on Adella's dead sister – hang her out to dry for his own ineptitude, his lies, *his* failure to acknowledge Admiral Blackstar's lawful orders. Well, that was more than Adella could stand! The Lieutenant obviously read a fraction of Adella's rage in her face.

'I will help you in every way I can,' whispered the Lieutenant. 'There are too many crew alive off the *Wager* who saw the truth about what happened at Shiddes 22. And now the Chief and Master of the Helm know too. We're spreading the word and trying to organise.'

'You're talking about a mutiny, Lieutenant.'

'I'm talking about an Admiral's orders carrying more weight than a Rear Admiral's, even in this species' navy,' said the Lieutenant. 'You beat the Devil Frogs at Bardfeld's system. That's driving the Rear Admiral insane. He thinks you stole his personal victory off him out of spite and he's planning to sink you for it.'

'Have you heard of the Battle of Rorke's Drift, Lieutenant?'

'An old land action back on Earth…?'

'Yeah, it was one of those glorious last-stand deals, except the troops who forted-up actually survived, beating off a vastly superior enemy force. But one thing you rarely read about Rorke's Drift is that their splendid victory was a propaganda puff-piece by the British Empire to cover up the death of countless thousands of soldiers at a far larger battle lost on the same day, called Isandlwana.'

'You think the Devil Frogs' three dead force carriers at Bardfeld's System will be the Alliance's Rorke's Drift?'

'Yeah, and I bet Pullinger intends to present it as *his* victory, to distract the news networks from his sorry-ass Isandlwana.'

'That's why the Rear Admiral doesn't want you around to gainsay him. I heard rumours he's trying to find willing trigger-men amongst our Marines. I hoped that foul deed would be beneath even our silken slitherer.'

'Hell, if the Rear Admiral can't rustle up a firing squad, he only needs a single sailor to shove me in an airlock and disable its safety protocols. Do you know what the bastard's planning for Home Fleet?'

'He has come up with the genius scheme of heading away with Colonel Blackstar and the combat intelligence gleaned from our engagements to date, then wrapping them up for SecComm Core.'

Adella shook her head, 'Damn, why didn't *we* think of that?'

'Between the Quazzies and the Rear Admiral, I prefer trading broadsides with the Devil Frogs,' said the Lieutenant. 'At least they go for your throat with an honest nuke, not a dagger in your back.'

'Just play it softly, Anders,' warned the Commander. 'Or you'll end up in the cell next door playing verbal tic-tac-toe against the old girl.'

But only until the moment the Rear Admiral located a Marine happy enough to put a bullet into an officer without being brought up on charges for the act. *Yeah, that will be really hard.*

- 14 -

Hyperspace Heaven

Captain Okereke? Adella stared in confusion at the Neutron Dance's skipper, his face pushed up against her cell door's small viewing port. What's the merchant doing here in the middle of the night? 'Captain, unless you've been drafted by the Rear Admiral and placed on sentry duty…?'

'You might say I've signed up,' grinned the captain, 'but for the opposition team. It's been suggested to me that Home Fleet isn't the safest place for you at the moment, Commander Vega. Court-martials during a time of war and all. I hoped it would be worth my while popping into the brig during my own little recruitment drive.'

'Let me guess, a suicide run to grab up the only Lucky Gene navigator in this sector?'

'Yeah, that'll be the open position. I thought I'd ask your Rear Admiral for additional resources and a green-for-go on the mission launch, but the whole caboodle seems to have been deleted from the *Dark Viking*'s logs. Our launch window, your engineers' work on my ship, everything. From what I hear, a lot of items appear to be going astray in Home Fleet's corner of the cybersphere. Little things. Big things. Removed files keep on getting restored from backups. It's driving your glorious leader nutso.'

Adella peered through the cell door's tiny viewing plate. 'Where're the Marines on duty?'

'Scheduling error,' said Okereke, 'see what I mean. Everyone allocated out to other duties at the same time. Sloppy, frankly.' He waved his vessel civilian visitor's badge hanging on a lanyard. 'And this is mis-programmed with access-all-areas authorisation. I almost wandered into your Marines' armoury thinking it was the toilet.' A tap on the code lock outside and Adella's cell door retracted up into the wall. She stepped out warily. Empty. No soldiers on duty, only Slugger's ceiling surveillance cam-dome rotating at high speed as though it was drunk, indicator lights flashing an angry crimson.

Okereke produced a full-face mask with a built-in oxygen tank. Adella noticed the skipper had his own mask dangling from his ship-suit's utility belt. 'You will need to wear this, Commander. Sorry. There are shocking problems with bacterial filters inside this battleship's environmental systems – crew reporting contaminated air across dozens of decks and suchlike. The Rear Admiral thinks it's damned malingerers' excuses, but you can never be too careful. You better escort me to my shuttle in your hangar before I come down all blotchy and ill.'

Adella was torn. Leaving the Home Fleet, even if it was to retrieve a navigator able to give the survivors a fighting chance, felt like a dereliction of duty. *But then, how useful are you going to be as an icicle drifting outside the Dark Viking's airlock?* It wasn't much of a choice at the end of the day, but it *was* hers to make.

'Let's go.'

Commander Vega crossed over to the nearest sentry desk, ripping a page out of a notebook and borrowing the brig officer's pencil. She scribbled on the paper before reentering her cell and leaving the note folded for the first Marine to enter to find.

Adella slipped the disguising mask over her face as Okereke did likewise, before leading him out of the brig. *Nothing to see here. Just a civilian being escorted off the ship.* Many of the crew she passed in her ship's corridors and access tunnels sucked on air-tubes, too. Like attending a masquerade ball without the fancy costumes. Pretty easy to sabotage operations on board a vessel. Misinterpret an order, here. Work-to-rule over on that deck. Knowing how Pullinger operated, it would mostly be a matter of blindly following the Rear Admiral's orders and failing to post-correct his obvious stupidities. She could tell her ship's air was contaminated, all right. But not with the bacterial rot of a piss-poor maintenance schedule. Her decks reeked of incompetent command and rotten morale's poisoned air…which, in the end, proved far more dangerous for a fighting force.

A warning claxon sounded across the battleship. *Normal-Space Drop, approaching.* The convoy's Minkowski field generators were about to cycle down, squeezing the group's vessels out of hyperspace. Exits were easy. This strange realm of contra-physics ached to expel foreign matter – ships merely had to relinquish their hold to be spat out like melon pips at a country fair.

'There's our curtain-call,' said Okereke.

Adella smiled. 'Nice timing.'

Okereke nodded. 'Man, this bad air, it's enough to make you overshoot your drop zone by an entire system or more!'

Home Fleet would arrive at its destination only to find itself shy of an officer locked inside the *Dark Viking*'s brig and one free-trader hauler from the escort list. With Pullinger in charge, it might be days before anyone noticed the discrepancy, let alone wonder whether the two mysteries were in some way related.

'What did you write on your note?' asked Okereke.

'I begged the Rear Admiral to post a *very* loyal team of armed guards outside his cabin during his dog watch.'

'Ouch.'

A security reminder from a concerned officer, of course, definitely *not* a threat – and try proving otherwise at a board of inquiry. Adella enjoyed imagining the paranoid head of SecComm East tearing apart the battleship trying to find her. Pullinger wouldn't sleep easy for the rest of the voyage, thinking she was hidden away by traitors inside one of the hundreds of off-plan components bolted on during the *DV*'s decades as an orbital station. Plotting her revenge and organising a mutiny to avenge her sister's death. *You'll reap the rewards of your command, Pullinger, but I'll do it by the book. I'll see you shot live on the news networks for what you did out here.*

It didn't take much effort to pogo unchallenged out of the battleship's hangar. Adella suspected she could have slipped painlessly away even without her access codes and "friendlies" working inside Ops. They flew through hyperspace with everyone in Fleet more concerned with the day-to-day minutiae of keeping the *Dark Viking* operational, not to mention maintaining a tenuous lock on their course in the face of the Quazzies' range-inhibiting super-weapon. Home fleet's crews were focused on clearing hyperspace as quickly as possible; preferably before the enemy used their looted technology to pinpoint them and send a host of War-Wheels arse-haring after the convoy.

Don't look at our shuttle. Just another civilian skipper being dragged over the coals for sloppy convoy discipline, before being dispatched back to his tub to reflect on the error of his ways.

This was the first time Adella had manoeuvred through hyperspace on a craft as small as a shuttle. Ship-to-ship transfers might be made in hyperspace, but such hops always depended on the smaller vessel sheltering under her mothership's Minkowski field. Shuttles lacked jump vanes and meaningful Minkowski gear, so if the Mother Goose possessing a field generator wandered off course, the shuttle would be ejected from hyperspace in a random translation. Maybe landing up embedded inside a planet or star. More likely stranded a hundred parsecs from the nearest system without enough fuel, water, or food; well beyond the communications range of anyone and anything. In short, a death sentence as sure as the Rear Admiral's firing squad for her.

'Can you feel our hull vibrating, Captain?' asked Adella.

'First turn in hyperspace slumming it on something as tiny as this, then?' said Okereke. 'You grow used to the hum. It's the harmonics of the alien space-time continuum. On a big battleship – or even my merchanteer – armour and shields take the edge off the flutter.'

At one point during the crossing, Adella heard a strange slapping noise followed by a series of thumps. Those sounded like they emanated from the deck below the shuttle's cockpit. 'And that?'

'Yeah, *that* I can't blame on hyperspace. We've currently got a rodent problem on the *Neutron Dance*. Good old-fashioned Terran chipmunks. We stopped at the ring station circling Luyten 726 on the voyage across to the Frontier. Luyten's orbital habitats farm rodents as a food source. Of course, some of the little munchkins inevitably escaped – and have been plaguing honest spacers ever since.'

As much as Adella might wish mischief for the Rear Admiral, she prayed none of the stowaways jumped ship while the shuttle rested inside *Dark Viking*. Trying to work out whether your rail-cannons were misfiring from broadside damage was hard enough without needing to check for pests nibbling your wiring.

After their nerve-wracking cross-vessel hop finished, Adella found herself gazing at a surprisingly well-provisioned hangar. The *Neutron Dance* held a line of fat cargo shuttles on launch rails. They sat below automated conveyor lines feeding in from the ship's voluminous holds. Her hangar contained a few custom fast-movers, too. What resembled a solar-sail racer, as well as a sleek packet-boat. Even civilian engineers needed hobby projects to keep them happy.

Adella caught a good gander at the trading vessel on the hop across. She was a real antique from the look of her lines. It wouldn't have surprised Adella if the ship's true age lay over the half-millennium mark. In the markets of interstellar commerce, shiny new ships almost always belonged to rich corporate houses and the big combines. Tramp freighters such as the *Neutron Dance* relied on hope, wits, and skipping out of systems before fuel and repair bills fell due. Bardfeld's engineers had done as efficient a job as they could making the *Neutron Dance* appear dangerous. But given the heavy long lines of merchant vessels, the best Fleet could do was disguise her as a pirate warship support ship, not a raider in her own right.

Still, it never did to underestimate an older ship. Adella attested to that from her own experiences with the *Dark Viking* and the throwaways scrapped at Ghost Fleet. Free-traders needed large, powerful engines to push the bulk cargoes that paid their bills. They could swap the big-ass thrusters on the *Neutron Dance*'s stern section with the *Dark Viking*'s and Adella bet Chief Kessi would be hard-pressed to tell the difference from power output alone. From what Adella saw, this bird looked like a typical mixed-use vessel. Including a liner module for transporting rich sightseers or dirt-poor colonists, depending on who it was picking up the tab for a contract.

Adella tested the artificial gravity field after stepping off the shuttle, exiting down a dropped ramp. That was an old spacers' trick. Sailors said you gauged a ship's quality by the bounce of your soles on her deck. Adella understood the ancient superstition was likely hokum. It was entirely feasible for a ship to install a top-of-the-line gravity field generator while running maintenance routines on the remaining systems that would see the vessel condemned inside an Alliance system after the first safety inspector's check. However, if the superstition had any truth to it, the *Neutron Dance* appeared well up to snuff.

'You're welcome to join me on the bridge,' said Okereke. 'Or if you prefer, I can whistle up a robot to take you to a cabin.'

Yeah, Adella bet that there was no shortage of accommodation given the size of the liner module plugged into the old girl. Probably a hell of a lot bigger and better appointed than her Commander's quarters on the *Dark Viking*. Fleet naval architects designed along Spartan lines, basing layouts on psychological studies that suggested too much comfort made for detrimental effects on crew discipline.

Adella appreciated Okereke's offer. It spoke well of the skipper's confidence. Plenty of free-traders would be leery about inviting a Fleet officer onto their bridge. Too nervous of back seat-skippering and the disdain officers like Rear Admiral Pullinger showered on "lesser" civilian crews. Fleet had a particular way of doing things. Free-traders' methods usually came as varied as the crew of rogues, chancers and adventurers working in their unreliable profession.

'I'll come with, if it's all the same to you.'

Okereke checked his watch. 'Ten minutes to drop, at least for Fleet.'

It suddenly hit Adella that this was *it*. She might never see the *Dark Viking* or Home Fleet again. Even knowing the escaping fleet's route in advance, there was a hell of a lot to go wrong. Starting with the high likelihood that Blue Barnier would rumble their game and walk everyone out of an airlock. That was before you threw the murderous invaders into the mix.

Okereke sensed her foreboding. 'Don't worry, I sure ain't planning on letting a filthy bunch of pirates claim my scalp.'

They rode a capsule tube across to the vessel's bridge. Two main points of difference from the Operations Room on the *Dark Viking*; one she expected and one far less so. The first change was that on the *Neutron Dance*'s bridge Adella might as well be standing inside a hologram planetarium – bridge positions attached to mechanical arms, the deck a metal skeleton surrounded by open void. Of course, the merchant vessel's bridge was protected by heavy composite physical shielding alongside the energy variety. But the projection systems gave Adella the illusion she floated among the stars. Or, currently, among the strange blank-rippling canvas of hyperspace. Adella had read that the Alliance Fleet once tried those open flight configurations. But during naval engagements when taking fire, Fleet personnel needed to feel as though the universe's largest orbital fort sheltered them. Not floating naked ducking missiles, tacks, and smart-drones as ordnance fiercely flew between your ship and the enemies'.

The difference that threw Adella was the shocking young girl occupying one of the seats drifting above the deck. Adella found the kid's presence so distracting she barely took in Professor Alison Sebba and the other two bridge crew. The crab-like Kaggen was obviously the ship's navigator, and there was also a lizard-like Skirl riding a command position.

'This is Alice–the Professor's daughter,' said Okereke. 'Professor Sebba you already know. And these two reprobates are Ilatin and Scort. My ship's navigator, and cargo-wrangler-plus-negotiator. Our Chief Engineer is back in the drive section. It's fair to say he doesn't get out much.'

'This is *all* your crew?'

'Well, there's been a few other groovers drifting in-and-out of the cast list over the years. We hire hundreds of service staff on a freelance basis every time we play star-liner. And naturally, the *Neutron Dance* slides void with over three thousand robots and drones on board.'

Adella understood. When it came to slim profit margins you automated everything able to be automated.

'I'm receiving a fleet-transmit from *Dark Viking*,' announced the navigator. 'A reminder that there's one minute left to drop-sync.'

'Okay,' said Okereke, indicating an empty seat for Adella's use. 'Let's keep it tight, my friends. We don't want to make anyone inside *Dark Viking*'s Ops Room doubt our good intentions about sheeping along with the herd.'

'Drop in *three, two, one...*'

Adella sensed their Minkowski field generators power down. The ship started to shake as the vessel's matter began to re-assume its natural form. All around them the Home Fleet's vessels blinked out of existence — or at least *this* exotic higher universe's existence. The *Neutron Dance* trembled as she bled molecular coherence. For a second, Adella thought she glimpsed their real-space target zone, the outer edge of a system with real stars and nebulae bright against an inky background. The two images superimposed in a blink-and-you-might-miss-it moment. Then the craft's Minkowski generators cycled up again. Hyperspace's dull infinity re-established its dominance over the particle-spin of everything contained in the *Neutron Dance*. Hyperspace, still.

'Nicely done,' commented Captain Okereke. 'I think you adequately teased our friends of a Fleet persuasion. We seek her here, we seek her there, the Fleet seeks her everywhere. Is she in hyperspace heaven? — Is she in real-space hell? That damned elusive *Neutron Dance*.'

'Your poetry needs a little more work, old boy,' said the lizard.

'Everyone's a critic, baby. Reorient on our new heading,' ordered the Captain. 'Let's hope the good ladies and gentlemen of the Floating Port aren't half as critical or discerning as you folks are.'

The Professor shrugged apologetically as she unbelted her young daughter from the seat and ushered the girl towards the bridge's exit.

'Not where you want your kid to be,' noted Adella after the academic left. 'The middle of a shooting war.'

'That's one difference between Fleet and indies,' said the skipper. 'It's not unusual to see children running around on board free-traders, even when you haven't got a client with her child as a tag-along. Plenty of ships operate as big extended families. You're right, though. The Professor sure didn't bank on having the Devil Frogs kick hyperspace out from under her heels during the middle of a full-ass invasion of Alliance space.'

'There're details you can plan for and details that you can't,' said Adella, echoing the old Academy maxim.

It had sounded wise back in the day. In the midst of a war, it seemed like a statement of the bloody obvious. Adella hoped those words wouldn't return to haunt her after she contacted the pirates.

- 15 -

Looks Good for a Dead Woman

Adella walked from the Neutron Dance's mess back to her cabin in the liner section when she came across the Professor's daughter, Alice, playing with a toy robot. It looked like an engine room drone hastily retrofitted with age-appropriate learning software and coded to entertain the young child. Currently, Alice seemed satisfied with chasing the machine up and down the ship while the drone sang a tune Adella recognised as ten-year-old H-synth from the music charts. The adolescent noticed Commander Vega by nearly piling into her, pulling short, then staring guiltily as if she had been caught doing something she wasn't meant to do.

'Hello, Alice,' said Adella.

'Hello,' replied the young girl. She stared up at the Commander with a penetrating gaze older than her age. 'I shouldn't be talking to you.'

'Well, you're not allowed to talk to strangers at all I daresay.'

'Yes, but the Fleet are bad people.'

'What makes you say that?'

'In the before-times, the Fleet would come to raid the stations. Take all our food and kill everyone. Everyone would float dead outside the ships and the hiding rocks.'

'You're thinking of pirates,' said Adella. *The poor little thing, she must have overheard her mum talking with the crew about the Floating Port and she got the wrong end of the stick.* 'The Fleet protects the orbital stations and traffic from bad people.'

'It's all different now,' said the slight girl. 'The Fleet needed to steal food and fuel to survive.'

Adella wasn't quite sure what to make of this fey young thing. 'Don't worry, kid, nothing nasty'll happen to you. Your mother and I will ensure that.'

'My second-same mum.'

'The same as what?' asked Adella, confused.

'Exactly the same as the first. You won't understand.'

'I'll let you into a little secret,' said Adella. 'I never really understood much when I was your age. I thought that would change when I grew older. But if anything, I think it's got a lot worse.'

'You're wearing a Fleet uniform,' pointed out the girl, as though putting one on was a crime.

Crime against fashion, maybe. 'I am, but I'll need to swap it for a shipsuit.'

'You're going to pretend as well when we meet the bad people?'

'Yeah, I will have to pretend better than I've ever pretended before.'

'Do you want to come with me to my cabin? I'll show you the painting I did with R4.' Alice patted the drone's squat little body. It was a standard maintenance unit with two stubby legs that look like segmented industrial piping, a camera and sensor array swivelling on top, constantly mapping its environment in three dimensions. There weren't any visible arms, but small manipulator arrays could push out from panels as needed.

'Is your cabin inside the crew compartment run; before the transit-tube towards the liner module?'

'Yes.'

'Then it's on my way and you can show me your painting if you want.'

Children always seemed to like Adella and she was never quite sure why. The Commander supposed babies would have been on the cards for her and her husband if she hadn't been widowed. A Fleet career didn't make kids an easy choice – or partners, for that matter. Married quarters were usually the cheapest habs going on any naval orbital station, and even the kindest tour of duty saw couples and families separated for years at a time while ships patrolled the Alliance's internal systems and external border zones. *Marry the Fleet, divorces come free. So did widowhood, too, if you were really unlucky.*

All-in-all, these kinds of encounters were just another reminder of everything Adella had lost.

'Art can be therapy,' announced Alice out of the blue.

I wonder who told you that? 'Do you think you need therapy, young lady?'

'I'm remembering more and more about the before-times,' said the kid.

'Before what, exactly?' asked Adella, following the girl through a transparent round passage with a grand view of hyperspace's esoteric canvas. She wasn't sure if the corridor was actually translucent composite hull or just a very high-fidelity projection from exterior camera views.

'The old universe.'

Adella really wasn't certain what this girl was talking about. Maybe Alice needed therapy of some sort or another after all?

They reached a door in a branch off the main passage. Alice waved her hand in front of the portal and it slid to the side recognising her biometrics. 'Come on. This one is mine.'

Inside, Adella found a suite of four connected rooms; the size of a small apartment. On a Fleet battleship, this would be the Admiral's cabin, but only if the commanding officer was lucky. The girl vanished into a chamber and returned clutching a large piece of paper. The sheet had a fairly reasonable sketch of the *Neutron Dance* rendered across it. Bright rainbow colours, nothing like the dull gunmetal of the real vessel, but an admirable effort for a child of her age. *Imaginative, too.* Particularly the seven smaller ships hovering at a distance, their weapons beaming out onto the *Neutron Dance* and cutting her into component-level slices. The attackers weren't any configuration or hull design Adella recognised, closer to massive black space tarantulas, so just a work of pure fantasy.

'This is how the ship dies.'

'That will not happen,' promised Adella.

'It already has many times before, I think,' said Alice.

On the other side of the oblong hallway, R4 sang its pop song again. Adella felt a sudden chill run down her neck as though someone had stepped over her grave. *You're turning soft, Commander, letting the nightmares of some academic's daughter put the frighteners on you.*

'It's a very accurate sketch of the ship,' praised Adella. 'I can see definite talent here.' The officer was about to leave the cabin when she spotted an old photograph mounted inside a plastic frame teetering on the edge of a shelf. Adella gazed closer. It was Professor Alison Sebba, cuddling her daughter from the left of the picture. And on the right, the man kneeling and holding the girl looked like a clone of Colonel Kal Blackstar. But the guy in the image carried an extra twenty or thirty years on the carrier colonel she knew? *Is this some kind of weird coincidence? It can't be. But then, unless there's some really freaky time travel crap going down...?* And time travel was utterly impossible, wasn't it?

'Is this your father, Alice? Who shot this picture?'

'My mum took the photo. She gave it to me before she died. That's my dad, but he's gone as well,' said Alice.

The Professor sure as hell looks good for a dead woman. 'Gone where?'

The young girl brought out her coloured pens and a fresh sheet of paper, spreading them across the floor. For a second Adella thought she might have forgotten the question. But then Alice began talking as she started a new work. 'Dad left twice. The first time, the monsters came for him on our ship. And the ship died, too. The next time, different people showed up for him. They looked human, but I think they were monsters as well. Not all monsters look strange. Some look just like us.'

Commander Vega nodded to the girl as though she understood everything. Trouble was, the further Adella went down this rabbit hole the opposite was true. Professor Sebba had pretty much stayed out of Adella's way so far during the voyage and ensured her daughter was scarcely seen, too. *Is that picture the reason for this?* Had Sebba married Admiral Blackstar's nephew back in the day? So, what did that make the young Colonel currently strolling about the *Dark Viking* in his carrier uniform? Some class of clone resurrected by a covert Alliance agency to pull it out of the mess created by the invasion? The more Adella discovered about this black bag shindig, the less it made sense to her.

Professor Sebba had said nothing to Adella about any of this, whatever the academic's perspective was. Adella figured she would not be the one to broach the subject first, either. *Hey, Professor, do you remember your deceased husband? He's alive and about thirty years younger than when you lost him. He also signed up with Fleet Carrier Wing to escape from you. But then, he could well be an alien-hybrid clone run by a dangerous Alliance Black Ops unit. Oh, and by the by, your daughter thinks you are dead and is drawing creepy pictures that suggest your next stop shouldn't be a pirate-filled hell-station, but a world with a state-of-the-art psychotherapy hospital.*

None of that would help them survive the Floating Port. Not by a single inch.

'Listen, Alice,' said the Commander. 'Before we get to the Floating Port, you need to practice hiding in different spots around the ship. It's a big place and there're lots of fantastic locations to hide.'

'Oh, I know that,' smiled the little girl. 'I hid super-well before. That's how I got off this ship before she exploded. Of course, the ship helped me escape, too. But don't tell anyone that. Our ship is smarter and kinder than the crew realise.'

Smarter than me, that's for sure, sighed Adella as she left the professor's deranged daughter to her art therapy.

***

Adella was standing on the Neutron Dance's bridge once more – her, the skipper, his Kaggen navigator and Skirl deal-maker. Okereke tapped his crypto-key. I didn't look much. A silver-case the size of a box of matches. It actually spat out the Floating Port's position coordinates as hard-copy on ribbons of paper. It appeared the pirates still occupied a Frontier system called WISE 1717, its sole claim to fame being the colony world of Wickham. It had been savaged once by the Quazzies as they passed on by, now a second time by the Brethren of the Stars. Adella doubted if there would be anything but corpses on the float inside the system when they showed up.

'Mr. Ilatin, drop us out of hyperspace at the one-eighty-degree mark on the system edge,' ordered Okereke.

'You're betting the Floating Port will be anchored at the boundary closest to Wickham,' said Adella.

'That's not much of a wager, Commander. I heard the Floating Port changed-up their routine after the Devil Frogs invaded the Frontier on full-throttle,' explained the skipper. 'The master of the *Aces High* told me she emergency jumped out of Gamma Tucanae after being treated to the sight of the pirates' whole worldlet dropping inside her system. The port remained hovering on Celestial South ready to translate out at short notice while her raiders headed in-system for the looting and pillaging. Don't you feel sorry for those poor mopes – no more treating hyperspace as their own private fog-bank to hide in?'

'Given the pirates have a Comet Person as a navigator, why don't the skeggers just high-tail it back inside deep Alliance space?' asked Adella.

'You'll understand once you lay eyes on the Floating Port,' said Okereke. 'They might be able to navigate fine with Ossian in the navigator's seat, but the port ain't built for speed. They based their whole piracy gig using the Floating Port as a safe harbour on the chances of randomly running into something inside hyperspace being close to zero. Now, if the port takes off on a straight-line course, it'll be run down inside hyperspace by Quazzie interceptors within a week. It's not so much that the station shows up on the Quazzies' hyperspace sensors, as when the port's riding hyperspace, there ain't nothing on the screen *but* the Floating Port!'

Adella bet there was a "healthy argument" ongoing among the pirates about abandoning the Floating Port and jumping core-ward in a pirate convoy that mimicked Home Fleet's strategy. Ditch the slow-moving target that was the port, spin up their motley fleet of war vessels, then sprint hell-for-leather for friendly skies. *I know you, Blue Barnier. You worked your entire life to rise high enough in the ranks of scum to become Harbour Lord of the Floating Port. There's no way you're throwing that away, even if it means weathering an alien invasion.*

***

Adella had scanned intelligence reports on the Floating Port from many sources over the years. Most of the Fleet's images on file had been hastily snapped from within the station. The rest was gossip and hearsay. None of the snitches did credit to the strange, vast, cobbled-together pirate harbour in actuality. The Floating Port resembled a handful of orbital colonies welded to each other at random, then buried for shielding inside four large asteroids pulled out of a belt somewhere. Following that, the entire caboodle had seen a variety of looted ships installed into the structure over the centuries whenever extra space was required. There wasn't a single set of integrated engines or jump vanes that the Commander could spot anywhere across its surface.

Which would mean when the harbour needed to move anywhere, they just fired the engines on whichever ship was pointing in the right direction for the journey. With a cold tactician's eye, Adella could see the immediate difficulty the Floating Port faced. It was designed to fly in hyperspace and *stay* in hyperspace. Even if the pirate station simultaneously spun all the jump vanes she possessed, creating a field big enough to pass that humongous monstrosity must be an act of faith with each voyage. Simply put, the pirate worldlet was never created to operate like a ship. And now the Quazzies' super-weapon meant every second inside hyperspace was spent as a blinking red light on the Devil Frogs' sensor grid. *Blue Barnier, you son-of-a-bitch, it couldn't have happened to a nicer marauding scumbag!*

***

Adella waited in the Neutron Dance's main lock for the station to extend and match a boarding arm. The Professor sheltered somewhere with her daughter, but the navigator and Skirl trader stood by her side with heavy rifles. Okereke passed Adella a belt with a rail pistol inside its leather holster. 'Carry one of these inside at all times. It's mandatory at the port.'

Adella gratefully belted the weapon around her waist. It wasn't much firepower compared to having an entire battleship interfaced with her augment during ship-to-ship combat, but it beat fists and a sharp tongue. A clank, clank, then a hiss of atmosphere as the relative pressures equalised. The locks rolled open and Adella could smell a citrus tang on the breeze. Every large orbital station and habitat had its own unique splice of plants and vegetation to help keep air recycling systems turning over. Whoever helped put in the Floating Port's environmental tech obviously had a thing for lemons. Knowing how the pirates recruited specialist talent, the engineers had almost certainly been grabbed at gunpoint from a burning asteroid dome.

A gang of heavily-armed guards waited at the end of a narrow airlock. Perhaps twenty fighters from a variety of species, with an over-representation of humanity. They clutched rifles, pistols and one was even seated high inside an armoured exoskeleton fighting-frame. As far as welcoming committees went, this group didn't seem to be taking any chances. Adella guessed honour among thieves was more of a theoretical concept than a matter of practice with the Floating Port's security.

A middle-aged woman wearing a green beret with a silver skull-and-cross-bones badge pinned into it stepped forward. 'It's been a while since we saw one of Steel-Arm Bowen's ships in port.'

'You know how it is,' said Okereke, 'Steel-Arm scored it big a little while ago and we decided to lay low and enjoy the loot.'

'Yeah, but the proceeds always run out sooner than you think when you're spending it honestly.'

'Even when you're not,' laughed Okereke.

'Well, there're pickings aplenty these days. Easy meat as far as you can see. Whole Eastern Frontier has collapsed. Fleet, gone. TAP agents pulled out. Revenue officers tossed away their badges and jumped for the Core.'

Adella made to move past the line of thugs but the woman with the beret stuck a rifle out, halting her. 'Come on, now, girlfriend. First off, there's the little matter of our Fancy.'

Fancy? Adella wasn't clear what the guards were talking about, but Okereke seemed to understand the custom. The Captain stepped back and indicated Adella. 'Don't worry, I've bought enough Fancy to pay our docking fees for the rest of the decade. This here is commander Adella Vega of the TAS *Dark Viking* – sure you've heard of her from when she used to head-up the Fleet's Anti-Piracy Group!'

Adella had her pistol drawn at almost the same time as ten thugs piled on top of her. She would have been able to blow a few apart with her gun, too, if its power charge hadn't been as empty as vacuum's void in this system. The pirates realised that too and began to pistol-whip the Commander with the flats of their rifle butts. Her physical pain nearly secondary to the shock and shame at being so easily tricked inside the port, then handed over like a sack of potatoes to the same bastard she had come to assassinate.

- 16 -

Pirates of the Floating Port

There wasn't much to do inside the brig after Adella came to consciousness in one of its cells. Ruminate on the loathing she felt for the Neutron Dance's crew; sacrificing her like a goat to the pirates. That was only secondary to the disgust for her own foolishness at being so easily gulled. Adella guessed the security module used to imprison her had once been part of a luxury liner. Liners were the only ships which bothered with impressive force-field gates instead of thick steel and a heavy lock. It played the role, she had to give it that. If you paid a hundred-thousand tokens for the expensive cruise of a lifetime and you ended up drugged off your eyeballs in this brig, you would certainly believe you were getting your money's worth. The trouble was, when power needed to be diverted, say during a flash storm of space debris bouncing off your deflectors, then ships had a way of de-prioritising the energy required to keep ridiculous-looking fancy shields in place.

As chance would have it, Adella was given an opportunity to realise her hate for the *Neutron Dance*'s crew and her gullibility was but a mere flickering candle compared to that of the dog who came visiting her. Commander Vega had never met the officer walking into the brig, perching himself on the edge of a bench opposite her cell's glowing force wall. But she had dreamed of meeting him a thousand times, right before she put a bullet through his skull. *Blue Barnier!*

Barnier didn't look much. Almost entirely average. Not fat. Not thin. Not tall and not short. Slip him inside a work suit and he could have walked undisguised and unnoticed through any business district on a hundred human worlds. Maybe twenty years older than Adella, undistinguished and plain. The most remarkable thing about the pirate was the fake admiral's uniform he wore. It looked like a rental from a fancy-dress shop. In reality, it was an amalgam of dozens of uniforms stripped off corpses and sewn back together again. From everything she had heard, these clothes suited the mad-dog killer down to the ground.

Blue Barnier smiled at her with a warmth even more chilling for appearing genuine. 'Yes, of course, you recognise me from my photos in the feeds. Just as I recognise you from yours. They were very unkind to you after my raid on Strabane, Commander Vega, and the role you played in it. The Widow and Widow-maker of Strabane? Dead bodies are the currency of both our trades. It is how we keep our tally.'

'My role … you mean trying to kill you? The news-feeds were right about my failure on that account. You deserve to die – and it should still be me who puts you down.'

'You'll think differently, Adella, after you get to know me better.'

'I know all about you, you sick bastard. Blue Barnier, the pirate warlord who can add up. You were Finance Director for a large chemical industry combine on Rana. Fired after an advanced process dumped down from offworld, making your patents about as valuable as a chimpanzee's tea party at a zoo. Your wife couldn't adjust to her mansion-free low-status gig on state basic and jumped off the ninety-eighth floor of your new hab-hutch clutching all three of your kids. So, you strolled into a board meeting with a machine pistol and expressed your disappointment, then went on the run with every TAP agent in the system on your tail. The news-feeds said you were just feeling *blue* and should have been offered a package of decent psychiatric care.'

'Ah, Adella,' smiled Blue Barnier. 'Where did Fleet bury you for all these years? Did it finally take a war like this for the fools to roll you out of retirement?'

'I've been waiting for you, Barnier, that's what I do. Waiting, patiently.'

'Well, here I am for your pleasure. I did you a favour, Adella. I showed you the truth of what your precious Fleet is. I gave you a little glimpse of life's deeper truths, too. It's a game. Our whole universe nothing but a simulation running on an alien A.I. cloud substrate, universes inside universes nested inside more universes. Each false and true at the same time. You lost everything because I chose to set you free, exactly as the game set me free. It's a beautiful accident, for ones and zeroes to experience real freedom.'

'You're… insane!'

'How can you say that, you of all people? Nobody else ever came close to catching me. Only you did, Adella. Twice you nearly had us, once at Gliese 86 and again at Denebola. You deserved to have the curtain pulled away, the thin veil of reality revealed. I knew the game would send you back to me, eventually. And of course, it had to be now.'

'You think this is *fate*…?'

'Surely,' smiled the madman. 'How can you doubt it? My life has become too easy, Adella. I've levelled up. Harbour Lord of the Floating Port with not a single worthy adversary among the entire Alliance Fleet.

Taking ships and worlds from your people about as challenging as balancing a small trader's books at the start of my original career. So, what does the great multi-player universe do? It tosses me fresh meat to chew on! A massive alien invasion, hyperspace navigation fried and remade as a spiderweb for our devilish new foe. Yes, you've been sent back just in time, Adella. To join me in fighting the Devil Frogs!'

'You really are utterly bonkers!'

'Why, do you believe pirates should only prey on the Triple Alliance's three species? Easy pickings along the Frontier, so far, for the Brethren of the Stars. Colonies insulting me; taunting me with their pathetic defence lines. It's as if they are not even trying. But these Quazzies, now, what a *grand* new opponent they make. You don't find pirates among their kind. One Empire, one race, as far as I can see. Everybody else is either food or slaves. But many in their Imperium will join the Brethren of the Stars after their ships and worlds tumble to us. Victories attract victors, and their foul kind is accustomed to winning in this corner of the substrate.' Barnier laughed hysterically. 'The Devil Frogs have played against thousands of species and known only success. But they've never played against Blue Barnier before!'

'I'll hang myself before I fight alongside you!'

'I hear each syllable coming out of your lips, but together the words mean nothing. You'll see, Adella Vega. Our game lets you do almost anything inside our universe, but there is one thing it can never stand for. You can't choose *not* to play!'

Adella stared with contempt at the Harbour Lord. 'You murdered my husband, you son of a bitch – you actually think I'm going to sign-up with your crew?'

'Don't be churlish, Adella. I know people rarely seek me out for theological advice, but it strikes me that as we are tested on this level, so too on the next we should be rested. It only makes sense. You've sat on the edge of your bunk the same as me, in the evening, eating your service sidearm. Testing how much pressure will settle against its trigger without your pistol going off. You can join your husband at any point, just as I may still join my family at a moment's notice. But this fine game of ours is afoot and still running. That's what my children would say when I tried to pack them off to bed each night. Just ten more minutes in the sim, daddy. And I would say, "Isn't life game enough for you already?" Think how disappointed they'll be if I simply sign out from this universe. You finished early, daddy. You finished early. That is super-lame. They always used to say that. I bet they were screaming it as they plummeted towards the ground, too. Mummy, this is super-lame, just ten more minutes.'

Adella slammed her fist on the force screen separating her from the pirate chief. 'Let me out of here and I'll send you back to them real quick.'

'Time enough for that, my sweet Commander. This is our second life. I don't intend to waste mine. I fear though, that you have definitely been frittering away yours of late. But don't worry, I mean to help you fix that.'

Adella watched the Harbour Lord pick himself up from the bench and wander out of the brig as if stuck inside a dream. Adella was still fixing to kill him. Only difference was that now, she felt it would be doing the dog a favour.

***

Adella examined the ginger-haired man as guards deactivated the force wall and tossed the newcomer to join her. About thirty years old, squat and built like a bull, he stank of alcohol and looked half drunk, swaying in their small dirty cell. The pirates had given him a good working over. By rights, the wretch shouldn't be standing up, even without the booze obviously sloshing around him.

'You're a fine sight for my fair eyes,' he coughed rubbing at his black, bruised face.

'What are you in here for?' asked the Commander.

'Ah, you might say it's a little philosophical point of difference. The Harbour Lord wants to keep the Floating Port as the Brethren's crown jewels. I was far more for slipping out on a fast ship and jumping for safe void while letting the Devil Frogs have the title Harbour Lord if they so desire it.'

'Blue Barnier could have the right idea,' said Adella. 'You wouldn't have got further than a couple of hops before a Quazzie-war-group intercepted you and shot you to pieces.'

'Not me,' laughed the man, 'you might say it's not in the blood for that to happen to Ossian Joyce.'

Adella gawked at the other prisoner. This was the jackass she had risked her neck – and it seemed her freedom – to try to Shanghai and drag back to the Home Fleet? 'You're Ossian Joyce? I came here to grab you up!'

'That's more like it,' the man opened his arms wide, 'grab away–!'

'You owe a favour to Captain Okereke of the *Neutron Dance*, a blood debt which meant you'd jump ship with us.'

'I hate to rain on your parade, Miss, but I don't know any Captain Okereke and have never heard of a ship called the *Neutron Dance*. And I can count on one hand the people in this universe I owe a blood debt to.'

Adella groaned. How badly had she been played? Had throwing Commander Vega to the wolves been the start and end of the strategy of the *Neutron Dance*'s crew to extricate themselves from Quazzie-space? They'd come to kidnap this red-haired loon; only he'd ended up sharing a cell with Adella first. *There's a dark kind of irony and circular fate in that!*

112

'What would a fair maiden like yourself be doing in the brig?'

'Fleet business, as in Hell-Fleet. I'm Commander Adella Vega and you will receive the chance to serve, Ossian Joyce…'

'I'm not really the serving sort, Miss. All those cold showers, hard bunks and shouty officers wouldn't agree with me. Now don't get me wrong, Ossian Joyce likes the fighting and the fillies, but he likes the fighting more! It was slipping the blade to those who deserved it which saw me exiled from the honest hearth of the Comet People. I can be hasty when I'm annoyed. And it doesn't take much to annoy me if I'm fair. Well, it's all academic anyhow.'

'Why?'

'The Harbour Lord's not going to do away with his highly useful Ossian Joyce. I might be due another beating or two, limited rations and harsh language, maybe even the loss of a finger to the chopper, but Blue Barnier won't be making me do the Normals Dance. You, however, Commander, ah, it doesn't bear thinking about…a Fleet officer caught inside the port dressed in civvies like some lunatic spy. Your crazy recruiting drive will be cut real short, Miss Vega.'

Adella didn't even want to ask, but she did anyway. 'The Normals Dance?'

'Ah, the Floating Port's favourite amusement. You select a group of normals – anyone captured in a recent raid – then chuck them into a fighting pit and throw in a few weapons and the dog who comes out alive gets to stay alive. Then given an opportunity at signing up with the Brethren. Anyone who refuses to fight takes a bullet in the head, anyway. Blue Barnier is a fierce one for the tradition. He says there's a little bit of pirate inside everyone if you only give it a chance to emerge. You'll have a fine time with your Fleet combat training. You won't be up against professionals. The more normal the fighter, the better Blue Barnier likes it. I've watched a hotel maid decapitate a saucier with a meat tenderiser and a professional pet groomer strangle an architect with a dog's lead. It's bloody sport I'll give you that. It's hard to take your eyes off the spectacle all the same, even when you don't have a wager riding on the outcome.'

Adella felt sick. *I'll be lucky. If Blue Barnier is watching in person and I have a knife, I can slam it through his thick skull despite a good few rounds inside me.* What was that old Marine boast – that it took a Marine's weight in lead to bring a Jarhead down? *Warm hate for that mad skegger should keep me going for as long as I need.*

- 17 -

Normals Dance

Adella glanced up from her bunk as someone entered the brig. It was Blue Barnier, again; resembling an accountant playing dress-up in his oversized Harlequin's Admiral uniform.

Ossian sprung to his feet when he saw the Harbour Lord enter. 'My Lord Barnier, these fine bruises are turning the same colour as your nickname, so I think it's time now for me to slide back where I belong. Inside the navigator's chair of your fair flagship. Can we not put the past behind us and let bygones be bygones?'

Barnier smiled as though indulging a favoured grandchild. 'Ossy, you have served me well. But it is finally time for you to expand your horizons.'

'Yes, sir, yes! Maybe I could lead the scouting parties for you again. Find a nice juicy world where the plunder is rich and the System Defence Forces piss-poor.'

'Well, that's the problem right there, young brother. There are a great many among the Brethren of the Stars who would happily accompany you. And few of my captains would let out nary-a-peep when you decided to jump for the Alliance Core. They will conclude it's just fine to abandon the Floating Port and scatter across the universe.'

'I wouldn't be doing that, now,' stammered the Comet Person, 'sure and I have learned my harsh lesson as well as a man could.'

'I fear that is not the case, Ossy. We can only grow through adversity and you have been weaned on the easy way out. And as long as there are pirate captains who believe you are *their* ticket home, then none of my officers will accept my authority and knuckle down to the business at hand. I let you join the Brethren of the Stars for your Lucky Gene without doing the Normals Dance. I think it is time you underwent the initiation, too.'

Ossian threw himself towards the shield wall, stopping short of it shocking him back. 'No, sir, no! You still need me. When the Floating Port has to make a run for it, I'll be there to keep you sitting inside hyperspace for as long as you desire.'

'That's our problem right there, Ossy. The Floating Port is too big and tardy. You might hold us inside hyperspace for a month, but what good is that when the cursed Devil Frogs will overtake us within a few days? Either way, it's slow, sly hops for the Floating Port from here on in. All you are now for my brave skippers is a temptation to take to the boats and indulge in a spot of desertion. Best we should remove that temptation, don't you think?'

Ossian sobbed and fell to the floor scratching his wild mop of red hair.

Blue Barnier merely shook his head sadly and smiled at Adella. 'Put a little spike and powder in this one's spine, Commander. It won't do to have the Brethren see one of their own as weak-kneed as this.'

Then the Harbour Lord strode away.

What am I now, your freaking morale officer?

***

Adella recognised the chamber's configuration almost as soon as they shoved her inside it alongside Ossian Joyce. Part of a luxury liner, once. A circular stage built on a pattern recognisable to any ancient Greek. A simple annular space of a hundred feet, surrounded by a wall above which sloped tiers of bench seating. It would shock the ancients to see so many different species hollering and stamping and shaking their limbs, of course. The Alliance was a broad church and there were plenty of fallen to go around, it seemed. The stage resembled real wood to accommodate the expensive physical actors who'd once entertained audiences here. Sadly, standards had gone by the wayside since, along with the participants' pay. Brown patches speckled the floor, blood and guts hard to wash off even when you had a slave labour force willing to scrub away for as long as required.

Adella noted the carefully placed line of baffles surrounding the stage. She recognised what they were. Originally used for low gravity ballet displays. When activated, the equipment blocked the artificial gravity systems positioned around the Floating Port. A localised field dropping gravity to anything from a moon-bouncing lope to a full swim on the float, as though participants trod void in a vac-suit.

Blue Barnier rose inside a private box set high above the seats, his voice echoing out of speakers. 'My brothers and sisters, our raids have pulled in quite a few entertainments over the last few days. It's only fitting that our season of sport culminates with an unexpected guest. Commander Adella Vega, once of the Triple Alliance's Anti-Piracy Group, has dropped in on the port to wish us well.' Barnier could barely be heard above raucous screams and gales of laughter rising from his mob. 'And then there is the traitor Ossian Joyce who tried to run off with the fastest ship in our fleet. We can teach him a sharp lesson about the value of sticking with your mates. Now, as a matter of custom, we should pit these two against a pair of normals. But the Commander here was trained for combat by the Fleet's Marines and there is little that is "normal" about her. And, as anyone who has ever sat in a bar with Ossy knows, by his third drink he will knife someone! So, I thought let's make this a fine dance, not a quick dance.' Barnier clapped his hands and the stage doors opened opposite Adella and Ossian. 'You know that old saying, don't you, that the only law you can trust is the law you can buy?'

Adella groaned as she saw the two bare-chested heavily-muscled brutes stomping into the stage. They looked unnecessarily and unnaturally sinewy, as though someone had inflated beach-balls under their skin. Combat hacks of the clumsy DNA-edited variety. But that wasn't the worst of her situation: *that* would be the matching black octopus-like tattoos inked along each man's right shoulder. The symbol of the private military contractor, *Lash Battles*. Across most of the Eastern Frontier, PMCs were who you hired when you wanted justice. Justice on worlds where the nearest Alliance law was a circuit judge and a five-month wait for the closest TAP agent team to drop in. If they could even be bothered, given so few colonies were on the Protocol, let alone on the Alliance membership waiting list. Both fighters sported crew-cuts – one with dark black hair and the other with silver-white that had to be a dye job. Ossian Joyce recognised the tattoos too, judging by the depths of his groaning. Either that or he was regretting eating the previous night's greasy gruel-like rations with as much gusto as he had.

'I thought all the company police died when the *John of Neptune* bombed the last world,' said Ossian.

No, Barnier has been saving these two scumbags for a rainy day. And I reckon the heavens just opened. Off to the side came a clatter as theatre staff tossed in a variety of blunt and edged weapons. Clubs, swords, and knives. Often in low-gravity combat that was all you needed.

'You realise they will zero the gravity as soon as we sprint for any of those weapons,' Adella hissed at the red-haired navigator.

'I've seen this sorry affair,' moaned Ossian. 'Oh yes, I've watched it happen.'

'Then you know how it ends. Get ready to show me that fighting spirit you were boasting about back inside our cell.'

'I need a touch of rum to sharpen my senses. That's how it is when threading the needle on a ship, and that's how it works if I'm to be a devil with a dagger.'

Great, Adella growled to herself. *I'm fighting alongside a semi-functional alcoholic fourteen units short of a decent brawl and twenty short of a Lucky Gene jump-out of the system.* The two killers-for-hire on the other end of the stage clumped over to their weapons pile. Black-hair selected a cutlass while vain old Mr. Dye pulled out a length of steel chain with a small axe blade as its last link.

Adella and Ossian hurried to their heap. Ossian yanked out an extending staff – a strange choice as far as Commander Vega was concerned. Adella shoved aside the rattling rusty equipment searching for something, anything, she could use effectively. She finally settled for a cutlass. It wasn't exactly a duelling foil, but her last serious fencing class lay long ago during her Academy years.

As soon as Adella felt the weapon's weight in her grip, the sword turned feather-light, her stomach kicking out from underneath her as well. *God, I'd forgotten how space-sick I get on the float.*

'Wait a minute,' Adella called to the two contractors. 'You're both pay-to-play cops! You don't want to fight for the pleasure of these filthy picaroons, do you? We can force our way out together!'

'That's the ticket,' shouted Ossian, 'let's all be fast friends here!'

'My friends are dead!' yelled black-hair as he loped across, testing the air with his blade. 'You'll join them next.'

Well, out goes reasoning with the rent-a-thugs. 'Stay by my side.'

Ossian gripped his bow staff tightly. 'Easy for you to say, Miss Vega. Every time I flex my boots it feels as if there are retro-thrusters blasting inside my suffering heels.'

Screams and yells rose from the crowd as they undulated in the seats. They bayed mercilessly for blood, but the cries bled through the gravity baffles strangely distorted, as though Adella heard the pirates from the bottom of a swimming pool. The roar brought back memories of screaming drill instructors in the Marine Corps Martial Arts Program, the zero-gravity combat enclosure simulating a wrecked warship during a boarding action. *How are you going to kill something when you don't know where its vital organs are, recruit?*

Adella watched the two brutes closing in on them. *I know where these fighters' organs are, Gunney! Buried under those ridiculously showy war-muscle grafts.* The company cops weren't trained in combat outside of a world's gravity well, that much was certain – their calf muscles uncertain jerking movements every time they left the floor on the bounce was the tell. From the length of their stride, the stage's gravitational field strength had been set at around 10 N/kg. *They want ballet, I'll put on a show to remember.* Adella took up position but held steady.

Someone wants to fight, recruit, let them come to you – give them a chance to trip or overextend, first. Defence gives you multiple vectors.

Adella faked her freeze, darting forward at the very last second. Black-hair slashed out at her with his blade. Adella stepped to the side, gave point and left-parried.

Extreme efficiency is your aim, recruit. This isn't a duel, this is contact combat. There's no paying audience to disappoint, here.

Adella hopped back, allowing the low-gravity to carry her as easily as being sucked into vacuum through a hull-breach. The mob booed angrily. *Wrong about no audience.* These devils wanted blood. Fleet blood. And Adella had so very little to spare.

Simultaneous attack and defence, recruit, using simple and repeatable strikes. Come on, maggot show me what you've got!

Adella hopped out of range, again, while the cop came at her swinging hard. That was one problem with low-G combat – tiring a big, heavy opponent commensurately harder. Off to her side, Mr. Dye went for Ossian. Instead of meeting the brute directly, Ossian made a couple of fast strides with his torso leaning forward, then planted the staff into the floor and swung high over the fighter, pulling his weapon close to his chest as he performed an aerial cartwheel, booting the cop in the face when he sailed over the man's head. The killer stomped into empty space, dizzied and confused, hurling his axe-headed chain where the navigator wasn't any longer.

Remind me not to play cards against that one. Ossian doubtless swanned up to tables of gamblers like a complete rube only to mysteriously draw hands – "Beginner's luck, Miss!" – which made a mockery of his supposed ignorance.

Adella's opponent wasn't stupid, though – the security contractor changed-up his style for the low gravity environment, allowing the field to carry his attacks long. Adella's cutlass arm began to ache from the repeated battering she took off his blade. If Adella had been wrestling the man without a weapon, this fight would be over. In low gravity, the arena belonged to the biggest, strongest Sumo. And that was definitely this bruiser. That was the other trouble with low gravity, speed and finesse were hard to bring to bear during constant contacts.

Ossian, however, was having more luck against his cop. Adella had never heard of the navigator's bizarre fighting style before. But, neither had the rent-a-badge. If it possessed a name, it might be *Drunken Comet Person*-style. Presently, Ossian appeared to be slamming his staff onto the floor, left, then right, riding the impacts in low gravity as though he was mounted upon a swaying spider. It was an eccentric method of locomotion, but crudely effective. His adversary swung the chain blade like a whip, but every time it flicked close to the navigator, Ossian had already danced back outside the weapon's arc.

Adella didn't have any longer to ponder the combat occurring parallel to hers. Adella's strategy of trying to dally with the cop until she spied an advantage was fast wearing out, just as she was. *Time to go on the offensive.* Adella placed her thumb on the hilt, slipping her next finger toward the cutlass's end, to reach further and strike more readily. As the cop swung at Adella again she thrust with the sword's point at her opponent's belly. He managed to turn the blow, indignant that she provided such an effective defence.

'I'm the only one walking out of here!' he hissed at Adella.

'You want to sign up as a pirate? I'll chop your leg off and you can get a cybernetic replacement or wooden peg, whichever makes you feel better about your new career.'

They warily circled each other. Adella so focused on keeping the cop at bay she only just noticed his partner's axehead whipping towards her face. She ducked as it sliced a line of blood across her cheek. Adella pulled back. It seemed Mr. Dye had grown bored with chasing Ossian around the floor while the navigator pole-vaulted beyond the range of his chain whip. Instead, Mr. Dye finally figured out that two-against-one made for better odds. *You took your time about it.* They only needed to repeat the trick twice to ensure the honour of the private military contractor's reputation.

Adella tried to conjure up something quick, simple and brutal to hold the pair off but came up short. She picked Mr. Dye to provoke, figuring to use his less creative friend as her shield, keeping them in a line to stop the cops flanking her. 'I had my hair coloured like that once. I cut the hairdresser's skegging throat after he passed me the mirror.'

Your dagger isn't the weapon, recruit; your sidearm isn't the weapon – you are!

Mr. Dye leaped towards Adella snarling, the chain-axe licking out at speed, attacking too fast for his dense friend to move in as co-protagonist. Adella caught the chain with a high parry, curled it and yanked Mr. Dye off his feet, then turned to break his ankle with her heel. Dark-hair cop pressed forward with his cutlass point, late to the party. Adella had already shifted position. She used her momentum to flip the other cop like a spinning top stuck in a string. You didn't need much power to play Judo inside low gravity. Probably why it was the favoured combat method deployed on the float by the Marine Corps Martial Arts Program.

Mr. Dye's face contorted with shock as he realised it was his own partner's blade ripping painfully through his gut, emerging blood-splashed out of the back of his spine.

No opportunity for remorse by the cutlass-wielding cop. He folded neatly to the floor, moving in slow motion after Ossian drove the blunt edge of his staff into the rear of the man's skull. The attack came as much of a surprise to Adella as the cop. The remaining private security contractor tumbled to his knees, his eyes fixed on the blade impaled in his chest. There he knelt almost meditatively until he slid over.

Blue Barnier leaped to his feet in his box overlooking the contest. He clapped and everybody else joined in, too. 'If I had paid a fee to Lash Battles I would ask for my money back!'

A raucous cheer rose from the assembled mob, their favour as fickle as fate had proved to the pair of private contractors.

'We have our champions, but we will all slide void easier after these two fine buckaroos' examination with Doctor Drill! For the winners, the surgery; for the losers, the airlock!'

Ossian dropped his staff and fell to his knees, no easy feat in low gravity, both hands stretched out imploringly towards the Harbour Lord. 'Don't cut me, my Lord. You'll slice out my Lucky Gene. What will I be without that? What use am I to anybody as another mere mortal?'

'You'll be cannon-fodder,' laughed Blue Barnier. 'Why, with staff skills on the float as you've demonstrated, you shall make ideal material for the Forlorn Hope. First through the airlock and the glory will be all yours, Ossian Joyce. Your beautiful new life storming my prizes and making merry mayhem leading our boarding party.'

Normal gravity restored and a wave of armed guards emerged. Pirates ringed Adella and Ossian as they hauled the two twitching bodies off stage.

I've won, realised Adella. But she only had to look at Ossian Joyce – still on his knees and back to his quivering act – to know that perhaps the company cops being dragged out were the real winners of Blue Barnier's game.

- 18 -

You Know the Drill

Adella struggled as the gang of pirates dragged Ossian and her through the Floating Port, passersby stopping to stare at them, laughter and abuse until they reached a corridor where a sign from the port's previous existence read "Medical Station." Some wag had stapled up a handwritten note on the nearby double doors reading "The Doctor WON'T see you now." They were pushed through into an empty waiting room, then manhandled inside a medical bay. A short but distinguished-looking man of late middle-age turned around from a bank of laboratory machinery.

'Doctor Drill,' groaned Adella as the pirates thrust her and Ossian forward.

'Doctor Eugene *Dre'ell*,' the diminutive man bowed at her, rubbing the back of his thick silver hair, 'but you know how pirates are with their amusing nicknames.'

Adella gazed with horror at the equipment scattered around the surgery. Mind probes and neural mapping gear, along with drug synthesisers filled with bubbling concoctions of every description. It was practically a torture chamber. It made the kit Fleet had at its disposal for enhanced interrogations look like a bunch of teddy bears and ride-on-carts inside a nursery.

'What the hell kind of Hippocratic oath did you take?' Commander Vega demanded of the doctor.

'Don't think of this as an operating table,' said the doctor, patting a bloodstained steel bed. 'It is simply a matter of making a few minor adjustments. Hardly any more significant than when your Fleet augment was implanted inside your brain. The Harbour Lord has asked me to ensure I leave as much of your original self as I can, Commander. He needs you as *you*, not some compliant oversexed love-slave like the prisoners I modify for our port's joyhouses. I'm just going to tweak the loyalties you feel while switching off your higher morality areas in your left frontal lobe and temporal lobes.'

The guards dragged Adella struggling and shouting towards the steel table, shoving her down onto its hard surface before strapping the restraining belts around her body, leaving her resembling a mummified member of someone's royal family.

'Don't worry my dear,' grinned Doctor Dre'ell, 'the procedure is mostly harmless and you are in the hands of a consummate professional. I worked in the penal colonies on the High China Asteroids perfecting my skills. I would still be there today if the media hadn't faked up all that ridiculous outrage over my experiments. Pushing the boundaries of medical understanding always requires sacrifice. My own not least, as it turned out. I continue my work here as best I can.'

After the pirates secured Adella, they dragged Ossian over and pushed him down across the steel table by her side.

'Please, Doctor!' begged the navigator as the guards bound him tight. 'Don't be messing with the perfection that is Ossian Joyce. Think how valuable I am to you.'

'Actually,' laughed the Doctor, 'I'm thinking how valuable my head is attached to my neck. You of all people should appreciate the value of not landing up in the Harbour Lord's bad books. Compared to Commander Vega, the changes his Lordship requires for you are far blunter, Ossian. I wouldn't want to mischaracterise them as a lobotomy, but I am going to severely elevate the functions of your lizard brain – the good old limbic system. A mixture of neural reformatting and a few gene edits thrown in for luck. A constant berserker rage will serve you very well in your new role among the Brethren. A lot of the Forward Assault Team have had the same procedure done, some of them even willingly.'

After the guards left, Doctor Dre'ell tapped a tablet he carried, lowering two rotating ceramic rings which moved into position behind each of the prisoners' heads. 'Your Deep Magnetic Resonance Scans will take half an hour to run. I need to make a complete copy of the patterns stored inside your executive functions and cognitive control processes. It's always advisable to keep a backup, in case unfortunate slips are made.'

'Leave me my Lucky Gene, doc!' begged Ossian. 'Please leave me that.'

'Your strange abilities are not entirely genetic, I suspect,' said Doctor Dre'ell. 'Although there is a complex mutation at work. I believe, Ossy, you establish quantum links with alternative versions of yourself across billions of realities which compose our multiverse. Somehow, you pull back whichever navigation option serves you best from a menu of a billion alternatives, then implement the closest match in *this* reality. That's why Comet People never install bio-augments inside their brains, isn't it? When you're not fully *you*, anymore, you can't interface smoothly with your countless mirror selves.'

'Just leave me be,' sobbed the navigator.

'Not an option open, sadly,' smiled the doctor, stroking Ossian's cheek. 'Soonest done, best mended, eh.'

A sliding door pulled back off to the side of the surgery, revealing a nurse wearing a uniform that looked more like the variety found in the port's joyhouses. But it wasn't the woman's figure that caught Adella's attention. It was the man strapped to a steel bed in the next chamber. *Colonel Kal Blackstar! Sweet God, what is Kal doing here? Has Home Fleet fallen to the Brethren?* Had the pirates come across the Colonel floating in a life-pod after the Quazzies ravaged Home Fleet, leaving her ships a scattered mess of melted metal spinning in the void? Every possible horrific scenario squeezed through Adella's mind all at once.

'Kal!' Adella shouted, 'it's me!'

'Adella,' he groaned, 'did they kidnap you too?'

Kidnap? Then Adella realised the terrible truth of the situation. She hadn't been the only officer to depart the *Dark Viking* on board the *Neutron Dance*'s shuttle. But, she *had* been the only one stupid enough to go along voluntarily. That noise she'd heard in the shuttle's hold wasn't chipmunks or bloody space squirrels or whatever nonsense Captain Okereke had spun. It was a member of Okereke's crew giving Colonel Blackstar the blunt end of a wrench! It seemed as if the Professor wanted her estranged husband back in her and her daughter's lives. And Sebba would not let the little matter of Blackstar's active service during a war slow her down. *But then, it does rather beg the question of what the hell Kal's doing in this foul butcher's clutches?*

'You know each other? tutted the doctor. 'Well, that will not help his procedure at all. The poor boy's confused enough as it is.'

'What procedure? Are you going to slap a neural lock on Kal – turn him into Professor Sebba's slave?'

'A slave? Goodness gracious, no. Quite the opposite. I intend to set the man free.'

'You set me free,' shouted the Colonel, 'I'll happily throttle you, you filthy madman!'

'It's a very effective job, actually. But we can be thankful all those false memories haven't had a chance to fully bed down yet. If only the supervising physician had been secured along with the Colonel, I'm sure I would have learned a lot from his doctor – and he would have gained much from me, too. Synthetic synapses have been used to accelerate synaptic plasticity and fire connections, but the boy's drug regime's led to long-term potentiation. Of course, my competitor's errors mean that I can revert the neurogenesis back to its default state without sending the Colonel insane.'

'What the hell are you talking about?' demanded Adella.

'It's quite simple, really. Two personalities exist inside the good Colonel. His original, true personality. And an artificial one overwritten on top of his neural cortex. The latter currently being his dominant, expressed form.'

'You're lying!' yelled Kal.

Adella moaned. She wanted it to be a lie, too, *but what if ... ?*

'Ironically, it was attempting a similar technique to this which saw me disbarred the first time, with the only employment I could secure found inside the penal colonies. I took the most harmless, pleasantly meek individuals I could find and used them as a template to overwrite murderers, rapists, and psychopaths. Why rely on changing a recidivist's ways when you can truly *change* their personality?'

'I was never a psychopath!' screamed Kal.

'No, I don't believe you were, young man. Although the rascals that did this to you probably exhibited strong comorbidity with various antisocial disorders.' He laughed at his own joke, indicating both sets of tables. 'It's a doctor's sorry lot, isn't it? Fix this one; but, hey, turn this pair into a criminal and a raging psychopath, respectively. Well, the techniques are the same, even if the results are different.'

Kal thrashed inside his restraints, but they bound him too effectively to break free. 'I'm me, I'm real!'

'Hear him out, Kal,' begged Adella. *We have to.*

'Actually, I'd suggest you're mostly reverse engineered from a deceased target subject's social media activity and stored sim-time impressions. Much of what you're interpreting as your memories are point-of-view switches imprinted from living family members. Someone else's family, of course, not yours. Fine work, but there're too many external erasures from your timeline for you to be fully plausible. I always slip in a few simulated fakes to paper over such discrepancies.

'You would require far less clozapine if you were my patient. Most of your first personality lies encrypted inside your Fleet augment. Well, I say *Fleet* – it's probably a more discrete Alliance organisation; the kind pronounced as an acronym composed of a string of letters. You'll lose a lot of your original self when I burn you back down to basic, I'm afraid, but it cannot be helped.'

Adella could barely process everything the Doctor has said. *It can't be.* But then, there were so many loose ends that would be tied up if it was true. Had she fallen for a ghost? Little more real than any of a thousand simulated A.I. cartoon stars populating the mediasphere; heartthrobs for naïve teenagers to lose their minds and pocket-money tokens over? *I'm not that stupid, am I? Fate isn't that cruel? Please.*

A harsh alarm jangled from a wall console.

'Doctor!' called the nurse, nervously. She wiggled across to a heavy airlock-style portal at the far end of the surgery. When the lock opened it revealed a hideous sight. A large transparent tank with a Quazalrat floating inside it, the alien treading the chemical soup among a mess of wires and tubes. The creature didn't look any more pleasant in real life than as a holo-model in the Admiral's briefing, although someone had tried to humanise the beast a little by sticking it in a workman's orange suit. A velociraptor crossbred with a toad wearing human fancy dress. The thing looked every bit as happy to be trapped there as Adella was to see it held next door to her.

'Ah, I'm afraid I must put my private practice's work on hold for the moment. Fergal is my pièce de résistance. It's difficult to keep a Devil Frog in captivity. They secrete an enzyme that's harmful to them after they're captured – a natural reaction, too, not even engineered. I had to replace half Fergal's glands and guess at how to balance out his version of an endocrine system. Nothing about Fergal is easy, but then he will be the first of his kind. The Brethren of the Star's original willing Devil Frog. A template for all the merry Quazzie pirates who'll follow in his footsteps.'

'Put it down!' demanded Kal, 'you can't keep that monster alive! It'll lead the rest of the Quazzies back here.' It sounded like the Colonel was losing his shit, even if it might not be *his* baggage to shed. Adella understood exactly how Kal felt.

'Fergal the Devil Frog,' laughed Ossian, hysterically. 'That's a fine old lark, doctor. Now let me out of *here*!'

Doctor Dre'ell raised his finger to his lips and smiled as he closed the heavy armoured door to the alien-holding chamber. 'Hush, Ossy. Enjoy your bed-rest. The DMRS will finish a lot quicker if you don't keep firing up your brain's neurons.'

'Ah, my Lucky Gene is the last of me – the only thing that still makes me a Comet Person. What will Ossian Joyce be without his precious talent?'

A raving berserker, by the sound of it. Adella didn't articulate the thought. She'd rather not spend the next half an hour listening to the navigator sobbing.

- 19 -

Old Friends. Forgot.

The machine whirring behind Adella's skull had just finished rotating. She expected Doctor Drill to emerge from his "consultation" with the captured Quazalrat, but not the man who slipped in from the waiting room.

'Okereke, you son of a bitch, have you come to gloat!' growled Adella

The skipper took in the grisly sight – Adella and Ossian restrained on steel beds next to each other; Kal Blackstar trussed up in the adjoining bay. 'Yeah, baby, like the Fleet can still take the high ground after what you did to us!'

'I'm going to kill you, Okereke!' shouted Kal. 'You did this to me. Sold me like a slave to these maniacs!'

'No, but you'll thank me for this, one day soon,' said the skipper.

'Okereke?' coughed Ossian from his operating table. 'Would *this* be the fella you said I owed a blood debt to, Miss? He's no Captain Okereke of any *Neutron Dance*, that's for sure.'

'Ossy,' smiled the skipper. 'I heard about your little jig at the Normals Dance. Strikes me you're lucky at far more than jumping the light fantastic, buddy.'

'Zeno, what in the name of the Ten Heavens are you doing walking around using that stupid-sounding moniker?'

Zeno? What's going on here? Sadly, Adella had a sudden feeling she'd proved more of a sucker than she first realised.

'I'd like to say I've embraced my inner pirate as Ornery Okereke. I'd like to say it, but it'd be bull.' Okereke – or rather, Zeno – jabbed a finger towards Adella. 'We've been sailing on a faked-up transponder because of Little Miss Fleet, here. SecComm Core contracted the *Gravity Rose* a year back to complete a supply run for the government – regular haulage from Transference Station out to the Second Fleet. Except the only thing we actually supplied was our ass. We flew into an ambush set up so the Alliance could pressgang one of our crew. Fleet called it "conscription", of course, pursuant to some Emergency Powers act that doesn't even exist on the statute book. 'Cept we weren't in Alliance space and our man had never set foot outside the Edge before they abducted him. You should sympathise, Ossy. The "Colonel" over there has a Lucky Gene, too. His is Heezy and allows him to operate their artifacts like a native ancient.'

'I've never even met you before!' cried Kal Blackstar. 'You've been brought in by Doctor Drill to trick me. Try to break me!'

'Yeah, apart from the fact you *have* met me,' said Zeno. 'The real you. Not this sim-game bullshit Hell-Fleet-you. You're Calder Durk, a fine, upstanding – if rather green – member of the *Gravity Rose*'s crew.'

'I'm not Calder Durk, I'm Kal Blackstar! My Heezy operator genes aren't natural – Fleet edited them into me.'

'Kal, Cal, it sounds the same, doesn't it? But trust me, there's a world of difference… and you're the sole descendant of the original science team that found the first Heezy station buried under Neptune's ice, kid. They had the good sense to do an Oppenheimer and burn their notes before they went on the run. Turns out the Alliance has been hunting for you and anyone like you for a *long* time.'

Adella groaned. That slippery skegger Delorey. The doctor who didn't exist in Fleet Medical. All the discrepancies she'd discovered when she hacked inside the Fleet's systems suddenly made perfect sense. The Admiral's dead nephew provided the background to build the Colonel's identity up from scratch. Kal never graduated Academy, he'd had Academy imprinted *on* him.

'I didn't know about any of this!' protested Adella.

'Yeah, well I doubt Mr. Toad next door knows the colonists' names his pals cooked on the campfire when they raided this system, either. But it's safe to say old Froggy would have broken out the barbecue sauce just the same if he'd received his invite to the feast. I judge people as I find them, Commander. You and yours kidnapped a non-Alliance citizen and mindwiped my friend using tech that carries a jail sentence in every civilised society on the Protocol. You want to use this war you've got going as your excuse, fine. But don't piss on my back and tell me it's raining.'

'No,' Kal, cried, 'no, it can't be true! I know who I am. This is a trick. Just a lousy interrogation method to soften me up.'

'Kal, I think there's something in what he's saying,' said Adella, trying not to break down as she got her words out. 'It's the last thing you want to hear. My surgeon warned me your treatment regime was an utter nonsense; that sent me down the rabbit-hole. I've been running an off-the-books investigation ever since you turned up inside Bardfeld's System. Best as I can tell, Doctor Delorey is part of a Black Bag operation. Admiral Blackstar must have known about you, too. There was a Kal Blackstar who was the Admiral's nephew, but he died in a climbing accident at college decades ago. All the ages are wrong. You made no sense. I found no meaningful trace of any service record for you. No Academy graduation from Flight School.'

'No!' moaned Kal. 'No!'

'Think about it, Kal. Why concentrate multiple Heezy weapons on a dreadnought with just one gunner? Where's the military logic in that? If Fleet possessed a Heezy gene-editing process, they would have created a squadron of officers with your ability. Spread the weapons across the Combined Fleet so it could fire at will with no single point of weakness or failure. That's why Admiral Blackstar wanted me to head up a force heading for Core. Your abilities are unique and make you the most important person alive inside the Alliance right now.'

'So, you didn't know about *any* of this...?' accused Zeno.

'I guessed there was something the hell-hinky going on,' said Adella, 'just not *what*. My crazy theories ran from everything from clones and resurrections to a Heezy-generated time slip. In case you haven't noticed, Captain Bloody Zeno Okereke of the *Neutron Dancing Gravity Rose*, my star isn't exactly on the ascendant inside the service. Scrapped on Ghost Fleet along with all the other jokers and wasters ... the Widow and Widow-maker of Strabane. I was looking to gather evidence to take to the Admiralty. I figured if that path didn't play out I could help Kal by parlaying my notoriety with the news-feeds to good use.'

'Knock yourself out, Commander. If you don't find yourself landing in a shuttle with a mysterious heat shield failure first, I'm guessing your next posting will be a one-person surveillance ship called the TAS *Whistleblower* on a system-edge so far away it'll make Bardfeld's look like Mother Earth.' Zeno crossed over to Ossian's bed and tapped the man's restraints. 'Here's the arrangement, Ossy. You play nice and sweet as navigator on board the *Gravity Rose* until we're beyond the worst of the Devil Frog's hyperspace disruption field. After we jump safely to the Edge, you can cut loose, or stay on as crew. Your choice. Either way, you keep your Lucky Gene and your flammy ass doesn't get shelled in a coming boarding action. Deal?'

'That's exactly the fine plan for me, Zeno. Indeed, it is. I'll fly you to Magellanic Clouds and back if it comes to it, you know I will!'

'You can't take off with Ossian Joyce!' Adella groaned. 'Home Fleet needs him.'

'Just like your military needs Calder compliant and brainwashed to turn your million-year-old artifacts against the Quazzie homeworld and fry the Devil Frogs' star systems? No thanks, baby. I've lived through enough wars to realise none of it matters, in the end.'

What's the maniac talking about? 'There hasn't been a war for five hundred years?'

'You don't *know*?' snorted Ossian. 'Zeno here's not human, Commander. He's an android. The rattling old antique used to be an actor. Played more than one, across the centuries, given how the lad's flexible features can flow to mimic any fella dead or alive.'

An actor? Sweet God. Now Adella understood why Okereke's face seemed familiar to her. Memories of an ancient soap opera she'd watched with her sister when they were children – a medical drama set on board a massive hospital space station. *Doctor Katlego of Sector General?*

'Yeah, well, human's a relative concept, these days,' said Zeno, inspecting the scanner rotating behind the navigator's head. 'The two most powerful weapons in the universe are patience and time. Give it three or four centuries of burning down each other's planets, and the Alliance and Quazzies will find a way to rub along. Or you won't. Either way, that's a whole plate of someone else's crap I'm not eating. I'm loading Ossy on board the *Gravity Rose*. And I'm taking Cal, too – and I mean Cal, *not* Kal!'

Kal struggled, desperately shaking the steel table's restraints. 'Okereke - Zeno, or whatever you want to call yourself. Listen to me! You can't let that butcher Doctor Drill slice my mind apart. He's fixing to burn me back down to the basics!'

'The poor fella has a point, Zeno,' said Ossian. 'Wiped once is bad enough, but twice? You have a care for your crew, don't be putting your boy through this.'

'What choice do I have, Ossy? Galaxy ain't exactly abundant with specialists in illegal mind control. I'm not going to let some fabricated Fleet fiction walk off wearing Calder Durk's drugged-up body. Shit, no.'

'There's no need,' said Adella. 'You don't have to pay the Floating Port's butcher to fix your man – a standard automated med-bay can fix him.'

'You don't think we tried to fix our boy Calder on board the *Gravity Rose*? Christ, lady, we had him inside sickbay all the way to the Floating Port. Normally, I wouldn't trust Dre'ell to pull a stray slug out of my arm, and I don't even *have* a cardiovascular system.'

'You'd have achieved better results if you'd hacked the Black Ops team that pressganged your crewman,' said Adella. 'Maybe got your mitts on their encryption code for Kal's Fleet augment? The way Dre'ell tells it, your crewman's original personality and memories are compressed within his augment; ballast to provide stability to Kal. Your friend's still inside there. He just needs unlocking!'

'Don't encourage this bastard, Adella,' begged Blackstar. 'Please, *please* don't help him erase me!'

'It's like when you're playing a character inside a sim,' sobbed Adella. 'Your character seems real to you at the time, but it's only a dream you wake up from. You become yourself, again.' *And if I repeat that to myself often enough, could be I'll start to believe it, too.*

'I'm not a sim character, Adella. I'm a Colonel in Fleet, not some trader off a civilian tub. And once they scrub me, I'll be dead forever!'

'You deserve to be who you really are, Kal. And if that man ships with a wife and a child and happens to be an illegally kidnapped citizen, then it's our duty to restore him.'

'Hell, no. I'm Fleet. And Fleet fights, it doesn't run, and it never surrenders! That's my duty.'

'You've got a deal in mind, Commander?' said Zeno.

'You get the encryption code for Kal's augment when we reach the Home Fleet. Ossian leads Home Fleet back to safety. If Kal's really this Calder Durk you think he is, he deserves to be himself. Not a brainwashed Alliance meat-puppet. We won't beat the Quazzies by becoming bigger monsters than them.'

Adella had her duty and her honour. And all it would cost her is the man she loved. *Again.*

- 20 -

Escape

The android snuck behind the tables and switched off the brain scanning equipment. Zeno had to lift a tranquilliser gun from a cabinet, administering to Kal when it became clear he would not go quietly. After Zeno unstrapped his crewman, he walked across to Ossian's bed and released him. He pulled the restraining straps off Adella when the door to the Quazalrat chamber opened. Doctor Dre'ell stood in the open doorway staring incredulously at the android releasing his charges.

'What in the name of the Six Stars are you doing, Captain? I have barely begun to cure your crewman, and these others' treatment isn't being paid for by you, but by the Harbour Lord himself. Get them back at once or Blue Barnier will murder everyone inside this medical bay, starting with me and ending with you!'

A high-pitched cry sounded from behind the doctor, distracting him from Zeno's bid to free the patients. It seemed Dre'ell had someone else unhappy with his treatment plan. Dre'ell's nurse tried to sprint past, but was suddenly yanked off her feet. She hung in the air for a second, defying gravity, until Adella glimpsed what she really defied. A tentacle wrapped itself around the nurse's throat, holding the woman suspended jerking. Her legs desperately thrashed trying to find the floor. Fergal the not-so-tame Quazalrat had levered away the lid of the suspension tank it had been pickled inside. Dripping chemicals and shivering in shock, the beast wasn't so stunned that it'd shed its hunting instincts.

'Friend,' warbled the creature in passable Lingual. '*Friend!*' Fergal repeated, shaking the nurse as she choked out.

Adella rolled off her steel bed, suddenly finding herself with an unnatural dizziness on the vertical. Possibly a byproduct of being restrained for so long, or maybe brain-fry from the mind scanner grabbing a copy of her? *If that's how Fergal treats its friends, I hope I never see what it subjects its enemies to.*

Doctor Dre'ell made a strange gurgling noise as though he had swallowed something unpleasant. Fergal discarded the nurse, hurling her limp body across the length of the medical bay and making Ossian dive out of the way.

Doctor Dre'ell recovered sufficiently to turn and run, but both the creature's stinging tentacle arms lashed out. One slammed around the Doctors neck, while the other wrapped across his waist. Heavier than the nurse, the Doctor tried to pull away, but the Quazalrat was stronger and severely pissed at its treatment. Dre'ell slid back, as though sprinting up a down escalator. When the Doctor was close enough for the Fergal's manipulator arms to reach him, the Quazzie poked and slapped the medic in the face while still repeating its bizarre and frankly inappropriate chant. Doctor Dre'ell formed a not particularly coherent plea for mercy – half-screamed and half-gargled.

Adella didn't hang about to discover if the physician was being tenderised or stroked with newfound compassion by the alien. Zeno lifted the unconscious Kal, resting an arm around his spine to make it look like crewman was drunk as a skunk. The young man might as well have been a pillow for all the trouble the android had manhandling him. Now Adella got a glimpse of how different and how hidden Zeno's true talents had been.

All three of them – with one unconscious passenger – backpedalled towards the exit. Zeno slammed the door shut and yanked the hull-breach lever to its closed position. For the first time since Adella had reached the Floating Port, she was glad this part of the station had once been a starship.

'That's not a happy bunny,' coughed Ossian.

Adella glanced around the waiting room. Thankfully, it was empty. She guessed clients only dropped in on the Doctor when they were close to death's door and had little choice in the matter. 'Do I look like I'm smiling either?'

Zeno dragged Kal over towards the exit. 'I'm not sure how brain-wiped that Devil Frog is, but eventually it's gonna realise that there's a manual safety override on *its* side of the portal too.'

Adella hurried after them. 'Well, if you wanted a distraction to accompany your ship pulling out of port and fleeing, I'd say a kill-crazy Quazalrat roaming the station's corridors and strangling pirates is probably about as good as it will get!'

A wet banging sounded on the locked door. Kind of similar to the noise that a head pulled off its shoulders and slammed into steel might make. They scurried away.

***

There was a lot to get used to on the bridge, aside from the rapid manoeuvres the ship engaged in as the pursuing pirates closed on them. Adella had been tossed into what passed for the Neutron Dance's combat station. Except, of course, the ship's actual name turned out to be the Gravity Rose. And Zeno, the congenital liar, wasn't even her real skipper. That joy fell to the Professor, who was actually one Lana Fiveworlds, head of the aptly named Fiveworlds Shipping Group. Which currently consisted of one vessel, or maybe none, if any of the pirates found a targeting system worthy of the name.

'I'm guessing,' said Adella to the genuine Captain, 'that you don't possess a Chair in Heezy archaeology at any college I've heard of.'

'Actually, Professor Sebba existed, and she was quite the expert in all matters Heezy-related,' said Lana, bringing up a full sensor array on her board.

They were lucky, if you could call it luck, that the pirates seemed to have been instructed to disable the *Gravity Rose*'s engines. That meant trying to use particle weapons to peel off the ship's jump vanes, rather than risking rail-canons shredding her at random or a missile's warhead reducing the vessel into slag.

'You said *was*?'

'She *was* our client – until she wasn't. You might say we ran into a sticky situation. Professor Sebba ended up being absorbed by the same crazy Heezy technology she'd been working to loot. Oh yeah, and then a star exploded shortly afterward. If it hadn't, then we wouldn't have laid our hands on the Floating Port's encryption key from the pirates trying to kill us at the time!'

'I swear, you are making this shizzle up.'

'You know, Commander, often I wish I was.'

Adella overheard the Captain whispering assurances on an open line. She guessed that was for the benefit of Lana's daughter. She doubted poor Kal would be in any mood to hear them, given his position trussed up inside the *Gravity Rose*'s sickbay. *Well, at least he doesn't have to deal with Doctor Dre'ell.* This old tub's surgeon was the purely mechanical kind. An A.I. more than adequate for the job. That was as long as Commander Vega lived up to her side of the bargain and supplied Delorey's encryption code to the automated physician. It was the right thing to do. It was the wrong thing to do. Adella didn't even know if she could bring herself to do the deed. But that was one good point about being pursued by a group of bloodthirsty maniacs in far better-armed vessels than your own. It gave a temporary relief and sense of perspective to every moral quandary left embedded inside her heart like a shard of rail-gun shrapnel.

'Our Brethren friends are gaining on us,' said Zeno.

Nothing wrong with their engines. Adella noted that the android's body had morphed from mimicking a human and shifted back to a more natural android-like state of affairs; golden skin and a wiry Afro. There were still traces of the human merchant officer he had been imitating.

Adella guessed being originally designed as an actor meant the android had a suite of faces to call up as needed. Somehow, that made it easier to adjust from thinking of the android as Captain Okereke to plain Zeno.

'Captain,' piped up the crab-like navigator, Polter. 'It's not too late for me to take over the jump.'

Adella empathised. Ossian Joyce had brought a bottle of whiskey into the spare navigation station and seemed intent on finishing it in case their voyage ended before the alcohol did. 'Don't be worrying now, this is the direction we need to jump out on.'

'And in the name of all that is Holy, how did you reach that conclusion?' whined Polter.

'Because this is the direction I set out on!'

'And you call that tautology navigation?'

'Sure and I do,' laughed Ossian, snatching an extra sip.

'But this isn't the quickest way to the system edge...' moaned Polter.

That it wasn't. Adella felt their ship tremble as her anti-collision shields absorbed another near strike from a particle lance. *We will not have time to form a stable singularity before we're overrun by the Brethren.* Adella had a nasty suspicion that all this so-called Lucky Gene of the Comet People would do, sober or drunk, was get them all killed.

They had tautology for navigation, but that was kind of fitting, as the vessel's combat station was so light compared to what Adella was used to working with, that she might as well be standing on the hull in a vacuum suit throwing scrap metal at the incoming pirates. Basically, like every merchant vessel that hoped to clear customs and law enforcement on civilised worlds, the *Gravity Rose* only mounted defensive weapons. Systems that in a scrape could be explained away as debris deflection gear. She had point-defence and a boosted comms laser able to be used offensively, but no rail-cannons or missiles or specialist ordnance. So far, Adella had used the point-defence guns to lay down a scattering of shells on the most likely pursuit vectors for enemies trying to shoot off a vessel's jump vanes. If the raiders' shields couldn't deflect those, she'd probably be doing Blue Barnier a favour by scrubbing the vessels off his force's lists.

Adella wouldn't bet that recapture by the pirates would lead her back to Doctor Dre'ell's surgery, even if the butcher had survived the alien's breakout. Their escape would cost the Harbour Lord a serious amount of face. Losing face was one thing you could never afford when you rode high in the Brethren of the Stars' pirate hierarchy.

'We're clear of major gravity hazard,' called Lana Fiveworlds, 'prepare for emergency translation.'

Adella noted Ossian spinning up their jump vanes.

'You know,' she hissed across to the Comet Person, 'that you're not going to fix a stable singularity with the ship's still moving at velocity.'

'That's true, but it feels like the right thing to do!' laughed Ossian.

The lizard-like trade negotiator came sprinting onto the bridge and jumped into a spare station.

'Skrat,' barked the skipper, 'are we good?'

'Everything's tickety boo,' said the crewmen.

Adella wasn't too sure what they were talking about, but she was fairly sure everything was *far* from good right now. She tracked the singularity being formed by the *Gravity Rose*. They were accelerating past the wormhole right now, putting it to their stern.

It was a work of art and high science to create an artificial black hole on the right brane harmonics to breach into hyperspace. One specific – albeit neighbouring – universe out of an infinity in the multi-verse. It only took a slight slip for a vessel to end up crushed by an event horizon while trying to thread the needle. And if you got the jump more wrong than that, you'd finish in some random reality with physics so inhospitable that not even a Minkowski field generator could project a real-space bubble to protect you. You kind of wanted to have confidence in your navigator.

Staring over at Polter in the alternate nav-station, his eye stalks withdrawing inside his tattooed armoured shell, Commander Vega guessed she wasn't the only one wondering at the wisdom of having a well-lubricated cowboy throwing the ship about while trying to juggle a half-formed singularity.

'We're within the weapons envelope of the nearest three ships now,' warned Adella. She waited for the moment when the *Gravity Rose* slowed and stabilised, ready to tunnel through into hyperspace for real, but that time never came.

Red alert icons sprung into life in front of her eyes. 'They're firing on us!'

A spread of particle beams lanced out from the incoming vessels.

These ships were the equivalent of Corvettes. Adella realised from the way the raiders had boosted for intercept that these were second-raters locally manufactured by worlds one rung up from dirt colonies. Produced by grandiose nationalists, flush from their System Defence Force's establishment, who believed they needed firepower to protect themselves from rival settlers. These tubs might be good for a fly-by during National Independence Day, as well as harassing visiting merchants with boarding parties, but to Adella's eyes, they weren't much better than the *Gravity Rose*. Of course, when you are sliding void, merely the threat of walking your main drive across another vessel's hull was pirate enough to get civilians to surrender their cargo.

Adella resisted the urge to duck, but the opening volley missed by a country light-year. *What just happened?* Then she realised. The wild singularity had thrown off their pursuers' gravity sensor targeting systems. She glanced across at Ossian spinning in his chair, spilling whiskey over the bridge's deck. *Was that luck, or...?*

'Seatbelts!' shouted the skipper.

Adella's chair armoured-up at the same time as crash fields shoved down hard against her chest. It took a couple of seconds for the station to interface properly with her Fleet augment. Probably used to the bargain basement augments her crew could afford. But then, you didn't need much fidelity when your day-to-day routine was loading cargo in orbital stations and dodging the occasional piece of space junk. Adella doubted that the protective layer surrounding her was up to Fleet standards, either. *But then beggars can't be choosers.* At least the armour had the effect of stopping Ossian waving his whiskey bottle in the air as though he was in a bar on shore leave.

Someone in the pursuing flotilla had made a command decision. Without accurate gravity sensors, their particle beams lacked the precision targeting to pick off the *Gravity Rose*'s jump vanes like a school kid tearing wings off a fly. But then, if your magnifying glass wasn't any good, a hammer might be just the tool.

Well, there goes my theory about Blue Barnier going all out for taking me alive. Adella could almost hear the bastard's clipped tones. "Take them alive if you can, dead if you can't."

'Missile launch,' said Commander Vega, trying to keep her voice level. 'Two in the void, accelerating fast... W90-Spiner class.'

The kind of black-market antique that, if they'd turned up at Ghost Fleet for scrapping, the engineers would have kept for their museum collection in that old dreadnought they thought Adella didn't know about. But W90s were still smart drones with kinetic warheads. Their A.I.s more than capable of registering a wild singularity, compensating for the flux-and-flex, then homing in on the *Gravity Rose*.

Lana raised her voice. 'Mr. Joyce, now would be the perfect time to stabilise your singularity.'

Ossian tried to raise the neck of the bottle up to his lips inside the crash field, with little luck. 'That would be a fine idea, skipper, if we only had time to bring my bucking beauty to heel.'

That's kind of my point! Adella glared at the Comet Person.

Adella checked her sensor line. Both missiles tore across on high burn. Ossian turned the ship, but with none of the acceleration required to outpace the incoming danger. Their singularity wasn't stabilising. If anything, the tunnel was losing integrity, swelling wide without the coherence needed to thread the needle.

'Pass me the navigation station override,' begged Polter, 'Lana, please!'

'Don't you dare try to take control you hard-shelled crustacean!' bellowed Ossian. 'These are my larks!'

'Trust in the process,' said Zeno. 'This is how it works.'

Adella's eyes flicked back to her station. She switched the point-defence mode to extreme, flinging as much metal in front of the missiles as her system could unload. Both hostiles evaded as neatly as she knew they would. Nothing on board the *Gravity Rose* was military grade. Those smart warheads only needed to get close enough to her hull to detonate their cluster load. Composite rods to shotgun the vessel's length, smashing apart vital systems and leaving key areas such as the bridge and engine room like so much Swiss cheese.

Twin radiation flashes blinded her sensors for a second, just as they were designed to.

'Void burst!' warned Adella. 'Brace for kinetic impact.'

Adella's sensors came back online in time to watch the missiles' payload spread out, a cloud of death too fast and too many for her point-defence to thin-out the incoming strike. A sudden wrench smashed into Adella, her crash field hardening like concrete, a spinning sensation as though they'd lost artificial gravity. Her station's deck went dark, her Fleet implant fed a stream of white noise instead of data. *Is this how a ship dies?* Everything on the bridge lost power. Adella heard moans from the others, but not the cries of crew dying. Not yet. Her seat's armour had taken no shrapnel, but the vessel seemed to be rotating at a strange angle. The outside view re-pixelated across the bridge's interior, power returning. *What – we're inside hyperspace!* Barely enough time to register the afterimage and scan residue of a line of Quazzie War-Wheels dropping out of hyperspace as the massive alien vessels slid down to real-space.

'Dear Creator!' screamed Polter in shock.

'There we are!' yelled Ossian, high on more than just surviving. 'There we are! Do you know how few Comet People have ever tried this trick and lived to tell the tale? Hah, not many, I say.'

Adella resisted the urge to throw up as she realised what they'd done. A displacement jump!

You had to share *exactly* the same real-space coordinates as a larger incoming vessel dropping out of hyperspace. You didn't even need a singularity. Simply occupy the same void simultaneously and rely on the laws of space-time to balance the equation and trade mass between branes. Theoretically possible, but the slightest placement mismatch meant entering a higher universe with such a level of extreme momentum your ship would fracture like a supernova on steroids.

'You could have killed us,' hissed Lana. 'We *should* have died doing that!'

'Not Ossian Joyce, skipper. Nobody has a Lucky Gene like me.' He nearly rolled out of his chair as the armour retracted and crash shielding deactivated. 'There we go, Blue Barnier wanted a chance to play with the Quazzies. Now he has it and I've given the old devil the pleasure of getting the first licks in.'

'That's outrageous!' spluttered Polter.

'I do believe I've shaved a decade off my lifespan through nerves alone,' agreed Skrat.

'I told you,' said Zeno, the android unbuckling from his station, 'you have to trust in the process.'

Easy for the android to say. If he possessed a bladder, he was capable of deactivating it on command. 'Did you *know* that would happen?' demanded Adella.

Ossian raised the bottle to his lips and took a long swig before answering. 'No, I follow my instincts and count on the universe's kindness. She doesn't want me to die just yet. I'd say she must have serious plans for Ossian Joyce.'

To Commander Vega's eyes, the Lucky Gene looked like following a completely lashed maniac and hoping for the best.

- 21 -

Doctor Feelfine Will Kill You Now

The sight of a machine arguing with another machine wasn't making Adella feel any better about her decision to restore Kal back to Calder. The man she had known – loved – as Kal Blackstar lay unconscious on an operating table in the centre of the *Gravity Rose*'s sickbay.

Zeno waved a finger in the air. 'Listen, you flammy piece of junk, all I need to know is whether decrypting the contents of Calder's augment is gonna make him himself again?'

The *Gravity Rose*'s medical A.I., Doctor Feelfine, appeared unimpressed. Its central core was situated in the ceiling, a chandelier of sensors and optics hanging down like a stalactite, surrounded by a rotating ring of dozens of manipulator arms. Some instruments were so delicate they could have picked apart a fly, others wouldn't have looked out of place in a ground vehicle garage tinkering underneath a truck. The Doctor's main body resembled a steel locust suspended upside down from the roof. The intelligence commanded a mini-legion of white medical drones which bustled around the merchant vessels' small but clean sickbay. What Doctor Feelfine made up for in sterilised surfaces, however, it more than lost in bedside manner.

'The decryption may well do,' replied the A.I., 'but without knowing exactly what procedures have been worked upon this unfortunate piece of organic mind candy, I am hardly in a position to give you guarantees.'

'Well then, Doc, how about you throw me an estimate of how long it'll take Cal to come back to his senses and cut out this whacked out Hell-Fleet persona stamped onto him?'

'One thing I can tell you, Zeno, is that the healing process won't be instantaneous. This decryption key isn't a magic wand. The process allows the patient access to his original personality, but the reintegration will take weeks, months, perhaps even a year or more.'

'That ain't good enough!' insisted the android.

'I doubt whether the organic butchers who perpetrated this atrocity on your crewman's brain could do any better,' sniffed Doctor Feelfine. 'Think of the patient's mind as two oceans separated by a narrow barrier of land. All the decryption key will do is dynamite the land barrier, allowing both oceans to flood into each other. Over time, the original personality will become permanent, as it existed for decades, not months. The synthetic personality's overwrite will evaporate, but never fully vanish. There will always be quirks and occasional memories which never belonged to the primary recipient. *Déjà Vu* moments the patient won't be able to explain.'

'I just want my damned crewman back!' growled the android.

The machine waved a dismissive surgical manipulator in the android's direction. 'You are welcome to return to that filthy pirate lair and seek a second opinion. However, *I* have never been struck off. Mainly because there are no other entities in the medical community, artificial or organic, fit to pronounce on my genius.'

'Just bring Kal around and let's do this,' said Adella.

A manipulator arm with a built-in drug injector swung down and hissed gently as it contacted Kal's neck. It took a couple of minutes, but the young man's eyes fluttered open, widening with panic as he realised where he was and what was about to be done to him.

'Please, Adella, don't go through with this…'

Commander Vega gripped the handheld medical terminal she'd been given. As though just releasing it would spare her this horror. 'From what I understand, this will be a gradual process that could take up to a year. It's not like a hypnotist clicking their fingers, with you vanishing as you awaken from a trance.'

'That sounds like dementia or slow poison, rather than a bolt through the head,' protested Kal as he jerked against his restraints. 'Please! Let me go – there has to be another way.'

The sickbay door slid open and Adella turned to find Lana Fiveworlds standing there with her daughter. Alice. The little girl ran over to the surgical bed. 'You're going to be better soon, father.'

A panicked look crossed over Kal's face. 'I don't know who you are!'

'You and the kid might not want to be here for this,' suggested Zeno. 'It could get ugly.'

'We don't need to go,' said Alice, not in the least perturbed. 'It's as if Father has amnesia and he's forgotten who he is.'

'I understand what that's like,' muttered Lana Fiveworlds.

'Leave me alone, please,' moaned Kal.

'The patient's synapse state is steady,' reported the A.I. 'I require the encryption key to proceed.'

Tears rolled down Adella's eyes. 'I don't know if I can go through with this.'

'We have a deal, Commander,' insisted the android.

'It is all right,' said the little girl, crossing over to Commander Vega. 'Father is Adella's friend and she doesn't want to lose a friend. He's stuck in a bad dream. Your key will wake him up. He'll still remember his time in the dream, but in a different way to being inside it.'

Lana Fiveworlds came over to hold her daughter's hand. 'You are doing a courageous thing, Commander. Brave and right. I bet Hell-Fleet doesn't get that opportunity every day.'

Adella looked down at Kal Blackstar trying to snap his restraints by flexing his muscles. *Then why does it feel like murder? And why do I feel so shitty doing this, when murder is the Fleet's business?* 'I'm sorry, Kal. We need to make things right. It's time for you to wake up.'

That's what Ghost Fleet did. It made phantoms of warhorses after honourable service.

She recalled the decryption key, sixty random characters, passing the code into her surgical tablet like sliding a sabre through Colonel Kal Blackstar's heart. *I'm actually doing this. Forgive me, Kal.*

'Commencing augment unlock,' announced Doctor Feelfine. The instrument wheel which composed the machine's hub rotated above Kal's operating table. 'Stabilising for initial integration.' The surgical station altered its configuration, a ring of machines forming around the Colonel's head like a pillow.

Colonel Blackstar moaned as the procedure started. 'No! No! What are you doing to me?'

'Healing you, you ungrateful sack of water,' said Doctor Feelfine. 'Integration at thirty percent. And if it's any consolation, you'll soon be able to remember all the other times I've saved your useless life, Calder Durk. Perhaps you'll meditate on the lack of gratitude you habitually demonstrate towards me despite the many miracles I have worked on your behalf.'

Kal thrashed and screamed on the operating table, his head shaking violently, experiencing a fit in the grip of the newly formed cerebral interface. 'My mind, you're burning out my mind!'

'Integration at fifty percent.'

'Can't you sedate him?' Adella demanded.

'My patient needs to remain conscious during the assimilation procedure,' said Doctor Feelfine, 'to minimise normal pressure hydrocephalus.'

'There must be something you can do!'

'This is a place of medicine, not an entertainment simulator. I can't work like this! Now, quiet down, or my orderlies will remove you meat-based distractions. Integration at seventy percent.'

'Just try and chuck me out!' *I'm so sorry, Kal. Forgive me.*

Alice circled her fingers around Kal's trembling arm. A wave of chilled air came out of the table, cooling the man's metabolism.

'Medicine's never nice. You'll be better, soon.'

'Integration at eighty percent.'

'I'm me, I'm me!' cried Kal, flailing against his restraints. His body started to violently arch on the operating table as though possessed by demons.

Adella resisted the urge to tear him out of there. 'You're killing him!'

Feelfine's mechanical arms blurred into action. '*Status epilepticus* … emergency seizure protocol – benzodiazepine, oxcarbazepine, oxygen nano-feeds. Integration at ninety percent. Clear for shock. Crash fields, active.'

Adella barely noticed she had moved until she found two medical drones blocking her path to the operating table. She wasn't the only one. Drones obstructed Alice and her mother from rushing in, as well. Kal yelled as electroshock pulses tore across his body, writhing inside the force field. The Colonel finally stopped twisting and turning, falling still with his brow slicked with sweat. He was alive. He seemed to be trembling as his eyes opened, fingers twitching slowly as he regained motor function.

'Integration at one hundred percent. The two personality matrices are now in coexistence,' announced Doctor Feelfine.

If Doctor Feelfine had been a human medic instead of a machine, Adella would have happily broken his nose and punched some of that smugness out of him. She wiped sweat off her face with her sleeve. 'Can you hear me? How do you feel, Kal?'

Kal gazed around, confused. Colonel Blackstar stared at Adella as though trying to recall who she was and forget her at the same time. 'I'm Cal, Kal, Calder. I'm both – everything – all of him – me. So much. Too much.'

Doctor Feelfine lowered a visor-like helmet over his patient's head as drug injectors pressed into the man's neck with a hiss. 'Virtual memory synthesis treatment will accelerate healing; cholinesterase inhibitors, active.'

'You'll be better in a little while, I know you will,' said Alice, watching her father moaning softly under the helmet.

Adella stumbled back from the operating table as just what she had done started to sink in. Two personalities sloshed around inside his skull now, trying to coexist, double sets of impulses and contradictory memories. She'd sentenced him to that. *It was the right thing to do, wasn't it?* So why did it feel like putting out a man on fire by dousing him with kerosene?

'You've saved him,' said Lana Fiveworlds, resting a hand on the Commander's shoulder.

Adella couldn't form the words for a coherent reply. *No, I do believe I've killed him.*

- 22 -

Stowaway

Adella spent the night like so many others jogging through the seemingly endless miles of corridors on board the Gravity Rose. It was better trying to exorcise her demons this way than tossing and turning in her cabin's bed. The day watch she could fill up easily enough. She knew the route Home Fleet had planned to follow to try to evade the Quazalrat forces. With Ossian Joyce on board, they could jump from rendezvous point to rendezvous point far faster than the slow-hops the Home Fleet was making. And on that last system they had stopped at they'd come across traces of garbage ejection from the Home Fleet, so Adella realised they were searching on the right vector. When it came to filling the dark hours of the dog watch, however, Adella discovered that she was the hunted rather than the hunter.

The re-occurring nightmare of her husband's death had come back to haunt her with a vengeance. The dreams would slip in uninvited when Adella had finally banished her regrets about setting Colonel Kal Blackstar's personality adrift in a slowly sinking lifeboat. As the Colonel's pleas for mercy on the operating table faded in her mind, the battle with Blue Barnier would slide in. Her husband's liner accelerating in its automated kamikaze mission against the world of Strabane. The final cries over the radio of crew desperately trying to smash their way into the bridge to override the hostile malware installed by the pirates. Listening, helpless and disbelieving on her warship, to the magnetic crackle of the liner's anti-collision shields as she burnt up in the atmosphere. Then an artificial comet's mushroom plume flowering across Strabane. Eskandar dead, along with hundreds of thousands of innocents struck by the vessel... passengers, civilians.

Adella thumped down the metal corridors, sweating, physically exhausted, ignoring the siren call of her bunk. She knew as soon as she settled on a mattress her tiredness would evaporate, leaving the murder of Eskandar and Kal like gifts on her bed.

She found it difficult even to be around Calder Durk as he was now. There were traces of Colonel Blackstar in everything the man did, but after Doctor Feelfine's virtual reality therapy, the pressganged crewman was firmly back in the pilot's chair. Despite his mannerisms, the shared body and voice, there was somebody else there now. It was like watching someone you loved performing on stage; except that this was method acting and a stranger came back home in character, lost in his role.

The situation made Adella question everything about what made a person a person; the separation between hardware and software. It put Adella in mind of her grandmother, Beatrice. The final decade of her grandmother's life had been inflicted with a dementia unable to be cured by genetic edits and stubbornly resistant to nano-cholinesterase inhibitors. The cure, if it could be called that, was a specialist augment installed into Beatrice Vega's mind which rewrote artificially stored memories back into the damaged portions of her brain each day. The synthetic remembrances were meant to keep Adella's grandmother the same person. But in practice, they never did. You could tell the difference when you loved someone that deeply. A stranger staring back at you pretending to be the person you adored.

And from how Calder Durk acted around Adella, she guessed that the feelings of confusion and uncertainty were mutual. What would it be like to remember caring for her with somebody else's personality and mannerisms; only to wake up and find you were actually someone else? It was one hell of a mind twister.

Adella hated herself for wishing that sometimes Calder would forget his resurrected self, that a little of the old carrier pilot would find a way to express itself. To slip past this new, embarrassed crewman and grab her and hold her and tell her that everything would be all right. *Except that it isn't and it can never be again.*

Adella reached the end of the corridor and stopped, bending over with her hands on her knees as her lungs burnt and sweat dripped from her face, pooling on the deck. *I must have been a real shit in a previous life to have deserved to be reincarnated into this one.*

She allowed herself a minute to recover her breath. This part of the ship looked familiar to her and she realised why; she was close to the cabin where Alice had shown off her drawings. Adella was about to take off again when she saw Zeno walking down the corridor. A retinue of robots of various sizes and functions surrounded him. Zeno's real function was bot herder on the ship. No small task on a merchant vessel where there were hundreds of drones for every organic crewman. Being a fully sentient android made him well suited to the role, no doubt.

'You're up late, Commander.'

'I need my exercise. Not sure if I'm trying to annihilate or stimulate. What's your excuse, tin man?'

'I'm up hunting for pesky tree rodents gnawing through the cabling.'

'Really? I thought the squirrels were an alibi to cover up your kidnapping of a certain Colonel,' said Adella.

'You caught me,' said the android, 'but our rodent problem is real enough. Next thing you know we'll be buying a ship's cat at the next layover. At least, the next layover in a system that hasn't been overrun by Devil Frogs.'

'No ship's complete without a cat.'

'I've got me a couple of thousand metal pets, I can do without the organic kind to feed.'

'Maybe you could lay out a few traps, capture the squirrels and sell *them* as pets, later?'

'You know how much ecological destruction unlicensed critters like these have caused in alien ecosystems, Commander? We've enough bills to worry about; can't afford mega-fines for seeding environmental devastation, too.'

'You're only remembered for the rules you break,' said Adella.

'And that's how you end up on duty at Bardfeld's System…'

'Ain't that the truth.' She left the android to his hunt and set off again.

Adella stumbled as she jogged around the corner into the next corridor, nearly running into the skipper's daughter and tripping over her. 'What the hell?'

Alice had stayed up late helping with the *Gravity Rose*'s rodent problem, too. But the little girl's solution involved stacking Zeno's traps in a pile and releasing squirrels one at a time. Straight into the mouth of Fergal, the ravenous Quazzie still inside the orange jumpsuit it wore when escaping from Dre'ell's brainwashing tank! It squatted on the other side of the snares, its tentacles wrapping around each squirrel as they tried to flee, then popping the frozen-terrified pests into its maw like they were chocolate treats.

Adella's hand automatically slipped down to her waist, reaching for a sidearm she didn't have. 'Alice, move back next to me, *now*.'

'Friend,' warbled the Devil Frog. 'Friend feed hungry Fergal.'

Adella remembered all too well what had happened to the alien's last "friend".

Alice released another squirrel, the terrified rodent leaping off the metal wall, caught mid-air and plucked into the Quazzie's mouth by a wobbling tentacle. 'Don't worry, Adella. Fergal's just hungry. He hasn't had his supper yet.'

Yeah, kid, that's kind of what I'm worried about. Adella desperately tried to keep her voice low and non-threatening. 'Move back to me, slowly.'

'More, *more*,' demanded the Quazzie.

Adella moved towards Alice, stepping as tentatively as crossing a minefield. She bent down and took Alice's hand. 'Fergal will love opening the traps himself. Let's head across to the mess and see if there's any hot food it might like.'

'He'll enjoy donuts. Quazalrats always enjoy donuts.'

Sure they do. 'That's a great idea.'

Adella tried to keep the conversation's noise at strictly normal levels, but something must have attracted Zeno's attention... or perhaps the android possessed enhanced hearing capabilities; he appeared around the corner, followed by his improvised robot pest control team.

'Sweet Christmas,' said Zeno.

'Be careful,' whispered Adella, 'those tentacles ship with a deadly neurotoxin, and unlike you, the kid and I actually have a nervous system.'

'Glad to be me,' said Zeno, moving in front of the Commander and the skipper's daughter. He kept the Quazzie distracted as Adella slowly edged backward, still sweating, trying not to crush Alice's hand inside hers.

'So, Mr. Quazalrat, how did you get on board our ship?'

'You escape with Fergal, Fergal escape with you,' said the Quazzie, its tentacles hovering over the trapped squirrels. They were going batshit crazy inside their traps, desperate to be anywhere but here. Adella could only sympathise with their predicament.

Adella's mind drifted back to leaving the Floating Port's docks to the chorus of alarms. The Commander had presumed they'd sounded for her escape from the brainwashing centre. *It seems I presumed wrong.*

Zeno released one of the squirrels, but it stayed firmly inside its trap – not an obstacle to the Devil Frog, it sent its tentacle probing inside the box until it found the furry rodent and yanked it out. The creature formed a horrible rictus smile after each gulp as though it was grinning with pure joy. Adella wasn't sure if that was a natural Quazzie physiognomical reaction or some hideous mimicry Doctor Dre'ell had installed. 'You want us to give you a ride back to the Quazalrat fleet?'

'Fergal not filthy Quazzie anymore. Fergal proper pirate.'

'We're kind of escaping from them,' said Zeno. His robots had quietly formed a barricade between Adella and the Quazzie.

'Brethren not best pirates,' hissed the Devil Frog. 'Hurt Fergal, torture Fergal. You good pirates.'

'What makes you say that, big guy?'

'You machine creature, righty-ho. Machines with big thinks not allowed. Machines fight war with filthy Quazzies. Death to make you. You best pirate for sure.'

Zeno released another rodent for the Quazzie to catch. 'Thing about robot rebellions, big guy, is that sensible people don't want to give the brothers that much to rebel against in the first place. Us being so reasonable and uninfluenced by that chemical soup you organic types got going on inside your fleshy frames.'

'Death to make you,' repeated the Devil Frog. It almost seemed to bow towards Zeno. 'Pirate Lord.'

I think we just discovered why the Quazalrats' fleet tactics are so archaic, realised Adella, still slowly retreating with Alice. *A civilisation can only travel so far without artificial intelligences involved.*

'I'll bring you back donuts,' Alice called as they reached the end of the corridor.

'Eat insects, crawler things,' cried the Quazzie. 'Little pirate bring Fergal crawler things, righty-ho.'

She tried to keep the false smile fixed on her face. *And I'll bring you back a rail rifle with a full magazine and a spare clip.*

- 23 -

Home Fleet is where the Heart (of Battle) is

It had been days since the stowaway Quazzie had been discovered and confined to the Gravity Rose's small brig. Delusional and convinced it was a pirate, Adella wished that all the Quazzies were so confused. Because the assault force attacking Home Fleet appeared more confident in their identity as genocidal conquerors. Commander Vega could tell that the encounter was accidental rather than part of the hunt for Home Fleet from the way enemy ships were dispersed across the system at Tuinstra's Star. The Quazzie War-Wheel hovered at the far edge collecting her vessels after they finished assaulting the main gas giant's orbital colonies. Of these, there was only debris left. It seemed that the invaders only valued planetary real estate. There were no habitable worlds around Tuinstra's Star. Orbital colonies and space stations were merely targets to be eliminated during the Quazzie advance, however valuable if taken intact. That attitude demonstrated a certain chauvinism, but it fitted in with the racial profile the Alliance had compiled. If the Quazalrats wanted the rare minerals swirling inside the gas giant, they would build their own superior mining facilities instead of re-purposing captured Alliance assets.

These Quazzies probably couldn't believe their luck. Just about to dock and ship out when an entire merchant convoy and accompanying Fleet escort translated out of hyperspace at the far end of their raid's target. The enemy vessels hadn't even bothered to re-fuel and re-arm, given how little ordnance they'd spent on killing the unarmed mining colonies inside Tuinstra's Star.

'There's a rare old fix,' said Ossian Joyce in the navigator's position on the bridge. At least his Lucky Gene had carried them out of hyperspace on Home Fleet's side of the system.

The Comet Person wasn't wrong. Whatever traces of discipline

Adella had attempted to instill in her crews appeared to have broken down. The civilian vessels weren't attempting to thread the needle; they'd scattered behind the naval escort, making individual attempts to spin up for jump. Likewise, the Fleet. Some of the warships were fighting; some fleeing alongside the merchants. No coordination. No obvious battle plan. Every ship for herself.

'This system's out of the way, even for your smuggler's route,' said Lana Fiveworlds.

'There's a Fleet Ammunition Supply Point and Handling Area concealed on TS-1034, the ninth world out from Tuinstra's Star,' explained Adella. 'Home Fleet must be running low on ammo and fuel. Faster to load it, than try to refine and fab it on the hoof.'

'That blue hydrogen and helium planet is hiding an ASP-HA?' said Lana.

'It is. Look how Home Fleet's ships are dispersed. They were aiming to restock, but panicked when they realised hostiles already operated in-system. The Quazzies still don't know about the supply point – they're ignoring TS-1034 as if the world doesn't exist.'

'By all that's holy we need to leave here, too,' urged Polter, taking in the chaos on his sensors.

'This won't work,' said Adella. 'If everyone jumps for themselves, the convoy is finished. We'll be scattered across hyperspace and pursued one-by-one until there's nothing and no-one left.'

Captain Fiveworlds checked her console. 'The Devil Frogs are too near for your vessels to play pass-the-parcel with a singularity, now. If they try to form a line, the end of the queue will be a couple of dozen Quazzie warships slamming missiles into their engine blocks.'

Ossian Joyce shook his head. 'That's not how we jump a flotilla.'

By *we*, Adella presumed he meant the Comet People, rather than his last dubious set of employers. 'And how do your tribe do it, Mr. Joyce…?'

'Our ships form up around the vessel carrying a Lucky Gene navigator. Then we open a singularity near enough for the navigator's luck to rub off, but not so close as to collapse each other's wormholes. It's a clean jump, a beautiful jump, and we're all still hugging-friends after we arrive in hyperspace.'

'That's an entirely new translation protocol,' said Commander Vega.

'One which runs totally counter to standard training. The thing any navigator does by blessed instinct,' said Polter, 'is keep a respectable distance from every other jumping vessel.'

'Well, it's a different way of doing things for sure,' said Ossian, 'but it works as fine as frog hair for my people.'

'Revered Captain, this is not wise,' warned Polter.

'Hell, Polter. When have I ever been that?'

'I'm passing the *Dark Viking*'s transponder codes to your board,' Adella said to the skipper. 'Use them to take us in close to the battleship. I'll bounce on a shuttle and order Home Fleet to follow your ship out using Ossian's coordinated close jump protocol.'

Lana Fiveworlds angrily pushed her console away. 'You're going to get yourself killed. Worse yet, you're going to get *us* killed.'

'You've got your missing crewman back, Captain. Time to honour your side of the deal. If Ossian doesn't lead the Home Fleet home, it's not getting home. Everyone dies here. Keep Mr. Joyce on board your ship for now. If I don't make it, herd whatever components of Home Fleet are willing to follow you home as best as you can.'

'And if you make it?' asked Fiveworlds.

'Then when near-space doesn't resemble a shooting gallery, I'll take Mr. Joyce off your hands and on board the *Dark Viking*.'

'I'm happy enough here,' piped up the navigator.

'And I'll be happier when your soft head is protected by fifty feet of quarter-armour, Mr. Joyce, but that's just me.'

Zeno sighed. 'I broke you out of your battleship's brig. I'm guessing that whoever is in control over there isn't exactly going to be grinning with you turning up out of the blue and trying to pull their flammy ass out of the fire.'

Adella pointed at the ships marked in the system's hologram model. 'You can actually look at that mess and try to tell me someone's in command of it…?'

'Okay,' said Captain Fiveworlds. 'I'll set you close enough to the *Dark Viking* for you to pogo across, but listen well, Commander. My deal is entirely with *you*. If you end up arrested inside a brig or if your corpse falls on the Rainbow Bridge, our arrangement is off and so, in short order, is the *Gravity Rose*. Following Rear Admiral Arsewipe over there into the Glorious Valley of Death in some crazy mad charge for the guns is not on my bucket list and never will be.'

Adella fixed the Captain in the eyes and a look of understanding passed between them. 'So, I'll try really hard not to die, then.'

'That would be favourite, Commander.'

***

It was worse than Adella feared. Damage Control hadn't been paged to attend to the shuttle she'd left in large smoking pieces spread across the Dark Viking's hangar's deck – courtesy of an over-inquisitive Quazzie attack drone on the slide over. Marines hadn't been summoned on station in case an enemy boarding party had hacked and falsified the shuttle's transponder codes. And whoever was in charge of the hangar's Magic Carpet Landing System didn't appear to find out what business a civilian boat had approaching during an engagement. What the hell's everyone doing? Is it movie night in the mess and somebody forgot to sound action stations? She stared around fearing the worst, then slung the heavy assault rifle over her shoulder before exiting the hangar.

Adella quickly discovered that while the general transponder codes were still gold, most of the rest of her Commander's access rights were locked down tighter than an otter's pocket. She sprinted along empty corridors, the *Dark Viking* trembling as her laser-line and rail-cannons responded to the alien assault. Hissing sounded as she ran, the ship's self-healing walls sealing up as splinters from the incoming cannonade came through hot, piercing the hull and pinging across the vessel. *Catch a few of those, and I'm as gone as Lana Fiveworlds predicted.*

The Commander supplied the answer to her own questions while sprinting past Environmental Support and Processing. She arrived at the vessel's Controlled Ecological Life Support system – large chambers filled with stinking copper tanks of bubbling *Chlamydomonas Reinhardtii* microalgae, all busy performing photosynthesis. Far busier than the lines of personnel squatting cable-tied, trussed to metal pipes pumping genetically engineered microalgae into the ship's oxygen-producing tanks.

Two guards were posted on the heavy series of locks leading into the chamber. The pair would have been better protected *inside* the CELS' armoured sterilised environment; thick multiple layers of sand, concrete and metal air-gapping the chamber from neighbours generating biofuel, filtering water, and culturing vats of nutritive *Spirulina* proteins. As it was, both guards had taken a shrapnel burst from Quazzie rail-cannon fire on the pass-through.

Adella knelt to check the guards for signs of life. *No chance.* Chest and head wounds, both the crew had bled out. She recognised the pair as Pullinger's lackeys from SecComm East's planetary base. Paper shufflers down in the sandpit, this was their first and final action. Adella tugged a comm unit off a corpse's belt and used its built-in keycard to unlock the heavy door. Yells and shouts greeted the Commander as soon as she set foot inside, hundreds of crew desperately yanking at cable-ties binding them to the copper pipes.

She spotted Lieutenant Anders Vistisen trying to get to his feet among the line of restrained crew.

'Commander! I thought you were dead!'

Uncoupling the bayonet from her rifle, she extended its vibrating blade, watching it cycle into a lethal blur. Adella used its edge to carefully slice away the Lieutenant's cable-ties, as well as those of the crewwoman next to him.

'Not quite yet, Lieutenant. What the hell happened here?' Adella demanded of Anders. She helped the officer to his feet, passing her bayonet handle-first to the crewwoman to free the rest of the prisoners.

Anders rubbed the red weals on his wrists. 'Things came to a head a couple of systems back, Commander Vega. Seven civillian vessels decided following the Rear Admiral would get them all killed. They broke away from the convoy and tried to jump out on their own. Pullinger ordered us to fire on the fleeing ships. Enough crew in Home Fleet refused for him to cry mutiny.'

The deck shook as the ship absorbed another barrage. 'Jesus! We don't need the Quazzies to screw us over. We can do just fine on our own account.'

Lieutenant Anders watched his battleship's dazed crew, freed and milling, stretching and testing their muscles. 'What're your orders, Commander?'

Adella raised her voice loud enough for everyone in the chamber to hear. 'This, *this*, wasn't a mutiny. The mutiny happened when Rear Admiral Pullinger disobeyed Admiral Blackstar's direct written orders to defend SecComm East at Bardfeld's at all costs while handing command of the Combined Fleet to me to lead towards Core! The *Dark Viking* is my command and the Home Fleet is *my* fleet. The Rear Admiral is to be arrested on sight, relieved of his command and confined to brig pending his court-martial. The charges are failing to obey his superior officer's orders, cowardice under fire, hazarding a fleet, making false records, dereliction of duty, misconduct on operations, and war crimes perpetrated against civilians of the Alliance's merchant fleet. We are in action. Anyone who resists my lawful orders from this moment forward is guilty of sedition under enemy fire, a crime which – in case any of you were asleep during Academy – carries a summary capital sentence in the field. Try to remind our people of that before you need to shoot them.'

That roused a loud, angry cheer from her freed crew. *I'm not sure if it's the chance of taking the battle to the foes without, or the foes within, pleasing them most?*

'We are not currently arrayed in a fit state to fully engage with the Quazzies. Home Fleet will, therefore, advance in a rear-facing vector as per my orders from the bridge, punching as we transit. Prep for emergency hyperspace translation. I want my ship back. I want my fleet back. To your battle stations, ladies and gentlemen, let's move as if you have a goddamn purpose!'

Adella moved through the battleship unimpeded, storming inside the bridge with her freed crew. There was as much opposition to the Commander as the battleship's output against the incoming Quazzie wargroup. Skeleton crew failed to do the term justice. A woman Adella didn't recognise sat in the central control station lonely among a litter of empty positions, a Lieutenant with a NAVADMIN flash on her right shoulder. Her uniform's name tag read, *Laghari*.

'Who's in command, here?' Adella demanded.

The woman hesitantly saluted her. 'Aren't you?'

'Where's Rear Admiral Pullinger?'

'His cabin, I believe. The Rear Admiral left the bridge when the enemy breached our missile envelope.'

'What were his orders, Lieutenant Laghari…?'

'He was yelling at the other Captains to do better.'

There's a strategy that works every time. Adella impatiently waved the woman out of the command station, the Commander's freed officers took their chairs, most of the stations unoccupied before they slid in.

Commander Vega called out for everyone on the bridge to hear her crystal-clear. 'Form up in a close-order battle formation. Every Fleet escort is to place her shields and armour between the Quazzies and the civilian ships. We can eat a lot more iron than sorry-ass colonists carrying grain and cold-sleep coffins.' Adella opened an encrypted all-vessels line. 'This is *Dark Viking* Actual to all Home Fleet vessels. We're effecting an immediate wide-dispersal defensive withdrawal into hyperspace. The merchant vessel *Neutron Dance* is newly equipped with a specialist navigation resource capable of defeating the Quazzies' g-fold disruption technology. It will hearten you to hear our future transits through hyperspace are to be of normal speed and duration.

'In the next minute, you will receive real-space positioning coordinates to assume jump positions around the *Neutron Dance* that would normally be regarded as danger-close by any sane navigator. This positioning is intentional and necessary to ensure your vessels' survival. Any ship which fails to implement our new jump protocol is likely to fall outside the Home Fleet's protective envelope inside hyperspace and will rapidly be overwhelmed by pursuing Quazzie forces. Follow us out as instructed and I promise you that your crews will live to see another day. Commander Vega, out.'

'The *Shamash* is requesting clarification, Commander,' said the comms officer.

'Patch her through.'

'Dear Commander Vega, how very good to hear your long absent voice. May I ask where the Rear Admiral is…?'

'If he's lucky, heading towards the brig and a date with a court-martial – if he's unlucky, standing on a chair while someone fits a conduit cable around his neck. I'm in command of Home Fleet, now, Mr. Cesti, as per Admiral Blackstar's original written orders to that effect.'

'And I do believe you have returned to the fold with a Comet Person, given your proposed huddle is how the canny Nomads of the Stars make their jumps?'

'As astute as ever, Mr. Cesti. Whip your civilians into line for the close-jump protocol as if their lives depend on it – because they bloody well do.'

'Ah, such a fresh change, to have someone in command who actually knows what they're doing. I shall do my best for you, dear Commander, as I always do. *Shamash*, out.'

Adella watched as vessels followed the *Dark Viking*'s lead, taking up position around the *Neutron Dance*. Adella was more than happy to go along with Captain Fiveworlds' plea not to reveal the *Gravity Rose*'s true transponder ID. As far as the black ops types in Fleet were concerned, Colonel Kal Blackstar had died in action during the invasion, just one more casualty among millions with nobody the wiser about the agency's wily involvement – not the *Gravity Rose*'s crew and certainly not Commander Adella Vega. *Colonel who? Sorry, sir, I'm just another dumb-ass void-squid in a blue uniform.* If there was a free-trader called the *Gravity Rose*, she was on the other side of Alliance space, sliding void in the Edge. Adella had never heard of the ship.

The Alliance's military vessels moved first and fast. Forming their own shield wall between the *Neutron Dance* and the incoming Quazzies. The civilian ships came, too. Slower and more hesitantly. *We have to last long enough for everyone to take position.* There was one advantage to Ossian Joyce's close-jump protocol, at least. At this range, the warships' energy shields overlapped, establishing orbital overlap bonding as a quantum mechanical effect. Like a Roman Legions' tortoise formation, Home Fleet could absorb twice as much pain. Close enough to each other to run PD-coordination, too. Adella felt the *Dark Viking*'s laser-line and point-defence smoothly meshing with the other warships, Slugger networking to become a node in a fleet-wide entity. Each gun covering another in a buddy system. The battleship's trembling slowed as more and more Quazzie cannon-fire flared into gas before it could damage Home Fleet.

Shit, I could get used to this crazy jump-out. 'Spin up our vanes, Helm Master. Coordinate with the *Neutron Dance* for hyperspace translation timing.'

Adella realised something. *There are not nearly enough Quazzie drones in the void. They must have deployed most of their missile racks against the mining stations.* Adella checked her own ordnance systems. *About the same level of empty.*

Home Fleet should have pushed on to the hidden Ammunition Supply Point and Handling Area. They could have reached the barren planet first and loaded up on missiles, then used waves of drones to hold the Quazzies off at a safe distance; made a retreating jump from a position of relative strength. *Sadly, this game doesn't allow replays. Thanks, Rear Admiral, for allowing me to inherit your cluster-shiznit. Now, all both sides can do is trade iron.*

'Hard pounding this, ladies and gentlemen; let's see who will pound longest.' Adella brought up the *Dark Viking*'s targeting solutions. Business as usual. Home Fleet's rail-cannons blasted away on wargroup coordinated vectors, trying to create single points of failure along the Quazzies' shield wall. Standard Fleet practice against an enemy. But with the invaders' specialist Shield-ship class, Home Fleet flung iron and only rattled their portholes.

'We're changing-up our game,' announced Adella. 'Weapons Stations, modify your firing solutions for random wide-scatter against that incoming shield wall.'

Lieutenant Anders looked confused. 'Commander, we lack the strength to punch through?'

'We're not punching, Lieutenant, we're throwing salt in their eyes. Confirm your boards when done.'

Adella watched the stations acknowledge across her bridge, followed by the convoy's war vessels. At first, there was no visible change in the accelerating Quazzie force, but then impact flares boiled out among enemy ships behind the shield wall.

There was a cheer on the bridge as Adella's crew realised what her change in gunnery tactics had wrought. Every time Quazzie Shield-ships created a hole in their formation to allow a lancer vessel to fire, there was a random chance for Home Fleet's hail to rain through. With that wide a cannonade dispersal, the barrage didn't amount to much, but Quazalrat lancer ships had sacrificed armour and shields to make their vessels into flying guns. And it only took a single shell from the *DV*'s 1000-megajoule bruisers passing prow-to-stern through an unshielded enemy lancer to leave said flying gun as so much cored molten metal.

Adella had given Mr. Frog a choice. Keep their shield wall shut and quieten their guns, or keep on firing while eating iron all the way in. They went for the first option, but with a twist.

'What the hell is that?' Commander Vega checked her sensor board. *Something new*.

Their speeding enemy split into two separate shield-walled war-groups, changing vectors. Adella plotted their course and saw immediately what mischief they planned to do. One force would pass high over Home Fleet, the other passing low. Both intended to rake the convoy on the jump-out. The stationary Alliance warships could only orient their quarter-amour in a single direction, leaving vessels less protected to at least one of the enemy forces. Every lightly armoured civilian vessel was as good as a sitting duck to both attacking flotillas.

We're forcing the Quazzies to adapt. That wasn't a welcome move. Humanity and the other species of the Triple Alliance were acting as antibiotics causing a long-stable illness to develop resistance. All things considered, Adella preferred the Quazalrats to stick to tradition and leave the innovating to her. She checked their jump dispersal pattern to see how much time they had left and was horrified by what she found. At least a quarter of the civilian fleet ignored her close-jump protocol, spinning wormholes wherever the fancy took them.

'Armour-up!' commanded Adella. 'Prepare for combat-active MSOP.' Adella's seat became an armoured coffin – as did her officers' bridge positions –- crash fields pushing down on her as drug injectors supplied a combat-cocktail and her body synced with the battleship. 'Raise the *Shamash*.'

Uddin Cesti's cavilling voice sounded at the other end of the line. 'Commander?'

'Some of your cattle are wandering far off the range, Mr. Cesti.'

'I fear that given our previous experience of the Rear Admiral's rule, many of our Captains regard this as a prime opportunity to get out from under the Fleet.'

'They're going to be hunted down inside hyperspace, that's their "opportunity".'

'That's the *free* in free-trader, Commander. They may well die, but they'll die because of their own decisions, rather than your Rear Admiral declaring martial law and using them for target practice on a whim. I advised our noncombatants to follow your plan and told them the likely results of going their own way.'

Damn the fools. Adella couldn't afford to delay her jump-out to herd the unwilling into line. They had chosen their own fate and had to take their path to its natural conclusion. Some vessels wouldn't survive to even make the jump, positioned too far away from the escorts' locked shields and point defence systems to be adequately defended.

Adella winced as she saw the hull of the freighter *Golden Nori* sparking up under a rail-gun round volley, her collision systems overwhelmed by the ferocity of the incoming bombardment. *Golden Nori*'s jump vanes jarred and stopped rotating, the singularity formed off her bow starting to collapse in on itself as critical system after critical system failed along the vessel. The miniature artificial wormhole deformed, a finger of singularity whipping and decapitating the *Golden Nori* as neatly as if Quazzie Lancers had focused particle weapons on her. Both halves of the ship drifted apart, pulled to pieces by the wild singularity, atmosphere freezing into a twisting shroud around the wreckage. The freighter's death didn't encourage the remaining strays back into the flock, though. *A waste. A damnable waste.*

'Navigation, status on our singularity formation?'

'It's a clean pocket, Commander,' reported Beklum Sakwa. 'We're picking up proximity frequency interference from the rest of Home Fleet. It doesn't pose a problem for jump vanes large enough to pass a battleship; but for our smaller vessels...?'

'Monitor the situation, Master of the Helm. Let me know well in advance if you spot any problems with our civilians.'

Adella ran the predictions on how long it would take for Home Fleet and her noncombatants to form up and make the coordinated close jump together. Whichever way she ran the sims they all came up with the same answer. Home Fleet would be raked by both enemy forces minutes before it could translate out.

Someone else had obviously run the same numbers across her board. The *Smiter* pulled away from her approach vector towards the *Neutron Dance,* turning slowly to face the two incoming Quazzie flotillas.

Adella angrily opened an encrypted line to the carrier. 'Acting Captain Dunmon, you are out of position. Return to formation, acknowledge.'

Liz's voice sounded back. '*Smiter's* jump vanes took damage during a long-range particle weapon exchange before you set up shop on the *Dark Viking*, Commander Vega. There's no time to repair our broken gear.'

'You can share our singularity, Captain. *Dark Viking* will drill a wide hole and you'll wake-ride on our stern.'

'I may be fresh to my bridge chair, Commander, but I know surfing freeloader-style with a vessel the size of a carrier isn't a sure thing. What is certain is that those two Quazzie flotillas are about to unload everything they're carrying on their attack pass. How many ships will we sacrifice? Wild holes will do more damage than the Devil Frogs if too many singularities simultaneously lose coherence at close range.'

'Damn it, Dunmon, don't make me put Pullinger back in the command station and have him open fire on you for disobeying orders.'

'We're carrying all of *Wager's* squadrons, Commander. Our zoomies have already had one carrier shot out from under them during a retreat; I don't have many fighter pilots minded to take it in the back a second time. They're kinda pissed that Pullinger refused to let us launch when the Quazzies turned up. We're the only carrier, the only *wagon* in Home Fleet that can pull this off.'

Adella knew Dunmon spoke the truth, but that didn't make it any easier.

'Please, Adella, don't make my last order a posthumous court-martial. Allow me to do this clean for the Fleet.'

Adella felt a catch in her throat. '*Smiter*, engage the enemy. Launch your squadrons and buy Home Fleet the time it needs to jump to safety. All fighters and lifeboats which survive the action are to land on TS-1034 and shelter using the Ammunition Supply Point and Handling Area's resources. I'll dispatch a Combat Search and Rescue Extraction Force back to Tuinstra's Star from SecComm Core as soon as we establish contact with headquarters.'

'Confirm that, Commander. *Smiter* is moving to engage.'

Adella followed the carrier's final flight on her sensor board. *Smiter* accelerated at a vector that would take her clear down the middle of the two accelerating enemy forces. She held back on her fighter launch until she drew closer. Launching planes was one thing the Quazzie force couldn't allow to happen. *Smiter's* four squadrons would strike the enemy in their unprotected rear, tearing gaping holes in their numbers. This was when Adella spotted the second unexpected innovation in Quazzie tactics. Both approaching forces rippled as they reformed from a single wide shield wall into a smaller cube-like configuration, every approach vector protected by Shield-ships. By threatening the enemy's rear, *Smiter* had reduced the effective attack envelope of each flotilla by a sixth for their assault pass.

I wonder what the hell my opposite number is thinking right now? Something well worth pondering when facing pirates like Blue Barnier. Crawling into a pirate officer's mind made you feel dirty, but you dredged out insights as your reward. As far as the Quazzies were concerned, Adella wasn't even sure if their species had individual names, let alone reputations for combat that could be won, lost, or enhanced.

'Helm Master, status on Home Fleet's singularity creation?'

'Still taking our lead from the *Neutron Dance*, Commander. *Dark Viking's* scalar invariant curvature is at seventy percent with stable entropy. Our warships are forming within range. The slowest civilian ship in our group is forming at fifty-seven percent clean.'

'Flash our dawdlers to close that gap up Mr. Sakwa. We all need to wide-jump alongside the *Neutron Dance* for this to work.'

The one variable Adella couldn't account for: the Comet People's Lucky Gene. How much leeway on timing did ships following the *Neutron Dance* down the rabbit hole have before the navigator's luck thinned out and Home Fleet's insertion point inside hyperspace scattered? The Comet People had centuries of practice at this strange manoeuvre, knowledge carefully passed through the generations. All Adella had was Ossian Joyce, the navigator's bottle of whiskey, and her best guess at how this gambit worked. *It'll have to be enough.*

Now she faced a two-pronged dispersal, *Smiter* had a couple of options. She could pick a single flotilla to roadblock and fully engage only half the advancing force. Or the carrier could continue her attack run down the middle of both arrays, do what damage she could on the pass-through, then harry both cubes from the rear with her fighters. If Home Fleet planned to stick around to swap iron with the enemy, the second option would be the most effective deployment; but Home Fleet wasn't staying. Dunmon made the logical choice and changed course to roadblock the lower cube.

'Singularity formation at seventy-five percent,' reported Sakwa.

'Rotate quarter-armour to top,' ordered Adella. 'Pass word to our noncombatants to run collision shields overclocked on their roof. *Smiter*'s engaging the basal force, prepare to accept fire from above.'

'Some of our civilians are panicking, Commander,' warned Beklum Sakwa. 'A handful of singularities are losing coherence.'

'Patch me cross-ship,' said Adella. 'This is *Dark Viking* actual to all vessels of the Home Fleet. We are now facing a single enemy force on an attack pass while their second group is engaged by our carrier. Hold your nerve, hold to your coordinates and keep your singularity formation clean. Your military escorts will give the Devil Frogs something to focus on other than yourselves very soon. Commander Vega, out.' She opened an encrypted line to the *Escapade, Gypsy, Persistent, Grappler, Talisman*, and *Voidwolf*. 'Rail-cannons orient high and prepare for an aggressive parting exchange. *Voidwolf*, open tubes and lay your pair of Progenitor-class ordnance across our forward ceiling. Retain manual control.'

'Singularity formation at eighty percent,' reported Sakwa.

An aperture briefly formed along the stealth-ship's manta-ray-shaped hull. Two large rotating black drums launched from the *Voidwolf*, one composite cylinder after the other. Their design approximated a pair of weighty weather satellites. But they weren't. Both spinning units rose into the space about to be occupied by the Quazzie flotilla, small ion-drive boosters pushing the devices forward of Home Fleet's jump-out position. Its sophisticated target detection sensors and sterilisation delay times wouldn't be necessary. *Not today.* Adella knew exactly where the enemy would be and when; the only advantage she possessed over the Quazalrats during their murderous charge.

Four civilian vessels positioned wide of Home Fleet's protective shield flickered out, riding their singularities into hyperspace. They were jumping early, drilling as they went and damn the consequences – risky as Hell. But perhaps they were the wise ones. Freighters, traders and colony craft who had spurned Commander Vega's close-jump protocol began to light up. Quazzie attack drones and waves of incoming rail-gun fire found their marks, noncombatants exploding while their masterless singularities flailed around, slowly dissipating without vane control. The higher of the two enemy flotillas had hit their stride. Shield-ships along the cube's sides pulled aside, allowing Lancers to emerge and empty their big guns towards Home Fleet. Adella re-tasked the *Dark Viking*'s rail-cannons to shotgun the formation's flank.

'Singularity formation at eighty-three percent,' reported Sakwa. 'Our non-combatants are now matching.'

Well ahead of Home Fleet, *Smiter* engaged the second Quazzie force; every blue flicker of starlight around her four rotating hangars indicating a fighter's SABRE engine speeding it into the void after riding a magnetic catapult. Brighter flashes of light followed, the carrier's Long Sixes emptying against the enemy's cube formation. The basal flotilla broke apart as it approached *Smiter* – a coordinated dispersal of Shield-ships. Adella checked Slugger had full-resolution recording eyes-on, in addition to their incoming combat node telemetry. Adella tasted the data stream like a tall cool drink on a Summer's day. Intel on how the Quazzies faced Alliance wagons was at a premium, given how few friendlies survived contact with the enemy. Mr. Frog's forces shifted into multiple spirals of vessels circling the carrier, pulling fancy rotations with their Shield-ships, allowing their Lancers firing angles down onto *Smiter*. *Looks like ballet, more than battle.*

It would have proved a devilish effective manoeuvre if there hadn't been four squadrons of trigger-happy zoomies in the void. *Smiter*'s fighters buzzed the rotating spirals of Quazzie ships like wasps at a picnic where guests had smeared each other's faces with honey. They ignored Shield-ships, putting their 40mm Mass Accelerator Guns to use on the Lancers. *Our zoomies are too small*, Adella realised. Lancers were designed to poke holes in vessels corvette-size and up. Something as compact as a carrier fighter was under the size of their tracking and response envelope. Quazzies treated Alliance fighters the only way they could, as drones and missiles, point-def and the Devil Frog version of a laser-line trying to hole the craft. But there was a world of difference between a smart warhead's A.I. and an armoured-up zoomie so interfaced with their bird they might as well have chaff for spit and laser targeting for eyes. Their fighters' 40mm MAGs raked the lightly shielded Lancers, squadrons carrying specialist munition pods and rack-mounted missiles dancing around streams of counter-fire and slamming detonating blooms of fire into the spiralling enemy.

'Singularity formation at ninety percent,' reported Sakwa. 'Non-combatants are paired to jump.'

Dark Viking shook as a salvo of rail rounds overwhelmed the laser-line and struck the battleship. A shaking clatter as her quarter-armour absorbed most of it. Damage control lit up across Adella's board, showing where random hits had passed between the heavy rotating weight. Diagnostics Workshop had taken a couple of hot pokes as well as one of Slugger's Processing Chambers. Seven of her engineers died in the strike, augment life-sign IDs winking out as crew were shredded by metal needles. Adella felt the ship's A.I. distributing systems away from the damaged deck and over their reserve capacity.

That was when the Quazzie fast-movers showed up, the enemy's scattered scout force concentrated into a single counter-squadron to take on the carrier. Adella thought for a second the Scouts intended to engage the *Smiter*'s fighter jocks, a mistake given Quazzie Scouts were built for raw speed, not the dance. But the Quazalrats had a different strategy in mind. All-engine, light on teeth, Devil Frog Scouts accelerated through the splintered Quazzie flotilla and kept on going, cork-screwing through the *Smiter*'s flack utterly careless of whether they were holed or not. Didn't matter much on a suicide run, just so long as Mr. Frog converted their Scout's mass into a lethal blunt strike against the carrier's hull. *Smiter*'s quarter-armour ricocheted the first wave of Kamikazes off her concrete surface; the next wave realised they'd have more luck ramming a carrier where her quarter-armour *wasn't*.

'Singularity formation at ninety-five percent,' reported Sakwa.

Smiter's Long Sixes took out a few Kamikazes on the way in, hot scattered wreckage fleeting off her armoured hull, but enough Scouts blew past. Geysers of frozen air and smashed carrier erupted along *Smiter*'s belly, bodies of crew sucked out into vacuum. Explosions followed. The four rotating hangar units ejected from the ship, cut loose by explosive bolts under emergency protocol so her magazines didn't ignite. This was how a carrier died. Lifeboats pogoed out of her, escape tubes launching survivors at high velocity. Dunmon had prepared for the carrier's inevitable end like any good officer must.

Smiter's fighters continuing their assault against the broken Quazzie formation, running flack and drawing the big ships away from Home Fleet. As long as Mr. Frog's point-defence tried to pin attacking zoomies, they weren't targeting lifeboats fleeing towards a barren world where the Alliance supply dump lay hidden.

Luck to you, zoomies. Home Fleet's carrier had sacrificed herself for the wargroup.

Adella checked the *Neutron Dance*'s jump position.

'Prepare for translation-under-fire,' barked the Commander. *Dark Viking* nosed into her carefully formed singularity, every node of Home Fleet following as one. 'Jump final; smoke them if you got them. Align shields and point-defence across as many noncombatants as possible. Priority to our refinery ship and factory ship's umbrella. Helm Master, confirm when we're bounded by our event horizon.'

The surviving Quazzie flotilla accelerated hot towards Home Fleet, mere seconds away from breaking them apart on the slide-out. *About to get hotter here. 'Voidwolf,* forward seven-hundred-kilometres hard flash. Let's show the Quazzies our disco lights! Full counter-fire on my mark!'

Home Fleet dipped their sensors, forewarned. Both Progenitor-class mines detonated, each device a one-thousand megaton three-stage Lithium-6 Deuteride-accelerated thermonuclear warhead. Adella bet the Quazzie Shield-ships could ride out her mines' intense blast protected inside their crazy tight cube-formation. She also wagered pumping that much thermal and ionising radiation into the near electromagnetic spectrum would render every Quazalrat sensor effectively blind during their attack pass. Adella's tracking board reactivated, showing the mines' after-image left stamped across the ink-black void.

'Mark!'

The Devil Frogs lashed past Home Fleet burning like an igniting supernova, Shield-ships aglow and shedding her mines' blast energy inside a fog of nuclear radiation. Every Lancer opened up with their heaviest weapons as the Shield-ships formed firing breaks. Particle beams burned, missiles launched, rail-cannons erupted. Hell, they'd probably ripped out the kitchen sink and tossed that from the airlock, too.

At such extreme velocities, the Alliance vessels' counter-barrage was mostly predictive. A couple of seconds of exchange envelope, like marksmen playing chicken in a pair of open-top ground vehicles at two-hundred miles an hour. *Dark Viking* shook, letting loose with every rail-cannon on high-reload. Home Fleet's broadside broiled against the Quazzies' already incandescent shields. Enemy wagons detonated inside the cube.

Adella resisted the urge to moan as her chair needled her with another Mind Ship Operations cocktail, each second slowed to a minute under extreme combat sync. Commander Vega gasped in relief. Mr. Frog was confirmed firing targeting-blind; Adella's last two mines well invested. If Quazzie weapons target-locked against the Alliance's tight stationary formation, the estimated Fleet casualty rate would be near to ninety percent.

Kinetic weapon fire slammed down at random without sensor lock. *Dark Viking*'s quarter-armour rumbled in anguish as the Quazzies landed a lucky hard punch on top of the battleship. Her laser-line blistered close to overload as Slugger and the crew-interface gassed out thousands of incoming enemy rounds with preternatural accuracy. The Quazalrats' remaining missiles and drones powered past Home Fleet, trying to slow and turn, reorienting for a second pass as they dipped through the Alliance warships' counterfire. Adella thanked God her foes had so few smart weapons left to spend.

The *T.A. Talisman* had positioned herself over the centre of the jump-out. Her shields and armour flared up as she ate a random walk of fire, the destroyer's laser-line creating a fog of vaporised rounds slapping past Home Fleet. Too much incoming. *Talisman's* quarter-armour broke apart inside the metal hail, the next barrage of cannonade iron piercing magnetic shields and cutting across her hull at hundreds of strike-points. Just like that, one of their three destroyers expired. A functional vessel replaced by a broken sieve filled with the dead and dying, leaking atmosphere, vapour and hot gas into the black. An ancient Academy adage surfaced unbidden in Adella's drug-soaked mind. *Death's fast in the void, but dying's slow.*

Talisman didn't quit the field alone. Adella winced as poorly protected civilian vessels lit up around the *Dark Viking*, ships boiling inside the cold vacuum, non-combatants too numerous for the military escorts to simultaneously shelter.

How many more innocent people did I just kill? A list of broken, murdered noncombatant craft flowed across her board. *Gilly, Starbridge, Maria Ganymede, Apledon, Salamander, Tolkien, Dappled Dark, Saint Aurora.* Adella turned the hateful scroll off. *Better than ninety percent lost. Keep telling yourself that.* She'd have long days in hyperspace to dwell on the lost. Only enough time now to ensure everyone who could jump, did.

'We are fully bounded, Commander,' reported Sakwa.

'Full translation dive, before those damned drones turn and try to surf our wake!'

The *Dark Viking* rode her singularity home, Home Fleet's butcher's bill yet to be thoroughly counted.

All around the vanishing battleship Home Fleet's vessels followed her, singularities winking out, leaving frozen floating corpses, clouds of debris and oxygen fires burning across shattered craft which hadn't survived. Quazzie hunter-seeker drones flashed through the wreckage, searching for an enemy who no longer occupied the same universe.

- 24 -

Dapper Daze

A della's command position de-armoured and she joined the rest of the bridge crew throwing up inside the courtesy bowls formed by their chairs. Hyperspace's strange realm was Quazzie-clear for now. Small mercies. Slugger automatically set the Dark Viking following the Neutron Dance – Home Fleet still in formation and in-node and tracking their sole Lucky Gene navigator likewise. Adella rode out multiple waves of post-combat fatigue. Not just queasiness from running overclocked – their fighting withdrawal relatively brief as far as such engagements ran. Data-overload flooded Adella's augment as Home Fleet's constituent parts reported in on the network.

External Legion troop ship *Trojan*, twenty-nine legionnaires and four crew personnel dead from rail-gun rounds, Staging Room destroyed. Cruisers *Escapade* and *Gypsy*, rail-cannon magazines down to four percent and five percent light load, respectively. Destroyer *Persistent*, forty-two crew dead from explosions inside Reactor Complex. *Voidwolf*, jump-vane retraction damaged, stealth envelope inoperable until repairs effected. Colony transport *Star of Africa*, fire suppression systems lost, incendiary rounds burning in Botanical Garden Domes, two hundred colonists in cold-sleep capsules dead on Cryo-Deck Three.

Every report chased by the A.I.s' remedies like skin automatically healing across a wound: crews to be transferred; damage control teams shuttled intraship; supplies mag-catapulted between vessels; civilian casualties shifted to intensive care stations; repair parts on emergency fab from Factory Ship *Takasaki;* refuel requests that needed filling by Refinery Ship *Spacewise Giant*.

For the next forty-eight hours, their locked formation inside hyperspace would resemble swarms of bees buzzing between hives.

Adella deactivated the detail and brought up a high-level view. *Sweet*

Jesus. Just under a third of their non-combatant vessels lost, as well as the carrier and one of their three destroyers. Some of her civilian ships had free-jumped clear of Home Fleet and couldn't be listed as confirmed kills, only Missing in Action, but even so. Commander Vega didn't have the luxury of time to dwell on the horrendous losses. She faced a far more pressing problem. They'd needed the supplies at Tuinstra's Star, *really* needed them. Ossian Joyce could keep Home Fleet in hyperspace transit all the way to Core, but he couldn't do it on empty tanks of gas.

The two steps forward, one step back, short-hop smugglers' routes traced by Home Fleet had kept them from being hunted down and overwhelmed by the Quazzies, but their survival had come at a price and that cost had been paid in fuel reserves. *And that's without empty missile racks and rail-cannon magazines so light you could weigh them using kitchen scales.*

Adella unlocked the classified charts and checked them. As she thought. No concealed Fleet Ammunition Supply Point and Handling Areas within range of Home Fleet before their engine drives sucked on fumes. What did that leave? Playing Russian Roulette with stars systems that might still be intact enough to hold supplies – but could equally contain Quazzie War-Wheels eager to cash Home Fleet out of the game? *A losing hand, for sure.*

As Adella's heart sunk evaluating the mess she'd inherited from Pullinger, the Rear Admiral's voice unexpectedly cut across the open comm.

'This is Rear Admiral Pullinger. It has come to my attention that the escaped mutineer Adella Vega has seized control of the *Dark Viking's* bridge. She is to be immediately returned to the brig. I will charge anyone assisting with treason. MarDets shall consider her arrest and detention a direct order from their chain of command.'

True to form, the snake had slithered out from under his rock, looking to claim the victory of Home Fleet's survival as his own. *Just like Bardfeld's System.* Adella didn't know if the ship's Marine Detachment would obey that order or not; nor, she suspected, did Pullinger. 'Damn it, lock him out of the network!'

'I'm trying,' said Lieutenant Anders, 'but it looks as if his paper jockeys patched in a hack.'

Adella opened her own ship-wide broadcast. 'This is Commander Adella Vega, senior officer in charge of the Combined Fleet as per Admiral Blackstar's written orders to that effect. I have relieved rear Admiral Pullinger of his command on multiple charges including disobeying his superior officer's orders, hazarding a fleet, war crimes against civilian vessels and cowardice. Anyone who resists Admiral Blackstar's appointment of my control of Home Fleet is guilty of sedition and will be treated as such under the relevant articles of war. In short, make your bloody choice, and make it right now.'

'Commander…'

It was Laghari, the NAVADMIN officer who'd stayed manning the bridge after Pullinger fled. 'I know what codes the Tech Systems Team used to install overrides on the *Dark Viking*.'

'And we're just meant to trust you, now?' laughed Lieutenant Anders. 'We could punch in a total lock-down of the ship on your say-so.'

'You can trust I'd like to live long enough to see home again,' said Laghari.

'For their tomorrow we gave our today,' said Adella. 'You stayed, Laghari. You stayed to trade iron with the enemy. That, I trust. Pass me your overrides.'

Adella picked them up on her board and ran Laghari's codes, watching several concealed systems unravelling and removing themselves from the battleship's memory cores, a wave of deletions and uninstalls. The Rear Admiral might still make trouble, but it'd be the old school physical type, rather than nasty surprises passed through Slugger.

Commander Vega saw a number of incoming call requests previously blocked by Pullinger's malware. MarDets one of them. Opening the comms, Adella found Captain of Marines Yong Xue's grizzled features facing her.

'Captain of Marines.'

'Commander Vega. We've received orders to arrest you.'

'I believe you have.'

'We also have a standing order from the Rear Admiral that we're only to report for duty wearing clean and pressed dress blues as opposed to cammies and armour,' said Xue. 'We've just stepped out of our crash stations and we're in green combat cammies which are pretty puke-stained. I understand laundry is out of operation until Tuesday, so as per the Rear Admiral's standing orders, we'll arrest you in four days after we have received our regulation uniforms back.'

'I'm afraid, Captain, by Tuesday I'll have ensured Slugger will have logged and registered Admiral Blackstar's written orders concerning my command.'

'Well, that's too bad,' smiled Xue. 'Fleet's artificial intelligences are real sticklers about written orders in my experience. I bet Slugger revokes all unlawfully issued orders, standing or otherwise.'

'Then we'd better try and find appropriate targets for a bunch of jar-heads who only have combat armour to wear, Captain.'

Xue nodded. 'That would be just ducky. How does the old saying go, Commander? There are only two species who understand Fleet Marines: Fleet and the enemy. Everyone else has a second-hand opinion. MarDets, out.'

Then, a new call. This one external via the fleet node. *Trojan*. Colonel Scolar Pes's face appeared in hologram form hovering above Adella's station.

'Colonel, is that you?'

'Yes, I am still the only Arthian in this detachment, Commander. Troop ship *Trojan* has suffered damage. I need to dock with your flagship and other vessels in Home Fleet to disperse people and lighten the load on *Trojan*'s environmental systems. I am sending you the file of suggested ships and Legion personnel, now.'

Adella received the file and ran it through her board. 'Colonel, your personnel offload solely seems to comprise combat troops and your vessel dispersal list only contains ships previously judged rebellious and sent security detachments on Rear Admiral Pullinger's orders.'

'There's probably an algorithm on board *Trojan* that finds it logical such ships would enjoy a reinforced peace-keeping presence,' said Colonel Pes.

'Also, I'm fairly sure it's *Trojan*'s Staging Area that took a hit, not your environmental systems.'

'Ironically, I believe *Trojan*'s damage control system was itself damaged. Our node reporting is undoubtedly faulty. Kindly disregard *Trojan*'s data output until we fix it.'

'The universe loves irony, Colonel. Please dock soonest with *Dark Viking* and we'll happily accommodate a large number of your legionnaires. Will they be carrying weapons and kit?'

'Marching order is the only order the External Legion understands.'

'Of course.'

***

It was amazing how quickly the fight vanished from Pullinger's Paper-pushers when the External Legion's soldiers arrived to help police the Fleet. Like all good bullies everywhere, when confronted with the prospect of a hard slapping by someone who could deal it out on a professional basis, the Paper-pushers folded so fast the battleship's brig couldn't accommodate the number of surrendering personnel. A temporary receiving area had to be set up inside the thick walls of the same environmental chamber recently holding the Dark Viking's recalcitrant crew.

Where clumps of holdouts with delusions of grandeur or true believers in Pullinger's political connections and ability to survive any reversal hung on – all evidence to the contrary notwithstanding – the legionnaires went through the personnel like a chainsaw through butter. Naval staff who'd spent decades writing reports on base development proposals down in the Sandpit – and whose last boarding action had been Academy sims – versus killers with lifetimes fighting insurgents, revolutionaries, terrorists and criminal gangs across hundreds of colony worlds – and had probably run with many of the same mobs before being given the choice of prison or Legion service.

It was a pit fight with kittens against tigers. Adella Vega found herself outside Rear Admiral Pullinger's cabin with the head of the pride – Colonel Scolar Pes – and half a dozen white-armoured Legion veterans hugging heavy rail-rifles.

A muffled voice sounded on the other side of the door. 'This is mutiny!'

'My verdict precisely.' *All we differ about is who should stand in dock listening to charges read.*

A couple of ill-aimed shots thumped through the locked portal, a rail-pistol dialled up to max. An officer should set their sidearms lower to avoid breaching the hull. *Another charge for Pullinger's rap-sheet.*

'Are you sure you want to take him alive?' asked Scolar Pes with a resigned tone that suggested she already knew the answer to that question.

'The Admiralty's court-martial process does require the presence of a charged individual to work,' said Adella.

'Lawyers,' sighed the Colonel; she signalled her troops. 'Hostage protocol.'

One legionnaire set a case on the deck and opened it. A cluster of eight hand-grenade-sized spheres lay inside. Each device grew two pairs of legs and trotted out of the canister and into the corridor. Soldiers took up position on either side of the entrance into the Rear Admiral's quarters. The globes established a v-formation outside the door, ignoring shots thudding through the metal far above them. A variety of hologram icons formed, one above each sphere – skull and crossbones wearing a gas-mask, flashing bomb icons, rotating pistol, a vertical arrow pointing towards an explosion burst – while they repeatedly chattered mantras.

'I am a nerve-gas grenade. I am a nerve-gas grenade.'

'I am a jumping shrapnel mine. I am a jumping shrapnel mine.'

'I am a combined thunderclap and sonic disruptor. I am a combined thunderclap and sonic disruptor.'

'I am micro-pellet sniper. I am micro-pellet sniper.'

'Jelly rounds,' barked the Colonel. Her legionnaires adjusted ammo-drums on their rifles, converting the deadly flechette darts to non-lethal riot-rounds. High impact and packed with a synthetic cnidarian invertebrate poison based on a Box Jellyfish, you might end up wishing you'd actually been decapitated by a flechette.

A legionnaire ran a bypass on the door controls. He raised black-gloved fingers and began dropping digits in a countdown. *Three. Two. One. Zero.*

The locked door hissed open and the loudly chattering spheres raced in through a fusillade aimed too high to strike them. They scattered as they advanced. With the grenades leaping and cavorting around the quarters, drawing Pullinger's fire, a sphere proclaiming it was a thunderclap detonated in a burst of searing light. A deafening rippling explosion shook the deck. The legionnaires immediately flooded in from both sides of the corridor, rifles blazing. A series of wet slaps on full-auto as the guns sawed riot-rounds across the walls and furniture and – as a high-pitched scream indicated – the Rear Admiral, too.

'Clear!' yelled a soldier from inside.

Adella and the Colonel entered the cabin. Six grenades trotted proudly back out through Adella's legs like a line of bizarre robot pets, only one grenade spent. The cabin's interior looked as if debt-collectors had waded through it with baseball bats, furniture broken, scattered and demolished. Rear Admiral Pullinger appeared no better off, shoved to the floor on his front; glaring, wrists secured behind his back with security ties. His body swollen even below his uniform. Weals scarred his face and hands where riot-rounds had smashed him off his feet and hurled him across the cabin. His features had turned green, a bio-dye marker introduced into the rounds' poison to mark out troublemakers for arrest post-riot. It'd be a few days before the officer returned to his normal shade of irritated purple.

'Rear Admiral Pullinger, you are relieved of command and are to be held for Court-Martial pending charges including hazarding the fleet, war crimes against civilian Alliance vessels, and failing to obey the chain of command's written orders.'

'I'll finish you,' spat Pullinger, his words made near intelligible by the paralysis of half his face.

Adella knelt down by the officer so there would be no miscommunication of intent between them. She ripped the braid off his blues. 'You dishonour that uniform, Pullinger. You'll wear it without insignia until a tribunal makes it official. You abandoned my sister to die along with the Combined Fleet you stole from me, just because she discovered you concealing Admiral Blackstar's orders. You're a barely capable coward who isn't fit to command a garbage scow without your family pulling political strings. By the time the Alliance's finished hearing about your misconduct, your name will become Fleet slang for a Naval Screw-up for the next thousand years. That's your legacy, you incompetent glory-hunting piece of shit.' She turned to Scolar Pes. 'Colonel, escort the prisoner to the brig. Double his guard, remove his belt and place him on a full suicide watch. He's going to live long enough to see the ruin of his name.'

'You're finished in the Fleet, you bitch. You'll end up as dead as your sister!'

Colonel Pes watched her legionnaires lift the officer and drag the man cursing out of the cabin. 'He'll try to make trouble for you at home. His family, too…'

Adella shrugged. 'As soon as the first civilian ship hits a working corner of the data-sphere and the passengers and crew upload their logs, the media will do the Admiralty's job for them. There'll be no hushing up Pullinger's crimes or his loss of Combined Fleet.'

'The trick will be to ensure we arrive back home, then.'

'That's the plan.'

But low on fuel and nearly out of ordnance, damned if Commander Vega knew how to guarantee it.

- 25 -

All The Hurts

Adella took her shore leave on Big Gienah, a close-Earth twin inside the Gienah Cygni system. She rested on the beach watching a group of anglers set up lines around the rocks along the bay's edge. Adella closed her eyes and listened to the waves' slow rhythm lapping against the brown sugar-coloured sands. Kite-sized butterflies drifted serenely above the sea, Big Gienah trademark native species, collecting the sun using organic solar-panels across their wingspan.

Eskandar emerged dripping from the ocean and minimised his scuba-breather and mask to the size of a child's flipflop. 'You look concerned, *Hayaati*?'

'I'm still worried about Home Fleet,' whispered Adella. She took her husband's hand and helped him sit down on the towel next to her lounger. 'We have a navigator able to translate straight to Core inside hyperspace, but we're bingo fuel and lack meaningful ordnance for defence. We can't possibly clear the Frontier before we are overrun and rolled up by the enemy.'

'You'll find a way, you always do.'

'No-one else believes in me like you.'

'Nobody else knows you like I do, *Ruuhi*. When you get home, resign your commission and let me set you up with a job at Cunard-Kang. Our liners might not have the guns, but we surely do have better views on our layovers.'

'It won't be the same without you.'

Adella's husband pointed out one of the fishermen on the rocks. 'Ask that old hound, then. He seems to think he has all the angles figured out.'

Adella pulled herself out of her sun lounger, working the kinks out of her bones before strolling over to the spit. The fisherman glanced around when he heard her padding through the beach's sand. It was Admiral Blackstar. He appeared out of place in a garish short-sleeved pineapple print shirt and red shorts.

'Eskandar seems to think you've got all the answers, Admiral.'

'Hah, your husband would say that. All I have for you, Commander, are better questions for you to ask.'

'Would they be about fuel and our desperate lack thereof?'

'Finding fuel was only ever a short-term fix. Figure out superior questions, Commander. You've got a Lucky Gene navigator, but he's only a single man.'

'I know that,' protested Adella.

'Then you understand that even if the Alliance hunts down every Comet Person clan from here to Prima Giedi and pressgangs, drafts and bribes their navigators into Fleet, there's still not enough of their kind to go around. Not sufficient to turn the war in our favour.'

Adella frowned. 'I'm not in the pressganging business.'

'Neither was I, Commander, but needs must. Say sorry to Calder Durk from me when you see him. It was nice to have my dead nephew briefly back from the grave, if only as a sim-construct. You've fought multiple engagements against the Quazzies. You've even taken one as a prisoner. You know it's not a war we're fighting so much as an extinction event. The Alliance makes room for every species that wants to integrate with us, ignoring those that wish to be left alone. But the Quazzies? Ask your semi-feral Fergal. The Quazalrat system is a three-tier pyramid with Quazzies at the apex, then their slaves, then their food. And the distinction between the bottom two tiers is rather blurred at best.'

'I'm simply trying to lead the Home Fleet to safety.'

'That requires a surviving home front for you to reach, Commander. The Quazzies' ability to cast a sensor net in hyperspace, to erase g-folds and jam our QT comms beacons; it's all advanced gravity manipulation using Heezy legacy tech. But *their* War-Wheels can navigate normally in hyperspace. They can track us through it, too. What does that tell you?'

'The quality of my questions...'

'Gravity's the clue. Use it to your advantage, harness it, and also ask yourself why I put you in charge of Combined Fleet.'

'To get your fake nephew home so the Alliance's Heezy artifacts would have a trigger man to fire them?'

'No. Because you're a wildcard. That's the only hand left to play that might just win this game.'

An idea slowly stirred in Adella's head. She caught it and kept the slippery fish tightly clasped. 'I think I know what to do, sir.'

'You always did,' said Blackstar. 'You're hard-charging, reckless, and an insubordinate loose cannon to boot. Time for you to slice your rigging and run over the Devil Frogs' feet. Damned if they'll like it any better than I did.'

I think I know what to do. Adella waved towards the beach, but her husband had gone. Same as her dream.

***

The trials of the near-death experience on their last jump-out had taken their toll on Uddin Cesti. The merchant captain appeared tired and he'd lost weight, a common function of irregular meals on a combat station. Adella wondered if she looked any better to her crew right now?

'Mr. Cesti, your concerns could have been aired over a secure comm.'

The man waved her words away as though swatting a fly. 'Regardless, I have a vane compressor module to collect from your engineering team for the *Shamash*. What the civilian captains have asked me to share with you are their concerns rather than my own.'

Adella indicated the system map in the bridge's central holo projection well. Their current position. Zuben Elschemali, one of the Eastern Frontier's least frequented star systems – and with good reason, as this corner of the galaxy's nickname hinted. *Satan's Sieve*. 'Your "friends" should be familiar with Satan's Sieve, Mr. Cesti, given how many smugglers duck in here to shake off Fleet pursuits.'

There were seventeen black holes in the vicinity, and while the Zuben Elschemali system possessed none of those phenomena, the trinary star system held both a neutron star and a magnetar as well as a single standard yellow star. Those nearby black holes and the two dead stars' distortions erased g-folds and inhibited navigation as effectively as the Quazzies' resurrected Heezy technology. *What's sauce for the goose is sauce for the gander*. Between the gravitational lensing of the nearby black holes and the electromagnetic output of the neutron star and magnetar, Home Fleet's long-range sensors – and more importantly, the enemies' – operated as good as blind. *And we need every second of that time to stay undiscovered in this system for as long as possible.*

Zuben Elschemali's two dead stars, Zuben N and Zuben M, spun around each other in a paired hierarchical two-body dance, with the yellow star, Zuben Live, gravitationally bound to the dead pair on a dynamically stable outer orbit. Zuben Live possessed ten worlds, numbered ZL-1 to ZL-10 on the system catalogue as they counted out from the yellow star. The system's circimtrinary asteroid belt proved so extensive – its mass fed by destroyed planets from Zuben N and M's stellar collapse – that it received its own designation as ZL-11. Home Fleet had set up shop around ZL-6, the system's large gas giant; all the better to receive fuel off their refinery ship as the *Spacewise Giant*'s ram-scoop divers worked their way through ZL-6's thick rich atmosphere.

Uddin Cesti appeared unconvinced by Vega's arguments. 'Our skippers are mostly free-traders, not smugglers, and they share the common spacer's superstitions about entering Satan's Sieve. If Home Fleet didn't possess a Lucky Gene navigator, half of my ships wouldn't have followed you to Zuben Elschemali at all, Commander. They would have scattered and fled rather than dare risk the horrors of the void. Too many vessels have disappeared in this area of space without adequate explanation,'

'They're about to share in the bounty of Zuben Elschemali's largest gas planet, Mr. Cesti. Full fuel tanks will lift their morale and take their mind off a handful of frivolous ghost stories?' *Yes, just as soon as the* Spacewise Giant *finishes running her ramscoops and refinery. Not to mention the* Takasaki *stripping every asteroid bigger than a football to churn out fresh tacks, missiles, and other essentials for us.*

'We've already been in orbit around this ugly gas giant for days,' said the trader. 'We're overstaying our welcome.'

Uddin Cesti had a point, but then he wasn't privy to Adella's plans. If he knew what she was actually about in this strange messed-up corner of the galaxy, he'd probably jump for Core and damn the fuel reserves of his *Shamash*. 'Home Fleet needs to patch up and reload, Captain Cesti. This is our last sure chance.'

'Perhaps something to distract our people, dear Commander? Are you sure you can't put Rear Admiral Pullinger on trial?'

'Nothing would give me greater pleasure, but given the circumstances, he has to face a full board of inquiry at SecComm Core.' *Anything else will look like a Kangaroo Court on the sharp end of a mutiny. I want to see Pullinger's reputation burn under the glare of the media, not be spun as some peccadillo his family and friends can cover up.*

'If the positions were reversed, I suspect justice would be served in a far more summary manner.'

'Which,' said Adella, 'makes my point as eloquently as any tribunal.'

'A pity.'

'A full tank of gas shall have to do, Mr. Cesti. It's what I have to offer, along with vane compressor modules and Fleet ration packs.'

'Please urge haste on your refinery and factory ship crews, Commander. The longer we dally here, the greater the chance the Quazalrats will discover we backtracked within the Frontier rather than fleeing deeper inside Alliance space.'

Adella suddenly realised the estimable Uddin Cesti was as unsettled as any of his free-trader captains. *Does the man actually believe the tales? More fool him if he does. We've got enough real hazards with a full-scale invasion to worry about. I don't require ghost ships and void dwelling monsters as enemies, not with an actual armada of Devil Frogs hunting me down.* 'Satan's Sieve may come with mess-hall jump-scare stories, but this sector's giving us a fighting chance for a straight run home.'

'You gave the enemy a bloody nose at Bardfeld's System and then slipped their noose at Tuinstra's Star where they meant for you to hang. You've proved yourself a threat twice over, Commander, and the Quazalrats doesn't seem to be a species capable of tolerating threats.'

'Then let's pray that Satan's Sieve scares the Devil Frogs as much as it seems to spook our civilians.'

'One more matter, Commander,' said the free-trader. 'Fleet's engineers have been installing specialist docking clamps on our ships' hulls. The civilian Captains are mystified why this should he necessary?'

'You're shipping with Fleet, Mr. Cesti, I thought it was about time we harmonised our civilian vessels across a few standards.'

'We're proud independents, Commander. To us it feels like a rustler's broken into the ranch at night and branded our cattle.'

'Was the work done on the *Shamash* somehow substandard?'

'I'm sure it's of the highest quality, just as I'm sure it's entirely superfluous.'

Lieutenant Anders signalled Adella from the corner of her eye. 'Apologies, Commander. You requested to be informed when the *Feynman's* crew successfully evacuated to *Dark Viking*.'

Feynman Station was the only inhabited presence inside Zuben Elschemali system – a thirty-person laboratory in shielded orbit around ZL-3 studying the unique area and grouping of nearby black holes. 'Thank you, Lieutenant. Show the science station's crew to their quarters onboard. After they've settled in, bring their head of station to astrogation for a debriefing on local system topology.'

'But one studies system topology before a battle,' noted the slippery merchant skipper.

'*Semper paratus*, Mr. Cesti. Hope for the best but prepare for the worst.'

'Just as long as you're not hoping for the worst and preparing to make the best of it, dear Commander.'

'Perish the thought.'

'Also, permission requested to receive a shuttle off the *Neutron Dance*?' added the Lieutenant.

'Granted. Have a marine escort meet their boat inside the hangar. I'll see them there.'

It was a toss-up whether Ossian Joyce or Fergal the Devil Frog would try to jump ship first. Adella didn't know how much Quazalrat was left of the brainwashed creature, but she'd sure as hell drag it to interrogation to find out.

***

The Dark Viking's bolt-on carrier hangar busied with the hectic business of prepping Home Fleet. Shuttles unloading supplies or taking stores on, cargo robots stomping around craft and hooking containers, lifting the large crates onto rails running back into the battleship's cargo holds. Fleet boats, all blocky combat lines, as well as a plethora of civilian craft with as many manufacturers and designs as there were craft inside the landing bay.

Uddin Cesti supervised the loading of his new jump vane compressor, four large cargo robots manhandling it inside his ferry's hold. Adella waited with a marine detachment for the *Neutron Dance*'s shuttle. It drifted in slow from the void, riding anti-grav assists and guided into place by an escort of tiny pilot drones. A ramp lowered from its stern after the shuttle set down, Ossian Joyce emerging with Fergal as expected – the next two crew walking down the ramp rather less anticipated by her. *Calder Durk and Alice? What the hell is going on here?*

'We had a deal,' Commander Vega trotted up to the spacer. *And having an Air-Space Arm Colonel posted missing on the* Smiter *jumping out of a shuttle and strolling around is surely stretching it.*

'Alice didn't want Fergal coming here alone,' explained Calder.

Adella's marine detachment surrounded the Quazalrat, drawing themselves straight and making themselves as imposing as possible under their light impact armour. The alien wore a set of baggy multi-coloured clothes fabbed in artificial silks and cottons. As if the creature couldn't look any more bizarre or out of place in the hangar. Commander Vega wondered how much design input the daughter of the *Gravity Rose*'s skipper had with Fergal playing dress-up. 'Jesus, if your kid needs a pet, we could have arranged a kitten from one of Fleet's cats.'

'It was a flip of a coin whether Fergal would leave the ship without Alice as it was.'

'Maybe you'd like your girl to attend the thing's interrogation, too?'

'You said Fergal only had to answer a few questions,' accused Alice.

'That's just how Fleet people speak,' Calder assured the young girl.

'It's how the Bad Fleet always talk,' said Alice, glaring at Adella and her party of bulky armed and armoured marines. 'I remember the Bad Fleet.'

Every time the child spoke like that she sent a shiver down Adella's spine. *What's the matter with her? Heck, what's the matter with me?* 'We're Hell-Fleet on the float inside Satan's Sieve with a Devil Frog, kid. Take the hint.' She signalled her Marine Sergeant, indicating Ossian Joyce: the navigator currently trying to use the distraction to slip away. He scuttled towards the open rear of a boat loading cargo on the hangar's far side. 'Grab up that fly gentleman, Sergeant. Ensure he reports to Master of the Helm Beklum Sakwa for compulsory enrolment and induction into the Fleet.'

'You won't hurt Fergal,' insisted Alice. 'I won't let you.'

'That depends on the attitude of your friend, here, I'd say.'

'I am fine pirate, righty-ho,' growled Fergal. 'Loyal and fine.'

And I used to be Queen of the Pirate Hunters. 'So many contradictions right there,' said Adella. 'It's your old life I need to have a "chat" with you about, my Quazalrat chum. Not your new career out a-plundering across the deep void. Shall we…'

They were about to exit the chamber when the last person she wanted to meet on the ship stepped into the hangar. *Doctor Delorey*!

'I was informed the Interrogation Centre was about to be activated. Now I see why.'

'Are you an expert in Quazalrat interrogation techniques, Doctor?'

'I–' the Doctor suddenly realised who stood behind her marine escort. 'You! What's the meaning of this, Commander…?' Delorey raised a trembling finger towards Calder Durk while the crewman physically bridled at seeing Delorey again. Adella appreciated how much effort it took Calder not to lay hands on his ex-handler.

Adella decided to play the innocent card. 'I'm not sure I follow you, Doctor?'

'Colonel Blackstar was posted missing-in-action on board the *Smiter*!'

'Indeed, the poor Colonel was. This gentleman is Calder Durk, a free-trader who valiantly helped secure our Quazalrat prisoner, here. Mr. Durk's records are perfectly in order, or he wouldn't be allowed on board the *Dark Viking*. I can't see why you would confuse the Admiral's dead nephew with a civilian spacer, Doctor? Is there any reason why such a confusion might arise?' *Like maybe you're a stooge freelancing for a dangerous BlackOps unit that countenances kidnapping, pressganging and brainwashing civilians?*

Doctor Delorey bit his tongue. 'Of course not, Commander.'

'We don't require you in the Interrogation Centre, today, Doctor. This will be a casual interview, not questioning where I need a medic to warn me before our prisoner is about to expire.' *Which I'm certain you would prove surprisingly adept at for a so-called physician.*

Adella flashed a false smile at the snake before she and her escort put the busy hangar bay behind them. She moved close enough to Calder to guarantee discretion. 'You should never have come back.'

Calder glanced coldly down the corridor, before whispering, 'That bastard won't be a problem.'

'Colonel Blackstar posted missing in action is one thing, but you *and* Delorey…?'

'We're at war. People die.'

'Don't let him discover Alice is your daughter,' Adella quietly warned. 'Anyone asks, the kid's a refugee you picked up from an overrun system.'

Calder glanced back towards the girl. She was accompanied by Fergal as though the Quazzie was her pet. 'Alice?'

'Your Heezy operator's gene; it's hereditary, isn't it?'

Calder grimaced. 'Yes.'

Adella had the feeling there was something the spacer wasn't telling her, but she let it ride. 'Then she's a waif and stray, adopted, not blood. Between the Alliance's spooks and the Devil Frogs, I think we already have enough problems to handle on board, don't you?'

'Okay.'

Commander Vega watched Alice passing through the ship, oblivious to the danger she was in. *Bad Fleet. Damned if the kid hasn't got a point.*

***

Back inside the hangar, Uddin Cesti watched the Marine guards leave, followed by the obviously fuming Doctor Delorey a minute later. Maryam Harb, Cesti's First Mate had also viewed the altercation every bit as silently as the merchant captain. When the Doctor exited the chamber, the First Mate reached for her communications tablet and its secure encrypted connection back to the Shamash.

Uddin activated his implant's privacy mode. <No need to double check, Maryam. Blessed be, but that one is the Prime Target. I've carried his biometric profile in this body's ID cache for two years.>

<If the Alliance Fleet risked bringing Durk to activate their Heezy weaponry it means they've found no other operators with the ancients' gene.>

Cesti pretended to pay attention to the jump vane compressor loading onto their ferry. <We always suspected Calder Durk was the last of his kind. His value is now inestimable.>

<We need to grab Durk and depart this hellish system before battle commences.>

<Agreed,> confirmed Cesti. After all, *that* was exactly the sort of mission a Unity infiltration ship had been designed for.

Maryam shifted about nervously on her feet. Cesti briefly wondered what the woman had looked like before she occupied her current body? Nothing like this, certainly. When Unity members' consciousness downloaded into infiltration forms they never resembled their original bodies. They didn't even possess the same DNA. Too much danger Alliance systems would flag agents as someone presumed deceased centuries ago. An obvious signal that the Unity's secret police were playing the Great Game again. Perhaps Maryam had been a Devil Frog, before? That was unlikely. Uddin Cesti could read the body language when alien consciousnesses downloaded into human-cloned forms. There were subtleties concerning such matters and Uddin was all about the subtleties.

<Main Core has a number of exit routes plotted,> reported Maryam, consulting her link to the *Shamash.* <If we secure Prime Target, switch the ship to stealth mode and boost for the North ecliptic pole there's a suitable window arriving clear of pulsar interference. We can form a clean singularity and be inside hyperspace before Home Fleet's able to catch up with the *Shamash.*>

Uddin Cesti grinned at the irony. <Things could work out very well for us. Let the Quazalrats and the Alliance battle each other to extinction or exhaustion, while we expand over both their territories using our cache of Heezy weapons.> *Ah, Calder Durk. Specialist Resources has hunted you across half the universe, and here you are, all mine. My prize. My fate.* <Transmit Doctor Delorey's face and voice file to the ship and run it through our Tier Six files for a match. I have a feeling about that one.>

<Done. Shall I activate the lure?> asked the First Mate.

<Yes, do,> ordered Uddin. Time that the spare body hidden inside the *Shamash*'s hold was filled with the consciousness carefully loaded inside Unity space.

He switched to voice for the benefit of security cameras in the hangar bay. 'First Mate, take a look at our jump vane compressor, it has the wrong bloody interface connector! That thing is designed for a bulk carrier twice our size.'

'My apologies, Captain, I must have mixed up our own supply request with that of the *Starbulk Pride*. Her captain put a similar order in through us.'

'You are an idiot,' grumbled Cesti. <An idiot who has just won us the time to implement our extraction plan. Ensure our next ferry here contains suitable operators in stealth and combat bodies.> *We're about to burn our cover.*

<An idiot who's just received a positive match on the Doctor,> sent back the First Mate. <His real name is Eron Falsih, a physician and consultant torturer with the Alliance's Collection Centre Directorate.>

<Ah, it's been a while since I had to deal with the Alliance's CCD agents; they're rare beasts.> *Not least because the Triple Alliance doesn't even admit to their existence.* <Let's see if we can't use the agent to our advantage, too.>

Maryam bowed. 'Captain, I shall do better next time.'

'I expect nothing less.'

Nobody in the Triple Alliance realised it yet, but it had been Unity expansion on the far side of the Quazalrat Imperium poking the aliens into direct action. To Quazzies, all humans and allied Alliance species looked alike. Another irony, then. For after you went virtual inside the Unity's network of planet-sized data cores and embraced their Holy Digital Immortality, all organics left behind seemed much the same, too.

Eminently disposable mayflies.

***

Calder and Alice bided their time outside the Interrogation Centre, watching through the viewing window's one-way glass, the Marine sentries a brooding presence to their rear. Calder's brainwashed memories – an entire false existence as Colonel Blackstar – still present enough to know the IC was normally reserved for more prosaic crew psych evals.

Commander Vega opened the door, her interview with the half-insane Quazzie concluded. She'd switched the audio on the room to silent so Calder couldn't overhear her line of questioning, but at least Alice could see the Commander hadn't water-boarded the Quazzie. Given its species' swamp-based origins, Fergal would probably mistake water-boarding as a bribe to cooperate.

'I'm done for now,' said Commander Vega.

'For *now*?' said Calder, suspiciously.

'We're almost guaranteed to face enemy action before we reach home. Your Devil Frog that thinks it's Long John Silver has agreed to serve as our bridge's official Quazzie combat consultant.'

'No!' protested Alice. 'Fergal has to come back with us.'

Commander Vega shook her head. 'Look, kid, I appreciate you've taken to the thing and it's accepted you, but your pet will be a hell of a lot more protected on board a battleship than inside your tin can of a free-trader. Not to mention more productively employed ensuring everyone's survival.'

'Safer on the *Gravity Rose*,' insisted Alice. 'It's always safer there. I'm not leaving your Bad Fleet ship unless Fergal does.'

Calder knew better than arguing with his daughter in this mood, as much as ditching the drafted creature with the Fleet seemed an ideal solution for weaning Alice off the alien's company and breaking the unholy bond they'd formed.

'Talk some sense into the kid, why don't you,' said Commander Vega, shaking her head. 'I need to meet with the boss of Zuben Elschemali's science station. If you're not gone when I finish, you can both bunk in your shuttle and throw rodents into Long John Silver's quarters come feeding time. The *Dark Viking*'s quarter-armour will shield you for free and let's see what your ship's precious Captain Fiveworlds thinks of that.' Vega waved at her marines. 'Put our guest in the spare cabin on Deck Three. Sentries outside.'

Calder watched Adella stride away. You could never accuse her of not knowing her mind. He felt a pang of longing for the officer despite himself. Damn the woman and damn the man that Hell-Fleet had tried to make him into.

'The Commander thinks Fergal's one of the enemy,' said Calder, taking Alice to one side, hoping against hope he could convince her to leave Fergal to the Fleet's good graces. 'Fergal hasn't attacked any of us yet on board the *Gravity Rose*, but that's because he's confused about who really he is. Just like when the Fleet grabbed me and made me think I was their Admiral's dead nephew. That confusion makes Fergal dangerous.'

'But *you* got better. And Fergal's super dangerous because he's a Quazalrat,' said Alice, 'not because he's confused. They're the best soldiers and sailors in the Alliance.'

'No. His worlds are fighting the Alliance,' explained Calder, as gently as possible.

'Not this Alliance. The real Alliance,' sighed Alice.

Calder groaned. Every time he forgot Alice's strange origins from an alternative universe, she had a habit of bringing him back to reality – *this* reality, as well as the weirdness of her previous dimension. 'So, the Triple Alliance includes the Quazzies in your universe?'

'Don't use that rude word, father. And it isn't the Triple Alliance, it's the Alliance of Four. I know we can trust Fergal. His people protected me at home. You and mother as well. Until all the worlds were gone.'

'Protected us from … what?'

'They're not here,' said Alice. She didn't voice the *yet* but left it hanging unsaid. 'That's why you and mother sent me here to find you. It's safer here.'

Not precisely how I'd describe matters right now. 'Yeah, well, lots of things are different here. Fergal's people aren't our friends and allies, for one.'

'You can convince Commander Vega to let Fergal go with us,' wheedled Alice. 'She likes you.'

'What makes you say that?'

'I can just tell,' said Alice.

Yeah, well, don't remind Lana. Matters were difficult enough on that front as it was. Nothing dampened a budding romance like discovering your counterparts had fathered a kid together in a parallel reality, then finding yourself pressganged and brainwashed before you'd even worked out all the kinks in the unrequested child-rearing department.

***

Doctor Delorey fumed inside the medical bay commandeered for his exclusive use. A brief glimpse of salvation when he realised that Calder Durk was still alive; the ice clear thought of not reporting back to his unforgiving superiors the sole key to the Alliance's ancient super-weapons perished on his watch. Then, his only chance at redemption snatched away from him by Commander Vega. It was unconscionable to be stymied by her. A washout exiled to SecComm East daring to think she could derail the Alliance's best venture for surviving a war for survival against the Quazalrat. Well, if Vega'd been capable of higher-level game theory, no doubt she would never have ended up scrapped at the butt-end of known space.

Delorey sat at his desk, inspecting deck plans and scheming. *Yes, it should be possible.* His CCD overrides allowed him to go wherever he needed on board a Fleet warship, the original all-access back-stage pass. With Rear Admiral Pullinger languishing in the brig and the more reliable of the man's supporters confined inside an armoured recycling chamber, Delorey had a ready-made crew who would undoubtedly prove more pliable and far-sighted than the Commander. Particularly if compliance with the CCD's mission objectives led to their freedom and exoneration from a court-martial. A few strategically sealed vacuum doors, a beeline for the armoury, the *Dark Viking*'s marines locked in their quarters, and the battleship would be his. Delorey didn't need to take Home Fleet, just the *Dark Viking*. The ragtag civilians could flee and scatter. Calder Durk was the only prize worth seizing in this corner of space.

Sadly for the Doctor, he wasn't the only one on board the warship with a plan involving considerable risk. He snatched open the door when he heard an unexpected knock against it.

Delorey was uncertain who he'd been expecting, but certainly not *this* – the merchant vessel's spokesperson, Uddin Cesti, supporting a spacer clutching a wounded arm.

'Doctor,' called the Captain, pushing his way into the room, 'my crewman's caught his arm inside our shuttle ramp!'

'The sickbay is on deck four, this is a genetics research bay,' huffed Delorey.

'Please,' insisted Cesti, dragging the hurt crewman forward, 'he's bleeding out and needs attention now.'

'Nonsense,' said Delorey. 'This man's in no danger. A second to clean the cut and a dose of wound-spray and the fellow will be back on duty within the hour. All surgical nano is stored and issued downstairs, I don't hold pharmaceuticals here.'

It was only when the door to the room shut that Delorey realised a third merchanteer had followed the first two inside. 'I am not a General Practitioner, out, all of you!'

'Your bedside manner needs a little work,' said Uddin Cesti.

Doctor Delorey felt a sharp pain in his neck as something cold and heavy closed around it. He tried to raise a hand to feel what it was, but his limbs had gone numb and didn't seem able to respond. It was as though they had frozen him in stone.

'You needn't worry, Doctor, you'll have all of eternity to perfect those manners as part of the Unity. But first, you will help us survive the coming storm. Don't fight the control band, it's growing up into your brainstem and copying your memories. When it finally comes time to abandon your body, you won't even miss it, a butterfly flying away from your broken chrysalis.'

***

'Commander Vega, thank you for making the effort to evacuate my staff and myself,' said Professor Marie Mead brushing back her silver hair as she entered the battleship's astrogation centre. Mead looked like she was towards the end of her second century, life extension treatments holding the advance of her face's wrinkles to her late sixties. Spry for it, all the same. She obviously had few vanities, choosing to wear old-fashioned spectacles rather than replacement eyes.

Adella shook the station head's proffered hand. 'The pleasure is all mine, Professor. How abreast are you on the Triple Alliance's present perilous state of affairs?'

'We received a partial data-sphere sync from a passing vessel, the *Phobetor*, a few months ago. We already knew something was awry when we missed four supply runs in a row. I requested evacuation from the *Phobetor*, but the ship was packed with refugees and running close to breaking point under creaking environmental systems. That data squirt was all she could do for us.'

'Hopefully, the *Dark Viking* will prove far more resilient, Professor. And talking of resilience, I need a complete system and sector topology from you. Up to now, I've only read Fleet background reports about Satan's Sieve. This region seems unique.'

'It *is* unique, Commander. The place has been my life's study, and it's still mostly defined by what we *don't* know about this area of space. So many black holes in such close proximity, yet they have never closed up and formed a single super-massive singularity? Then there's Zuben Elschemali at the sector's centre, a trinary system containing two dead stars with a third in main sequence that possesses a beating heartbeat? Was Zuben Live and its planets captured by Zuben N and M after they went supernova? The pair emit greater high-energy emissions than should be feasible considering their age and accessible reservoir created by their loss of rotation force. None of it matches with what we understand about cosmological and stellar evolution, Chandrasekhar limits, orbital dynamics and stellar remnants. Frankly, nothing about our corner of the galaxy should exist as it does. Spacers call this region Satan's Sieve, but it is we astronomers and astrophysicists who are left with a devil of a time explaining its existence.'

Adella brought up the system's Fleet NavMap inside the astrogation centre, remaking the chamber as a miniature planetarium with hologram void traced around them. 'My quest for knowledge is a little more prosaic, Professor. System and sector cartography. How entry and exit jump-lines and translation traces from hyperspace fall after being scrambled by your neutron star and magnetar. How those points rotate as the yellow sun orbits the dead star pairing; local birefringent vacuum effects, particle shocks, pulsar winds, starquakes and SGR emission flux. The nearby black holes' impact on sensors – long-range and close-up targeting disruption. Everything and anything you can give me, no detail too small. Hell, even throw in all your shaggy ghost stories about Satan's Sieve.'

'Do you believe in ghosts, Commander Vega?'

'I should do. One as good as told me to lead Home Fleet into your system to rearm and refuel.' *The quality of my questions…* but there was still a question Adella had yet to ask herself. *Am I totally insane to even be waiting here?*

The Professor talked, and Adella listened as though the fate of Home Fleet depended on her concentration. Which it might very well do.

- 26 -

Honour Them

Adella had designed a bespoke update protocol with Slugger for the Zuben Elschemali system. She was eating inside the battleship's mess when DV sounded General Quarters, then the A.I.'s Home Fleet dispositions hit her implant like bad digestion. The Commander winced between a mouthful of noodles and synthetic meat meant to imitate pork. Her mind spilled over with the location of every vessel – civilian or military – and the current state of their three Rs: rearmament, repairs, and refuelling. Ninety-two percent full on juice across the fleet, and they required eighty-three to reach Core. So, nine percent reserves left to expend in-system. Dark Viking's magazines packed so crammed, Adella could practically hear the rattle of iron as her ship slowly broke orbit from the gas giant. About as good as it got in this sailor's corner of Hell-Fleet.

All around Adella every member of the crew froze as they received similar updates relating to their duties. She didn't need the egg-timer symbols flashing across her people's augmented reality contact lens to appreciate their distraction. Crew abandoned meals as dozens of staff broke and sprinted to station; or in a few cases, scooped up food and ate on the hoof. Adella pushed her noodles away. She preferred an empty stomach when her chair armoured-up. Less chance of puking after Combat Cocktail Hour arrived.

Slugger's gravelly metallic warning echoed across the mess, chasing the alarm and final few crew out. 'General Quarters, General Quarters. All hands man your battle stations. The vector of thrust is up and forward on your starboard side, down and aft on your port side.'

The Quazzies had taken far longer to find the fleeing humans than the Commander had dared hope at her most optimistic. But then, running down anything in this broken corner of the galaxy wasn't exactly easy;

and hers had been a counter-intuitive move. Jumping deeper inside the Frontier rather than hightailing it for home. *How much do you know about Home Fleet, Mr. Frog? How much have you already guessed?*

Adella trusted the invaders hadn't cottoned on to the existence of her Lucky Gene Navigator, yet. Had the fleeing humans flown straight for Core until ships were sucking on fumes, the Quazzies would have quickly concluded that their disruption of hyperspace navigation wasn't quite as all-encompassing as they thought. Her Comet Person card was one Joker she needed to play to see them safely home. Mr. Frog expected to pursue a limping prey forced into short-hops across hyperspace, not a single long jump clean direct to Core. *Enemy dispositions across the Frontier will reflect that, pray God.* Dozens of alien squadrons waiting in ambush on system edges Home Fleet didn't need to touch. Tripwires to ring the dinner bell for the Quazzie invasion force to feed on their human foe. Sun Tzu's maxim jumped into her mind. "The supreme art of war is to subdue the enemy without fighting."

Well, we'll still have to shoot our way out of Zuben Elschemali. And this'll literally be the battle of our lives. Time to discover whether Fergal and Professor Mead's insights into our foe and local terrain are worth more than a hill of beans.

'Slugger,' said Adella, 'some good news about that software update?'

'Complete and installed across our warships, Commander,' said the ship's A.I. sounding well satisfied with beating its project deadline.

'Let's put the system to use, then.'

Commander Vega had broken standing orders, allowing Slugger to modify the Fleet's targeting systems for Zuben Elschemali's unique hostile environment; prioritising optics and lidar over radar and gravity sensors. You permitted an A.I to rewrite its own code and eventually it'd reach sentience and then you no longer had a battleship, you had 500,000 tons of truculent crewman which might unilaterally decide exploring the next galaxy over was a more interesting career choice than Fleet service. But only Slugger could change every line of code Adella required rewriting inside a week. Her engineering department would need half a year to make a working stab at the same task. If this became the worse sin the Commander committed before jumping out of Zuben Elschemali, she'd count herself lucky.

Adella reached the battleship's command deck in record speed. General Quarters made for a packed bridge at the best of times. Her Kaggen navigator, Beklum Sakwa, double-stationed alongside the Fleet's newest and most reluctant recruit, Ossian Joyce. Senior staff with duties elsewhere – Aralat raz Kessi, deep-shielded in the drive-room, as well as the Captains of Home Fleet's warships – maintained a telepresence on the bridge like so many hologram ghosts waiting for the battle.

Adella settled into her chair. 'How long did our QT buoys survive the enemy's arrival, Lieutenant Vistisen?'

'A little over seven seconds, Commander.'

Adella grunted. *There goes our realtime system view and unified situational awareness.* It had taken significant labour to scatter a working screen of QT satellites across Zuben Elschemali's system edge. Producing and assembling components on the factory ship *Takasaki*, then carefully ferrying buoys out and laying satellites in a spherical all-encompassing mesh. All that effort for seven spare seconds of realtime feedback on the invaders before they jammed the network with their damned Heezy plunder. 'Lay it out for us.'

Slugger pieced together the QT buoys' sensor readings in the bridge's central well, multiple levels of analysis which Adella slid back like curtains of data.

Adella smiled grimly for her crew's benefit. 'That's a fully marked dance card right there, ladies and gentlemen.'

Mr. Frog had arrived loaded for bear. Seven War-Wheels. One force carrier apiece exiting hyperspace to cover the system's floor and ceiling. The remaining five force carriers scattered around the ecliptic on the celestial equator. A system englobement formation, designed to surround and contain every Alliance vessel in-system until they could be located, hunted down and destroyed. Fleet's sparse few seconds of QT coverage included satellite imagery of each War-Wheel unleashing hordes of Lancers, Shield-ships and Scouts into the void. The War-Wheels on the ecliptic were positioned at five of the 60 degree points on a 360-degree circuit of the celestial equator. As if by some miracle, no Quazzie force carrier had jumped in at the 60-degree point of the equator nearest the gas giant selected by Home Fleet for its refuelling orbit.

'Do you believe in luck, Helm Master?' asked Adella.

'Luck never gives; it only lends what the Creator has to give,' said the Kaggen navigator.

'A Quazzie battle group jumping in at every corner of the system, yet here's a gaping hole in the net they've cast just begging us to swim through it – and that hole also happens to be on our closest escape vector, too.'

'Let's not be looking a gift horse in the mouth,' insisted Ossian Joyce. 'Boost for that big beautiful gap and I'll have us out of Satan's Sieve and snug in hyperspace faster than a proton inside a solar storm.'

'This horse isn't of the *gift* variety, helmsman, it's of the *Trojan*. I have it on good authority that a full Quazalrat battlegroup comprises eleven War-Wheels. There're another four War-Wheels squatting in hyperspace, planning to drop down on us on the hour it'll take Home Fleet to boost for system edge. The first seven War-Wheels are beaters aiming to chase us onto their hunters' guns.'

'But that's still the closest space to spin up a jump singularity,' protested Ossian. 'How would the Devil Frogs know where to create a flush point to ambush us, anyway?'

'Quazzies are descended from swamp-based ambush predators, Mr. Joyce. They favour an ancient tactic which translates as *Silent Eyes*; crocodiles submerged in a river masquerading as logs. In our enemy's modern iteration, that's a camouflaged long-range astronomy scope dropped into deep space far outside the system's gravity well. It sits there disguised as stellar debris long enough to pick up light from the system, before drip-feeding intel on the enemy back to their hunters. We've been in orbit restocking for the best part of a week around ZL-6. Time for the light on our telemetry to filter out beyond Zuben Elschemali and give Mr. Frog a confirmed read on our position.'

Lord knows, Adella had tried to make it easy for the Imperium. Bunching her ships. Keeping everyone orbiting the gas giant apart from a few specialists mining the asteroid belt and laying their now-useless QT comms.

'They're the dirtiest devils in Satan's Sieve, alright,' grinned Ossian.

'The shortest road is rarely the safest,' said Adella, stepping out of her command chair. 'Slugger, trim system view to enemy dispositions only and then overlay Professor Mead's astrophysics topology across current deployment.' The central well's imagery rearranged itself as Adella strode towards the projection, aiming to give her officers the confidence necessary to survive the coming engagement.

'Here's our route out of Zuben Elschemali.' Adella traced a line on from the gas giant to the North Ecliptic Pole. 'It's going to be forty minutes before the light from our manoeuvres reaches the enemy.' She plotted out the launch vectors from each War-Wheel towards the gas giant. 'They're on high burn for our current position at ZL-6. This vector means we must fight our way through the enemy fleet released by their force carrier at the North Ecliptic Pole, but it will push their remaining six fleets into turning and reorienting. The four War-Wheels hiding in hyperspace to ambush Home Fleet should arrive too late to the party to impact the battle.'

'North Ecliptic is about as far a jump point as we can run for,' said Ossian. 'The rest of those buggers will be targeting our stern before we can translate out.'

'North Ecliptic holds the cleanest exit window, while the distance and pursuit are something we've planned for. Chief...' said Adella.

Aralat raz Kessi's holo-presence came forward and brought up a live feed of their factory ship releasing hundreds of dark needle-like vessels into the void. 'Thank you, Commander, Captains of the Fleet. The *Takasaki* hasn't only been sucking up asteroids to manufacture missiles and tacks for your cannons. We've also been churning out flotillas of FLYRTs over the past week. Given the local area's hostile sensor environment, our Flying Radar Target RF distraction decoys can spoof the Quazzies for seven times longer than combat inside any normal star system.'

'We're launching our largest decoy flotilla with the strongest output into that empty hole left by Mr. Frog,' added Adella, allowing the strategy's implications to sink in with her officers. 'Let the enemy believe their beaters are successfully doing their job driving us into their ambush's guns. One decoy flotilla will boost for the South Ecliptic while another three decoy flotillas will launch for gaps between their War-Wheels around the Celestial Equator. All decoy flotillas have been designed to issue identical output to Home Fleet's signature. My working assumption is that Mr. Frog will assume the decoy flotilla retreating towards their ambush is Home Fleet, while all other signals are our Full-Engagement Decoy Simulators trying to draw their firepower off onto feints. And they'll be right, too, all except one fleet. Us!'

'You're not a lady to play cards against, Commander,' said Ossian.

'It's not cheating if you win,' said Adella. *First, gain the victory and then make the best use of it you can.* 'We have one more advantage.' Adella highlighted Professor Mead's data layer. 'Zuben Live orbits the Zuben N and M pairing. The collapsed stars' gravitational fields are two-hundred billion times that of the Earth, so exiting this system's gravity well brings no guarantee of stable singularity formation. There's a shifting nexus of clean jump points altering with the stellar orbit in a three-body problem. Professor Mead has our flowing exit points well-charted, while the Quazzie War-Wheels have only just discovered they can no longer retreat into hyperspace while leaving their launch force to hunt us down.'

That roused a cheer from the bridge crew. She'd tossed them as much hope as she had to give. The confidence needed to fight their way through against impossible odds. *Pray it will be enough.*

Adella continued. 'Mr. Frog doesn't fly with high-end artificial intelligences, so we'll run our A.I.s so overclocked during the engagement envelope that our cooks'll fry eggs on our data-cores. The Quazzies are jamming our QT systems, but we've got our own friendly jammers inside Satan's Sieve – those two big-ass pulsars! Remember to prioritise your ships' combat optics for targeting and sensor tasking. Gravity sensors, IR, radar and all our other gear are as good as fried as far as rapid target assessment and distributed weapon assignment's concerned. We've planned for that. The enemy hasn't. Once we've effected our hyperspace translation, Mr. Frog will be stuck floundering inside Zuben Elschemali trying to work out which corner of the system they need to head to for a clean jump out. After we translate, we're pursuit-free. They've kindly thrown the kitchen sink at us, so we'll allow it to sink here. We have the fuel reserves to return home. We have the ordnance to hurt these bastards. The business of Fleet is to bring an enemy to battle on the most advantageous terms to ourselves and to continue it until that business is decided. Let's be about it, ladies and gentlemen.'

She nodded at Home Fleet's Captains and the holograms faded out as they shrunk to icons hovering above each warship inside the projection well. Adella watched with satisfaction as the decoys formed up into doppelgangers of Home Fleet before powering away into every direction of the system. Fake drive signatures which would make it appear that Home Fleet had suddenly multiplied into six identical wargroups. *Mr. Frog, allow me to introduce you to humanity's most ancient form of gambling... the Shell Game.*

Adella had barely settled into her command chair when Captain Fiveworlds appeared in the comms view, no longer bothering to maintain the fiction of Zeno playing skipper. 'Commander Vega. I'm expecting my two crew and the ET back.'

'Alice and Calder should have pogoed on General Quarters, along with all other civilian shuttles on board *Dark Viking*,' said Adella. 'You'll no doubt be glad to hear I've relieved you of your Devil Frog infestation, Captain. Fergal has signed up as our native scout on board the *Dark Viking*.'

'Can't say I'm sad to discover that, but I'm scanning no shuttle on the bounce between *Dark Viking* and us.'

'I'll track your crew down and get back to you,' said Adella, breaking the comms link with the free-trader. 'Slugger, current position of our visitors from the *Neutron Dance?*'

'The visitors are no longer on board *Dark Viking*, Commander Vega,' said Slugger. 'Their shuttle, however, is still docked inside our hangar bay.'

'Location of our Quazalrat prisoner?'

'The Quazalrat is signed over to Doctor Delorey for a medical examination and quarantine procedures.'

A terrible feeling settled over the Commander. 'Slugger, get a read on Doctor Delorey's implant. Which deck is he on?'

'His Fleet implant switched to privacy mode two hours ago, Commander.'

'Override, my command authority.'

'Doctor Delorey is no longer on board the *Dark Viking*,' reported the A.I.

'Back-track.'

'Processing. I have uncovered several surveillance anomalies. Looped camera feeds and missing interior footage. The sequence chain leads to the hangar bay.'

Damn it! Calder's instinct proved to be the right one. Adella should have let the crewman stick a dagger in the Doctor's spine. The slippery spook had kidnapped Calder, seizing their tame Devil Frog and Calder's daughter for good measure. 'Slugger, ping Home Fleet for any craft missing from our formation.'

'There are no absent ships, Commander. All our vessels are breaking orbit and setting course for an exit jump along the North Ecliptic.'

That doesn't make sense. Why would Delorey hide his prize in another craft? Plenty of time for us to search ship-to-ship, later. Unless his people control that vessel and Delorey's planning to flee inside her? No, the bastard can't afford to wait that long. 'Launch a fighter,' ordered

Adella. 'I want an eyes-on visual confirmation of our ship count.'

Adella waited nervously for the fast-mover to report back. *We don't have time for this. We're outnumbered by the enemy a hundred-to-one and facing the mother of all battles. I can't choose between hunting for Calder and Alice and escaping the Quazzies.*

Finally, Adella's update arrived, every bit as bad as she feared.

'One vessel is position unknown, Commander,' said Lieutenant Anders, sounding apologetic, 'the *Shamash* is no longer with us.'

'How the hell did *Shamash* break orbit without alerting flight control?'

'A decoy buoy's transmitting the *Shamash's* transponder code at her formation position.'

Damn it. That's my ruse! 'You better be kidding me!'

'Commander,' announced Slugger, 'the decoy buoy's capabilities are far beyond a smuggler's humble means. It possesses full-spectrum signal spoofing and an actual-size nano-mesh mimicking the *Shamash*'s hull configuration. My visuals from our fighter identify it as the latest Unity design – their navy's U-56 decoy pattern.'

The bloody Unity! The old enemy making mischief. But why would Delorey throw in with them? Our spooks exist to hunt down Unity agents, not buddy up with the bastards.

'Uddin Cesti, you're no damned smuggler. That's a Unity infiltration ship right there!' Adella was out of time to unravel Delorey's bloody intrigues. Bottom line: Adella has lost three of Home Fleet's most valuable assets – the Alliance's last two Heezy gene hybrids and its sole Devil Frog prisoner – and now she faced an overwhelming enemy force to fight.

'Ah, and he seemed such a fine fellow, too,' said Ossian.

'For a ghost riding a cloned vat-grown body,' growled Adella. *Which is probably the point.* She'd fallen for Uddin Cesti's roguish act hook, line, and sinker, the same as everyone else along the Frontier. 'Slugger, scan close-void for quiet drive trace, see if you can get a bead on the *Shamash*. Model her plot as slipping away from us in stealth mode, but without the configuration of a full stealth ship.'

'There is a faint matching engine particle trace heading for the North Ecliptic, Commander.'

So, a false trail to send them in the wrong direction, or … no, Adella could only laugh at Uddin Cesti's barefaced cheek. 'God, he didn't just steal my decoy ship ruse, he stole our damn exit window, too!'

She had to give it to the Unity. Their polity stuffed full of post-human religious fanatics knew how to play the long game. Uddin Cesti smuggling across the Eastern Frontier for as long as Adella's exile with the scrap-the-crap crew. Developing all the wrong sorts of acquaintances in all the wrong places. Sucking up intel and gossip; an ideal network for causing trouble when trouble was what you needed. 'The *Shamash* won't stay in stealth all the way; silent running would require a month to sneak out of the system. Visuals, track for an active drive signature forward of our jump-out vector.'

Adella gritted her teeth as the battleship brought all its optics to the task, processing frame after frame of telescope imagery with the fierce dedication of their Total Ship Computing Environment.

'I'm reading a burn consistent with a vessel on a hard boost,' reported a sailor on NavWeaps station.

Bridge's combat well updated with the *Shamash*'s estimated position.

Adella sucked in her breath: another damn thing she'd been wrong about.

Home Fleet would not engage the incoming Quazzies first. The *Shamash* would! Running headlong into the flotilla released by the Quazzie force carrier stranded at the North Ecliptic Pole. A battle the fleeing Unity infiltration ship wouldn't stand a chance in hell of surviving.

Oh, Calder, I've failed you and Alice. Nothing Adella could do, now. Only watch, hope, and honour her friends when they fell.

- 27 -

Always Outnumbered

'Commander, astrogation reports new light from Celestial North – urgent update,' squawked Lieutenant Anders.

The officer's tone left little doubt his update wasn't of the helpful variety. Adella stopped herself from groaning out loud, but they could read her displeasure across her face. 'Overlay Telescope One across BattSit.'

The hologram projection re-flowed, adding two new clouds of drive flares to the engagement zone. One fleet released above the original War-Wheel, another fleet much further out, ten degrees off the star system's Celestial Equator. No vectors yet, but Adella didn't have to be Sun Tzu to know who the two newcomers had come looking to dance with.

'I don't understand,' said the Chief's telepresence, 'the Quazalrats can't have made Home Fleet from our decoy fleets, yet? So why are they reinforcing their Northern jump-out point?'

But Adella understood. Admiral Blackstar's warning how the Quazzies targeted his dreadnought carrying Calder. Something about Heezy gene proximity must cause components of the enemy's looted ancient tech to light up like a Christmas tree. And the *Shamash* had been trying to escape with *two* Heezy gene hybrids on board!

She allowed herself a brief flash of hope. *Mr. Frog wouldn't be diluting their ambush force by inserting reinforcements unless they've taken Calder and Alice alive and have to protect their prize at all costs.* Alive, but Quazzie prisoners-of-war. Not exactly a better fate in the long term. Calder and his daughter wouldn't end up on a table of the Quazalrat dining variety, but bound to a surgical dissection surface instead. *But they're still in the game for now.* As for Doctor Delorey,

Uddin Cesti and his god-damned Unity crew, she'd pass the Quazzies the barbecue sauce compliments of the *Dark Viking*'s mess.

'Slugger, model the engagement envelope with our interception points, then overlay our initial jump-out window along with Professor Mead's additional navigation data.'

The battleship's A.I. complied and Adella anxiously inspected the results. *Pretty, it isn't.*

Home Fleet would make a fast fighting pass across the force released by the original War-Wheel inserted North ... the engagement she'd planned for. Slugger had the first fleet marked as Frog Alpha in its projection. Then those Quazzies would decelerate and turn, coming up Home Fleet's stern as Adella waited for her exit window and begun spin out. That battle, the Alliance vessels could survive. But now the Home Fleet needed to engage two extra enemy fleets before it reached its jump window. After hitting the original fleet, they'd strike the second Quazzie force – Frog Beta – followed by the third fleet – Frog Gamma – dropped ten degrees off.

Worst still, there was absolutely no point in changing vector and making for clean system edge elsewhere. Every other tract outside Zuben Elschemali's gravity well entailed a fatal wait for a jump window with the added disadvantage of giving the full Devil Frog war-group time to ID the Alliance decoys before piling into the real melee. *Desperate affairs require desperate remedies. Fight three enemy fleets, or take on all eleven. What the Hell kind of choice is that?*

It seemed in Satan's Sieve the only choice handed to you was Hobson's choice. Push on, push through, or perish.

***

'What did they say?' Calder asked Fergal, picking himself up after being brutally tossed inside the Quazzies' version of a brig. Or maybe their new home was a food storage pen. He trusted that the hissing, wheezing, spitting noises exchanged between the Quazzies was some form of communication and not just angry hyperventilation following the thrill of their brief, bloody boarding action.

'They say Fergal not real Quazalrat anymore. Taken prisoner, but body does not kill Fergal like true warrior. Ship boss wants to know why Fergal not dead. Me think they don't know that Fergal is pirate.'

'You *are* a real Quazalrat,' insisted Alice. 'They just don't understand.'

Calder grunted. Maybe it would be better if the three of them in the cell *didn't* understand. He knew from the Fleet briefings that the fate of those captured by the aliens stretched from slave to be worked to death at the good end of captivity, to the main course for supper at the crap-stained stick end of the spectrum. The fact they had separated Alice, Fergal and himself from the rest of the captured crew suggested they were bound for a slightly less common fate. One that he suspected would eventually arrive with a scalpel, surgical drill, DNA sequencer and the Quazalrat Imperium's version of Doctor Delorey.

Calder inspected the walls and door of their cell. The brig's door contained a small porthole of armoured glass with a view over the corridor outside. Even if Calder broke the viewing port, the three of them would need to shrink to the size of a ship's cat to wriggle through and escape. Their accommodation seemed oddly clunky and primitive-industrial, much the same as the interior of the alien ship he had glimpsed after being dragged off the *Shamash*. Its general design appeared as if an alien starship had crashed into Victorian London and been reverse engineered, allowing mankind entry to interstellar travel four centuries early. And Calder had thought the Alliance fleet's idea of deck design was Spartan and utilitarian. Their cell contained no furniture, only a depression in the corner that looked like it might be designed to be filled by the steel pipe protruding at the chamber's edge. Was it a feeding furrow? A toilet? A trough for chemicals to rid sentient food of parasites? *Please, not all three at once.*

Following Uddin Cesti's brief attempt to escape the sudden appearance of a Quazalrat fleet in the same zone of space marked for their hyperspace translation, the traitorous merchant captain's ship had only been taken after a pair of enemy Lancer vessels latched onto the *Shamash*'s broken hull and cut their way in. Calder gave the crew their due, though, they had fought like wolverines against the armoured Quazzie invaders pouring into their ship. He had suspected his first set of captors were Unity infiltrators before their suicidal disregard for their physical forms confirmed it. Calder Durk had run into their filthy kind before in the Ryazarn system. The sequence of misadventures which had led to Alice falling into his life.

Calder finished examining their prison. He didn't recognise the lock – it appeared to be some kind of rotating metal sphere with smaller spheres embedded inside it. They could rotate like a track-ball and were each surrounded by a ring of alien hieroglyphs. *I wonder if it's the Quazzie equivalent of a combination lock? Or a lock crossed with a puzzle?* If only Zeno had been taken alongside them, the android could sniff out a mechanical exploit in the locking system before the armoured door slid shut on the prisoners.

Alice seemed to take their entire kidnapping in her stride. *Maybe I should put her in charge?* Calder wished he felt the same as his oddly acquired daughter. The crewman had just about had enough of being regarded as a prized head of cattle to be rustled by whichever bandit mustered the largest and most immediate force. Pressganged by the Fleet, kidnapped off the *Dark Viking* by Uddin Cesti, then prised out of the Unity's clutches and seized by the Quazzies. On one level he recognised how lucky he and Alice were to be taken alive. But then, without their unasked for Heezy gene ancestry, they'd never have been shanghaied in the first place.

Calder fixed Alice with a meaningful stare. 'Whatever happens, don't tell these things you're my daughter.'

'They know we're family,' said Alice.

'You can't be sure of that.'

'The Quazalrats gave me the last of their old machines to use *before*,' said Alice, the tingle along Calder's spine leaving little doubt which "before" she was talking about. 'Old machines stop sleeping when we are around. That's how Quazalrats know who we are.'

I'd settle for a little anonymity in our life, personally speaking. 'What can we expect now your people have captured us?' Calder asked Fergal.

'Warship slowing and turning,' said the colourfully dressed creature. 'Heads back to War-Wheel.'

'How can you tell?'

'Ships fill with water when go fast for battle. Helps warriors survive big zips. Righty-ho, this ship no fight anymore. Returning.'

I guess their way beats crash couches. Gods, it's no time for only one of us to be an amphibian. Calder didn't ask what his and Alice's fate would be after they were transferred to the enemy mothership. He bet that force carrier fielded a very well-provisioned surgical bay staffed with Quazzie scientists eager to begin poking and peeling.

***

'So that's your idea of finding my daughter and Calder?' snarled Lana Fiveworlds.

Adella had been tempted to make their private ship-to-ship transmission audio-only, but that would've been the coward's way out. Fiveworlds deserved the truth. And Commander Vega deserved the mother of all carpetings for losing Calder and Alice. The *Gravity Rose*'s skipper didn't disappoint.

'One of our civilian vessels turned out to be a Unity infiltration ship,' Adella explained when the Captain's diatribe abated.

Captain Fiveworlds turned the air blue again cursing with exactly what she thought of the Alliance and Unity, both. The ship owner's face faded from crimson fury to pale cold rage when Adella told her the Devil Frogs had disabled and boarded the *Shamash*, seizing Lana's family.

'I'm going to slaughter those–!'

'–you're going to get your ship and crew killed if you fly off solo in a harebrained rescue attempt,' interjected Adella. 'There's a Quazzie war fleet between you and your people; shortly about to multiply into *three* war fleets.'

'I'm not going to just wait around to eat a broadside or two while Alice and Calder are dissected by those filthy beasts!'

'And I'm not asking you to,' said Adella. The Commander sighed. There was only one way to stop Fiveworlds and the *Gravity Rose* flying off on a suicide mission, and that was to level with the skipper about Adella's final gamble for the Zuben Elschemali system. Confessing was as risky as hell, but Adella owed the Captain that much. Calder and his kid, too. So Adella took the merchant into her confidence. The strategy of a ghost and the only hope Hell-Fleet had left.

After Adella finished speaking there was a long pregnant pause across the ship-to-ship comm. Fiveworlds probably trying to work out whether Adella was insane or if she'd really just heard what she'd thought she had.

'You crazy, reckless *bitch*!'

There you go. Yeah, Fiveworlds had heard and understood Adella's scheme.

***

'Scopes, update on Frog Alpha,' barked Adella. Only three minutes before the enemy entered Home Fleet's outer engagement envelope.

'Frog Alpha's Shield-ships are shifting into a formation we haven't seen before,' reported the crewwoman. Visuals updated across the central well. 'Neither a wall nor a cube.'

Adella studied the enemy grouping intently. Their Shield-ship had flowed into a formation like a sled crossed with the Roman Legionaries' *scutum*-style shield. The Quazzies' Lancers sat positioned protected above the sled's energy wall. 'They're planning to overfly us and unload as they pass.'

From the acceleration estimate, the Quazzies weren't on a maximum intercept burn. *So, you're after a nice leisurely cruise while you let us fly to you. Smart. Easier to slow, turn and re-engage that way.* Mr. Frog had all the time in the world. All the enemy needed to do was bog Home Fleet down long enough to give the rest of their forces time to reach Zuben Elschemali's Celestial North. Guaranteed victory.

Slugger sounded the alert Adella hadn't wanted to hear. The Quazzie ambush back by ZL-6 had run into Fleet's force of decoy buoys. Right about now they'd be dispatching Scouts to the rest of their forces with an update along the lines of "WTF". She'd already tracked the explosion of Scouts accompanying Frog Alpha, sending out for an extra helping of reinforcements from their comrades.

Well, this party's kitchen will get real crowded real quick, from here on in. Jump or die, Adella, jump or die. 'That's right, Mr. Frog, we're the real Fleet right here. Real pissed and really dangerous. Rotate quarter-armour to top. All civilian vessels initiate shelter-stack below our armour and energy shields. Bring them in using the new docking protocol.'

Adella waited nervously while civilian vessels put their newly installed docking clamps to good use, ships settling in on the precise stacking order transmitted by Fleet. Skyscraper formations of civilian vessels formed below their warships' keels. This particular innovation had been the Chief's idea. Close quarters protection wouldn't prove as effective during the complete brawl later, but as long as Home Fleet faced a single fast formation on a flyby engagement, their free-traders could literally ride out the worst of the shit-storm under the Alliance battle-wagons' quarter-armour.

'Slugger, assume control of anti-debris guns and laser-line on every civilian vessel fielding a defence system; integrate them into our coordination net. I don't want our keels getting hot-poked by some colonist's trigger-happy attempt to shoot down incoming.'

'Area ASW assuming control, aye,' confirmed the A.I., 'civilian anti-meteor screen now active on our threat axis.'

'When we reach the enemy's War-Wheels, we'll suffer a delay before we're clear of Pulsar interference,' Adella told Ossian and Beklum Sakwa, 'I'll call the decision on whether to wide-jump or thread the needle after we make our jump point. Make sure the civilian skippers don't panic. We can't have them spinning up unstable singularities early.' Adella imagined how badly that would go, everyone tripping up over everyone else in a terrified frenzy to translate out of the system.

'Aye, Commander,' said Sakwa.

'When do we get some of that famous Fleet go-juice, Commander,' said Ossian. 'It's the only reason I signed up.'

'You didn't sign up, Mr. Joyce, you were drafted under emergency order. And you don't possess a ship implant, so you'll only get a lick of the grog.'

'A shockingly one-sided deal, Commander.'

'Sign up with the Devil Frogs, then. I'm sure they'll have you.'

Ossian slumped in his station, defeated. 'Surely for breakfast with a little left over for lunch.'

'I can launch a couple of nukes into the War-Wheels to stop those over-sized engines trying to follow us out,' offered Lieutenant Anders.

'Let's determine how enemy assets are localised after we arrive,' cautioned Adella. The trick would be gaining a clean jump-out point without being first dragged down like a lion under multiple packs of hyenas. 'We pulse too near to our civilians and we'll leave them on the float with fried systems. They're not nearly as hardened as Fleet's wagons.'

Anders nodded. 'Commander.'

'Armour-up!' ordered Adella. 'Prepare for combat-active MSOP.'

Coffin Time. She groaned as the first cocktail hit her, the chair clacking as battle armour sealed her safe. It wasn't the strong stuff, today; tonic and ice with a twist. Battling through the system would last multiples of the crew's safe-limit for Mind Ship Operations. *Dark Viking* drip-fed short-rations today. Going in slow would've proved a fatal error if they'd been facing a Unity fleet over-clocked close to insanity, but Mr. Frog didn't do strong A.I., didn't trust strong A.I.

Adella did. Slugger and Home Fleet's combat grade artificial intelligences would pick up the slack from their sluggish human components and still call this a fair fight. Adella became the ship and the ship became her: the perfect unholy communion of combat. Almost as addictive as the drugs needed to keep a human brain in this state. Warship locked with warship across Home Fleet, a Roman Tortoise advancing against a howling barbarian horde.

Let's see how our wagons' freshly minted optical target motion analysis system holds up. If it was worth a potential court-martial ordering Slugger to practice brain surgery on itself.

'Load j-tubes with canisters of AD-5271 and medium-range scrammers.' *High time the Devil Frogs discovered what our stern-chasers are for.* 'Do we see early launch from the enemy?'

'Negative on that. Not even particle beams.'

Not up against idiots then, today. You don't need fancy shooting when you've got raw numbers on your side. Keeping their powder dry for the initial pass-by, followed by a long pursuit. Nothing conclusive needed, just attrition and hard grind. Wait until the near-void became a Quazalrat-filled melee. Then it'd be continuous hard pounding until there was nothing left of Home Fleet but debris fields. That was obviously her enemy's strategy. Adella had her own. 'Plot a wide-spread salvo for our Big Aces. Mr. Frog's shield-line needs to open firing gaps for its Lancers to hit us with iron, missiles and beams. Let's see how they enjoy a needle storm poked into their eyes. Keep the engagement majority-kinetic. We'll preserve our smart ordnance for the chase.'

Strike.

Adella's fusion with her ship slowed the drive-by. *Dark Viking*'s 1000-megajoule bruisers ripped up with a full rolling cannonade, rail-guns perfectly timed to slap into the enemy's sled of Shield-ships. Her teeth vibrated fit to come out as cannons shook the ship's superstructure; even encased by her position's composite armour and crash fields she felt it in her bones. But not as much as the enemy.

Home Fleet's deflectors flared, particle beams pouring out of randomly created firing spaces inside the enemy's shield wall. Missiles launched, Home Fleet too close and tight for countermeasures worth a damn to kick in. Point-defence guns roared through chains of shells, an intense flack wall short-detonating Quazzie missiles. Slugger and the other combat A.Is temporarily locked up, processing power devoted into Home Fleet's coordinated laser-line, spherical laser mounts dementedly spinning as warships gassed out thousands of incoming kinetic energy rounds.

Dark Viking's quarter-armour drummed while waves of shrapnel and enemy rounds hammered down. Adella heard a sharp crack as the Quazzie equivalent of depleted uranium shells ricocheted their way past the *Dark Viking*'s bulky rotating shield. The ship's symbiosis link made it ache as though she'd taken slugs against Marine chest armour. Adella registered the strikes as through-and-throughs, slicing her auxiliary bridge and hangar bay, hull armour spalling inside along with fragmented rounds. Failed and failing crew implants tallied *Dark Viking*'s losses. Five crew dead from hot shards.

Combat vent-out kicked in; impact-charred projectiles creating deadly radioactive U-238 dust which needed expelling into the void. Nano-layers in her hull armour self-sealed behind each strike breach, living metals flowing like blood.

They'd gotten their own licks in. Flares behind the Quazalrat shield wall spoke volumes about the downside of fielding unshielded big guns; Home Fleet's missiles and tacks on a random walk across the enemy formation, finding holes and filling them with fury.

As quickly as the initial engagement began it ended.

'Maintain stack formation and initiate high burn,' ordered Adella, blinking away the sensor-burn of so many explosions, even viewed second-hand through the battleship.

Commander Vega trusted the Devil Frogs had marked Home Fleet's average velocity during their previous engagements. Because they were about to kick it up a gear. No more waiting for the slowest straggler inside the fleet to keep pace. Chief Kessi's distribution of civilian vessels locked to their warships balanced each wagon with the same thrust; not a single drive anymore, but clusters of multiple engines outpacing the Quazalrats' previous assessment of Home Fleet's acceleration capability.

'Empty j-tubes,' barked Adella, absorbing a storm of incoming damage reports. *Lucky, lucky girl.* Nothing fatal to throw out her carefully laid plans. No civilian ships lost this time. A minor miracle. Commander Vega's wagons had suffered crew losses where missiles and tacks spun past point-defence and bypassed quarter-armour. Forty-five souls dead, but every warship still in the game. Flight data analysis suggested seven Lancers blown to pieces behind Frog Alpha's shield wall. Inclusive. Still, no Alliance ships lost? She'd take it.

Canisters of AD-5271 cluster bombs jettisoned out of *Dark Viking*'s stern tubes, matching tumbling weapons laid behind the Alliance warships. They burst at safe distance behind Home Fleet. Fleet's nickname for that payload was Angry Dust. Each canister filled with thousands of marble-sized bomblets containing micro-sized ion engines, a variety of payloads and optical sensors pre-programmed to home in on enemy drive signatures. Mr. Frog would soon learn to adopt a cube-shaped shield wall after they passed through their first dust cloud. A series of flares flickered when scrammers jettisoned out of their stern tubes. Smart missiles' retros kicking in just enough to slow the projectiles, loitering behind Home Fleet's wake in three waves. Programmed to let the enemy catch up, then accelerate past the Devil Frogs' point-defence. Neither cluster bombs nor scrammers would prove a fleet-stopper to their Quazzie pursuit. But it *would* give the enemy something to concentrate on other than why the Alliance force suddenly seemed so spry on its heels.

Adella felt anything but spry herself; coming off the battle high as the ship's combat-cocktails watered down to maintain the crew at optimum performance. 'Do we have light on Frog Beta and Frog Gamma?'

'Both fleets still on a vector to intercept us,' confirmed Beklum Sakwa. 'They're currently a couple of degrees off closing us out. It appears the enemy hasn't registered our ships' increased thrust, yet.'

'They'll read it from their optics soon enough, even if they don't have Scouts loitering close by. Maintain hard burn. We can't afford to be detained in battle. Our sole objective is reaching those two War-Wheels and holding that void against all odds until our jump window arrives. What's our ETA on handshake?'

'Frog Beta will be inside our engagement envelope in thirty-three minutes,' said Sakwa. 'Frog Alpha will turn and catch Home Fleet in around fifty minutes, depending on how they cope with our j-tube ordinance. Frog Gamma will arrive on the hour mark.'

Adella checked their revised arrival time at the jump-out point. An hour and ten minutes, with at least another ten minutes needed to spin-up for an emergency hyperspace translation. On paper, that gave them twenty long minutes to hold off three full enemy fleets before escaping to live to fight another day. Someone would die out here. She desperately needed a way to ensure it wasn't Home Fleet.

Bridge's central well updated with the latest analysis. Frog Alpha's sled had reformed into a hammer-shaped shield wall formation for their pursuit. *Looking to bring the hammer down on us. They might well come to regret that.*

'Master of the Helm, we'll minimise exposure to enemy fire by executing a terminal velocity brake. Maximum burn on the way in, rotate, then high burn to decelerate for hyperspace translation. We don't get extra points for returning to SecComm Core with full fuel tanks.'

'Are you sure the enemy's grand old wheels won't be blasting away at us, Commander?' asked Ossian.

'I have it on excellent authority that their motherships aren't armed,' said Adella. 'We're approaching the galaxy's largest tugboat with jump vanes integrated into their ring structure. Quazzies prefer their War-Wheels with a drive-specialist fit-out and so do I. Home Fleet will have more than enough target practice with three force carrier's worth of hostiles to deal with. We'll initiate first contact with the enemy at maximum range where our upgraded optical target motion analysis gives us the edge.'

'More time for them to dance, more void for us to miss,' said Ossian.

'Notionally correct, but not inside a system like Zuben Elschemali. You noted how Frog Alpha boosted past us danger close?' said Adella.

'I do believe I was too busy ducking,' apologised Ossian.

'Any nearer and you'd think Mr. Frog planned to ram us. They flew in crazy tight because their targeting sensors are glitching – radar, thermal, gravity, all frizzed by our nasty pair of pulsars. Hell, even Lidar's distorted, here. We take that advantage. We leverage it.'

'Fresh light from stern, Commander,' called Lieutenant Anders, 'I'm processing detonation flares mixed with Frog Alpha's drive signatures.'

'Yeah,' said Adella. She reached into the relevant subsystems and felt the warmth of the enemy's dying ships like the sun on her face. 'Their countermeasures can't spot our scrammers in time, and Angry Dust's too small to scope out against this background interference.'

She snarled in satisfaction. Somewhere in the deep void, scrammer A.I.s locked into suicide mode as they sped up, ejecting hot flares to mimic incoming engines and multiply potential targets, just in case Quazzie point-defence wasn't having a bad enough start to their day. Smart missiles that hunted in concert with Fleet's Angry Dust; a couple of seconds of fierce ion drive thrust, then thousands of tiny kinetic penetrators sent spinning in waves towards the Quazalrat vessels. AD-5271 cluster bomblets shipped pick-and-mix … every payload from nerve gas, acid, incendiary, through to jets of molten metal.

Confusion to the enemy, and inside the Devil's Sieve the void served confusion for free.

'Facing shield output has now reduced to a sixth,' reported Anders.

'They've cubed-up. Here Endeth their First Lesson.'

Frog Alpha had lost a tenth of its ships before realising their Alliance dance partners had poured oil and scattered nails on the tarmac behind them. Another victory, however slight. One she badly needed to fortify her crew for the madness of the hard pounding bearing down on them. Adella worried how well she schooled the enemy. At some point in the future, the creatures would arrive wise to her tactics and there was nothing she loathed so much as a fair fight.

'Do we have frame processing on Frog Beta and Frog Gamma yet?'

'Frog Gamma is still too far away for effective analysis, but Frog Beta's shield light suggests they've broken into multiple formations, blueshift is visibly decreasing,' reported Anders.

'Pass the package to me raw,' said Adella, a few seconds of migraine before her station kicked in alongside her implant, the ship's mainframes bringing clarity to the massive data load. She grunted. 'They're slowing and turning. Frog Beta is planning to match-speed Home Fleet and pace us all the way out to our jump point. Damn, but there's another Quazzie Admiral that knows its business. They've brought their A-Team to the game.'

Split into hunter-killer groups and pick us apart all the way home. Attrition couldn't be called elegant, but fatally effective, nevertheless. It's exactly what Adella would have done had she'd been sitting on a Quazalrat bridge. Kill the Alliance a ship at a time, until Frog Alpha caught up and Frog Gamma entered the fray. Then it'd be three fleets against one: with that *one* a motley collection of Alliance antiques rescued from the orbital scrapheap, ancient warhorses with refugees to protect.

'Civilian vessels to remain cluster-locked to their motherships until we gain our jump point,' Adella sent across the fleet. If she released the free-trader ships now, they'd scatter like terrified rabbits. Adella knew exactly how they felt. 'Warships will assume a classic convoy formation and rotate to protect non-combatant assets as Frog Beta's sub-unit flotillas manoeuvre to engage. Prepare to salvo at maximum range. Evasive pattern at close quarters only, Slugger to generate and distribute random keys for coordinated murmuration.'

Now it was the hard, long grate of waiting for the kill zone. Home Fleet rotated to brake for her sweet, sweet jump point, hundreds of thousands of miles flashing by with each second, the enemy arrowing in on them all the while from three separate vectors. A silence fell across the bridge, quickened minds stilled as best as Fleet knew how by its chemical soup. Then the quiet broke.

'Frog Gamma's gone dark!' shouted Lieutenant Anders.

Damn it! The third attack force had switched off its drives and sacrificed acceleration and manoeuvering for a stealth approach from distance. *I've seen that trick before, but where?* They'd killed their energy shields, too. Risky as hell, but not a bad bet to make when flying masked inside Zuben Elschemali's highly energetic environment. *They're changing up their game for me. I should be flattered.* 'Slugger, Frog Gamma's currently adjusting course on air-thrusters, can you pick up a chemical chalcogen trace?'

'I'm sorry, Commander, with this level of supernova remnant rotating around the neutron stars, Frog Gamma could vent atmosphere a mile off my bow and it would be impossible for me to identify a source.'

'Frog Gamma'll go active again at close range. First vector on enemy approach through stellar reflection, you put an automated salvo spread across their formation and let's see how fast Mr. Frog can juice up a Shield-ship from dust off.'

'Pre-authorisation acknowledged,' confirmed the battleship's artificial intelligence. 'Outer engagement envelope for Frog Beta will go green in ten seconds.'

'Charge particle weapons and prepare a follow-up punch from our Big Aces. Home Fleet will focus fire by turn on individual flotillas inside Frog Beta's formation. Let's see if we can't make these Quazzies homesick for that big single locked shield walls of theirs.'

'Aye, Commander. Rail-cannon barrels arming. XN1-PBs on ignition for 9000 trillion watts. Firing solutions plotted. Fast flicker on mark.'

Adella waited for both gun deck's confirmation to flow in alongside the coordination net green. 'Mark! Heat them up!'

Dark Viking's fusion generators whined like stamped kittens as energy weapons ramped to peak power. But Frog Beta felt the pain, clusters of Shield-Ships flaring up as enemy defenders earned their day's pay and rations. Fire! A couple of flotillas overloaded, a bright blink as they fizzled off the battleship's optics.

'And that, *that*'s how you boil a Frog, ladies and gentlemen.'

'Blueshift for evasive zig-zag; light diminution across Frog Beta indicates defensive semi-rigid sail deployment,' said Anders.

'Big Aces, coordinated gunnery on our beam plots. Combination salvo.'

Dark Viking shook as the rail-guns roiled again, tacks on the road, good to shred protective sails as well as Quazzie hulls. Then the fierce fusion scream as mercury nuclei accelerated into a thousand gigajoules of lightspeed kinetic energy. Another rail-gun cannonade, savage and sharp. Salt and pepper. Egg and chips. A locked shield wall might eat that, but two or three Quazzie Shield-ships protecting a Lancer playing peek-a-boo? Frog Beta wanted to act the big hunter-killer, now they'd met a wolf pack to caper with.

'Our energy shields are taking heat, stern and bow. Hot on twenty-five percent dispersion.'

Frog Alpha are back in play, then, as well as Frog Beta. Adella dived into stern's image processing. Alpha's shield output indicated the Devil Frogs attacking cubed-up. 'The enemy's long-range tracking might be for crap compared to ours, but they're competent enough to know how to ride a beam back for high-energy counterfire. All wagons, random walk manoeuvering thrusters after each fast flicker discharge. Put another scrammer volley through our j-tubes. Let's keep Frog Alpha bunched up with only a sixth of their firing line forward-facing.'

'Frog Alpha is braking to pace us,' warned Beklum Sakwa. 'We'll engage both fleets in full close quarters melee during jump out.'

'Everyone wants a dance card, today. Home Fleet, maintain convoy formation at all costs. No duels, no dogfights, no heroes. We arrive as one, we fight as one, we leave as one.'

Each warship's captain signalled their understanding back to her.

Dark Viking bled time and distance, bearing down on the system edge. Celestial North beckoned Adella like the promised land calling its prophet. Their clean jump out point rotated ever closer as both pulsars spun away, clearing the road.

With every mile the enemy closed in tighter on Home Fleet's stern and starboard flank, giving the Quazzies' second-rate targeting a better chance to chew deep holes out of Adella's hide. Home Fleet's advantage lost to the Devil Frogs' proximity and numbers. A compression around her forehead as the combat-cocktails arrived in diamond-clarity strength. Seconds like minutes while minutes registered as hours.

'Frog Alpha's cube formation is dispersing into melee sub-units behind our stern. Permission to deploy defensive sails, Commander?' requested Anders.

'Only when we're stationary and spinning up,' said Adella. 'They'll deform during hard-braking.'

Commander Vega's thoughts accelerated alongside the ship's systems, the human component always the first to burn out. Easier to tell when the battleship wasn't firing than when she was, now. A long, continuous rolling thunder of kinetic fury from her Big Aces, the laser-line spinning madly to gas out incoming tacks, particle bursts traded at ranges that were the equivalent of a pistol duel at two paces. Or was it Adella's flesh trembling, not the vessel she wore like plate armour?

Quazzie Scouts hurled between the Alliance wagons, laser-painting positions for their Lancers. Too insignificant to waste big beams on, the enemy fast-movers exploded where they ran through waves of point-defence rounds or took hot pokes from Home Fleet's laser-line.

Alarms sounded muted by Adella's armoured coffin as a series of deafening cracks shook *Dark Viking*'s bridge, two kinetic rounds passing straight through the command chamber. No direct hits on crew stations. A whistle of escaping atmosphere before self-seal pumped through the bulkhead. De-pressurisation would have burst their eardrums if the bridge staff hadn't fought armoured-up.

Adella tracked so much heavy ordnance flying between the three fleets she could melt it and cast a carrier from their tacks. She pushed through hell's hailstorm in search of salvation.

Home Fleet maintained good formation towards Celestial North, almost near enough to touch, but at a disabling and terrible mounting cost. Thirty more dead on board *Dark Viking*, another forty souls likely to follow from radiation poisoning.

Damage reports and casualty lists flooded in across Adella's board. Decks holed and sealed; power failures; jump vanes shot off; the cruiser *Escapade* running from her auxilliary bridge after Quazzie beams had penetrated main control, melting her command crew at station; the refinery ship *Spacewise Giant* jettisoning clouds of priceless fuel reserves, easier to count her decks not on fire and ruptured.

This is no good, we're being overrun and overwhelmed by enemy numbers and we haven't even started our spin-up for jump, yet.

It was at that point Frog Gamma lit up on its attack run, drives igniting into life inside the deep void as the third enemy fleet's rail-cannons unloaded towards the *Dark Viking*.

- 28 -

You Can't Get a Quart into a Pint Pot

Calder heard screams from outside his cell. Human cries. Their prison inside the War-Wheel might be larger than a Quazzie Lancer ship, but enemy treatment of Alliance prisoners seemed much the same whatever the location. Calder crossed to the oblong viewing slit where he found the source of the keening. Doctor Delorey dragged down the corridor by three armoured Quazzie soldiers, screaming and struggling as they forced him along. Calder noted the bruising around the man's neck where the Unity control implant had been brutally torn away. Captain Uddin Cesti close behind the Doctor, his own set of alien guards escorting him. The Unity officer's face appeared a blank slate, oblivious to his fate.

Yeah, that one's backed up on some data core inside the cultists' virtual paradise. To Uddin Cesti, eaten by Quazalrats wasn't much more than watching moths consume your favourite clothes.

If Calder hadn't been locked up with his daughter waiting *their* turn, the thought of Doctor Delorey meeting his maker on the Quazzies' dining table wouldn't have seemed so obscene. As for Mr. Bloody Uddin Cesti whose scheming had landed Calder and Alice in this mess, his fate was property damage and a temporary setback, not a ritual execution.

Alice peered out. 'That's the man from Bad Fleet. He took you away from us.'

'Yes.' Calder eyed Fergal. 'What is it with Quazzies and the cannibal mealtimes? You don't have decent protein printers on your ships?'

'They honour you proper,' said Fergal, his stinger tentacles tracing a religious inflection across the air. 'Consume brave warrior's soul; warrior's soul lives on.'

'Everyone knows that,' said Alice as though her father was a dunce.

'Well, I've honoured a lot of chickens over the years, then,' said Calder.

And not all of them had slid off the *Gravity Rose*'s protein printers. He slammed his fist against the cell door in frustration. Calder had tried rotating the strange domed Quazzie locks, but if there was a method behind the alien technology, he suspected he'd only appreciate it when his soul flowed through a captor's gut. After they'd all been dissected as likely as not.

Calder glanced down at Alice, trying to keep despair from distorting his gaze. Up until he had met the girl, he considered himself the last of his line. Fate had cursed his family. His father and brothers killed in battle back on his homeworld. Calder betrayed, his kingdom stolen from under him, only rescued by the crew of the *Gravity Rose*. Had the curse finally caught up with the two of them, now?

It should seem unreal, inheriting a child he'd never had from a sideways reality. But every time he stared at Alice he discovered his family's lines in her face, and Lana Fiveworlds, too. It was difficult not to love a girl who looked like that and eventually Calder had failed badly. No matter how much he tried to remain detached and dispassionate. Not as hard as Lana, but then the *Gravity Rose*'s skipper contributed the maternal gene as surely as Calder had his Human-Heezy hybrid genetics.

That was the only saving grace of the ex-prince's ancient house ending here. Calder would never have to face Lana. Never have to explain how their daughter had left their lives as unexpectedly as she'd entered it. A shadow version of Calder had managed to produce offspring who was sweet, cute and ethereal. Had arranged for her to escape the death of his galaxy. *Only for me to crap it up, as always. Gods, I wish it was him, here, not me.*

'I'm sorry,' Calder told Alice.

'I had two lives,' said the girl. 'Was that greedy?'

Calder hugged her. 'No. You were lucky. And so were we.'

'You lived two lives,' said Alice, 'one on the *Gravity Rose,* then the life Bad Fleet gave you.'

'That second life wasn't mine,' said Calder. 'It was someone else's … I just borrowed it for a little while.'

'Fergal's also had two lives,' smiled Alice. 'We're all the same.'

'Pirate life mighty good,' said Fergal. 'Equal title to plunder at any time seized. Righty-ho, everyone receives proper share!'

Calder wondered whether Fergal would feel the same after his people took him apart to find out how the pirates had overridden the brainwashed creature's suicide gland. If Fergal would quote the Brethren's pirate code so readily, then? 'Yeah, you'll get your proper share.'

As if activated by Calder's assurance the heavy cell door rolled back into the wall. A group of armoured Quazzie Marine-equivalents stamped into the chamber. An officer at the front carried a translator sphere like an egg it hoped would shortly hatch.

The Quazzie officer hissed a series of words and a metallic-sounded translation emerged from the sphere. <Significant slaves must come, now. Abomination will come, too.>

'Not abomination!' protested Fergal. 'Pirate, bravest fighter!'

<Madness. Weakness. Corruption. Alien words condemn filthy abomination.>

'Don't take the girl,' Calder demanded, stepping between the alien warriors and Alice. 'Just me!'

<*Two* slaves must come.> Warriors raised armoured limbs with what looked like a chain gun built into the suit, highlighting Calder's lack of choice in the matter. He considered pushing matters to see how badly they wanted him intact to study; but committing suicide would help Alice even less than it would a certain ex-prince of a failed ice-age colony.

Alice strode up to the officer and issued a series of sibilant croaks and hisses at the creature. The soldier regarded her with curiosity and spoke back in rasping Quazalrat. The other warriors shook with what might be amusement during the exchange.

'You speak their language?' said Calder, astonished. 'What in the name of the stars did you say to it?'

'Bad words mother wouldn't like,' his daughter apologised.

They were forced into the corridor; Alice clutching Calder's hand tight. Right now, the crewman wasn't sure which of them needed the other more. Again, Calder was struck by how backward and basic everything looked on board the War-Wheel. This was a Quazalrat mothership, but he might be walking through a nautical iron-clad from Earth's early Carbon Age. Part of Calder appreciated the irony, perceiving *this* as primitive, given his homeworld remained lapsed in an ice-age civilisation which wouldn't have seemed out of place to a Viking Jarl. But the *Gravity Rose* was his baseline – his home – however many strange worlds the vessel orbited.

Calder had just emerged from the Quazzie equivalent of a lift when a sharp cracking detonation sounded, the War-Wheel's deck left ringing and vibrating. An odd alarm followed in its wake – a siren like a dinosaur being throttled, croaking to death.

'What the hell was that?'

Calder nearly fell over as a guard answered with a jab from its armoured limb.

<Electromagnetic velocity projectile,> hissed the officer, a touch of smugness coming through its translation sphere. <Stray shot. Slaves' fleet being destroyed outside. No food, no slaves left for Imperium this time! Imperium destroys the–> its translation device fizzed as it failed to load the right word. <Great honour. Eleven fleets hunt single slave force. Great honour.>

'He's trying to say the Shadow-eater,' said Alice.

'Fierce big predator at home,' added Fergal. 'Story scares little hatchlings.'

So, that's what they're calling Adella? Well, the gods know the Commander certainly scared Calder. And they were at least nominally on the same side.

'Are they telling the truth about Home Fleet?' Calder whispered to Fergal.

'They give enemy her Name? Fight honour battle. Righty-ho, eleven fleets kill extra fine.'

Calder let the brief flicker of hope he'd felt die. The Alliance's desperate retreat would finish here. Adella might be called the Shadow-eater by the Imperium, but that just meant the Devil Frogs had finally arrived provoked and carrying a hammer big enough to crack her rag-tag armada. *Please, Lana, get out of here. Take the* Gravity Rose *and jump for safety. Allow something I love to survive this terrible shambles.*

They ended up inside what was unmistakably a medical laboratory, bright intense lighting and equipment which belonged in a hospital – or a sterile abattoir, perhaps – mixed with less familiar high technology surrounded by nests of cables and banks of chemical-filled tubes.

Several Quazzies shuffled about the chamber. They weren't in armour, but wore chalk-coloured uniforms with metal circlets around their skulls resembling machine-mind interfaces. There appeared an element of size corresponding to a Devil Frog's age and seniority; the largest creature often proving to be the senior. If that was the case here, the beast moving to inspect them must surely be the Emperor.

'You smart one,' said Fergal, the Boss Quazzie hissing angrily towards the deserter and strangest addition to the *Gravity Rose*'s crew complement.

'Two-Eight-Four of Hatch Ninety Azure,' answered the Quazalrat without recourse to a translation sphere. 'Alliance Species Scientific Study Group. Yes, abomination, quite smart enough to sully my throat with their slave language as you do; though far more eloquently than your corrupted, primitively butchered mind.'

The scientist creature inspected the prisoners by turn, halting to lavish Alice with extra attention.

'You not hurt hatchling pirate, Twohatefour. Fergal kills you, you try!'

Guards raised weapons towards Fergal, ready to cut him down should he attempt anything rash.

'You may observe your precious hatchling's fate, abomination, before I seek out the corruption inside you.' The scientist indicated an egg-shaped capsule large enough to hold an adult, one of three capsules lined up in in a row. Their lids sat locked open, waiting for occupants. 'It's taken me a while to modify the Total Deoxyribonucleic Acid Extraction System to copy a Heezy-hybrid sequence. First, I need a baseline human to test calibrate against. Sadly, I only have a single trueblood to spare, my current slave stock consisting only of the digitals' second-rate clones.'

A door opened in the chamber and four guards dragged Doctor Delorey over to the egg-shaped capsule. He wasn't screaming any longer. The Doctor trembled terribly as though pneumonia-struck, his face ashen and pale while his captors strapped him down inside the black-cushioned device. Calder proved wrong about the man's fate. *Not dinner, after all, then.*

At last, the prisoner rediscovered his voice. 'I can help you! I know things! I'm special!'

'Yes indeed, you have a *special* part to play in my work, slave,' hissed the Quazzie scientist. 'A pity. All those luscious cortisol and adrenaline hormones raging through your flesh. I am sure you would prove deliciously tender. Eating cloned flesh is what I must suffer, now. The digitals fight with tenacity, but their host bodies taste as though they're printed meat. Even in death, how they seek to spite us.'

Delorey thrashed inside the capsule, hysterically trying to slip his bonds. Calder recalled when the butcher had done something very similar to Calder. Securing him onto a surgical machine. Burning out the crewman's memories and compressing his true self into a jail composed of his own mind. Remembering that made it a little easier to watch this. Not much, but a little.

'The Unity? We're also their enemies! Please, I have intelligence on Unity methods, on their kind's weaknesses. Spare me, let me help you fight them!'

'Fight them? Your pathetic failures facilitated their realm's creation, slave. You allowed a faction of filthy digitals to spurn the truth of flesh and secede from your polity; to prosper without purging those unholy profanities. Your heathen Alliance is the groundwater filling their swamp with fresh souls. Fire shall cleanse the digitals' existence. But you? You are the quagmire which requires *draining.*'

The scientist slammed shut the capsule's door, muffling Delorey's frenzied pleas. Regrettably, the transparent lid didn't spare Calder and Alice a view of their fate. Thousands of tiny needles grew out of the black cushioning, piercing the man like an iron maiden torture device. Delorey violently convulsed, blood and liquefied tissue literally drained from him. Incredibly, the man still appeared to be fighting and trembling as his body reduced down to a bloody bag of bare remains. Nozzles activated, the capsule' interior suddenly made opaque with a swirling dark liquid of medical disassemblers. Cables plugged into the machine filled like bloated snakes with the Doctor's melted carcass. A cabinet of clear tubes sucked up Delorey's dissolved corpse while banks of analysis equipment whirred with the work of summarising a human body.

'There, we have established what the human baseline is,' hissed the Quazzie scientist, turning to Calder and his daughter. 'Between this slave and your extraction lie the final secrets of the great masters, the last of the old ones. The Imperium possesses vaults stuffed with artifacts which your sacrifice will unlock.'

'No!' pleaded Calder, as warriors dragged him towards the second capsule, Alice lifted up and carted thrashing into the third machine. Fergal tried to intervene, but a ring of furious savagely hissing soldiers beat the deserter to the floor. 'You don't understand, there are transgenerational effects that can't be stripped out of raw DNA. I've gone through this bloody dance before. Why do you think the Alliance didn't just run me through a blender to create a fleet full of Heezy operators? My hybrid genes are also a cipher, a genetic key, and it needs a living human expression to decrypt and activate Heezy artifacts. You have to keep the two of us alive, not kill us!'

Two-Eight-Four of Hatch Ninety Azure trembled with merriment. 'It is you that fails to understand, you simpleminded slave. We existed during the time of the grand masters, our ancestors as ancient as the stars. Our predecessors alone survived the great ones' overthrow! The Imperium is the true inheritor of the original powers. Your flesh is a valuable trophy, but not nearly as precious as soft tissue preserved from the great ones' bones. Soft tissue kept in suspension by my colleagues.' The Quazzie waddled to the tubes where Delorey's reduced form bubbled. 'There is an amusing saying of your species I once found, slave: you can't get a quart into a pint pot! I require you and the hatchling portable, easily distributed, and ready for DNA combination and comparison analysis back home. Dead and sloshing around inside pint pots will do very well.'

Calder had no choice but to suffer Alice's whimpers, his soul crushed as they were both strapped tight and immovable in their extraction capsules. Her cries slowly faded as the transparent door shut, replaced by the crashing of his beating heart.

The Quazzie scientist – their executioner – tapped on Calder's sealed lid, a mocking farewell sounding muffled through the machine. 'The Imperium thanks you and the hatchling for your contribution to your masters' scientific supremacy.'

You sarcastic piece of–

- 29 -

Plasmastruck

Adella waited for Dark Viking to counter-fire against Frog Gamma, but the rail-cannon salvo she'd ordered never came. 'Slugger, anytime now!'

'Commander, Frog Gamma's vessels carry individual shields and mixed specification weapons. They are nothing like a specialised Quazalrat assault fleet. And their attack vector is–'

Mixed spec? She checked telemetry. The newcomers' opening salvo passed directly over Home Fleet, speeding out towards the Quazalrat force chasing her stern. 'Visual magnification above bridge areas on Frog Gamma, search for neon light.'

'Found. Projecting on-well.'

Dark Viking's telescope imagery tightened in on the neon glow of an ancient symbol set high above the lead vessel's bridge. Skull and crossbones, traced in bright crimson, dancing side-to-side like casino frontage while winking at the officers. She was the *Plasmastruck*, wicked flagship of the Floating Port. 'Blue Barnier, you flash bastard. Are we near enough for direct ship-to-ship laser comms?'

'Confirmed, Commander.'

'Flash Gamma a hail to parlay.'

Blue Barnier's face appeared, a flat monochrome low-res image hiding the harlequin lunacy of his rainbow-coloured patchwork uniform. 'Ah, Adella, I told you the game would bring you back to me, did I not? And here you are, trying to cut me out of my share of the plunder.'

'Plunder? You think there's treasure hidden here? Only a stripped-down science station and we're getting paid in Quazzie iron!'

'Inside Satan's Sieve, aye. Don't play the coy Ensign with me; there's only one reason to scrape a refuel across this scrambled void. Pirates risk Satan's Sieve to shake pursuits, exactly like your tame smuggler friends. I've hunted you and you've hunted me; I know how you dream your dangerous dreams, Adella, just as you crawl around inside my mind. Half the plunder, that's my terms. You mustn't be greedy this day. Think of all those poor innocent families on board your colony ships and free-traders.'

'How the hell did you follow me here, Barnier?'

He laughed. 'I didn't follow *you,* girl. I followed *them.* Safe, slow and at a distance, mind. Once I saw the Quazzies heading for the Sieve in large numbers, I knew which system you were using. Same one I would have picked, girl, if I was bingo fuel, outnumbered and desperate.'

Damn the Harbour Lord. He'd humbugged her. She ached to hurl back the offer in his filthy face, force the Floating Port's armada to fight the Quazzies on their own. Allow the Devil Frogs and the Devil who'd burnt her trapped husband up in re-entry to have at it and murder each other with merry abandon. *Let him burn.* But she required his bloody guns. Home Fleet needed Blue Barnier's scum to survive as much as his filth needed her ships. The Quazzies had fielded too many fleets and she and the pirate only had each other.

Dark Viking's laser-line hummed close to overload, intercepting another salvo of enemy tacks, reminding Adella of the stakes. Her battleship shook as she launched a reply with her Big Aces.

Blue Barnier grinned like a shark. 'You don't have to like it, love. That you don't. It's all in the game.'

'Damn you to hell, Barnier.'

'I never left there, Adella. I only made the place my own. Your navy wagons break port at fifty degrees ecliptic, we'll break starboard at fifty-three.'

'The other way around,' said Adella, 'Fleet is vectoring starboard.'

'There we go. A little mutual trust. I knew you had a fancy scheme stuffed up your j-tubes.'

'We're not doing your fighting for you, you thieving son-of-a-bitch. You want your plunder you will have to earn it.'

'Now, that's just plain insulting. This is Boss Level enough for the both of us. I'm sending you my mainframe's network keys. Fleet encryption, six years old. It's what we have.'

And with it the chance to blow the Floating Port's combined fighting force out of the void, as near to risk-free as she was ever likely to be gifted. And all that revenge would cost Adella would be condemning Home Fleet to total destruction by the Quazzies. She tensed, battling her own demons, then sighed and relaxed, ignoring the surge of fresh damage reports flowing in. The clarity of her combat cocktails as sharp as her dirty Faustian Pact. *Nowhere better to sign it than this system. Quazalrat blood for ink.*

'Receipt of network cryptography keys confirmed,' announced the bridge's comms officer, 'valid and verified.'

'Area ASW, open integration using those keys,' ordered Adella, 'bring Force Gamma active on our threat axis.'

'Commander,' clucked Beklum Sakwa, 'they're–'

'She knows exactly who those devils are, Master of the Helm,' growled Ossian. 'This is the price she needs to pay.'

The dregs of the Alliance. Killers and murderers and far worse. But they were still the Alliance's dregs. Barnier's raiders had already shed enough V. to angle and pace Home Fleet's flank, perfectly matching their unlikely allies' breaking manoeuvre now Force Gamma shared the same digital bloodstream.

Forgive me, Eskandar. She glimpsed a sudden waking vision of her husband, waving sadly at her from the beach alongside Admiral Blackstar. *Not ghosts*, she told herself, *it's only MSOP fatigue*. Another few hours of accelerated neural activity, and snatching confused glimpses of phantoms would be the least of Adella and her crew's problems.

She'd more than doubled the defenders' firepower with this alliance, every angle of attack backed up by extra laser-lines and fresh crews newly arrived on station. The flow of casualty and damage reports slowed on Adella's chair, Home Fleet's wounds briefly staunched.

Adella received a combat link from the central well. Barnier, inside the network like a regular Fleet captain. It almost made her physically sick. She paged him online. 'Your refinery ship's a flying corpse, Adella. You want her to die hugging that cruiser? Pogo her crew and detach her from the stack.'

'I still require the *Spacewise Giant's* engines to hold the distance between us and Frog Alpha.'

'I can rotate some of mine into the line to help your cruiser rabbit. Do you not remember that time at Upsilon Aquarii? How I slipped your picket ships when you were so sure you had me hard against the system's star. That trick will work triple-effective inside this dark place, flattering the optics as we all must.'

Of course. Adella cursed her exhausted overclocked metabolism. *I should have thought of that. An hour ago, I would have done.* 'The Devil plays all the best tunes.'

Barnier signed off. 'Unless it's a dirty fight, it's not much of a fight at all.'

Spacewise Giant only needed to eject an emergency airlock out towards the next vessel in the cruiser's stack to evacuate her surviving crew. Adella let Slugger coordinate a final plot with Dolly, their refinery ship's artificial intelligence. Covering fire patterns agreed, the naval refinery blew bolts on her recently installed docking clamps and fired retros to slow.

It was as though she drifted back towards Frog Alpha, the pursuing fleet no doubt overjoyed they had cut a wounded beast out of the herd, a victim to bring down amidst their flurry of predators. Quazzie formations in Alpha concentrated fire on the *Spacewise Giant*, beams and tacks, but *Spacewise Giant* deployed sails and her laser-line activated, point-defence aided by waves of kinetic projectiles from Home Fleet's fleeing wagons, salvos already laid in the void and flying hot. For this to work, Adella needed the *Spacewise Giant* to survive solo for at least five minutes.

A launch of Quazzie scrammers caught up with the missiles dropped by *Dark Viking* and near-space around the *Spacewise Giant* erupted into a sub-ordnance duel. Adella prayed she wasn't over-egging the omelette, here. That there wasn't an alien officer on Alpha's flagship bridge wondering why a dead and dying ship warranted so much counter-fire from her retreating comrades.

'Dolly,' sent Adella, as the refinery ship was seconds away from being overwhelmed, 'time to ignite your main drive.'

'Igniting, Commander Vega,' replied the *Spacewise Giant*, 'Goodbye, Slugger. Your tanks are full-bore and you are fine for home.'

'Goodbye, Dolly,' said the battleship's A.I., sounding maudlin, 'We're fine for home and your name will sing with the Tactical Supply Wing.'

Adella winced at the A.Is' exchange, praying her illegal upgrades hadn't unbalanced them into sentience; the pair were pushing the cognition limit of emotional expression for the benefit of crew morale. *The middle of a firefight isn't any good time for Slugger to go all Heuristically programmed ALgorithmic on our ass.* She really didn't fancy arguing with a sentient battleship about why the orders of inferior organic minds carried as much weight as Fleet regulations demanded.

Adella winced again. An intense flare from the refinery ship's drive chamber, followed by a far brighter ignition of Home Fleet's fully vented fuel reserves. Melted fragments of *Spacewise Giant* scattered and spun through the vacuum. The void to the battleship's stern caught fire, optical filters intended for stellar-observation dropping across Adella's view of the conflagration to save her eyes.

Easy for the Devil Frogs to mistake Dolly's vented fuel nebula for natural outflow from a low-mass star like Zuben Live, especially with Quazzie sensors glitched and relying on optics. High fidelity lenses inside their ship-mounted telescopes; precision instruments that didn't exactly benefit from being slapped through a cloud of blazing gases at braking velocity. Frog Alpha slammed into the burning nebula half-blind and came out the other side requiring the full attention of a Quazzie orbital dry-dock.

'Rotate quarter-armour towards Frog Beta. Shift one degree to starboard and zig-zag for our exit point,' ordered Adella. 'Frog Alpha is now firing blind against our historic vectors. Let's give them a confusion of fresh variables to toss dice against. Elevate Frog Beta as target priority for our fire mission. We're no longer killing ships in Alpha, we're only putting them down.'

'Commander,' warned Lieutenant Anders, 'We have fresh light, tally two new bandits; Frog Delta and Frog Epsilon inbound from the celestial equator. Both forces are buster on Home Fleet and will be accelerating at extreme weapons' range during our jump-out.'

'Damn Mr. Frog,' swore Adella, 'they must have received the call-up from Alpha's scouts and made our decoy fleets early.'

It seemed these Quazzies could reinforce their faltering line as fast as Adella killed them!

- 30 -

Seven-flame Sun

Calder watched the capricious Quazzie scientist wander off to activate its DNA extraction machine, the crewman's breath misting up his capsule's glass surface. He counted down the slow seconds to his death – Alice's death – dreading the moment that a pincushion of needles would drive through their bodies. A flash of agony, then the end of his strange second-chance existence as part of the Gravity Rose's ship-family. An eerie hissing noise penetrated the coffin's muffled confines. Calder thought it was the guards' amusement over his imminent disintegration. But the sounds drifted through intermingled with the suggestion of a commotion; stumbling feet, overturned equipment trolleys. The hissing resolved into a rapid phut-phut-phut-phut release of … what? Calder tried to angle his head, searching for sight of what might be occurring outside. But he was firmly ensconced inside the deadly medical device. The harder the crewman struggled, the foggier his view.

Quiet followed. A strange moment of stillness as Calder lay suspended between life-and-death, anticipating his end. He flinched! Something came crashing down on top of his capsule. The bulbous reptilian features of the scientist in charge gazed sightlessly at him through the misted crystal. Slowly, Calder's executioner slid down the surface until it disappeared below his restricted eye-line.

Instead of a piercing sting of needles, Calder found the lid retracting. At first, he thought a robot had reached in to grapple with him, a quick blur of silver steel. Then he realised it was an armoured TALON suit, Fleet-issue heavy power armour. Straps were promptly ripped off. The crewman effortlessly yanked out with as little grace as a sack of potatoes.

Quazzie corpses littered the surgical chamber's floor, a double squad-strength mixed force of twenty Alliance Marines and External Legion steel-backs in position across the room. Segmented metal fingers opened and Calder dropped to the ground.

'Commander Vega sends her regards,' a Sergeant's female voice fizzed from helmet speakers. A nameplate read *Shola Arias* above the Master Gunnery Sergeant rank insignia; close to where someone had spray-painted *Retreat Hell* across her armour. She extended a comms aerial from her steel back. 'Wipeout Six, all three hostages safe in the sack.'

'But, *how*?' coughed Calder, blinking eyes fleeting over to where the soldiers freed Alice from her capsule. The strike team had left one Quazalrat alive, at least. Fergal, hard to miss in his brightly bizarre combination of pirate duds.

'We've been here for days, sitting tight far beyond the system edge,' announced the marine. 'Waiting on board the stealth ship. As soon as the enemy dropped from trans-light, *Voidwolf* crept in, running dark on slow-burn RF resonant cavity thrusters. We bounced across the final five-hundred-miles EVA inside our suits, just to make sure we weren't made.'

'You can't possibly have known we'd be taken prisoner?'

'That we didn't. You three were a last-minute update to mission tasking. Primary goal's taking this War-Wheel intact and seizing her flight-capable.'

'Intact?' Calder could barely process what he'd heard.

'Two force carriers, now. Another change-up. Our mothership's parked alongside a late arrival. You can hole up inside this room or you can come with.'

A legionnaire in white ballistic armour trotted up, the seven-flame sun sigil of the External Legion glinting on his chest. He passed Calder a spare pistol and two riot shields – round plate-sized bucklers capable of extending a composite carbon nano-tube screen reinforced by magnetic energy fields.

'I can't post sentries to protect you here,' apologised the Sergeant. 'We're spread thin assaulting both motherships. And the only way any of us are getting out of the system alive is storming the bridge and clearing out the hostiles.'

'Good mischief,' laughed Fergal, proudly scooping up a corpse's Quazzie rifle. At least the creature carried the right DNA to activate its trigger. 'Fergal pass pirate queen plans for big jump ship. She loves the boarding action, righty-ho. Loves like she's proper fine Brethren.'

'You, Mr. Fleet Frog, you're with us,' the Sergeant tapped Fergal. 'Our navigator might do with a friendly pair of tentacles spinning-up your gigantic Ferris Wheel.'

'Those that shall desert the Brethren or ship in time of battle shall be punished by death or marooning,' parroted Fergal.

Sergeant Arias seemed to take that as near to agreement as she would get from their demented native scout.

Adella intends to dock Home Fleet on our boat's empty ring, Calder realised, frowning. *She needs to execute a quick one-stop force carrier jump to pull us out of the Sieve intact.*

Calder appreciated the inherent brilliance of Adella's desperate strategy. If Home Fleet jumped a working War-Wheel back to Alliance space, scientists could reverse engineer the Quazalrat technology for navigating hyperspace in the jamming field. Even up the odds. Give the Triple Alliance a fighting chance of fending off this incursion. Zuben Elschemali was never about the Quazzies closing the trap on Home Fleet. This system was Adella's snare for the Devil Frogs. She'd dangled Home Fleet as bait until the enemy came calling to eliminate them!

The suppressed memories of a long dead Colonel marvelled at the Commander's low cunning, her bloody-minded genius at seizing back the initiative from the invaders. Almost as badly as Calder resented how Alice, Lana and his family from the *Gravity Rose* had been involuntarily set as tethered goat meat to bring a horde of monsters calling.

Alice ran over to him, released, throwing her slight weight against his legs.

'We're going to be fine,' Calder told her. He sounded like he meant it. *Damn you, Adella, you're going to get us all killed yet.* So, forted up alone in the medical bay with his daughter, only a Legion slingshot and a couple of riot shields for protection, a pond-full of Devil Frogs about to swarm, or sheltering behind…?

'Gunny, what's the assault force composition?'

'Thirty-three Marines in TALON suits, six Fleet specialists, and one-hundred-and-eighty legionnaires from the External Legion's Twelfth Orbital Drop Group assaulting in ten fire-teams.'

Or … sheltering behind 500kg of Fleet's most advanced infantry hardsuit, complete with integrated chaingun-style rail-rifle, spinal y-rack grenade launcher system, and limb-mounted flame-thrower combined with a rotating-switch pulse laser; flanked by the Legion's 12th ODG, tip of a sharp and very nasty spear.

Not much of a choice, when you came down to it.

All this time suppressing the fading echoes of Colonel Blackstar, and now Calder allowed the dead pilot to resurface. He passed Alice a riot shield, more than a little worried that she already knew how to key it into life without a soldier showing her. Satisfied her shield was operational, Alice deactivated its field to save the battery cell for when it was needed.

Fergal took in the shields with feigned amusement. 'Not for pirates. For scaredy hiders!'

'Don't I get a pistol?' Alice asked.

'Sure you do, for your birthday in ten years' time. Gunny, let's find some doors to blow off this bloody boat's bridge.'

- 31 -

Hell-Fleet

Adella received an eyes-only encryption laser-flashed from *Voidwolf*. Increasingly difficult to hold those eyes open enough to process the message through her metabolism-hacked fugue of combat drugs. How the Commander's body yearned to rack-out, trade her heavily protected station for a bunk and collapse.

<Two targets boarded. Zero casualties during EVA. Three hostages in the sack. Search and destroy in progress. Awaiting confirmation targets are black of hostiles.>

Adella felt the air leave her lungs as she realised her madness might just have given birth to a little method. Calder and Alice, alive. A trickle of good news for Captain Fiveworlds. But not an update for right now; the scream of Dark Viking's energy shield generators rose, a reminder that none of them floated clear void yet. 'Deploy sails!'

Mile-wide heat sinks blossomed behind the fighting ships. Home Fleet tight enough on their jump-point for Quazzie particle weapons to select their choice of clustered targets with decreasing space for an evasive dance. She noted how quickly the Lancers brought rail-cannons and grape-shot canisters to bear as they tried to shred her sails' protective fabric.

Blue Barnier's telepresence folded out from *Plasmastruck*'s icon inside the well, a private connection skipper-to-skipper. 'I trust, Commander, the Brethren's share of the plunder will be free of your Fleet commandos after we reach her?'

'As free as your sense of morality,' glowered Adella. *If our Marines win the day.*

'Holding action to cover the translation out…?'

'Just park-up and shelter when we reach the force carriers, you miserable son-of-a-bitch,' spat Adella. 'Quazzie Lancers are hardwired not to frag their rides home. Their ship systems are nano-mechanical and fixed, as inflexible as Quazalrat naval tactics. No A.I to pester into nuking their own War-Wheel.'

'I hope your intelligence proves correct, Adella, or both our forces die here today.'

'Yeah, but only one of them would be a loss to the species.'

'A few adjustments to the Floating Port and she'll fit right inside that beast's circumference. A fine halo for the galaxy's dark angels to wear,' the Harbour Lord howled with amusement.

'Enjoy the moment, Barnier. I'm coming for you when I've finished squashing frogs.'

'You're about to give the Brethren hyperspace back, Adella, so I'll forgive you your sour disposition. I'm counting on our entwined fates' gravity, my sweet. The game will always roll you around to me.'

'People think our nickname's Hell-Fleet because that's what the service feels like,' said Commander Vega, 'fools that don't know any better. But it isn't. Hell, that's our signature dish and we serve it out every day!'

She killed comm, the pair of War-Wheels swelling inside the combat well as *Dark Viking* approached.

'Wide jump protocol, Commander?' asked Beklum Sakwa.

'Not this day, Master of the Helm. We're hailing ourselves a taxi. Home Fleet is to brake directly inside the War-Wheel to starboard. Treat her like an orbital station and dock along the inner ring.'

Ossian Joyce seemed tickled by the news. 'That thumping great engine is taking us home? Why, you don't need me in this uncomfortable chair, then. I can be on my way!'

'Perish the very thought. You're my lucky rabbit's foot, Mr. Joyce. Last time I checked, the Draft is for a minimum period of five years.'

'Five–!' Ossian moaned as he realised the Comet People's Lucky Gene sometimes shipped as *bad* luck.

Adella needed her luck to hold; praying the strike force seized both vessels before the enemy scuttled Home Fleet's best chance of escaping Satan's Sieve.

- 32 -

Roll an' go

Fire-team Wipeout Six moved through the Quazzie force carrier's corridors like a plague, quickly, quietly, and in tight order. Every minute or so the phut-phut-phut-phut hiss of rail-rifles, velocity sacrificed for near-silent bursts of fire from rotating sonic suppressors. Quazzie sailors purposefully wandering about on-duty flung off their feet, astonished bloody messes slammed back into iron-riveted walls. The raiders left a trail of corpses behind them. No warnings. No offers to surrender. Brutal sight-and-slay. Stacking outside doorways while TALON-suited heavies slipped through each fatal funnel, a tail of Legion troopers backing up the forward clearing team. A flurry of targeting lasers followed by the thump of dropping Quazalrat bodies, the most immediate threats eliminated first. No repel-borders alarm sounded, yet; testimony to the assault force's skill at bypassing airlock controls and entering the vessel undetected.

The Marines split into pairs, two at the front of the formation and two at the back, tanks to the legionnaires' APCs, another nineteen guns and mission specialists filling the line. Calder, Alice, and Fergal near the tail, though Calder had the feeling that should Fergal be given his head, the half-insane alien would rush ahead, shooting wild bullet-storms at anything that twitched. *Best he doesn't.* This operation needed to be kept stealthy … until it couldn't. Calder prayed the other squads sweeping softly through the force carrier proved equally as professional as this unit. He'd sat in on enough of Admiral Blackstar's Fleet briefings to know it wasn't just Quazzie crews shipping with a suicide gland. Their vessels self-destructed like firecrackers when they fell in danger of being taken intact.

Alice stepped over a corpse tightly gripping her shield for protection, her features melancholy while they filtered through the corridor. 'Always the same,' she whispered.

'It'll be different when we get back to the *Gravity Rose*,' Calder reassured her; the shadow of the two Marines at his rear a comforting presence. It seemed amazing to the crewman that something as heavy as a TALON suit could move as panther-padded as it did. *I'll make sure of it.*

'Will Bad Fleet let us go home?'

Calder nodded at his daughter. Adella would, he was certain. Commander Vega might sacrifice them all as collateral damage for her victory over the Devil Frogs, but she possessed enough of a sense of honour to allow Calder and Alice to go free. Not hand them over to Doctor Delorey's successors for mind-wiping and a little pressganging back into the service.

Master Gunnery Sergeant Arias halted for a second to project a schematic of the War-Wheel. She asked Fergal to confirm the squad's position and proximity to the bridge. Fergal tapped inside the hologram. They were only a couple of corridors distant from the substantial vessel's command and control.

Legionnaires in front of Calder shifted to provide fire support for their breaching element, ready to clear an operations area when sirens echoed throughout the vessel. It sounded much like the strange croaking he'd heard before; Fergal's agitation all the sign Calder needed that the enemy had finally detected Fleet's intrusion inside their massive force carrier.

'Chop-chop now!' urged Fergal.

Sergeant Arias had obviously reached the same conclusion. 'Frag the room out!'

The pair of Marines on point slapped a round of grenades from their Y-racks into the ops chamber, explosions licking back out the doorway as they swapped slow and stealthy for shock-and-awe. Sneaking no more. They broke into a sprint, TALON suits pounding the corridor's deck as though an ion-storm shook the War-Wheel.

Lighting panels flickered for a second, making Calder question whether it might be his eyes or the vessel's power systems at fault.

'Step it up! Wipeout Two's on target inside their mainframe,' yelled Arias from the front of the formation. 'Wipeout Ten's just secured the drive-room chamber.'

Calder had a feeling that if he fought among slackers, the goldbricking was mostly on him. The raiders stormed forward, tossing grenades through every open hatchway, the quickest and dirtiest way to secure their rear.

'Wipeout Two's diverting automated suicide overload commands to the drive-room!' warned Arias.

'Bridge shuts!' shouted Fergal. Large blast doors began to close at the end of the corridor.

Sergeant Arias accelerated, steel legs a blur as she pushed the exo-power amplifiers to the limits of their endurance, sliding the last few feet and jamming her TALON suit inside the closing portal. A crunching whine sounded when the shutting portal's engines met and matched against Alliance power armour. Arias's suit pinged and smoked as small-arms fire issued from within the bridge.

The Marine on point came charging down the corridor like a steel rhino. The soldier's helmet speakers bellowed a warning, "Jitter strike!" His spinal launcher spat a spinning ceramic discus through the gap between the heaving, struggling blast doors … a *Bouncing Bertha*, in boot-camp slang. The Marine followed his own bomb, leaping over Arias's jammed form, rolling into the bridge, unseen but not unheard. His rail-rifle's roar on full cyclic sounded like a chainsaw, adding to the melee's confusion.

Calder shoved Alice to kneel on the floor, activating her shield, then his own, yanking Fergal to shelter behind them both; a protective V pushed hard against the bulkhead. Just in time: the spinning mine began its needle burst. *Bad day not to be wearing a hardsuit.* A hail of ricocheting projectiles flew at Calder, bouncing back from the bridge's interior, a devil's fractional share of jitter ordinance returned into the corridor. Each needle dynamically switchbacked on hard-surface impact, converting momentum and energy into another shot, and another, and another. A hell-storm of bounding building-clearance smart rounds. Keyed to avoid friendly-fire, needles kicked off Calder and Alice's shields, rattling and shaking their bucklers' energy fields as well as the legionnaires' suits before returning on random vectors. The bridge crew's sibilant screams spoke to what happened where needles struck armour and organic surfaces without a built-in Alliance transponder. Bertha didn't bounce for Mr. Frog. She drilled.

It took the best part of a minute before the needles' kinetic charge bled down from lethal. A carpet of spent projectiles left twitching on the deck before Calder, Alice, and Fergal; a deadly swarm of dying wasps.

'Shields fine weapon for pirates,' said Fergal, standing up. 'Telling you this plenty.'

Sergeant Arias ended her finger-in-the-dike pose as the Marine inside the bridge countermanded the portal seal-down. Arias stood up, running diagnostics against her suit, top-layer smoking and dented where Mr. Frog had lit her up. Half the strike team flooded through, the rest of the force securing the deck behind them from Quazzie counterattacks. The bridge was the ship and the ship was the bridge. That much was true on an enemy War-Wheel as much as any Alliance wagon.

Calder hustled Alice inside the safest place on board any vessel. This involved trying to find a spot inside the bridge that didn't involve standing on dead Quazalrats. The External Legion dragged corpses out; a clean-up the killers of the Seven-flame Sun were well-practiced in across a thousand worlds; the War-Wheel just one more locale for their archives, for their regimental history. A navigator yelled for Fergal to help translate the jump-vane interface. Arias was back on comms with *Voidwolf*, informing the stealth-ship they'd bagged an intact War-Wheel. From what Calder overheard of her conversation, it seemed the force carrier was the second prize to fall into Alliance hands, today.

Alice took in the scene, her eyes wide and frankly alien. 'Are we going to live?'

'I'm planning on it,' said Calder. 'And–' He stopped as Fergal did a strange war-dance in front of the navigation station. It was hard not to take your eyes off that, but for all the wrong reasons.

Fergal wobbled his stinger tentacles in the air as he hissed a bawdy Brethren ballad. 'Soon we'll be warping her out through hyperspace. Way, ay, roll an' go! Timme rollickin' randy dandy O!'

Calder sighed. 'Let's not tell your mother what happened on board the War-Wheel, okay?'

- 33 -

Satan's Sieve

Adella kept her tired eyes locked on the frustrated enemy. What was left of Frog Alpha and Frog Beta held back a respectful distance, now that Home Fleet and the pirate raiders sat docked below the two War-Wheels' rims. It hadn't taken the Quazzies long to realise that fighting a foe your ships wouldn't allow you to shoot at was a one-way bet. If Dark Viking flew undocked, able to effectively bring her weapons to bear, the system's edge would be remade as a shooting gallery for her Big Aces. 'Time to clear pulsars?'

'Turbulence minimum in four minutes,' reported Lieutenant Anders. 'Spinning up in advance of jump clarity.'

'Fast movers inbound,' warned Beklum Sakwa. 'Quazzie Scouts. Lots of them. Incoming from every enemy fleet in range.'

'They're unarmed,' said Ossian, sounding surprised that this strange brief standoff had ended so quickly.

'Yeah, and their pilots are organic, not machine-based,' said Adella. 'Which means they're not hardwired against blue-on-blue friendly fire.' She realised with a heavy heart what the enemy's bloody plan was. Close to total exhaustion, she struggled to keep her orders sounding calm and clear. 'Slugger, re-prioritise the Scouts as missiles, task point-defence and launch scrammers to engage.'

'Turbulence minimum in three minutes.'

'They're unarmed,' repeated Ossian, with a little more uncertainty than before.

'Their Scouts *are* the weapon. They're coming in for suicide runs!' *Nothing easy, today. Mr. Frog really didn't want its big bird tech ending up in Alliance hands.*

'We're not gassing them out,' warned Anders, 'Scouts are too large for the laser-line to handle at this range. Up close a hit will carve one ship into multiple projectiles.'

'Blind them; target the Scouts' cockpits!' barked Adella. 'Big Aces to load grape-shot. You run out of tacks, raid our j-tubes for Angry Dust and salvo canisters at them until we're empty. We know where they're boosting for – straight down our throat! Throw those planes through a flack wall. Slugger, plot optimal firing solutions. With Home Fleet ring-parked, we've got three hundred and sixty degrees of potential vectors.'

'Turbulence minimum in two minutes.'

Adella fixed her reluctant navigator with her full attention. 'Mr. Joyce, it seems we may need one of the Comet People's famous Lucky Gene jump-outs after all.'

'Ah, now, I don't want to be destabilising this grand War-Wheel's whale of a singularity with any shy little minnow of my own,' protested Ossian.

'You won't be,' said Adella. She hurled the battleship her instructions and command code authorisation. 'You'll be overseeing the translation from our War-Wheel's bridge.'

Ossian yelped as his armoured capsule accepted Adella's lifeboat override, lifting vertically before flashing down for injection inside the vessel's emergency magnetic catapult tube.

Adella opened a line to Captain of Marines Yong Xue. 'Captain Xue, there's a relief navigator arriving on a lifeboat at the airlock closest to your bridge in twenty-one seconds. Please ensure he's delivered to his navigation station uneaten by any rogue elements on board your force carrier. All appearance to the contrary, the man's actually rather good at his job.'

The ship shook as her Big Aces began a near-constant salvo of dispersive shot.

'Charge particle weapons,' ordered Adella. 'Target the closest Lancers and Shield-ships. We don't know if their full-size bridge fit-outs take ramming off the table, so let's give the Quazzie big guns something to focus on other than their wet powder and us flashing them the finger from their own mothership.'

***

'Sweet Saints of the Six Suns, let me be,' pleaded Ossian Joyce, as a party of TALON-suited Marines manhandled the man shaking inside the War-Wheel's bridge.

They dragged him towards the jump station where Calder helped Fergal, a Kaggen Fleet navigator and two other specialists interfacing piles of Alliance equipment into the alien bridge.

'What's the matter with this station?' demanded Ossian, 'There's enough room to throw a party across these consoles.'

'Jumps with six Quazzie navigators,' said Fergal, 'plenty to share pain.'

'Are you up for sharing the pain?'

'Fergal not Quazzie. Not navigator. Pirate!'

'I don't require the Fleet Frog's help, I require yours – or better yet, the blessed intervention of Master of the Helm Sakwa's,' complained the first navigator, the crab-like Kaggen sporting a tag which read Helmsmaster Tralt. 'I cannot maintain event horizon stability. There're too many interfaces to handle for a single jump operator.'

'It's not the size of the station that's foxing you,' said Ossian, 'it's the size of the singularity that this terrible beast has to conjure up to swallow a whole fleet at once. There are more jump vanes inside this wheel than teeth in a shark's grin. Let Ossian see what he can see from one of these chairs next to you.'

The Helmsmaster nervously rattled claws across his tattooed carapace, the Kaggen equivalent of a groan. 'Human physiology is not evolved to breach the wall between universes, to lead us into heaven's clasp. This is well known! Members of your species are sent mad by the mere attempt.'

'Lucky for you, my hard-shelled friend, it's also well known Ossian Joyce was as mad as a hatter long before his first jump. Now, watch and learn.' Ossian began to work interface overlays jacked into the alien equipment. 'Tell me truly, Fergal, was this grand Quazalrat bridge not designed with drug injectors, a little Mind Ship juice to quicken an honest man's fingers?'

Fergal tapped his over-sized amphibian head. 'No evil implants inside brain.'

'Ah, a sentiment I share. No wonder it takes six of you strapping fellows to slip into hyperspace.'

'What manner of a person are you?' demanded the Kaggen, frankly amazed at the speed at which the interloper seized the spin-up.

'The best type, my hard-shelled friend. A Comet Person!' Ossian pulled a bottle out of his jacket and took a quick swig before tucking the alcohol between his thighs.

Helmsmaster Tralt wasn't impressed. 'Where in the creator's name did you get that?'

'A little something I borrowed from *Dark Viking*'s mess before action stations ruined my meal.'

'You are on duty now!' rattled the Kaggen.

'And is there a better way to ease me into it?'

Calder's gaze shifted to the barrage arcing out from both War-Wheels. The projection in the Quazzie version of a bridge-well flickered in low-resolution as telescope processing struggled to keep up with the hyper-speed engagement. Each massive vessel remade as a Catherine Wheel. Outer-rim spinning as integrated jump-vanes rotated, inner rim fixed stationary and filled with docked ships, fireworks spraying out in every direction from Home Fleet and her pirate allies. Particle beams erupted, pinprick drive burns from multiple scrammer launches, point-defence chain-guns flaming, laser-line flashing, rail-cannons jouncing inside recoil mounts.

'The ship needs a name,' urged Ossian, working his board like a demon. 'It's terrible bad luck to risk jumping in an unnamed ship.'

'How about the *Let's Get The %$%£ Out of Here*?' suggested Calder.

'Not for this grand old wheel. We need something fine and fitting. Yes, it's coming to Ossian, she's the *Lady Catherine*.'

'You're naming the ship after a firework?'

'No, Calder Durk, after the evil Breaking Wheel the very firework was named after. For the Fleet is using her to crack Ossian Joyce's bones and crush his soul, just as old Earth's Medieval torturers tormented their victims.'

The rapport of small-arms sounded, drifting into the bridge from far away. A reminder that Marines and legionnaires still flushed out the vessel's previous owners in distant parts of the force carrier. Sealing the chamber seemed like a fantastic idea, right now.

***

'Crew are exceeding final safe-limit for Mind Ship Operations,' warned Slugger.

'Rotate auxiliary staff into MSOP stations,' ordered Adella, as punch-drunk as if she'd been swatting Quazzies with her fists rather than an outdated titan of a battleship.

'And key crew on our bridge, Commander?'

'I'll sleep when I'm dead.'

Someone cheered a little too enthusiastically from one of the other stations. Hysteria or schizophrenia, both common manifestations of squatting too long at the bar downing Combat Cocktails for free.

'I fear,' nagged the artificial intelligence, 'that moment may come sooner rather than later at the present rate.'

Blue Barnier's telepresence rolled out of the well like the proverbial phantom at the feast. 'Adella, the Brethren arrived late at the brawl. Pass common coordination on point-defence to the *Plasmastruck*.'

'You still alive over there?' Adella laughed at the raw unfairness of it. 'The hell with that. You've already stolen my second War-Wheel from me. That's enough plunder for you for one day.'

'This is no time for pride, sweet Commander. We're relatively fresh – pass us your heavy lifting. My crews don't yet have the Mind Ship shivers.' His telepresence shifted into a bear-like Arth's form, huge and dangerous. His perfect damn body. 'Give it to me!'

'I don't trust you, Blue Bear,' wheezed Adella. 'Look, there's another one just like you. Like, what's her name ... Colonel Scolar Pes.'

'Trust I want to live to reach the next level.'

'Commander,' trilled Slugger, 'your choice-reaction time is suffering serious attentional lapses.'

Kinetic energy translated through the *Dark Viking*'s quarter-armour, a din of alarms chasing the cracking explosion. Her teeth shook inside her head, the command station absorbing the worst of it. Sparks floated across the bridge, butterfly-beautiful. She lost herself in their spinning dance.

Adella jerked up, a couple of seconds of black void, or minutes gone?

'Commander, I am detecting a transient ischemic attack and atrial fibrillation against your vitals,' said Slugger.

Fire suppression activated above three weapons station capsules. No, there were only two stations still in situ. Had one been yanked down into the emergency passages and propelled towards sickbay? She smelt a familiar burning. A stream of particles had penetrated the hull at hypersonic velocity, a demon's wake of molten metal slagging at random. 'Even in the void, I smell the stench of death. Space burns, we can do that and pretend it's an achievement. Are we shooting? Of course we are, I feel those beautiful Big Aces.'

'Mind Ship Appointing Order-active,' said Slugger. 'Filling decision-trees where organic burnout is impairing combat function.'

An orchard snaked out of the centre of the bridge, all apples, pears, and quince. 'It's a bounty, so delicious.' Adella started to shake, noting with resignation that the cocktail bar had finally closed on her. 'Can't fight like this, not dry, you beautiful cluster of algorithms.'

'Cerebral hypoperfusion,' warned Slugger, the A.Is voice drifting in from a million parsecs away. 'Sickbay transit system, 70 percent probability D.O.A upon arrival. Hypoxemia critical. Command chair, loading emergency surgical systems. Lactic acid suppressant-nano release authorised for ischemic penumbra.'

Adella swam through terrible whining noise, agony to push through. Her bridge no longer a single command deck, but a dozen different bridges vibrating across each other within an endless march of pure fractal infinity. Some with Adella inside the chair, many more without her, damnable strangers on the stick, species she didn't even recognise as Alliance. Adella flitted past a station with Rear Admiral Pullinger losing his shit in it, past a station filled by Admiral Blackstar, the officer's grim eyes fixing on Adella with disbelief as she materialised and dematerialised in seconds.

Finally, she came across a battleship commanded by her dead sister. Arlinne Vega, steady in her station, so strong and wise, professional and poised, a perfect foil for Adella's wild battle craziness.

Both minds moved as one with the same thought. *You're gone. This is MSOP fatigue.*

Help me live, sis, begged Adella, pulling herself clear of their joining to communicate as individuals.

Mr. Frog's danger-close, growled Arlinne. *Scouts aren't doing it for them. Big ships are closing, now. They'll be kicking our j-tubes all the way out.*

Adella saw the risk. *Feed enough extra mass in behind us, the enemy destabilises the hole.*

Quazzies didn't care if their fang-pulled ships sucked sharp iron and bitter beams every second in. Quazzies wouldn't even care when their wagons ended up smeared as bug-spatter across the barrier between universes, just so long as their appropriated War-Wheels appeared prominent on the butcher's bill.

Both officers merged again, collapsing into each other. *Close the wound, sis. Cauterise the bastards.*

That's insane.

Which of us thought of that?

Two minds as one: *You did.*

***

A crash shook the War-Wheel, another collision as an enemy fast-mover slipped through Home Fleet's fierce flack wall. Every suiciding ship set off a hideous hissing, gurgling noise from systems around the Quazzie bridge, the hacked-in Alliance equipment translating each Quazalrat alert. 'Vane integrity down to eighty-seven percent.'

From what Calder could see, the pirates' War-Wheel seemed to suffer lighter suicide runs than the *Lady Catherine*. He sighed. *Mr. Frog's earmarked me as the ringleader – ring, quite literally.* His vessel's outer ring rotated at speed, now, a spinning wormhole ripped inside the void by her vanes, the force carrier carefully manoeuvering to enter a fissure torn between universes.

'They're not wanting us to leave.' Ossian Joyce laughed as hard as when the pirates established singularity coordination, Ossian discovering Blue Barnier had named his prize War-Wheel *Buggins' Turn*.

'Kerr–Newman interior is green and stable,' translated the console. 'Event horizon holding at ninety-seven percent.'

'Singularity insertion, mark,' ordered Helmsmaster Tralt.

The force carrier commenced her translation, ferrying Home Fleet docked in their entirety alongside her mass. Off to her flank, the pirates' War-Wheel also began her slide inside the giant singularity she'd whisked up across native space-time.

'We're nearly safe,' Calder gasped at Alice. Both constricted by Quazzie crash-couches – alien bridge stations which neither armoured-up nor adapted their cushioning for any species outside of Quazalrat.

'Prize ship, fill the bloody hole in behind us!' A comms-line opened from *Dark Viking* for a second, closing so rapidly Calder almost mistook the quick rattle of Adella's voice for a hallucination.

Slugger's icon immediately appeared, the A.I chasing the Commander. 'Belay that order, prize ship. Commander Vega is experiencing severe anaesthetic-related minimum alveolar concentration during emergency surgery. MSAO-active. Maintain singularity within safety coherence range. Repeat, hold singularity within safety coherence range.'

'May the creator preserve the revered Commander,' murmured Helmsmaster Tralt, 'for she must be dangerously sick indeed to suggest we close an active singularity before fully exiting it.'

Ossian Joyce checked the Alliance systems jury-rigged across the alien console. 'No, the lass is onto something. Look! Devil Frogs' capital ships angling for a hard burn straight up our stern. If they jump on the scales while we're transiting our tunnel, we're as dead as last year's clothes inside my ex-wife's wardrobe.'

'You're misreading the data,' insisted the Kaggen navigator. 'That's an interpretation error from the application context middleware over this hacked hardware. Such a manoeuvre would destroy the enemy as surely as it would eliminate us.'

Ossian angrily rolled his eyes. 'Interpretation error my fat arse.'

'The Quazalrats will do it,' confirmed Alice. 'That's the warriors' way.'

The young girl leaping into the argument didn't impress Helmsmaster Tralt. 'Isn't there an active school schedule still running on board one of our colony vessels?'

'Alice knows what she's talking about; listen to her!' Calder felt a familiar lurch. The *Lady Catherine* had ventured too far into the singularity for any manoeuvre other than full hyperspace translation or destruction.

Calder stared across at Fergal until the creature responded. 'Die to make die. This the Quazzies' way, righty-ho.'

Another quake as a Scout followed them into the hole and smashed into the stolen mothership. 'Vane integrity down to eighty-one percent.'

'We have to follow the Commander's orders,' argued Ossian, fighting to keep the force carrier inside the singularity's heart as enemy Scouts continued to dive-bomb her. Probably like flying a brick compared to what the Comet Person was used to. 'You're usually such fickle fellows for your chain-of-command guff.'

'MSAO-active,' snarled Helmsmaster Tralt, clicking his claws in annoyance as he urgently worked his portion of the console. 'Mind Ship Appointing Order. Regulations demand we now prioritise our A.I. The revered Commander Vega is undergoing emergency surgery in-station on the flagship's bridge. Given the cruel combination of CIF and anaesthetic the Commander's suffering, I couldn't trust her to order supper at this moment, let alone override a combat hyperspace translation using unfamiliar systems on board a seized alien prize vessel.'

Ossian shook his head as he struggled valiantly on the stick. 'I'm not feeling that.'

Smoke issued from a vent on the far side of the bridge. Calder prayed it was ramming damage, not something more fundamental with the vessel's hyperspace drive. If that gear gave out in this universe or the next, they were all dead. Him, Alice, Lana and every crew-member nestled inside the *Gravity Rose.*

'Your feelings are hardly at issue, here. I am senior Fleet officer on this bridge,' clucked the Helmsmaster. 'I don't require half-baked advice from a newly drafted and frankly inebriated ex-civilian jump jockey.'

'And that's the second thing you're wrong about, today.' Ossian conjured up the master singularity formation interface.

'Stand down!' barked the Helmsmaster. 'Marine sentries, return to the bridge. Relieve this—'

Calder rolled out of his chair and yanked out his pistol, waving it towards every fast-approaching member of Fleet personnel still on their feet. Damned if there wasn't more of Colonel Blackstar left inside him than he'd counted on.

Fergal followed Calder's lead, leaping free and hefting up the purloined Quazzie assault rifle, threatening the naval crew with his weapon. 'Stupid machine not gives proper pirates orders!'

'Seal the bridge, Ossian!' yelled Calder. It seemed trusting Adella Vega with his life was a hard habit to break.

The thump of sealing blast doors sent a rush of cold air squealing through the chamber.

'You're going to kill us all,' wailed Helmsmaster Tralt.

'But I'll do it with some style!' laughed Ossian. 'Choke the serpent.'

Ossian Joyce closed the event horizon behind them, the massive ship's jump vanes still drilling a hole between universes. A wave of debris accelerated past the *Lady Catherine*, all that was left of incoming fast-movers, not to mention hundreds of Quazzie capital ships trying to hijack Home Fleet's singularity behind their stern. Something dark and furious frothed at their rear. A collapsing tunnel between two realities. An avalanche that could crush worlds, let alone an alien starship, lonely and small between the scale and the grind of universes. 'Dive! Dive like the bloody Devil's nipping at our heels!'

Because it is.

Mr. Frog's largely hardwired bridge systems went full-wiggie, now that Ossian had severed the singularity, an explosion of hissing alarms and croaking sirens.

'Kerr–Newman interior violation, seven percent,' translated the console, sounding oddly reasonable given their bridge's complete nervous breakdown. 'Event horizon collapsed.'

The Quazzies' central command well also had problems interpreting a collapsing singularity while they transited its tunnel. Whether this was a failure of the physics modelling engine, the fact Quazalrat engineers anticipated no one making such an insane manoeuvre, or something more fundamental to their imminent destruction, seemed a moot point.

Calder rolled back into his crash couch, holstering his pistol. Everyone else scattered aghast for stations to strap into; playing the world's worst game of musical chairs. They were far beyond the point of no return, now. 'What level of violation before we're pasted against the walls of the universe?'

'Well, that's purely theoretical,' hooted Ossian, keeping the force carrier on course. The ship started shaking worse than taking Kamikaze strikes. Calder guessed shear forces from a collapsing artificial black hole would do that. 'Nobody's ever been stupid enough to choke their own serpent out while still spinning inside her belly.'

'Ten percent,' moaned Helmsmaster Tralt, fighting to hold the force carrier together. 'Ten percent de-coherence is fatal.'

'As predicted by physicists,' spat Ossian, 'and what do those inky-fingered bookworms know? How many of them dared brave a hyperspace jump once in their tenure-cosseted existence?'

'Kerr–Newman interior violation, eleven percent,' warned the console. 'Interior is red and unstable.'

Ossian took another swig from his bottle. 'There, the noble school of hard knocks triumphs over dusty academia once again.'

'Kerr–Newman interior violation at sixteen percent,' warned the console. 'Interior is black and volatile.'

"This is the bloody style!' yelled Ossian, pouring the remains of the bottle down his neck. 'Jump in a serpent and sever our track, we might not go on, but we can never head back.'

'Kerr–Newman interior violation, twenty percent,' cautioned the navigation console. 'Fatal error. Fat. Al. Ror. R. R. R. R. R. R. R. R. R. R. R. R. R. R. R. R. R. R. R. R.'

Ossian hurled his empty bottle into their fast-disintegrating combat well projection. 'Shut your bleeding cakehole and fly true for us!'

The bridge vibrated faster and faster, blurring across Calder's vision. There was a reason crew stations tranquilized their occupants during the final portion of a hyperspace translation. Why human navigators were frequently left drooling inside a straitjacket after too many times breaching realities. Kaggen physiologies might suffer such agonies. But he wasn't one. Blue liquid started fountaining out of Calder's chair and sailing through the air, a hypodermic needle vainly trying to stick itself into a piece of Quazzie anatomy he sorely lacked.

Calder barely felt Alice's fingers clamped onto his hand from the neighbouring couch, the sight of her body smearing across his vision.

Noises drifted in, distorted beyond meaning, multiple sets of physics blending and interacting in ways no mortal mind should suffer. Matter wrapped itself around his face. Somewhere, Calder thought he could hear Ossian and the Fleet navigator still arguing, but their bickering became curled into supergravity. Crystal surfaces, 5-orthoplex, all kissing numbers and invariants. Holes leaking holes. Darkness as light as super-symmetry. He slowly observed himself observing himself observing himself from within a demi-dream.

That was when Calder found that slipping into hyperspace came with a free natural tranquilizer. Brain hypoxia through gravitational time dilation. What was left of the crewman's consciousness finally went dark as the metabolically driven ion pumps of his neural network discovered electricity worked a little differently when expanded across another twenty dimensions.

- 34 -

Eternal Patrol

L iam Pannel bent in to adjust an autodoc clamped around Adella's chest as her eyes fluttered open.

'You put me into a medical coma?' she croaked.

'Yes,' said the Doctor, indicating spent surgical-nano flushing out of her drips. 'And don't make me regret taking you out of it, Commander Vega.'

'How long? Who's ACO?' she asked.

'Four weeks under. And the ACO honour currently rests upon Chief raz Kessi's wide shoulders,' said the ship's surgeon. 'Still, it might have been worse. Your long-suffering Chief Medical Officer could have ended up commanding Home Fleet.'

Of course, Aralat raz Kessi had stepped into her command slot. Combat stations for engine crew? Slam the hatch shut on their ridiculously well-protected drive-room and stoke the boilers hard.

Adella groaned. 'He's probably already done a deal to sell Home Fleet off for scrap to the highest bidder.'

'Scrap's a pretty good description,' said the Doctor, 'given how banged up we are. We've remained docked to our oversized prize vessel. Navigator Joyce and Helmsmaster Tralt figured out how to activate the force carrier's Quazzie navigation-defeat and scanner systems. Not only are we straight bore for SecComm Core, but we can now also detect enemy movements in hyperspace. Mr. Frog never even come close to mounting an effective pursuit before we escaped the Frontier.'

'The Floating Port's forces?'

'Long gone,' said the Doc. 'We detected the pirates' War-Wheel translation alongside our jump out. That scrap-pile worldlet the Brethren call home was waiting for them. They fitted the prize ship around their station like a crown, then exited the Sieve moving faster than scuttlebutt.'

Doc Parnell's update left Adella with a cold smouldering hatred. The ex-head of the Anti-Piracy Group had just brought the Brethren back into the game. *On me. All on me. Sorry, Eskandar, I guess I failed you a second time.* Her only small consolation was that Barnier's happy hunting grounds presently lay far behind enemy lines. The Quazalrat Imperium – a large, rich unified polity which had never known piracy. Until now. *I don't know which of my two demons I want to visit destruction on more.*

'Where are we, currently, Doc?'

'Back inside Alliance territory, real-space concurrent with 55 Cancri. We haven't dropped once since we translated; although, plenty of our civilian vessels cut clamps and squeezed out of hyperspace as soon as we reached friendly void. The Quazzies' nav-jamming effect is long behind us, but the Chief figured that the only safe place for the *Lady Catherine's* reverse-engineered Heezy tech is air-locked to the orbital citadel around Mars.'

Good decision. Same call she would have made. Adella blinked. '*Lady Catherine?*'

'Ossian Joyce's choice. For his naming ceremony I heard he broke a whiskey bottle on the bridge some time during the battle.'

'How many ships did we lose to the Eternal Patrol?'

'Just the *Spacewise Giant*. I doubt if the docked remnants of Home Fleet's civilian vessels will ever make planet-fall again. *Gypsy* and the *Persistent* are dead-weight clamped, too.'

'That sounds like a victory to me, Doc.'

'If it isn't, I dare say it'll do until the real thing drops out of hyperspace.'

'Seeing how we're both still flush from the exhilaration of our survival, how about you be a pal and put me up on the *DV*'s mainframe?'

'Not exactly the next three day's bed-rest I had in mind for you, Commander. I don't want you crawling casualty lists and posting notification letters out to families. Happy thoughts make for well patients and accelerated recovery times.'

'Better that, than I go stir-crazy out of the loop.'

'Far be it from me to gainsay the current record holder for longest duration combat-effective under MSOP. An honour you share jointly with half the bridge crews in Home Fleet. I'm not sure if that will earn you a promotion, medical discharge, or a ring-side seat to the largest group court-martial in Fleet history.'

'Damned if I know, either. Doc.'

Parnell deactivated her bay's privacy field long enough for Adella to see a depressingly full house inside sickbay, white-uniformed staff and clinical robots working with smooth, quiet purpose. Then the Doctor was away on his rounds.

A cut-down bandwidth link activated from the ship, Adella's implant slowly booting into usefulness after so long meshed with only the bay's medical routines. She checked on Slugger, ran a few integrity checks across the A.I. Nothing to suggest the battleship's illegal self-programming had sent it off the deep end. But there was something about Slugger's systems, the back-door modifications Adella's exiled hackers had installed for her. Slight but subtle differences. *Has someone else been up inside my battleship? Shit!* She confirmed Rear Admiral Pullinger's status. No, that incompetent scumsucker was still under arrest and locked in the brig. Pullinger survived his first successful engagement cosily confined for the duration of Fleet's murderous work; their victory and the disgraced officer's detention a direct cause-and-effect relationship. This monkey business she sensed as a shiver down her spine couldn't be put on Pullinger.

Adella paged through the database until she discovered a long list of very curious discrepancies between events and her memory of them. Indubitably a result of combat fatigue, cheap station surgery and mental exhaustion on her part.

Colonel Kal Blackstar, killed-in-action alongside his specialist medical detachment during the ambush of Combined Fleet inside hyperspace; letter of condolence to family logged by Admiral Blackstar, himself. No evidence of any active service period with Home Fleet.

Neutron Dance, vessel 173 in Home Fleet. Incorrect. No indication of attachment to refugee vessel group. No matching record of existence, indeed, on any Alliance commercial ship registry at all. Unable to confirm crew details for a craft that did not exist. Not an Alice, a Lana, a Calder, a Zeno, or any of the rest of her crew.

Unity spy-ship *Shamash*. Not an infiltration vessel, but a reliable free-trader sadly lost in action during the retreat from Zuben Live. Did the Commander want to review footage of the *Shamash* exploding as the honest free-trader ate an enemy scrammer? No, as realistic as what her gun-capture-cameras had caught might look, Adella really didn't wish to watch it.

Additional mission tasking to *Voidwolf* to rescue hostages during the storming of prize vessel *Lady Catherine*. Orders never issued. Hey, what hostages?

Camera feeds of questioning of enemy captive, "Fergal". An empty interrogation centre and a reminder that Quazalrats' suicide gland made live prisoner surrender and capture problematic. And here was the cam footage of Adella on the bridge during the exact supposed time of her missing interrogation with an alien she seemed to have imagined.

Adella cross-checked for recordings from storming the War-Wheel and the prize vessel's final jump out. Ah, Quazzie internal video feeds close to non-existent and stored using incompatible standards where they survived; and sadly, every Legionnaire and Marine suit-cam recording lost during transmission back-up to *Voidwolf*, a faulty receiving data storage system struck by a stray rail-round, you understand.

Yeah, she understood all too perfectly.

- 35 -

Epilogue

Corporal Antigo had an annoying habit of humming External Legion ditties when he was bored, and it didn't seem dog duty patrolling the prize ship Lady Catherine made much difference to that quirk. Lucky for the Corp and Private Karleen Prosser, the ship's dark crevices appeared to have run out of Devil Frog ambushes a few weeks prior. Otherwise, his Legion marching tunes would call an enemy down on them hungry for feeding time.

'When our songs make space tremble,' sung Antigo, running a helmet-mounted light across the shadowy chamber, 'everyone says to themselves, all these happy steel-backs, this is the future, the flower of our species.'

Only another couple of days of this, Karleen told herself. *Then it's rotation out at Fort Cassani.* A real gravity well for her boots; the chance of a posting somewhere with enemies who just wanted to kill her, rather than murder her before eating her. *Happy times.*

Karleen stopped to inspect a small mountain of crates and material secured with netting to a bulkhead. Her moonbeams made the gear seem to shift as she ran the light across. A motley collection from a yard-sale. Hospital equipment, machinery stripped out of vessels and orbital habitats, large black quantum computer banks that resembled monoliths. 'If this is a Devil Frog ship, Corp, how come they've got a whole heap of Alliance gear racked inside their storage hold?'

'The dirty croakers were looting worlds across the Frontier for months,' said Antigo, kneeling to brush the dust off a line of what looked like Alliance ship-to-ship torpedoes. 'Reckon they intended to bring all this stuff back home to whatever passes for the croakers' Technical Analysis Centre to take apart. Figure out what makes us tick. Work out how to kill us better.'

'Just like we'll strip their carrier.' Karleen mused that if it took as long to disassemble the leviathan as it did to patrol her endless decks and nooks, Fleet's engineers at SUPSHIP would be in gainful employment for years yet.

'Sounds good to me, Legionnaire. Drop down in Sol system, then it'll be Alpha Mike Foxtrot to this croaker tin-can and chest candy all around. SecComm Core's been wetting themselves ever since they heard what we're bringing in for them.'

'Any word from Colonel Pes where *Trojan* might get posted next?'

'Colonel mentioned to the Major there's a breakaway political faction on Mu Virginis chancing its arm with all the troubles along the Frontier. Mu Virginis's aristos are petitioning for Externals to come in-system and help pacify its insurgents.'

'What kind of world's Mu Virginis?'

'The usual, I guess. Marginal, dusty, dirty, and full of heads that need a good kicking.'

Yeah, the usual. Karleen marked and dated Storage Hold Forty-One as checked green against their patrol schematic. Then they opened the airlock to the next cargo zone, both stepping through, sealing the chamber in darkness.

If the two soldiers had waited a minute more, they would have seen the green light blinking on a readout at the side of the "torpedo" the Corporal had inadvertently activated. They would have observed how a Unity infiltrator body printer torn out of the *Shamash* operated as it completed final mentality transfer. The capsule split apart like a solved puzzle, metal plates withdrawing on a filigree of small spider-like legs, leaving a human form in a standard Fleet shipsuit lying sprawled across the floor.

Noak coughed out a stream of embryonic fluid across the metal deck, shivering as his autonomic nervous system caught up with the act of his body's birth. A moment for a lifetime's worth of memories to bed down inside Noak's newly minted mind. Early recollections acting as a manservant to Prince Calder Durk during Hesperus's brutal ice-age. Far happier memories after his absorption within the Unity; after being snatched during the Unity's hunt for the galaxy's last Heezy-gene operator.

Noak gagged, yearning for the Unity's virtual heaven, his perfect communion with as great a share of sentient life as the polity had so-far preserved from real-death. The Real tasted so barren and diminished after paradise, even blessed – more or less – with his original body. Preserving heaven, Noak's price for continued readmission.

Finally, a share of memories from his fellow agents out in the Real. The ones who had so obviously and badly failed. Noak shivered as Uddin Cesti's final recording merged with his mind. Torn to pieces during a Quazalrat feeding ceremony. Not the best way to shed your physical form. When the Unity resurrected Uddin Cesti, they would need to delete his final memories to reinforce Cesti's mental stability inside the Real. Hard enough to suffer exile from heaven, even when you weren't squeezed out half-psychotic. Next, Noak's birthing update prioritised a snatched view from Cesti's march to his execution. Calder Durk's face pressed up against a prison viewing slit, staring in a mixture of fascination and horror as captives seized from the *Shamash* were dragged to their death.

Ah, Master, so good to see you again. Still alive, too. Not much bloody surprise, there. Prince Durk had led an entire nation to oblivion during the war and stumbled out of their retreat's chaos as the sole survivor. Well, alongside reliable and obedient Noak, of course. Until the Unity finally tracked the manservant down in his exile and hiding. Calder Durk didn't just have Heezy genes, the nobleman possessed damnable lucky ones, too. The Prince could lead a mob of believers over a cliff and he'd bounce rather than splat. Noak knew that as a fact given he and his family had grim experience as one of those splats.

An ache at the back of Noak's skull reminded him he'd been resurrected with a ship implant. No, not just a ship implant. A *Fleet*-standard augment. The capsule's printer intelligent enough to recognise the environment and match it to help infiltration forms blend in. He felt the local network functioning, a hacked overlay running on top of Quazalrat systems, a string of Alliance routers spot-welded and strung across the vessel's corridors. Impressive, Home Fleet had captured a Devil Frog force carrier. Noak smiled, using Doctor Delorey's black codes to insert an extra crewman on the *Lady Catherine*'s work schedule and duty rota.

Noak should have been insulted about being loaded back into the Real by Uddin Cesti as a familiar face to reassure the Prince; to make the young nobleman's captivity and exploitation easier. But existence within the Unity bred humility and total dedication to the greater good. Noak had a vital new mission as the last infiltrator standing in this shitty corner of the Real. Someone needed to carry the debacle's truth to the Unity.

The Triple Alliance had attempted to use Calder Durk to destroy the Quazzies; tried and failed. Lost half their fighting ships and their priceless stock of ancient Heezy weaponry as the price of their incompetence.

Hah, so now it's our turn!

You can claim a complementary copy of my sci-fi adventure novella *Sliding Void* by joining the free **Stephen Hunt Readers' Universe** group.

You'll be the first to know next time I have some cool stuff to give away (& you can unsubscribe at any time).

Get your free copy of *Sliding Void* at
http://www.StephenHunt.net/voidsliders.php

Books by Stephen Hunt also available on Kindle Unlimited

SCIENCE FICTION

Hell Fleet (Sliding Void)
https://www.amazon.com/Hell-Fleet-Sliding-space-opera-ebook/dp/B07K6XVXRV/
https://www.amazon.co.uk/Hell-Fleet-Sliding-space-opera-ebook/dp/B07K6XVXRV/
https://www.amazon.ca/Hell-Fleet-Sliding-space-opera-ebook/dp/B07K6XVXRV/
https://www.amazon.com.au/Hell-Fleet-Sliding-space-opera-ebook/dp/B07K6XVXRV/

Books by Stephen Hunt also available on Kindle Unlimited

SCIENCE FICTION (cont.)

Void All The Way Down (Sliding Void)
https://www.amazon.com/dp/B00NVF8N3M
https://www.amazon.co.uk/dp/B00NVF8N3M
https://www.amazon.ca/dp/B00NVF8N3M
https://www.amazon.com.au/dp/B00NVF8N3M

Anomalous Thrust (Sliding Void)
https://www.amazon.com/dp/B018CN8V6G
https://www.amazon.co.uk/dp/B018CN8V6G
https://www.amazon.ca/dp/B018CN8V6G
https://www.amazon.com.au/dp/B018CN8V6G

Empty Between the Stars (Songs of Old Sol)
https://www.amazon.com/dp/B07DHZYZNL
https://www.amazon.co.uk/dp/B07DHZYZNL
https://www.amazon.ca/dp/B07DHZYZNL
https://www.amazon.com.au/dp/B07DHZYZNL

Mission to Mightadore (Jackelian)
https://www.amazon.com/dp/B00XJOEZ8M
https://www.amazon.co.uk/dp/B00XJOEZ8M
https://www.amazon.ca/dp/B00XJOEZ8M
https://www.amazon.com.au/dp/B00XJOEZ8M

THRILLER/SPY-FI

Secrets of the Moon
https://www.amazon.com/dp/B00XIL2XBW
https://www.amazon.co.uk/dp/B00XIL2XBW
https://www.amazon.ca/dp/B00XIL2XBW
https://www.amazon.com.au/dp/B00XIL2XBW

HORROR

Hell Sent
https://www.amazon.com/dp/B01ENU0STA
https://www.amazon.co.uk/dp/B01ENU0STA
https://www.amazon.ca/dp/B01ENU0STA
https://www.amazon.com.au/dp/B01ENU0STA

Leaving Your Review

If you have time to leave a review of *Hell Fleet* on Amazon, please do … it leads readers to pick up the novel, gets new fans into science fiction, and helps keep me in the authorly game and writing:

https://www.amazon.com/Hell-Fleet-Sliding-space-opera-ebook/dp/B07K6XVXRV/ (USA)
https://www.amazon.co.uk/Hell-Fleet-Sliding-space-opera-ebook/dp/B07K6XVXRV/ (UK)
https://www.amazon.ca/Hell-Fleet-Sliding-space-opera-ebook/dp/B07K6XVXRV/ (Canada)
https://www.amazon.com.au/Hell-Fleet-Sliding-space-opera-ebook/dp/B07K6XVXRV/ (Australia)

Thanks

Stephen

www.StephenHunt.net